BLOOD LOSS

BLOOD LOSS

THE DIVINE VAMPIRE HEIRS, BOOK FIVE

by

GINNA MORAN

Cover design by Silver Starlight Designs
Cover images copyright Depositphotos

For Inquiries Contact:
Sunny Palms Press
9663 Santa Monica Blvd Suite 1158
Beverly Hills, CA 90210, USA
www.sunnypalmspress.com
www.GinnaMoran.com

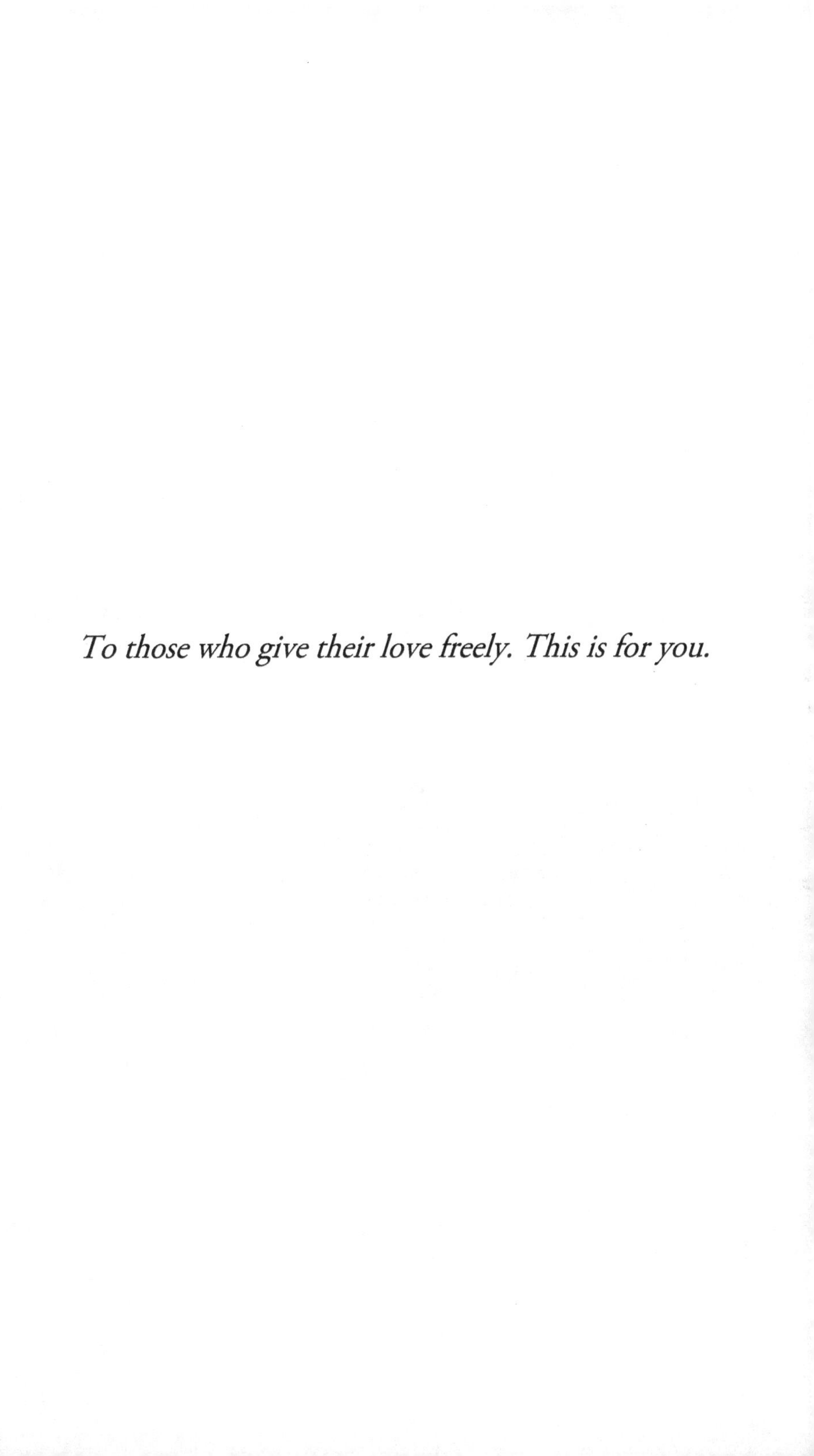

To those who give their love freely. This is for you.

STARVED

"YOU'D STOP STALKING ME IF you knew what was good for you." Peering over my shoulder, I peek at Orlando strolling behind me at a slow human pace.

He purposely stalks me, keeping a bit of space between us, triggering my human fear instincts like crazy. He smirks at me, his blue eyes flashing silver. "I do know what's good for you."

Goosebumps prickle over my skin, and my even breathing turns into a pant. Annoyance washes through me that I can't manage to keep myself in control. "Like starving me?" I ask. "Because this shit sure doesn't feel good."

I could stop in place and turn to face him, but if I do, I know he'll want to wrestle or something. He'll attempt to pin me down just to instigate me to get me to fight back. Working out and learning new fighting techniques has always been mine and Diego's thing. I don't know what Orlando gets out of trying to get me to fight him, but I don't like it. For one, his T-shirt is too damn tight, showing off his muscles. And two, he looks ready to push me to my limits, and none of my guys are here to reward me with cuddles and kisses.

"It serves a purpose." Orlando's smile widens, and he rubs his hands together.

"Yeah, if pissing me off is what you wanted to get out of it." I turn back around as not to get trapped in his gaze. He promised he wouldn't manipulate my mind anymore without my permission, but I still have trouble holding his stare for more than a few seconds.

He hums his amusement. "I do love when you fight."

"Asshole," I mutter. "If you knew me at all, you'd know I'm a lover and not a fighter."

He chuckles. "Exactly. It's too bad you resist letting it turn into something you know you'd enjoy. Things don't have to be so tense between us all the time. You can lighten up."

I groan. "Shut up."

Picking up his pace, Orlando closes a few feet of distance between us. "I will if you make me. At least try."

Fear blasts through me at his sudden movement. I break into a sprint despite knowing how it'll wear me down faster than if I just fought against the fear my human rationale ignites in me. Where Diego will do everything in his power to stop that part of me from running rampant and controlling me, Orlando seems to enjoy stabbing at it to get a reaction. Starving me doesn't help.

"You know, acting like such a dick will only make me continue to dread any and all time I have to spend with you," I say, risking looking over my shoulder again.

He dashes closer and touches my shoulder, causing me to swing my arm back and run faster when I miss him. "You sound like Austin, precious Jewel. Just this morning we discussed this. He thinks you need to be coddled."

I frown. "Austin was helping you?"

"No, he was trying to help you by raising his concerns, which I considered. Your other matches see things differently, though."

His words make me slow down a bit. "Why are you telling me this?"

"To help you understand the purpose behind tonight. You might not believe me, but I would love nothing more than to see to it that you enjoy our time, but your wellbeing takes precedence to me. If you can't fight, you will die."

I clench my hands into fists. "I can't fight when I can't concentrate. Just give me a break. I need to eat. I feel sick."

"You had the option to eat. You chose not to."

I stop in my tracks and turn to face him. "You know what? This is enough. You're freaking me out and making me miserable. I don't deserve this."

I friggin' hate everything about this night. I don't even

have to ask Orlando to know that he instructed Kingston, Austin, and Diego to stay away. None of them have yet to ever interrupt one of my excruciatingly long nights with Orlando like they do on each other's. And tonight has been the worst one yet. Orlando refused to let me consume their blood. It was his blood only or nothing tonight for whatever asshole reason he has. So now I feel like I'm dying, because screw that. I want to make it clear that I would rather starve.

Orlando tightens his jaw, his amusement disappearing with his oncoming frown. I expect him to stop and consider my human rationale that screams at me to be afraid of a vampire, but he disappears inhumanly fast. Friggin' A.

Spinning around, I swing my arm out and hit empty air. I thought for sure he'd sneak up on me to tackle me. My muscles tense in anticipation, and I jerk my leg behind me. Again, I don't hit anything. I don't see Orlando anywhere, but I can hear his heart picking up pace as he moves out of my vision every time I try to find him.

"Seriously? You need to stop. I don't like this—"

Two strong hands latch onto my shoulders and rip me off my feet too fast for me to even react. My back hits the wall, and I gasp out all the air from my lungs. Orlando flashes his fangs at me, pinning me in place, his icy blue eyes searching over my face.

He leans in super close, his cool breath blowing strands of my dark hair that spilled from my ponytail from my face. "Good. You're not supposed to."

I press my head to the wall, trying to get space between us, but I can't properly move with how close he stands. "Let me go. I mean it. This is not cool."

He stretches closer, tilting his head to the side. His soft breath pants against my mouth, his heartbeat thudding against mine. "I want you to make me...unless you like it."

Jerking my head forward, I head-butt Orlando so hard that my vision shadows. The movement surprises him, and he drops me. I hit my knees on the mat and hang my head, watching small droplets of my blood pelt the slick material.

And then I push up and run.

I make it all of ten feet.

Orlando hooks his fingers to the back of my shirt and drags me toward him. I skid across the mat, flailing my body, trying to find something to grab onto. I manage to pinch my fingers into his arms, digging my nails into his skin hard enough to get him to let me go. I drop back to the mat with an oomph. Using his foot, he rolls me from my stomach and onto my back.

He pins my hands over my head, straddling me, putting me in a position that makes me feel so out of control and vul-nerable. "You're making it too easy."

My fear turns to anger, and I grit my teeth, glowering at him. "Do you get off on making me feel like this?"

My words shock the hell out of him, because his fingers loosen just a bit. He doesn't get off me but stares so intently that for once I don't avert my eyes until something splashes right on my forehead. He stiffens, flaring his nostrils. My body reacts just as quickly as his, and I realize what has him on edge. Blood drips from a gash on his forehead, and I can't take my eyes off of it. The dark ruby liquid trickles into his eyebrow, pooling into a drop again. I gawk at it, waiting for it to fall, wishing and practically begging for it to.

"Fight me," he says when I don't move. "I just want you to fight. Please."

I don't respond to him. I still can't manage to avert my gaze from the blood. It's so close to spilling. I can almost taste it.

"Precious Jewel," Orlando whispers, his voice going soft.

The blood drop releases from his brow, and I yank my hands free and shove them into his chest, knocking him on his back. I launch up and at him, fire burning so intensely inside my stomach that I can barely think straight. My body moves without my mind's permission, and I tackle Orlando.

He extends his hand out, pressing it into my cheek, keeping my face away from him. "Control yourself."

"I warned you!" I scream, my voice screeching so loud that I'm sure everyone here at the Shadow Crest Villa can hear me.

Snapping my teeth, I attempt to bite the side of Orlando's hand. He recoils, pulling back, and I grab onto his wrists, pinning him down for once. He snarls at me, his fangs flashing. My mind and body start a war with each other. My mind begs for me to chill the eff out, but my body wants nothing more than to taste Orlando's blood, to satiate the pain he ensured would burn through me by starving me.

Bending his knees, he jams them into my back, somersaulting with me. I land on the mat, disoriented from the sudden shift of the world. Orlando's weight falls on top of me, and he holds me down with one hand.

He doesn't get a chance to stay on me long. I manage to break free and punch him straight in the throat. The move surprises him so much that his eyes widen, and he falls off me. I don't think I've ever seen him scramble to his feet like he does now, the force of my punch knocking him down a peg.

I get back up and swipe my hair from my face. Charging forward, I launch myself at him and cling onto his back. I lock my hands around his taut chest and hang on for dear life as he spins me so incredibly fast that I can't see anything but the world blurring around me.

"Jewel, enough!" he yells, trying to throw me off.

The scent of his blood tantalizes me, pulling at the deep need inside me. And I wish it didn't. I wish he didn't put me in this position. I feel so out of control, so hungry, so... All I want to do is sink my teeth into Orlando and make him bleed. I've never wanted anything more. But fuck.

Inhaling a sharp breath, I get my shit together and release him. I scream out and brace myself, expecting to crash hard into the wall. Big hands lock around my waist midair, jerking me to a halt a moment before I find my footing.

I growl. "Shit! Get away! I'll hurt you. I'm out of control."

"Orlando, what the hell?" Diego's voice cuts through the pounding in my head.

"Listen to her and stay back," Orlando warns.

A hand touches my shoulder and spins me around. I jump and collide into a solid body. I open my mouth to bite down and stop short, the sweet yet slightly spicy scent of Kingston tickling my nose. I relax and sink into him, catching my breath.

"Fuck, babe," he whispers, reaching up to push my hair behind my ear. "I thought you were going to devour me."

I release another deep breath and lean in to brush my lips to his throat. "I want to so bad. You have no idea. Please, push me off and get away."

"Not a chance," he murmurs, his breathing panting as hard as mine. "Think of this as a moment of restraint. If I can resist—"

I flip off of him and curl in on myself, the temptation harder than I expect. Everything inside me hurts. I don't trust myself not to lose control and bite Kingston. He jokes about accepting the risk, but I don't want to go there with him. "You have too much faith in my capability," I say. "Now, please. Get away. I hurt too much. I'm starving. I don't want to accidentally hurt you."

Kingston pouts his lip out at me as I lie on the ground, counting the seconds between my breathing. One, two, three—breathe in. One, two, three—breathe out. It's all I can do to stop my body from launching from the floor in search of a vampire blood source, most definitely Kingston because he risks standing the closest.

I wave my hand out to him. "A couple more feet, dude."

His brows lower on his head. "Not a chance. If you're hungry—"

"Please," I beg, my voice softening.

"That's it. I'm risking it." Kingston flashes his fangs and lifts his arm to his mouth. "I can't stand another second seeing you like this." He turns his attention away from me. "I'm feeding our girl."

Austin materializes next to him and holds out a cup. "Not straight from you."

I release a breath of relief. "What he said."

"But—"

Austin whacks Kingston on the shoulder. "I know you have a lot of faith in Jewel, and I know she wouldn't hurt you either, but if she feels out of control, it's a dick move to test her restraint."

"We wouldn't have to if that asshole didn't starve her," Kingston says, glowering at an ever so silent Orlando. I can feel Orlando's gaze on me, studying me just as intently as Austin does as Kingston fills up the cup with blood. Diego steps a bit closer too, like they're fully prepared to tackle me if I can't wait for Kingston.

Orlando straightens his shoulders and stands with his arms crossed over his chest, staring at the four of us. I wish he'd take the hint and leave, but he doesn't. Or he's ignoring the hint. Probably the latter. It is his night after all.

"I know it's tough to see her like this, but Jewel needed to be tested," Orlando finally says to Kingston. "And the safest time is during my care."

"Tested?" Kingston's voice rises in irritation. "You starved Jewel as a test?"

Austin shuffles closer to me, gingerly extending his arm to hand me the cup of Kingston's blood. I snatch it from his fingers and gulp it, tipping it upside down with my head tilted back to assure I get it all. My guys gape at me as I stick my hand into it and run my finger along the inside until I swipe up every last bit.

Kingston releases a strange cross between a deep breath and a growl. "Fuck."

I turn my gaze to him, still sucking my finger, and my face burns with embarrassment as he gawks at me.

"Babe, you're a savage," he says.

Diego shoves him in the back, sending him crashing to the floor next to me. He startles, our eyes meeting, and I flare my nostrils at him. Kingston raises his hands in surrender, his midnight eyes so wide that I can see the whites around his irises.

"Careful, bro," Austin says.

I fake-glare at him. "Stop treating me like a wild animal, Austin. I'm—"

Rolling over, I throw myself onto Kingston and grab his

hands, lifting them over his head to pin him to the floor. He tenses beneath me, his eyes flashing silver, but he doesn't push me away or fight. He stares at me with a good intensity, waiting to see what happens next, his body reacting to the closeness of mine.

I smile and bend down and kiss him. "Thanks for taking care of me," I whisper against his mouth. "Even if you did call me a savage."

He relaxes beneath me, letting me melt into his arms for another kiss. Sliding his hands around my waist, he pulls me into him, ensuring there's no space between our bodies. "A sexy savage who I'll let devour me in...fuck. Too many hours." Tipping his head back, he glances at Austin. "Trade days with me, Austin. You can still have the night."

Austin's mouth tightens for a second before he smirks. "Not a chance."

I lean up and pat Kingston's cheek. "You already got an extra day, dude." Because there is no friggin' way I'd sleep in the same room as Orlando. So now, I rotate the one day that's supposed to be mine alone between Austin, Diego, and Kingston.

"You know you want another," Kingston says, sliding his hands lower to squeeze my ass. He jumps the both of us to our feet, making me squeal and pat his chest until he lets me down.

"I always want extra time with all of you." I turn my attention to Austin and Diego. "But right now...I just want to eat. I'm still so hungry."

Orlando strolls a bit closer. "And I have dinner ready. Care to join us, brothers?"

I close my eyes for a second at his use of the term. I don't think I'll ever get used to it no matter how often Orlando refers to my guys as his brothers. And what's even weirder is that they'll call him brother back. Not often, but I have heard all three of them say it, though Kingston calls Orlando asshole more often than not.

"If Jewel is okay with it," Diego says, smirking at me, knowing my answer.

I give him a long once-over, taking in his flexing arm muscles before working my gaze to the rest of him and back to his smile. "Of course I'm okay with it. Why would you even ask?" I flick my gaze toward Orlando and realize that this must be some sort of rule between them. I sometimes wish they'd all give me a rulebook or something, so I know what the hell is up between them, but then again, I'm not sure I want to know.

Diego turns expressionless. "I just didn't want to assume, beautiful."

"Because it is our night together after all, precious Jewel," Orlando says, cutting between me and Kingston. He holds his arm up to me. "And things change."

"Maybe in another hundred years," I quip, faking a smile. "I don't care if you think your dickishness serves a purpose, but like I said, it's not going to make me like hanging out with you."

"I'm incredibly patient. You never know, perhaps you'll change your mind sooner if you choose to remember."

"Perhaps," I respond. "Perhaps not."

Kingston snickers as I allow Orlando to guide me from the makeshift gym that once was supposedly a carriage house, whatever that is. I can't imagine humans traveling by horse. Diego swears they did, but this was long before The Divide. He told me Orlando might know more, but I don't want to ask. I don't care enough to open a conversation that could make him think he has a chance with me beyond our agreement of my blood and company in exchange for protection for me, my guys, and my family.

Orlando and I lead the way to the formal dining room where familiar voices trickle through the air. With my family under the same roof, and in a vampire household no less, they've become accustomed to the night schedule despite the amount of shade in Ombre Noire.

"Lighten up, Ramona." Uh-oh. I wasn't expecting Ramona to be with my cousins.

"Lighten up? You both need to smarten up. This isn't Dark Terrace Ranch or Haven Springs. We are not safe here."

I stop in place, the familiarity of my sister's sharp voice cutting me through the heart. I knew she was here. I knew Orlando kept the contract of the blood debt from Donor Life Corp because of the Blood Rebels, and as long as I remain here, Orlando won't obligate her to anything. She usually sticks to her room and in the human section of the estate since she can't leave, so having her in an area I frequent weirds me out. Something is up. I haven't seen Ramona for more than a quick peek to make sure she was okay.

"Jewel won't let anything happen to us," Fallon argues.

Bringing his finger to his lips, Orlando motions for me to be quiet. I shift and peer at my guys standing behind us and reach out my free hand. Austin takes it, squeezing my fingers and rubbing his thumb up and down the side of my hand in an attempt to keep my heart in check.

"She let all of this happen." Something slaps the table, possibly Ramona banging her hands on it.

Dana huffs. "That's not true. Uncle Noah—"

"You will not place blame on my dad."

I inch forward and stretch my neck to peer at my cousins and Ramona huddled at the far end of the table with empty plates in front of them.

"He's why all of this happened," Fallon says, pushing her chair back.

"Don't be delusional. My dad had a plan. Hayden told me so. If Jewel had just listened to me in the first place, we'd be free of all this bullshit."

Dana slams down her fork. "You're being unfair, Ramona. Uncle Noah abandoned us. Jewel did everything she could, so stop being ungrateful. This place is a million times better than The Boxes."

"We shouldn't be here!" Ramona's voice rises with her

anger. "We should be in Haven Springs, especially now that Jewel is here. The blood debt is hers, not mine. Hayden said it was always intended that way."

"No one is making you feed Orlando," Fallon says. "I don't see the big deal. I don't want to go to Haven Springs. I like it here. I like that we can do what we want and that we get to see Jewel all the time. And you know what? I like that we get to be around her guys too. They're awesome if you'd give them a chance."

"Ugh, don't talk like that. They feed on us. We're nothing more than a blood source. They use Jewel, and she lets them. You two need to see that we're prisoners here. Jewel assures it."

"Jewel is—"

Orlando vanishes from my side and enters the dining hall. I rush after him and freeze in the entrance. Ramona jerks her attention to me and glares, not even seeing that Orlando looms behind her. Something dark lines his face, making me clutch onto the wall.

He flicks his attention to me for a second and then leans his hand on the table next to her. "You should thank your sister, dear Mona. Without her, you'd have lived a far different life. One you'd appreciate a lot less than what you take for granted now."

Ramona stiffens, tipping her head back to stare up at Orlando. Her brain catches up with her, and she whips her chin down to break her gaze. Picking up her butter knife, she grips it in her hand while glowering at her plate in front of her. "Screw off."

Orlando swipes the butter knife from Ramona and stabs it into the table. "Hearing you sound like your father is a lot less endearing coming from the mouth of—"

I clear my throat. "Orlando, that's enough."

"Aw, come on, babe. This was just getting good," Kingston says, stepping up beside me.

Diego slides his arms over my shoulders. "It kind of was."

"Fuck off!" Ramona yells, pushing back in her chair despite Orlando being behind her.

"Ramona," Dana says. "Don't be a bitch. If you didn't act like this, they'd be nice to you. You should appreciate that you don't have to donate. Ever."

"Because Hayden does it for us. Without him—"

Something inside me snaps, and I launch forward and crash into Ramona. We fall into Orlando, who doesn't try to intervene and lets the two of us land on top of him. All he does is restrain Ramona, stopping her from attempting to push me off.

And then she freezes, her blue eyes widening in fear. "Oh, shit. They were right about you."

My brows pucker. "What do you mean?"

Her eyes harden, and she glowers at me. "You're a monster. A threat. A traitor. A—"

Strong hands encircle my waist and pull me from Ramona. Orlando lifts her on her feet and spins her around, pressing her back to the wall. He growls in her face, capturing her with his eyes. "Return to your room and appreciate all that Jewel has done for you. Remember that it is Jewel who pays your debt, not Hayden. He pays only his own."

Ramona heaves a breath and rushes from the dining room without looking back.

I catch sight of my reflection in the ornate mirror hanging on the wall. My silver eyes flash at me, and even with the light, a darkness lingers beneath them. I can't stop thinking that Ramona might be right about me.

"Why don't you two go get some dessert from the kitchen? I might have made a cheesecake with your names on it," Austin says to my cousins.

The two of them bob their heads and get up from the table. Despite everything, they come to me and each gives me a hug that I had no idea I desperately needed. I ruffle Fallon's hair and kiss Dana's cheek, forcing myself to smile as I watch them go.

It took me a week to get used to them walking around this deathtrap of a mansion on their own, but they navigate it better than I do. And surprisingly enough, the few vampire guests Orlando allows on the premises leave all the humans alone. They don't ever test his or my guys' power. They respect them. Something that didn't often happen under the authority of Donor Life Corp.

A gentle hand touches my shoulder, and I flick my gaze to Orlando. "I'm sorry you had to hear that, Jewel."

"I just don't understand why she hates me so much. Did you mess with her head too? If you did, you need to tell me." I still can't process why Ramona flipped like she did. She can't get past whatever it is she holds against me.

Orlando stares at my reflection as I continue to gaze at my silver eyes, unable to look directly at him. His eyes soften for what feels like the first time since I've arrived. "The only manipulation I performed on Ramona was to keep her from attempting to hurt others, but I do wish I could tell you I had turned her against you. That could be fixed. Her attitude now? It arose naturally. Something so deep-seated will linger regardless of emotional manipulation."

"Oh." It's all I can manage to say.

He motions to the table. "Try not to let it bother you too much. Ramona has a lot of things to learn, as do you. Now, come on and sit down. You'll feel better once you eat."

"I'll feel better when I get some answers from you. You promised me. It was part of our condition," I say, hugging myself.

My guys watch us quietly, and I turn my gaze from my reflection to meet their eyes. They give nothing away apart from smirking their encouragement.

Orlando follows my gaze to look at them and finally nods his head. "I suppose this is a good time if you feel you're ready, Jewel. You know I'm surprised it has taken you this long considering that I know you have been holding onto a lot of questions."

"She always has a ton of questions," Diego says, stepping closer.

Austin heads toward the table. "It has always been one of my favorite things."

Kingston pokes my nose as he passes, following Austin. "Not mine."

I gape at them as they settle down at the table and look at me expectantly. I can't help feeling a little thrown off. I mean, I know Orlando invited them to join us, and I'm friggin' grateful as all get-out, but they seem so damn comfortable like we do this all the time. Orlando doesn't move from my side, and I shift on my feet as everyone gazes at me.

"Is something wrong? Do you have questions you'd prefer to ask me privately?" Orlando says, lowering his voice to a pitch intended solely for me.

"Uh, no. We don't need privacy. I'm just—I wasn't sure you would be willing to talk in front of my guys. I thought that's why they haven't been around on our nights." The last few nights with Orlando have been utter torture. I've wanted answers so badly, but a part of me always freaked out about opening a line of communication with Orlando without my guys.

"This has been an adjustment for you. I did ask for space from my brothers but not with the intent to keep things from them." Orlando flicks his gaze to Austin, Kingston, and Diego.

I purse my lips. "Then what was it for?"

"That is between my brothers and me. You must understand that we also have to figure out our relationship and infrastructures as a coven." Orlando nudges me to stroll toward the table and pulls out a chair for me across from Kingston, Austin, and Diego.

The narrow table allows Diego to touch my knee, and I meet his smiling eyes and run my foot up his leg. Orlando slides into the chair beside me but scoots it slightly away to give me some space.

I lean on my elbows. "I expect you guys to tell me when you figure it out. But right now, I want you to start with—"

Orlando bites his arm, cutting off my words with the distraction. He lets the dark red liquid partially fill a glass before handing it across the table to Austin. I find myself leaning closer, practically climbing from my chair and onto the table. The anticipation pains me. I don't even think I acted like this while starving in The Boxes. Back then, I had better control. Now? I'm pretty sure I'm drooling.

"Babe, control yourself," Kingston says, softly kicking me with his foot. He tosses a cloth napkin at me, and it lands on my head, breaking my concentration on Austin as we watch each other. "You know how much you've been testing Austin's restraint lately. He will happily let you latch onto him and suck him dry. I'm not in the mood to intervene."

Drooping my shoulders, I rest my head on the table. "Ramona was right. I'm a monster. My dad made me a monster."

"The only thing your father made you was a donor." Orlando gently touches my back between my shoulder blades. "Everything else, well, you were born this way."

I turn my head at his admission, resting my cheek to the cool wood to peer at him. "What? What do you mean *born this way?*"

I stretch my neck to gaze at my guys' reactions. None of them hide behind serious expressions. Austin gawks at Orlando, his mouth partially open. Kingston scrunches his nose, mirroring my *what the hell* expression. Diego squeezes my knee under the table, rubbing his lips together in thought.

Straightening his shoulders, Orlando removes his hand from my back and places his elbows on the table. He takes the now full glass of blood from Kingston. "Here, drink this first, Jewel. You overreact when you're hungry."

I stare at the glass, my insides burning, begging me to give in. But then I remember Orlando added his blood to the mix. I swallow. "I—I don't want to. Your blood—"

"Is strong enough to satiate you longer."

I flick my gaze to my guys again, but all of them quickly soften their expressions so that I can't tell how they feel about the new addition of blood Orlando insists is added to my diet. "It is?"

Orlando offers me the glass again. "I know you struggle to trust me, but I wouldn't lie to you. Just give it a chance. It will help you."

"He might be right," Austin says softly. He offers me a

smile when our eyes meet. "You managed to go longer without when...in Haven Springs." He doesn't say the words I know are on his mind. The two weeks Mitchell purposely kept them away from me before they knew that vampire blood was important to my survival were excruciating enough. I don't like to think about our time there either.

Diego reaches across the table to rest his hand on mine. "I know it's weird for you, beautiful, but if it could help...we just know you've been miserable. We want to do the best to change that and don't want you to feel like you have to deny your needs for our sakes."

"And if you hate it, you know I won't fucking protest if you say you'll never drink it again." Kingston smirks at me, trying to combat against my persistent pout. "I'll risk getting devoured by you and your zombie bite."

I inhale a sharp breath. "Fine, but I'm not drinking blood alone while you all watch me."

"I can go grab some gen. pop.," Austin says, getting to his feet.

I shake my head. "No, get your kit. You're going to let me feed you all, and then we're going to get answers. Right, Orlando?"

"She's so hot when she's bossy," Kingston murmurs to Diego.

Orlando smirks at me. "For today, I'll give you what you want."

ANOMALY

"YOU'RE SHITTING ME," I SAY, watching Austin fill up Orlando's cup. "Bitten? With venom? That's crazy. A vaccine would make more sense."

"It's a similar concept," Austin murmurs. "Being exposed to vampire venom in utero could possibly create a strengthened immune system. I can't imagine the survival rate to be very high, though. I know how much a toll venom takes on a healthy human. Not all people transform. Like children. The sick or elderly either. At least, as far as I know."

"Wait, what? Not everyone?" Austin's info bomb stops me from thinking about how I'm apparently a descendant of a woman bitten during pregnancy. I never thought much about it, but I guess he's right. I've never seen a child vampire, and

Donor Life Corp has strict rules when it comes to age and donations. It keeps the donor population from flipping their shit as well. "So, my ancestor—"

Orlando lifts his hand to touch mine but stops short and drops it to the table. "I'm sorry, Jewel. Austin is correct. Yvonne died during the first wave of the uprising during the chaos. But her daughter—Jade Jewell-Jordan—lived. "

My dad never mentioned her, but if she's my namesake, he had to have known. I wish he were alive for me to ask him. It makes me even angrier that he kept such a huge part of my life from me. "And she was like me?" I ask.

Nodding his head, Orlando says, "Yes, born into a half state of human and vampire. A dhampir, some might say. You look a lot like her, you know."

Surprise lifts my brows. "You know her? She's alive? That's how you know I'm immortal."

His frown cuts off the million questions that tumble through my head. "Unfortunately not. She died decades ago. I did know her, though."

Disappointment sweeps through me, and I slump in my seat and rest my head on my arm. A hand touches my knee under the table, and I link my fingers through Diego's as he silently takes in what Orlando has said.

Kingston pushes back from his seat and plops into the empty chair beside me, engulfing me in a hug. "Maybe this is enough revelations for tonight, babe. If you get more worked up, I can't properly cuddle you."

Austin reaches to brush the hair from my shoulder. "But I can...and I might make a small exception."

I offer him a weak smile, trying my best to keep my shit together. I mean, it's not like I knew my ancestor. My parents never told me any of this. The only pictures I have are of my grandpa and grandma. They lived in the city before The Divide turned it into Dark Terrace Ranch.

"I'm fine," I manage to say. "Just a little overwhelmed." Shifting away from Kingston, I glance at Orlando again. He captures me with his blue eyes but not in the way vampires do to manipulate a human's mind. He just studies me so intently that I can't get myself to pull away. "So, what happened to her?"

"Blood Rebels. Jade died protecting her blood source...one of my coven brothers. She made quite the impression on my entire coven, to be honest. Not unlike you."

I raise my eyebrows. "Don't you friggin' tell me you were in love with her."

He chuckles. "Most definitely not. She never let anyone get close enough to try apart from..." Sighing, he lets his voice trail off. "No matter. Jade carried a fear of herself that led her to people she shouldn't have trusted. Fell for one, too."

It takes everything in me not to reach out and demand he tell me every single detail. "So, what happened? I mean, to your coven brothers?"

Orlando shrugs, eyeing Kingston. "Maybe some other time, precious Jewel. That information doesn't involve you or your ancestor."

I grimace. I have so many questions.

"But as for Jade, she had a son with your great-grandfather before she was killed."

My mouth falls agape. "He turned against her?"

"I don't know all the details apart from knowing that he was a Blood Rebel. They found out about Jade and couldn't understand her desires not to follow their fight. She believed in co-existence."

"I bet that went over well," Kingston says.

Orlando leans back. "They considered her a traitor against humanity and took your grandfather to raise. I kept track of him as...let's just say I owed my brother, but Chris was ordinary, purely human. So was Noah. And then you came. The mutation is passed through females."

"What about Ramona? We come from the same fami-ly...right?" We look alike. There is no doubt that she's my sis-ter.

"While you and your sister are descendants of Jade, you were born with the mutation, and she wasn't. Like I've said before, you're an anomaly. There aren't many like you, Jewel. Evolved. Even less who survive to maturity."

"Because humans protect their young and keep them from vampires," Austin says, trying to make sense of the in-formation. "They probably assume it's a sickness if they be-come symptomatic."

I frown. "How friggin' awful."

Orlando stretches his back and looks at the ceiling, breaking his stare on me. "You were lucky I agreed to help your parents, precious Jewel."

"I wouldn't call it lucky," I say, trying to process all of the information. It's so much to take in. "You took advantage of my parents."

"She's right. Fucked up is more like it," Kingston says, releasing a soft growl.

Orlando doesn't react. "I did what I had to."

"What you *had* to?" Anger rushes through me. "You forced my dad into exchanging blood for blood. You tried to use my weakness to your advantage by basically commanding that he give me to you."

Orlando remains unfazed, though the corners of his mouth twitch. "It was a fair request, and you were not against it. He couldn't see the future like you could."

I push Orlando's shoulder, making his eyes flash silver. "You kidnapped him."

He shifts out of my reach, pushing his chair away. "He planned to break our deal. I could not allow such a thing for your sake."

Clenching my fingers, I say, "He was only trying to take care of me to the best of his capabilities."

"You have no idea what kind of man your father was. He wanted to use you for his cause. He thought once you were mature, things would change and that you—" Orlando slaps the table, startling me. "You would've ended up dead like

Jade."

"You're wrong," I whisper to keep my voice even. The passion in his voice, the sudden protectiveness, prods at something inside me that begs me to see his reason. The human part of me struggles. I know—I knew my dad. My mom. They just wanted me to have the best life had to offer.

"Even if I am wrong, it doesn't change things. We had an agreement, Jewel. I did not put forth the effort to have you taken and used and killed. You are mine."

Shit.

All three of my guys growl at his claim.

I hold up my hand. "I'm not a piece of property. I don't care what kind of deal my dad made. I'm not yours, Orlando. Get it straight."

My words are enough to settle everyone down. Orlando looks like he wants to say more, but he tightens his lips and lifts up his empty glass from the table. "I think that's enough information about your family history for tonight. We have other important matters to discuss. But first, another drink if you're feeling up to it."

Orlando bites his arm and extends it over my empty glass, adding his blood to it. He slides it away, watching me watch the glass. Kingston takes it next, and then Diego, and lastly, Austin tops it off. The four of them watch me whirl the blood around, but I don't drink right away.

"Austin, I'm okay to provide more if you all want to join me." Because damn do I dislike drinking alone, especially with the way Orlando doesn't take his eyes off mine, expectantly waiting for me to either reject or drink the mixture of blood.

Austin relents to my suggestion and fills up all of their glasses halfway, claiming that I need to eat solid food before he's comfortable with drawing more. No one argues with him, and I kiss Austin sweetly, wishing I could move to sit next to him.

Orlando holds up his glass of my blood. "Here's to the start of our future together."

I tighten my jaw, still annoyed about everything. "If we choose to stay."

"If *you* choose to stay," he corrects, glancing at my guys. "I know your matches want to."

I glance to them too, and none of them react. I know their true feelings about the situation. We stay because it's the best option without our Divine name.

So instead of arguing, I clink my glass to his before my guys' and refrain from downing the mixture of blood in one gulp. I hate to admit that it still tastes good, even with Orlando's blood added, so I keep my face expressionless. Everyone watches me, and I sink lower into my chair under their scrutiny.

Austin lifts the lid on a tray brought in by the human chef and draws my attention by cutting a piece of meat. "Want a bite of steak?" His question is enough to distract me. My guys make it easy to pretend that everything is normal despite Orlando thinking he even has a chance.

I lick my lips and manage to set my glass down. "Sure. I'm still so hungry. You know, Orlando didn't even give me breakfast or lunch." I swing my gaze to narrow my eyes at him. "I felt lucky that he even gave me water."

Orlando sighs. "Jewel, it wasn't like that."

"You mean you didn't tell me no when I asked?"

Diego growls. "Are you kidding me, Orlando? You're supposed to take care of Jewel. It's not that hard to grab a banana if you're too lazy to put in a request to the kitchen."

Kingston twists his lips, slamming his empty glass down. "Shit like that makes it hard for me to want to allow you a moment of her—"

"Calm down. I was testing her capabilities," Orlando says, holding his hand up.

Diego scowls. "It's one thing not to feed Jewel when she doesn't ask, even if she's hungry, but it's another to deny her. You could've still given her something small to eat."

Orlando stares at the side of my face. "I offered my blood."

Kingston stands up and motions for Austin to take his place. I'm sure if Kingston sits this close a moment longer, he might do something he regrets. Plus, I sit in the middle. "Which you knew she wouldn't drink."

"I had a good reason. Right, Austin?" Orlando glances at Austin as he sits beside me.

"You knew?" Kingston practically shouts. He looks ready to shove his brother from the chair to take over.

Austin doesn't respond right away, quickly cutting up my food to hold up another piece of steak for me. I hum under my breath, the savory flavor making me already feel loads better. If I wouldn't risk choking, I'd start shoveling. Austin's way too slow, forcing me to chew.

"No, I didn't, but I've suspected that Jewel's capabilities might correlate with blood drinking. She gets more like us when she's hungry or hurt. Anger also brings out her...aggre— fiercer side." Austin's cheeks blush from his stumbling over words to describe me. Turning his gaze to me, he offers a smile, purposefully staying in control to offset the raging emotions consuming Kingston. He also continues to feed me, not even offering to let me take over for myself.

I play-hit Austin's leg under the table, sliding my fingers over his thigh to tease him into knowing that stating the obvious about my uncontrollable, crazy ass behavior won't hurt my feelings.

"That is correct," Orlando says, chiming in. "All I was testing tonight is to what extent."

Kingston slams his hands on the table. "You could've just asked. We're highly aware of Jewel's badassness. She outmatched Brayla. She managed to attack Mitchell. Hell, once she gets that hungry, pouty mouth on one of these guys, there's practically no stopping her without help."

I groan. "Kingston."

He bares his fangs to me. "What? I wish I could say the same about me..."

Diego bumps his shoulder to Kingston's. "Yeah, sure."

Kingston shrugs. "Okay, only sort of. I can't help it if I love our girl's gentler side."

I sigh and throw a dinner roll at him. "Enough with that." Turning to Orlando, I say, "What does starving me have to do with anything apart from making it easier to relent to drinking your blood?"

"As Austin said, you become more vampiric in nature, and I wanted to test your capabilities without having to provoke you too much."

"But why? You said I was born this way."

"You were bitten with venom. It's made you more powerful. Jade wasn't. If she was, she might have fared better. You regenerate faster now. She never could. Not like a vampire. She might have survived. It's what I want for you. I'm sure your matches would agree."

"Damn straight," Kingston says. "We'll keep you in my bedroom to assure it if we have to."

"Really, dude?"

He winks at me. "I can try."

Orlando brushes his hand through his hair. "Or we could move forward with my plan to assure Jewel continues to progress. To test her. Train her."

"Assure she can take care of herself," Diego says, offering me his brilliant smile. "I like it."

Austin feeds me another bite. "Me too. You can take care of us as well. Mitchell won't be a problem. We'll be stronger than ever."

Kingston groans. "I don't like it. I would rather just assure we take care of our girl so that we can spend the rest of eternity loving every inch of her."

I stick my tongue out at him.

Diego whacks Kingston on the back with a laugh. "You're just worried she'll make you look bad."

Austin chuckles. "Yeah, because she'll definitely be a better fighter than you."

I playfully run my foot up Kingston's leg. "He's right, dude. I can't wait to wrestle you."

Kingston flashes his fangs at me. "I might be able to get on board with that since I'm more of a lover than a fighter anyway. And you can wrestle me all day now. You know I'll let you win just to have you on top of me."

A soft knock on the doorframe draws our attention to Brayla. I was too busy focusing on my guys that I didn't hear her approach.

Orlando stands up and waves to a chair. "Join us, Brayla. We were discussing plans for Jewel's training. You might be the perfect person to help out seeing how well you've transitioned."

Brayla flicks her gaze to me. "I'd love to help Jewel learn how to take down the four of you. Us girls have to stick together, right, Jewel?"

I bob my head. "Right, Bray-Bray." It's still weird to see her as a vampire, but ever since my guys and I decided to stay,

Brayla doesn't piss me off as much. Sometimes, she still feels like the girl I knew in The Boxes. I don't know what's changed, maybe because we don't have to deal with the bullshit of Donor Life Corp and my guys have relaxed a little toward her, but I've managed to summon forgiveness for her. At least for now.

"Maybe on Diego's night. Orlando and I have something to attend to," Brayla says, glancing at Diego.

"I don't mind," Diego says.

Orlando places his hand on mine, surprising me, but I don't jerk away. "My apologies, Jewel. I forgot I had other arrangements for the rest of our night. If you'd excuse me—"

I lift and drop my shoulders and turn back to Brayla. "He's all yours."

Orlando turns to my guys. "Call if you need me."

"We'll be fine," I say, responding for them.

"I'm sure you will be." Bringing my hand to his mouth, Orlando kisses the back and then vanishes along with Brayla.

I shift in my seat and look at my guys. "This was an interesting night."

"You okay, Jewel?" Austin asks, draping his arm over my shoulders.

I shrug. "I don't know. I'm still letting things sink in."

"Would cuddles help?" Kingston asks.

"Possibly kisses." I tip my head toward Austin, and he grazes his lips to my temple.

Austin sinks deeper into me. "What about dessert? I can

see if your cousins left any."

"That sounds amazing. I want to check on them anyway. Maybe we can all watch a movie before bed."

Diego stands up. "Whatever you want, beautiful. I think it's the least we can do."

Kingston sighs. "Not what I had in mind with this unexpected Orlando-less time, but okay."

I laugh and shake my head, pelting Austin with my hair. "Thanks, dude. You're all the best. I'll figure out how to make it up to you."

Kingston purrs in his throat. "I can make a few suggestions."

"On your night," Austin says, kissing my throat. "She gets to hear my suggestions first."

Kingston growls.

I laugh. "But first the dessert."

Austin helps me to my feet. "First dessert."

This night might not be so bad after all.

RAMPAGE

"WHERE ARE YOU TAKING ME?" I ask, holding onto Austin's back, hiding my face in the crook of his neck to stop the wind from making my eyes water.

"It's a surprise." Austin slows and flips me over his shoulder and into his arms before setting me on my feet.

He silences my laugh with a kiss I can't help sinking into. I run my hands up his chest and bring him closer to me by his neck. Smiling against my mouth, he releases a soft hum of a breath, sucking my bottom lip between his, teasing me without getting carried away as much as I want him to.

"Come on," he says, easing away like the act tortures him to do so. "It's been so long since we've gotten to do this together."

I lift my brow at him. "Do what?"

Austin only smiles and offers out his hand for me to take. We stroll along a cement path through a garden I haven't seen before on the west side of the estate. I stop at a plumeria tree and pick a blossom, inhaling a small breath of the sweet scent. I tuck it behind Austin's ear, making him chuckle, and he leans in and kisses me again.

"I've missed you," I say, swinging our arms. "Feels like it has been forever since we've been alone." Having to give up time to Orlando doesn't help.

He pulls me to a stop outside a gate nestled within a wall covered in vines. I'd have missed it if Austin didn't show me. "That's why I wanted to do something normal. I know things have been unfavorable with the adjustment to our life here, and I promise to try harder now that things are settling."

"You mean...?"

Austin graces me with a smile that lights up his face brighter than the silver moon overhead. "Orlando and the Ortega Region have been accepted onto the Donor Life Corp board."

My mouth falls agape. "When? Why didn't you guys tell me sooner?"

"Just got word from Viorica while you were eating breakfast with your cousins. The vote swayed in Orlando's favor three to two."

"I bet Mitchell is furious."

Reaching up, Austin runs his finger over my lips. "You

could say that, but let's not talk about him anymore right now. We can save it for dinner with my brothers. I don't want to waste a single second of our time on things that make neither of us feel great."

Unfortunately for Austin, I'm nosey as all get-out. I open my mouth to tell him he can't just leave me hanging, but he wraps me in his arms and lifts me off my feet, silencing me with a kiss that leaves me craving more.

He doesn't stop kissing me as he carries me through the gate. He kicks it closed with his foot, the metal snapping against metal echoing through the air. I laugh and pull away, trying to look around.

"One more," he murmurs, caressing his lips to mine.

I smile and nuzzle my nose to his. "Maybe two. This is one of the best places in the world, you know."

"Hmm?" he asks, frowning for a split second.

"Not Shadow Crest Villa..." I kiss him again. "I meant in your arms."

Austin grins and finally sets me down, loving the cheesiness of my attempt at romancing him. He can't always be the one to make my heart pound like crazy.

He waves his arm toward an outdoor pool with a bubbling hot tub that cascades a steaming waterfall over the edge and into the glowing pool water. Under a billowing canopy, two lounge chairs await us. A small table with a collection of sweets and a bouquet of huge pink and yellow roses sits between the chairs. Glowing candles flicker from within glass sconces along the perimeter, illuminating the ground in sparkling fractals of blue light.

My cheeks hurt from smiling so much. "This is beautiful. Thank you, Austin."

"I'm glad you like it. I've missed our dates together," he says, sliding his arm around me tighter to walk with no space between us.

"I love it and you. This is exactly what I needed."

"Me too, Jewel. Just seeing you smile—it's the best part of my life."

My heart flutters at his words. "I can say the same."

Guiding me to the lounge area, Austin motions toward the swimsuit neatly laid out on a fluffy gray towel. He drops the privacy curtain, though we're the only ones around. I'm nearly certain no one would dare disturb us, not even Kingston and Diego. The huge walls around the pool block anyone's view too.

"Would you like to eat or swim first?" Austin asks, bouncing on his feet.

"Your choice. But be prepared. My whole body still aches from training with Orlando. You might have to swim with me."

"Is that so?"

"Mmmhmm. I might need help undressing too. But you first."

We both know I'm making an excuse to be close to him, and he's happy to play along with my little game. He looks like he could use it, especially with everything that's been happening in his life.

Austin offers the cutest shy smile and chuckles, running his fingers through his hair. He tugs his shirt off from the back of his collar. Pink tints his cheeks, reminding me a lot of what he was like when we first met. Without all the threats and nerves of being under the board's scrutiny, Austin can finally relax again. He doesn't have to hide behind his stoic façade.

He doesn't move, just letting me drink in the hard curves of his muscles in the candlelight. His green eyes flash silver, his fangs peeking from under his lips, and he shifts on his feet, rubbing the back of his neck.

"What's up? You nervous?" I ask, giving him a long once-over.

Unlike his brothers, he's more reserved. Even more so on our nights together since deciding to stay. And I think it has to do with my progression and need for blood. It doesn't help that Austin's been consumed with figuring things out and his place within Orlando's coven, as have I, and it's left us both in a state of trying to adjust to the change in our relationship.

We're still learning things about each other we couldn't open up about before—Austin and his life as a Divine, which he was saving for our Blood Vows due to Mitchell, and me, with this whole shit show I can't even wrap my mind around. We've been together for months, but things keep changing. It all feels so new again.

"Never with you, Jewel," Austin says a little late, pulling

himself from his thoughts.

I try not to react to the uncertainty in his soft voice. "I'm not feeling weird or anything. It's okay to come closer. I won't attack you with anything but kisses."

His brows furrow at my words, his lips parting as he tries to figure out what to say. "Oh, Jewel. I'm sorry. That's the last thing that concerns me with you."

I release a relieved breath. Because I'm sure dealing with me isn't exactly easy on him. It tests his control. He wants to give me what I need, no matter the consequence. And now that I know more about what's wrong with me, I can't stop thinking that my guys should be cautious. Our roles somewhat reversed. I'm far more dangerous. The thought unsettles me.

Austin must read my expression and the doubt in my eyes, because he adds, "I'm more excited than anything. I was a little worried about us, and I now realize it was all in my head."

I bite my bottom lip between my teeth. "Worried?"

"We've been through a lot. I know you didn't want to stay here with everything Orlando has done. I hate that we've put you in this position. You're sacrificing more than anyone."

"You didn't put me in this position, Austin. Mitchell did. Donor Life Corp. You've done nothing but try your best to make our lives livable and safe. And to be honest, it hasn't been so bad. I love having my family here. Things could be worse," I say.

He bobs his head. "We're going to do everything to assure that it doesn't get worse. I promise."

"As long as we're together and safe, that's all that matters." Even if it means staying. I don't say the words out loud, but I know it's true. Orlando wasn't wrong in his speculation about my guys wanting to stay. They don't have to tell me for me to know. This whole trial period as being a guest at Shadow Crest Villa was for me, not them.

Austin puffs out his incredibly kissable lips with a breath. "I want you to be happy too."

"I am seventy-five percent of the time."

"And I want to make it a hundred percent."

I nod and smile despite my chest tightening. I'm afraid to tell Austin that I'm not so certain that kind of thing is attainable as long as I'm sharing my life with Orlando. It's hard to get over the things he did no matter his reasoning. He manipulated my mind. Tried to erase my guys. Transformed my best friend. He scared me. Put me in a dangerous position and let me get hurt. Even if he did all those things to get me away from Mitchell and the Divine name, he was never part of our plan even if I've supposedly been a part of his.

Pushing the thoughts away, I take a small step forward, inching my way closer to Austin because he still doesn't move. I hope that his presence distracts me enough from the whirlwind of thoughts constantly spinning through my head. "What about you? How can I assure you're a hundred percent happy? That matters to me too."

Austin closes the space completely, hooking his hands to my waist. "This. Just being with you."

I slide my arms around his cool shoulders, slowly running my fingers over his muscles. "Is that so?"

He grazes his fingers under my shirt. "Mmmhmm."

"It makes me incredibly happy too." I stand utterly still as he drags my shirt up and over my head. "But so does this." Spinning in his arms, I saunter away from him all while unbuttoning my pants.

I hold my finger up to him, stopping him from getting closer, and shimmy out of my jeans, leaving them on the ground. Warmth blossoms through me, starting from my middle to work its way to the rest of me the longer I remain under the delicious weight of Austin's gaze. Desire darkens his eyes, his smile turning serious with the racing of his heart. His anticipation is so palpable that I nearly rush back to him.

Instead, I peek over my shoulder, listening to him intake a sharp breath as I unclasp my bra and let it drop to the ground. Austin inches closer, humming a breathless moan at the sight of me. He looks ready to rush me in the best way possible. My skin already tingles at the thought of his arms around me.

I laugh and wag my finger at him, hopping on one foot to kick off my underwear in his direction. "Nu-uh. You can't come any closer until you lose the pants."

"Jewel," he murmurs, trailing his eyes from my feet to my face.

Stripping down, Austin stands a few feet away, his lust and desire prominent through his boxers. He says my name again as a breathless plea for me to allow him to close the space between us, but I keep my hand up to him.

"I don't think I want to swim just yet," I say, clasping the corner of the privacy curtain that obscures our view of the pool.

"What did you have in mind?" he asks, licking his lips, taking another step closer, completely drawn to me.

I finally curl my fingers to him. "Come here and find out."

Before Austin moves, I yank the curtain open with a laugh and dash the few feet of space to the bubbling hot tub sending steam wafting through the air. Austin could have already caught me, but he jogs toward me at a human's pace, grinning as I splash onto the first step and flick the hot water at him.

All he does is laugh and then kicks off his boxers, leaving them on the ground. I move across the expansive hot tub, the waist-high, bubbling water feeling amazing on my skin, and wiggle my fingers for Austin to join me.

He splashes toward me, a huge, sexy smile plastered on his handsome face. I love everything about this moment and how light and carefree our world feels when we're alone together. It helps me remember that even though things aren't how we imagined, that life is still perfect regardless.

Standing on the step, I climb up the divider between the

pool and hot tub, uncontrollably laughing because Austin does. I'm ungraceful as hell, splashing water in his face in the process, probably looking all sorts of ridiculous. He jogs through the water in an attempt to grab me, and I jump backward into the pool, breaking the surface with a squeal.

Austin's strong arms slide around me, pulling my body to his, and we tread together with a few inches of space between us.

I shiver, the pool feeling a million times colder than the hot tub even though it's heated. Austin swims us to the waterfall where warm water engulfs us. He runs his fingers up my body to comb them through my hair, pushing my dark, sopping tresses over my shoulder.

Meeting his lips to mine, he kisses me softly, tasting of saltwater. His hand travels lower down my back until he can pull me as close as possible to wrap my legs around him, letting me feel his excitement graze against me.

I slide my hand between us and tease him. "I think I'm done swimming."

He moans, resting his forehead to mine. "Me too. It's a little cold anyway."

Smiling against his mouth, I kiss him deeper, caressing my tongue over his, not letting him break away from me as he tugs the both of us to the side of the pool. Austin lifts me from the water, setting me on the edge for a moment as he pulls himself out. Moonlight sparkles across his dripping skin I can't resist running my hands over. His muscles bunch and ripple under my exploration, and he scoops me up to carry me back under the canopy and to the lounge chairs.

"Is this okay?" Austin asks, gently setting me down.

I nod and pull him closer, silently giving him permission to lie with me. He drapes one of the fluffy towels over us and snuggles close, grazing his lips to my shoulder to work his way down to flick and lick and suck the sensitive skin of my breasts. Tingles blossom over my skin, his desperate touch showing exactly what he craves to do.

Desire flushes my skin, warming the both of us despite the chill in the air. Austin traces his fingers down the length of my body at a torturously slow pace. He kisses along the buzzing invisible line he creates, keeping his weight off me. I run my fingers through his hair and down his back, gently digging my nails into his skin. I press myself deeper into the soft cushion of the lounge chair, sucking my lip between my teeth to silence what I'm sure will be a loud ass moan the second Austin reaches exactly where he wants.

Whoa.

Austin squeezes my hips, keeping me in place, and releases a low moan while kissing my thigh. His voice vibrates against my sensitive skin in such a way that leaves me gasping. I manage to keep my rebel mouth in check as good shudders travel through me, setting my body ablaze with electricity that sinks deep in my core.

"I can't get enough of you," Austin whispers, grazing his hands up my stomach as he nestles down between my legs to lie on top of me. Resting on his elbows, he aligns to look down at me, running his fingers up my jaw and into my hair to push the loose strands from my face. "Especially when you look at me like this."

"Like I want you?" I ask, stretching up to kiss his neck. "Hopefully not like I want to devour you."

He chuckles and shakes his head. "Like you're in love with me."

A smile stretches across my face. "Because I am. Madly. Infuriatingly. Out of control in love with you."

"And you make me feel it without even having to say the words."

"Why do you sound surprised?" I can't help asking the words. Austin's always been guarded but honest with me.

"It's not that I'm surprised. Relieved mostly." He kisses me. "Happy. I don't think I've ever told you, but I never expected this. When I first laid eyes on you, I knew you were perfect for me. Then I thought I might not have been perfect for you. We didn't exactly enter the Blood Match Program for the same reasons. I had hoped I could prove myself to you, though."

I cup his face, searching his eyes for a moment. "Can I be honest?"

He nods. "Always."

"I never expected this either. It was so strange to me that you'd have such interest in a donor. And then to offer me forever after so little time—"

"Time means nothing to me, Jewel. You're my perfect match," he whispers. "What we've created together...it's all I've wanted. I feel lucky that you love me...after so little time to you."

I shake my head with a smile. "I knew I was spending the rest of my life with whoever I matched with, and if you think you feel lucky..." I pull him into a hug, begging him to sink against me to feel the weight of his body on mine.

"I love you," he whispers to my throat, brushing his lips to my neck. "Can I continue to show you?"

I respond by opening myself completely and kissing him. Austin whispers my name against my mouth, rocking his body slowly to start, just teasing and testing me until I dig my fingers into his hips and arch more to experience every amazing inch of him. He holds me tenderly, working his mouth along my jaw, continuing to whisper in my ear about how incredible and sexy I am.

Resting my mouth on his shoulder, I suck his skin just hard enough to leave a mark. His moans send shivers through me, and I graze my teeth, nipping him hard enough to make him pant harder. I move with his body, his desire turning into desperation, and I cling onto him, muffling the sounds of my own lust until he thrusts a few more times and slows to hug me.

He leans back and smiles. "I want nothing more than to let you bi—"

"Samantha, get back here!" Diego's voice echoes through

the air, pulling Austin's attention from mine. "Leave Austin and Jewel alone."

Kingston growls from somewhere nearby. "Let us handle it or wait until they return. They're on a date."

"Austin owes me and can make the time," Samantha snaps.

"Yeah, lover. We don't have all night."

I stiffen at the purr of Merrick's seductive voice.

"I'm not your damn lover," Kingston says, his voice deepening as it hums through the air.

"You're right," she responds. "I don't know what I was thinking. Without the Divine name, you're just—"

Something crashes. "Shut up, Mer. The last thing I need is for you to piss him off. Evora will never forgive you if Kingston decides to retaliate for your crap." Samantha's sharp voice whips through the air angrier than Kingston's.

Austin narrows his eyes, listening to the conversation outside the pool area unfold as footsteps draw closer.

"Austin, incoming," Diego calls. "Widows on a rampage."

Rolling off me, Austin grabs the towel from the other lounge chair and wraps it around his waist. "Wait here. I'll be fast."

I nod and gather my towel around me, listening as the metal gate creaks open. The arguing suddenly stops, turning from annoyance to whispers. I get to my feet and head to peek out of the curtain. Kingston grins at me, startling me. Covering my mouth with his hand, he nudges me back and enters, looking around at the candles, flowers, and dessert.

"Sneaky, babe," Kingston says, drinking in the sight of me in the towel.

"I'm the one who's sneaky?" I ask, smirking. "You're totally taking advantage of whatever the hell situation is going on. Why are the Vaduvas here? Should I be worried?"

Kingston glances behind him, staring at the closed gate. He doesn't take a step closer to me, though he looks like he really friggin' wants to. "Nope. It's under control."

"What do you mean no!" Samantha shouts, drawing my attention away from Kingston. "You owe me. This is all your fault."

"My fault?" Austin says.

"Yeah, if you would've just done what you were told, you wouldn't be in this position."

Austin growls. "Jewel's life was in danger. If you would've accepted that she was our match and didn't give the board a reason to question it—"

"Me?" Samantha says, cutting Austin off. "You're blaming me? It was Orlando. The Blood Rebels. Even Jewel. She's why all of this happened. I don't care—"

I startle at the scary ass roar that reverberates through the air. Something crashes and Austin yells. Kingston grabs my hand, stopping me from running out of the canopy. A loud thud echoes and then Samantha hisses. Merrick laughs.

"What the hell?" I ask, yanking my hand from Kingston's.

He materializes in front of me, making me crash into his chest. "Babe, don't you even think about it."

The gate clatters as someone enters the pool area. Hooking his arm to my waist, Kingston picks me up to drop me onto the lounge chair to stop me from running out to see what the hell is going on.

"Jewel!" Fear crashes over me at the sound of Samantha yelling my name.

"We need to talk. This is your fault, and I want you to deal with it."

Anger quickly suppresses my fear, and I scramble to my feet faster than Kingston has a chance to pin me in place. I don't make it far, though. He grabs the back of my towel, accidentally yanking it right off me. I spin, and he stares with wide-eyes before rushing to cover me up again.

He hugs me against him. "I'm sorry, babe. Sort of. But you can't go out there yet. Your eyes...she'll know something's up."

I stiffen for a split second and relax, leaning my head on Kingston's shoulder.

"Jewel!" Samantha yells.

A splash sounds through the air, and Kingston and I both turn to peek through the crack in the canopy. Austin and Samantha both pop up from the water. Diego holds onto Merrick, stopping her from entering the pool area. I glimpse a few figures behind them, but I can't get a good look over Diego's hulking frame.

"Just let me talk to her," Samantha says, splashing water in Austin's face.

Austin grabs her by the back of her shirt. "No. She's been through enough. She doesn't want to see you. Just leave us alone. We're finally happy here."

"Jewel, please," Samantha calls out to me, ignoring Austin. "It's about Cyprus."

Cyprus? I haven't thought much about the guy I met in Haven Springs since we parted ways. He went with his sister and the Vaduvas as a way to redirect attention away from the fact that we weren't running back to Dark Terrace Ranch to appease Mitchell.

"It's not a big deal, babe," Kingston says. "We don't owe her anything."

But now I'm curious.

Kingston spins me away and leans into me. "Oh, no you don't. I know what that look means, and I'm not Diego. You can't always get your way with me."

I poke him in the chest. "Is that so?"

Austin and Samantha splash each other in the pool as Samantha tries to swim in my direction. Just when she's about to pull herself out, Austin grabs the back of her shirt and yanks her deeper into the water. They both growl at each other, flashing their fangs, their silver eyes glowing like crazy.

"What is going on, brother? Do I need to intervene?" Orlando materializes from out of nowhere at the edge of the pool.

Great. I was hoping I could avoid seeing him for a few days or at least until dinner. He must sense my annoyance, because he shifts on his feet and glances in my direction, locking his eyes on me through the crack in the curtain. I step back and let it fall closed.

"Samantha was just leaving," Austin says.

"Austin, please. They'll kill him. You out of everyone should understand. Isn't that why you took Jewel's heirs away?"

"And we're the ones taking care of them," Austin says. "That's a huge difference. We've taken complete responsibility. What you're asking is a burden in these times."

Samantha groans. "You know I'd take care of him if I could. Mitchell..."

"What about him?" I ask, raising my voice to draw attention to me.

"Is none of your concern," Orlando says. "Let your coven handle this, Jewel."

Now that's the last thing I want Orlando to do. Kingston realizes it, because he heaves the loudest, most dramatic sigh. Austin groans next.

Diego chuckles. "Seriously, brother. You claim to know Jewel—"

I grimace at the term he uses on Orlando. "He doesn't know me."

"Jewel, please. Hear me out," Samantha says.

I tug Kingston a step with me.

"Don't be a brat, babe." Kingston smiles at me and leans in, brushing his lips to my ear. "Be the biggest pain in the ass ever. For the Vaduvas too. They all deserve it."

I smirk. "Fine, Samantha. I'll hear you out. But under one condition."

"Name it," Samantha says.

"You have to apologize to us. So does Merrick."

I don't think I've ever heard Kingston laugh so loudly.

NEW GUEST

"I'M NOT DOING IT," MERRICK says, crossing her arms over her chest.

Samantha touches her sister's shoulder. "Please, Mer. Do it for me and Evora. You know how much her brother means to her."

The gorgeous vampire crosses her arms. "She'll get over it."

"Come on. Is that really something you want to deal with?" Samantha shakes her sister softly, trying to get her to look into her eyes.

Merrick glares at me instead from over Samantha's shoulder. "She's your match. I don't care."

"Damn, I feel sorry for you," Kingston says, drawing my

attention away from the Vaduvas to him as he stands behind the couch, hovering over Evora and Cyprus. "They're currently discussing whether or not you'd forgive Merrick for not apologizing and sending your brother to meet his final donation. Merrick said she doesn't care if you do."

Evora frowns, her brows puckering together. "What?"

"Kingston," Merrick hisses, glowering at him for blatantly telling Samantha's match what she can't hear the Vaduvas whisper about.

"What? You're the one who said it. Can't blame me if I'm empathetic toward the situation." Kingston rests his hands on the back of the couch and leans forward. "My brothers would've already apologized a dozen times if our situations were switched."

"Because they're screwing her," Merrick snaps, flicking her hand at me.

Samantha whacks her sister in the arm. "They love her."

Kingston flies toward the archway to the foyer and points to the door. "Get out. You've had enough time to consider apologizing. I will not stand here and listen to you discuss how you think our relationship with Jewel works and the reasons we do what we do."

"Merrick!" Samantha's voice screeches through the room. "Please. Do this for me."

Merrick flashes her fangs. "Maybe if you'd share Evora like they share Jewel." The second the words escape, she slaps her hand over her mouth in surprise. Merrick's gaze darts from Samantha to Evora before turning to me for all of a second. She shifts, looking ready to flee the room.

"Whoa, shit," I whisper. "She's jealous."

Austin laces his fingers through mine. "Of course she is."

Diego touches my shoulder. "They all are, beautiful. What we have together is incomprehensible to most. Our devotion to you would tear many other covens apart. It's one of the reasons why the one-to-one is in place with the Blood Match Program. It's not only to keep the human safe. It'll be interesting to see how long the whole coven inheriting a human match if something happens to their vampire thing lasts."

"They'll most likely pass them to their leader," Austin chimes in.

Diego bobs his head. "You're probably right. Good thing for Evora if Merrick decides to murder Samantha."

Merrick's wide eyes narrow, and she glares at us. She slides around Samantha and struts in our direction. I half expect her to initiate a fight with how she inhales deep breaths through her nose, her fisted hands shaking at her sides. She stops a foot away and stares down at me, towering a few inches on her stilettos.

Austin releases a soft growl, tightening his fingers through mine.

I try my best not to react. The last thing I need is to lose control in front of Merrick. Diego massages his fingers into my bunched muscles to help me out, and Kingston closes the space just in case. Everyone else is as silent as Orlando is. He stands in the corner, watching everything unfold.

Merrick purses her lips. "Jewel, I'm sorry."

I blink a few times in surprise. I can't friggin' believe the words that came out of her mouth.

"For what?" Kingston asks, smirking at me from behind Merrick. He loves this way too much. I'll let him have it though, because I kind of do too.

Glaring at Kingston, Merrick raises her hand to shove him but stops short and turns back to me. "I'm sorry for my poor behavior since the moment we met. I was angry that the Div...I was pissed off that Kingston, Diego, and Austin matched before me. Please forgive me."

I nod. "Thank you. I accept your apology."

"Now, us," Kingston says.

Merrick huffs. "I'm sorry."

He lifts his eyebrow. "For?"

Now I laugh. I can't help it. This is way more satisfying than I expected it to be, and Kingston obviously feels the same.

"We accept your apology, Merrick," Austin says. Turning to Kingston, who looks ready to tackle him, he adds, "We'll be here for the next decade if she must go over the reasons. I'd like to get back to my night with our girl."

Kingston groans. I expect him to say he doesn't give a shit, but he surprises me and nods. "Yeah, yeah. What he said."

"Yup," Diego says, squeezing my shoulder. "And we'll do

what we can to assure the Blood Match Program starts up again soon so you can re-apply."

Samantha comes up and hugs her sister from behind. "Who knows, maybe we can have Mother convince the board to make another exception if another female comes along."

All Merrick does is nod. "Would be nice after all the bullshit lately." She side-eyes me, her eyes flashing silver. "Now, hurry up getting things settled. I can't stand here another moment and will wait for you in the car."

Merrick disappears without a word, and Samantha shifts on her feet, turning her attention to us. "So, will you care for Cyprus?"

I open my mouth to agree, but Orlando materializes next to us, finally moving from his spot in the corner. Taking an automatic step away, I lean into Austin until he wraps me in his arms, resting his head on my shoulder.

"I'll allow him to stay in my household if he agrees to sign a contract to become a member of my staff," Orlando says.

"What?" Evora asks from the couch.

Orlando smiles, lifting his brows in amusement. "Did you assume that Jewel ran my daylight household? Because she does not. She's merely a guest here. She can agree that she's comfortable with your brother staying, but she and her matches do not have the authority to bring in a human until officially agreeing to join my coven and accept the Ortega name."

Samantha frowns. "I thought..."

Evora stands up. "Samantha."

Orlando remains expressionless. "If you'd prefer, your brother could instead donate blood to cover his dues. Some of my guests would love—"

"No," Evora says, cutting Orlando off. Her bravery impresses me, but it makes sense. You'd have to be brave to enter the Vaduva household. I, on the other hand, am only brave with my back-up. "I entered the Blood Match Program to assure Cyprus would never have to do that again."

Orlando draws his gaze to mine. "Then I'm sorry, Ms. Vaduva. You must take your match's heir and vacate the premises. You wouldn't want to upset the delicate alliance your coven shares with the Divines...I guess just Mitchell."

For the first time ever, I feel bad for Samantha. I knew Orlando was an asshole, but I expected him to agree. It's not like he needs another staff member or someone to pay dues with me around. All the mysterious vampire guests, which I think might only be one or two, have their own sources. And now that Orlando's a board member and holds power in a region? He can bring in humans to live and donate to the gen. pop. blood pool for vampires interested in relocating. I know he'll eventually want to. My guys have talked about it.

"I can pay for his expenses plus anything else you require," Samantha says after a moment. "Please."

Orlando rubs his chin. "Ombre Noire isn't open to new residents yet."

Samantha frowns. Her eyes glass over for a second as she

accepts defeat.

"It's fine," Cyprus says, getting to his feet. It's the first time he's said anything, probably used to the new vampire customs he's had to learn at the Vaduvas. "I can take care of myself."

"But you helped Jewel. There is a target on you in and out of Haven Springs," Evora says. "Mitchell threatened the Vaduva alliance when he saw you."

"It's fine," Cyprus repeats. "I'm not afraid. I survived two weeks on Starlight Row. This is nothing."

"Ah, hell," Kingston whispers.

I catch him staring at me and realize he can read my thoughts the same time I even think them. Stepping forward, I touch Orlando's shoulder, making him turn toward me. "Maybe we can work something out."

Orlando's face softens, and he searches my eyes for a long moment. "That is what I'm trying to do."

"I meant with us." I shift on my feet and look at my guys, remaining utterly expressionless at my words. "Would you like me to give up my free day? My only thing is that I'll require separate sleeping arrangements."

He presses his lips together in consideration. "As tempting as that sounds...I want you to allow me to take the block off your mind instead."

I grimace, the thought stirring all sorts of unbidden, wild emotions through me. "I—"

"And agree to join my coven permanently," he adds.

Opening and closing my mouth, I attempt to tell him no friggin' way, but then I catch Cyprus looking at me. Samantha and Evora too.

I can't stand their silent pleas, so I turn and face Austin, burying my face into his chest for a moment. Diego and Kingston each take one of my hands, and the three of them sandwich me between their bodies just like I like.

"We'll do whatever you want, Jewel," Austin says.

I inhale and exhale his sweet, citrusy scent. "We haven't even discussed it yet." Peeling myself away, I turn to Samantha. "I'm sorry, Samantha. I can't do that. Not for Cyprus."

She frowns.

I turn my attention back to Orlando. "That's an asshole move, you know. If I decide to permanently join your coven, it'll be because I want to—and because Kingston, Diego, and Austin want to—not because you're trying to use my empathy against me."

Orlando steps closer and reaches up like he's going to brush my hair behind my face but stops himself short. "Point taken. And you're absolutely right. I owe it to you to make the decision on your own."

"Thank you."

"But there's still the other thing." He leans closer, gazing so intently at me that I can't look away.

I swallow my nerves. "You'll let him stay if I allow you into my mind? How do I know you won't—"

"Your matches can be there," he says, stopping me from

spilling my heart of all my concerns about leaving myself in such a vulnerable position with him.

I turn to my guys.

"It might be time, Jewel," Austin says, releasing a small breath. "I know you're scared of what you'll remember, but I know we can get through anything."

Diego reaches out and takes my hand. "We also know how much it bothers you that pieces are missing from your life. You don't have to keep the block for our sakes. We're good. It would be unfair to you if we weren't. You're allowed to have your life outside of us. We've had decades outside you in comparison."

Kingston nods. "And we'll love you no matter what, Jewel. We're here and aren't going anywhere. This could be a good thing."

But what if it's not?

I don't say the words out loud. I don't get the chance. My head automatically nods my agreement for me without my mind's permission. And then I say, "Okay. If I allow you to open my mind, Cyprus can stay here."

"Under your protection," Orlando says.

I nod. "Under my protection."

"I guess we have a deal."

"Jewel, why don't you and Brayla show Cyprus to his room and get him situated? My brothers and I will need to speak to the Vaduvas alone for a few minutes." Orlando gives me a look warning that I better not argue because he knows I will. We argue about practically everything like my survival depends on me picking a fight.

"Come on, Jewel. I'm sure your boy toys will spill their hearts to you later." Brayla materializes in the foyer, holding a black bag, which I assume belongs to Cyprus. "It'll make me feel better about my lover leaving me out when he knows I can handle the man-eaters."

"Perhaps you can join us some other time," Orlando says, smirking at her. "Right now, I need you to assure our new house guest knows his place. You are the head of the daylight household."

Brayla playfully sticks out her tongue, reminding me of what I sometimes do to Kingston. "Don't think you can use that excuse on me next time."

"This will be the last time. Promise," Orlando says. "And to be fair, you still need to work on your composure, especially around the Vaduvas."

She rolls her eyes. "Yet you allow Kingston to join you."

Brayla materializes next to me, taking my hand and tugging me toward Cyprus. Kingston mutters a slew of backworld words I can't understand, but it's enough to make Brayla tip her head back and laugh.

"What, dude?" she calls over her shoulder. "You make it so easy."

"Jewel is the only one who can call me that, Brayla," Kingston says. "And I fucking swear you better take care of my babe. I don't want her alone with that guy." He doesn't even look at Cyprus as he says the words, putting on his invisible vampire blinders that make him act like people who aren't worth his time aren't even in the same room.

I peek over my shoulder. "Seriously, Kingston?"

Kingston narrows his eyes at me. "Super serious. I don't even trust Brayla alone with you, but I have to suck it up. With him, nope."

I crinkle my nose and place a hand on my hip. "Sure, okay. That's totally it."

"It is for me," Austin says. "So we'll be fast."

"Twenty minutes tops," Diego adds.

I turn my gaze to Austin. "Try to make it fifteen, okay? I want to get back to our date."

He smiles. "You bet."

Brayla drags me along to keep her pace, motioning for Cyprus to take his bag. He slings it over his shoulder and strolls in front of us, only turning to smile at me when we enter a long, narrow hallway of easy riser stairs that lead to the second floor in what I think is a zig-zag design. The architecture of this house is so confusing that it's hard to tell.

"So, first thing's first. Don't wander the premises until you're familiar with where you're going," Brayla says. "If you choose to do so and get lost, I promise no one will go looking for you for at least a day."

Cyprus twists to look at me. "Is she joking?"

I press my lips together. "Probably. But don't worry.

You'll be staying in the same wing as me so at least you won't have to worry about plummeting to your death on one of the floor windows or having the roof collapse on you in the run-down part of the house."

He nods, unsure as to whether or not I'm joking with him now. "Okay."

Brayla waves her hand towards a closed door that I've never entered. "Most definitely stay out of the basement."

"Is that where you keep prisoners?" he asks.

Brayla flashes her fangs. "No, just the ghosts."

I side-eye her. "Don't listen to her. The ghosts only haunt the old séance room. But you'll never go to that section of the house. It's off limits."

"At least to you, new guy," Brayla says. "Jewel, on the other hand, can go anywhere she pleases. The benefit of being the best friend of the head of the household."

"Or because she's the blood source to the entire coven," Cyprus remarks under his breath.

I blink in surprise.

One second Cyprus strolls in front of us, and in the next, Brayla shoves him into the wall at the end of the hallway. He startles, his dark eyes widening, but he doesn't attempt to fight or move, just going slack as Brayla dangles him off his feet.

I take an automatic step back, fear blasting through me at how unsettling it is to see Brayla outmatch a guy a few inches taller and quite a bit heavier than she is.

"For your information, Jewel is not the blood source to

our entire coven. I have my own personal donor, thank you." Brayla releases him but doesn't move back, still pinning him to the wall. "And you better think before you speak again. It's impolite to comment on our household customs. Or have the man-eaters not taught you any manners?"

Cyprus doesn't respond, flaring his nostrils. He darts his gaze over Brayla's shoulder to look at me.

"Now apologize to Jewel. You're lucky I don't drain you myself and pretend it was an accident." Shit. Brayla standing up for me like this leaves me all sorts of confused. I know she means well, but she also knows I prefer no killing on my behalf.

"Brayla." My voice comes out a lot softer than I want, and I clear my throat. "I'm sure Cyprus didn't mean anything bad by his comment."

He continues to stare at me. "She's right. I didn't. I'm sorry if I offended you both. Vampire customs aren't exactly my strong suit. Samantha and my sister kept me away from most of her sisters. Tonight was the first night I even met Merrick."

Brayla moves away from Cyprus to return to my side. "Even the Vaduvas themselves know they're man-eaters. Probably the real reason why he ended up here."

"Not true." Cyprus risks stepping a foot closer. "Mitchell wanted Samantha to return me to Haven Springs for some reason or another."

Icy dread spills down my back at his words. "He doesn't

want to let the Blood Rebel thing go."

"Of course he doesn't," Brayla says. "The board currently vetoed his notion to split Haven Springs."

"They did?" That's new information to me. Last I heard, Haven Springs was days away from getting completely re-evaluated.

"Your boy toys didn't tell you?" she asks, her perfectly arched brows peaking on her forehead.

I remain expressionless.

"I bet they would've gotten around to it. Orlando probably asked them to allow him to tell you, and you weren't in the mood to talk—like always." Brayla flicks her fingers, motioning Cyprus to start walking again. Leaning closer, she brings her lips near my ear. "Which I don't get. He's been pleasant to you, hasn't he? He offered protection for your guys. Allows your family to stay here. He's not this awful person."

"That's easy for you to say," I mutter, trying not to let her words get to me. I knew sooner or later that she'd bring it up. Orlando probably put her up to it.

"It is. He's been good to me, Jewel. Even with his heart set on you." She slides her arm around my back. "But don't worry. I've known since the day we Blood Matched. The biggest thing we had in common was our love and loyalty to you."

Cyprus halts in front of us, and I nearly collide into him, because I struggle to process Brayla's words. She did not just say that Orlando loves me. I'm nearly certain she doesn't even know what that word means. Obsessed is more like it. I know and feel love on the deepest level with my guys and even mentioning Orlando is capable of such an emotion is more than ridiculous. It's friggin' ludicrous.

Brayla pulls me to a stop, preventing me from crashing into Cyprus. She hisses at him, making him step back.

"Knock it off, Brayla. It was an accident," I say.

"Yeah, well, you try telling that to your boy toys if I return you to them with even a scratch. They're overprotective and highly reactive when it comes to you."

I exhale a breath. She kind of makes a point. "I'll talk to them."

"Good luck with that," she says. Turning to Cyprus, she points down the narrow hallway. "Your room is the second on the left next to Liz's. If you need anything, ask her. I'm sure she'll be happy to see you. All the other rooms are off limits unless you want to be devoured by one of Jewel's matches."

"This isn't a human-only wing?" Cyprus asks.

"Orlando said you were to be under Jewel's protection, which means you get to stay in a room across from Austin." She glances at me. "But don't worry, he's much quieter with Jewel than Kingston—"

Swinging my arm out, I whack Brayla in the shoulder. She laughs, her voice echoing through the hallway. Cyprus doesn't react to her words, and it's then that I realize she didn't actually say the part about me and Kingston loud enough for him to hear.

My cheeks still flame like crazy.

"You are welcome to be on either a day or night schedule. It doesn't make a difference here," Brayla adds. "Though, the night is more fun. At least for me."

"I like the night too," Cyprus says.

Brayla smiles. "Well, that's pretty much it. Dinner is an hour before sunrise. It's up to Jewel whether you eat with her family or the staff. Any questions?"

Cyprus rocks on his heels and adjusts his bag. "Will you show me around more?"

"Depends who you're asking," Brayla says.

Cyprus looks at me. "No offense, Jewel, but I think I'd be safer if you let your best friend show me around. I don't think the Divines—"

Brayla closes the space to him and covers his mouth. "Shhh. Don't say that name. Just refer to them as Jewel's matches or their first names until things are worked out."

Cyprus nods. "Got it," he mumbles against her fingers. "So, will you show me around?"

Brayla offers Cyprus a huge ass smile. "If you can survive your first day here, I will tomorrow night if Jewel is okay with it."

I fold my arms across my chest. "If you assure he doesn't get hurt."

"Perfect. We'll see you tomorrow. Get yourself settled and enjoy. If you can excuse us, Jewel and I have somewhere to be."

I frown. "Huh?"

Without answering, Brayla surprises me by hooking her arms around me to lift me off my feet. The world blurs as she steals me away.

HUMANITY'S GIFT

"WHERE ARE YOU TAKING ME?" I ask, clinging onto Brayla.

"It's not often I get a moment alone with you, and someone wants to see you. But I need to ask you a question first." Brayla sets me down on a balcony with a view of the dense forest that edges the far side of the property where a river runs through, acting as a border.

"What?" I ask, frowning.

She glances behind her and leans into me, getting close to my ear. "Did you consume any of Austin's blood?"

I shiver as her breath blows my hair, her closeness unnerving me. "That's personal, Brayla."

Fear sneaks up on me, and I shuffle back in an attempt to

put space between us. Her eyes flash silver, setting off my human rationale that reminds me that even though I grew up with Brayla, and we've been working on our friendship since her transition, she's still a predator. She doesn't have the best history of self-control, either.

"Jewel, please don't be afraid of me." Her voice lowers, barely sounding a pitch above a whisper.

I inch away, reaching behind me to feel the grooves of a crystal window. "Then take me back. Diego said they'd only be away for twenty minutes. I don't want to be here. I don't exactly trust you, Brayla."

Her frown deepens. "I'm not asking you to trust me."

"Why do you want to know if I consumed Austin's blood then?" Because I can only think of two reasons. She's either worried about my inability to keep my shit together if I need more blood or she wants to use it against me in the way I fear most by breaking into my mind. Why she'd want to? I have no idea, but it couldn't possibly be good.

She doesn't respond right away.

I move away even more, resting my back on the window. If I have to, I can shatter it. "Tell me now or I'll scream. Did Orlando put you up to this?"

Pursing her lips, she peers around again. "He—"

"That friggin' asshole," I say, cutting her off.

Brayla closes the space to me inhumanly fast and covers my mouth with her hand. "Chill out. He didn't. This has nothing—sort of nothing—to do with him. It's about your dad."

I grimace in confusion. "My dad? What the—"

"Psst, Brayla," a familiar, masculine voice calls from below. "We're ready. Hurry."

Brayla yanks me from my spot and jumps from the balcony with me over her shoulder. The sudden move steals my voice, my stomach flying into my chest. She lands with a thump, and a hand slaps something over my mouth—tape.

I try to scream, but Hayden comes into view.

"Don't do it, Jewel. You're noisy as hell. If you promise to be quiet, and really mean it, I'll remove the tape. It's just a precaution. The last thing we need is for you to do something you'll regret." Hayden touches my cheek, digging his nail under the edge of the tape. "So will you be quiet? We'll explain things as soon as we relocate."

"Relocate?" I mumble, the words sound more like an indecipherable whine.

"Not for long," Brayla says. "We don't have a lot of time."

I inhale a few deep breaths through my nose, trying to calm down my racing heart. A part of me wants to scream like my life depends on it to hopefully attract the attention of my guys, but one look into Brayla's brown eyes leaves me confused and curious. I know she worked with Hayden before to help us leave Haven Springs, but I thought all of that was for Orlando. Seeing them together now? It feels like something else.

And my friggin' curiosity. It always gets the best of me. I can't help it. Living my life with so many secrets and missing pieces leaves me wanting to know everything.

I bob my head and mumble, "Okay, I'll be quiet."

Hayden rips the tape from my mouth, making me wince, and I swing my arm out and sock him hard enough in the shoulder to send him stumbling back. He catches himself before he eats shit on the ground and glares at me.

I glower right back at him but don't say anything, afraid he might try to silence me again.

Brayla laces her fingers through mine and tugs me along at a pace I have to jog to keep up with. We head to the trees, the sliver of moonlight above us making it nearly impossible for me to see anything apart from silhouettes and shadows. Luckily, I don't catch sight of any silver flashing eyes.

"Almost there," Brayla whispers. "The cabin is right through the clearing."

"Whose cabin is it?" I ask, spotting a light illuminating through the trees.

"It belongs to the groundskeepers. There are a couple of housing units out here for the staff with families. I handle all of them." Brayla steps forward, dragging me along at this point because my feet choose now to resist.

The last time I was taken to a cabin in the forest, I was imprisoned and nearly murdered. It's when Katherine bit me with her venom, starting this whole shit show with my blood hunger. I was lucky my guys insisted on giving me their blood to protect my mind. Things might have turned out differently otherwise. But I can't think about it now.

A figure emerges from the cabin and hovers on the porch. Shadows slash across the man's face, making it hard to see his features.

"Jewel," Brayla says.

I turn to look at her.

Cupping my face in her hands, she captures my gaze. "Don't fight me. The blood should be wearing off enough that if you allow it, I can enter your mind."

I struggle, bringing my hands up to try to tear her fingers away. "What are you doing? Stop it."

She leans closer, her eyes flashing silver. "Please, Jewel. It'll help."

"Help with what?" I clench my jaw, managing to break my stare. Brayla tightens her hold on my head, and I lock my fingers to her wrists, fighting to yank her away. All it does is make her hiss and bare her fangs at me.

"Jewel, stop being a bitch and let Brayla do this," Hayden says, stepping up behind me.

"What the actual hell!" I yell. "Stop. Let me go."

"Cover her mouth. Someone will hear her," another masculine voice says. I tense at the sound of Mr. Diggs.

"Don't you fucking dare!" Swinging my arm back, I elbow Hayden in the ribs. He falls back, releasing me.

Brayla waves her hands at me. "Jewel, Jewel. Look at me. You need to calm down. I'm only trying to fix what I did to you."

"Fix? Are you kidding me? You did this before? How could you?" Jerking my arm up, I punch at Brayla. She misjudges my action, and I ram my fist into her chest, making her gasp. Her eyes widen, and she scrambles back.

I don't let her get far, charging forward in her direction. She dodges around a tree, and both Hayden and Mr. Diggs call out my name. But I don't stop. I don't run in the other direction either. Instead, I push hard on my feet, catching up with Brayla. I manage to lock my fingers to the back of her shirt and yank her back.

"Oh, shit!" she yells. "Someone help! She's going to bite me."

"Hell yeah, I'm going to bite you," I scream at her, pinning her down. "You can't break into my head if I do. You should've thought about this before dragging me out here."

She yells again, ramming her hands into my chest. I fly back, only yanking her with me. She lands on top of me and growls, snapping her teeth like it takes everything in her not to attack. I buck under her, trying to get my knees up to kick her back, but her predatory nature burns at full force.

"Brayla, stop. If you bite her, it'll be over."

Brayla punches the ground next to my head, sending dirt exploding over my face. I cough and spit under her, and she hops off me. I roll over and push to my hands and knees.

"Jewel, honey. I need you to take a deep breath. I know you're confused and scared, but it's going to be okay."

I freeze at the deep familiar voice. "Dad?"

"That's right, Jewel-babewel. It's me. I was hoping you'd trust Brayla, but it looks like it's going to take more than a few weeks to mend your relationship," Dad says, emerging from the trees. I tilt my head up but don't get to my feet. Brayla stands behind my dad with her hands on her hips.

"I don't understand," I say.

Dad takes another step closer. "Will you please trust me and let Brayla help you out. We don't have a lot of time to explain. You gotta get back to the house before anyone notices you're missing."

A huge part of me screams to get to my feet to hug the man I thought I lost, but a nagging voice keeps me in place, warning me that he's supposed to be dead. And if he's not, it means that everything I've experienced the last few months, brought on by Orlando, was never supposed to happen. That my dad purposely put me in a terrible position.

I open my mouth to ask him how he could do this to me, but Brayla flies forward and catches me off guard. She tackles me and cups my face, capturing me in her gaze.

"Brayla..." I slacken under her, feeling my mind automatically open up.

"Jewel, remember our agreement," she commands, her eyes flashing silver.

Releasing me, Brayla gets to her feet and dusts the dirt from her skirt. My head spins as my mind whirls, trying to catch up. I can't move. I can't speak. All I can do is stare at the starry sky through the sparse section of branches through the towering trees.

"Jewel," Dad says. His boots crunch over the wild terrain as he strolls closer. "Honey, I know you're angry—"

"I asked you to leave me alone." I dig my hands into the ground and finally push myself to my feet.

Dad wrings his hands together. "Please, Jewel. You have to hear me out."

"I don't have to do anything." I rub my fingers into my temples, remembering how shocked I was when Brayla brought me out here the first time Orlando called my guys away to help him with Donor Life Corp. And now, as I look at my dad in this moment, the feeling of relief that had cascaded over me discovering that Brayla faked his final donation to get him away from Orlando doesn't confuse me any longer. It doesn't exist at all.

Brayla gazes at me for a second, her hard features softening in a pout. "You have five minutes, Noah. And so you know, I won't do that to Jewel ever again. Now, hurry up. I'm not going to risk my life if she's not ready." She abandons me and disappears into the trees.

"Not ready?" I ask. "Of course I'm not ready. I'll never be ready."

"Jewel, please. He got into your head." Dad steps closer and offers out his hand to me. "The others are only using you. You make them stronger. One of these days, they won't be able to help themselves. You're different."

I ignore my dad's hand and push to my feet. "I know that I'm different. I know about Yvonne. About Jade."

Dad's eyes narrow. "Orlando told you."

I nod.

"And did he tell you that they died because of vampires?"

"You mean Blood Rebels," I snap.

Dad tightens his mouth, and I know my words got to him. Because they're true. Orlando told me that Jade died protecting a vampire, her blood source. "A vampire got to her. Got into her head...like you. It was the only way. The world didn't gift humanity with dhampirs to serve vampires. You were born to stop the devastation and help humanity thrive."

I scoff, annoyance washing through me. He used the term Orlando used to describe me. "You have no friggin' clue, Dad. I'm done here. You ruined everything the second you left us in Dark Terrace Ranch."

Turning away, I stride a few feet in the direction of the lights illuminating through the trees.

"So that's it?" he calls. "You're turning your back on your family? On Ramona? You know you could do something about her."

"You're why she's here! What you did—it ruined us. Now, leave me alone. If you don't, I'll tell Orlando about you." I curl my hands into fists and spin around. My dad stands a dozen feet behind me. Meeting his glassy eyes, I point my finger at him. "Actually, I should tell him about you. If you want Ramona, turn yourself in. But leave me the hell out of it."

Tears burn my eyes, but I don't cry. I manage to keep my shit together and turn my back on the man who was supposed to do everything to see to it that I got what I needed in the world. The man who was supposed to protect me. He was wrong about my guys. They'd never use me. It's my dad who does. I hate to admit it, but Orlando might have been right.

"Jewel, this isn't over. I'm not giving up on you," he calls, risking raising his voice to yell after me.

"But I'm giving up on you." I don't say the words louder than a whisper.

Thoughts spin through my mind, and I feel even more lost and confused than ever. How can my life have turned into such a mess I can't seem to navigate? Mom would've never allowed this to happen. If she were alive, she'd have never let my dad do this—to choose the fight he thinks humanity deserves over me.

"Fucking traitor," Hayden mutters under his breath, watching me from beside Mr. Diggs. I realize he keeps his hand on his weapon, but I can't tell if he's ready to shoot it at me or Brayla.

I don't plan to find out. "Brayla, please take me back home before I call for someone to find me."

Brayla materializes in front of me, and I catch sight of Mr. Diggs startling. She turns slightly and waves to her father without approaching. I have so many questions that I won't get answered because I can't stay here a moment more. As much as I shouldn't care if my dad's caught out here, part of me doesn't want to prove Hayden right. I'm not a traitor to humanity. I'm also not a traitor of my heart either. Whatever these Blood Rebels seek to accomplish can't bring about anything good.

"Jewel," Brayla whispers, keeping her voice low to a pitch only I can hear. "I'm sorry. I really am. You have to believe me when I say that I never wanted to forcefully keep this from you."

"But you did anyway," I say, glancing at her.

"I need you to understand—"

I shake my head. "Not tonight. I need to process all of this."

"You won't tell Orlando, will you?" she asks, sucking her bottom lip between her teeth. Worry lines her brown eyes. For the first time in a long time, I can't help being reminded of the girl who really was my best friend in The Boxes. The girl who snuck me food when she wasn't supposed to, who stood up to Kingston on my day of Blood Matching, the girl who swore to be my best friend forever. I didn't know how much I missed that girl. And part of me misses the me who thought such things were possible.

I think for a moment. "I won't tell him, no. But you can't ever mess with my mind again."

"I won't. I swear. I only did so because—"

"They think I'm a traitor," I say. "I know. I get it. But they have to realize that to be a traitor I would've had to have been on their side."

"They're just trying to survive in this world, Jewel," she says.

"Is that why you agreed to a Blood Vow to Orlando? Do you love him?" I wish I didn't want to know, but I can't help myself.

She shrugs. "Our vow wasn't based on love. He's kind enough. Powerful. I love life. It was something I couldn't refuse. You have to understand that. You made the same choice."

"You didn't answer my question," I say.

She brushes her hair from her face. "No."

"Okay." It's all I can manage to say. "Now, will you take me home?"

Nodding, she turns around and bends forward enough for me to hop on her back. "Please pretend we just went for a walk if your boy toys ask."

"I won't lie to them."

She sighs. "Then I guess I better hurry, so they don't ask."

I jump on her back. "I guess so."

INSATIABLE

"YOU'VE BEEN SO BRAVE, JEWEL-BABEWEL. I'm so proud of you." Dad releases me and steps back, giving me a long once-over.

I hug myself. "Why did you ask Brayla to help you fake your death? You knew what would happen...Ramona, she—"

"She's as brave and as strong as you are, honey. And I never meant for it to turn out this way. I was trying to save you. When I got word that you matched with all three Donor Life Corp Heirs, I had to help you. I thought you were one donor to them. Easily replaceable. I knew Orlando would do whatever it took to possess you, so I gave him a reason to try. But I underestimated the outcome. I had no idea that you'd fall so easily for a vampire's charm. I taught you better than

that."

I gape at Dad, my mouth hanging open at his words. "What?"

"It's okay, Jewel. You didn't know better."

Anger washes over me. I never thought I'd see my dad again. I never thought I'd get the chance to find out his reasoning for abandoning us—and now? I'm not sure I want to try. The man standing before me isn't the man who raised me—or maybe because I'm no longer the girl I was before.

"But everything's going to be okay. I'm here now. Soon enough, you'll be ready to fight."

I step back, putting space between us. "Fight? What are you talking about? I don't want to fight."

"But you must. You have a duty to this family."

"What family?"

"Jewel."

I shake my head. "No. You have no right to just show up after putting me through this without even telling me what the hell was going on. I mean, Blood Rebels? I thought you were a conspiracy theorist."

"It was better if you didn't know."

"Fuck that."

"Jewel!"

Dad rushes forward, trying to snatch me by my wrist. I spin out of the way and race to the door. Mr. Diggs charges me next, but I shove him back, sending him crashing into my dad. I make it out of the cabin and down the gravel path to the tree line.

"Brayla, stop her!" Dad calls.

Brayla materializes in front of me. I screech and stumble back. Hooking her arms behind me, she catches my fall and sets me back on my feet. I spin around to face her, and she sucks in a sharp breath.

"Jewel, please. Don't attack me," she says.

"Then take me home," I say, glancing around. My guys won't be back for another twenty minutes. I could run through the forest and hope that I somehow manage to make it back to the estate, but I'm certain I'll get lost. I'm not invincible. Donor Life Corp could have vampires all around, waiting for their chance to get me.

Brayla bobs her head. "Okay, we'll go home."

"If you leave, you better damn make her forget, Bray-Bray. I don't trust her not to say anything. We'll be slaughtered. You don't want to see that happen to your father, now do you?" Dad asks from somewhere in the dark.

I stare at Brayla with wide eyes. "Don't, Brayla."

Her eyes glass over for a split second, and she captures me in her gaze before I have a chance to react. "Jewel, we were never here. You will forget the last hour and think we just watched your favorite movie, but you fell asleep, okay?"

I resist responding, her ability to manipulate my mind weak. "No."

She releases a small growl. "Jewel, you will forget."

My muscles relax, my body lolling. "Brayla, please."

"Jewel," she repeats. "Tell me what we did for the last hour."

"No."

She digs her fingers into my cheeks, her eyes flashing silver. "Tell me we watched a movie."

I groan, pain exploding in my head.

"We watched a movie," she repeats. "And then you fell asleep. You had an amazing dream."

My eyes water, my head fogging.

Narrowing her eyes, Brayla commands, "Sleep."

"Jewel, hey. Jewel, wake up." Diego's voice pulls me from the dark forest and Brayla. "You're having a nightmare."

"Perhaps we should've given her more blood." Orlando's voice trickles to me next.

I struggle to open my eyes, my whole body wanting nothing more than to snuggle under the blankets. A soft moan escapes my lips, and I turn on my side, reaching out for Diego but only feel the empty bed where he usually sleeps.

A cool hand rubs my shoulder. "This side, beautiful. I'm right here."

Orlando clears his throat. "As am I."

I shiver and blink the sleep from my eyes, flopping back over without getting up. Bright light seeps in from the window, silhouetting Orlando's form as he stands behind Diego.

"It's still light out. What's going on?" I ask.

Diego helps me sit up. "Something has come up."

I rub my hands into my eyes and suppress my unbidden

fear. "You're dressed." Finally, I turn my gaze to Orlando. "Is everything okay?"

Orlando steps closer. "Yes, everything is under control. I told Diego to allow you to sleep because we'd be back before you awoke, but he insisted that you needed to relocate to either Austin or Kingston's room."

I shift and rest my head on Diego's shoulder. "Thanks, Diego. I'd have freaked the hell out if I woke up to you being gone."

He gives Orlando a smug as hell look. "That's what I told Orlando."

"I look forward to the day when I'm on the receiving end of her concern, devotion, loyalty...and possibly desire." The last two words come out slow and soft, almost as a test to my reaction.

I give him none. All I do is glance at Diego and curl my fingers through his under the blankets. "I'm going to assume you two aren't going to tell me what you're up to?"

"I need Diego to go into town with me for an inspection," Orlando says, surprising me. "Word has already gotten around about our region, and it's important to remove any unwanted, unregistered guests. Donor Life Corp is excessive with protocol and must offer final approval to anyone wanting to transfer."

"So we're going to open to new residents?" I ask, gobbling up any and all information Orlando's willing to share. I'm surprised he even does.

"First vampires. Then donors. The laws we create must comply with Donor Life Corp's."

I frown. "Meaning?"

"Meaning that there is still quite a bit of work ahead of us. But worry not, precious Jewel. Today is not the time for you to start worrying about our future. You must decide if we have one together first. Now, if you'll excuse us, we must be going."

Diego pulls me in for a hug. "I'll be back for our night. Promise."

I tilt my mouth up to his and kiss him sweetly, letting him lift me off the bed to set me on my feet. "I look forward to it."

"Want me to walk you?" he asks, holding me close.

I shake my head. "I'm good. I think I can manage twenty feet."

Orlando waits for me to let go of Diego and takes my hand, kissing the back. I stroll with them out of the room and watch them disappear down the hallway. Closing my eyes, I listen to the world around me for a minute but don't hear too much considering it's still midday with the sunset hours away. I half expect either Austin or Kingston to meet me in the hallway, but neither of them does.

I head in the direction of my cousins' room and peek inside, seeing them fast asleep. A soft voice comes from inside Cyprus's room, and I press my ear to the door. He talks in a low voice, and I make out him telling someone, probably his sister, that everything is fine and not to worry. Apparently, he believes he can handle himself.

I turn away from his door toward the soft music humming through Kingston's door. I don't hear anything in Austin's room, and sneaking a glance inside shows me he's not there. Either Orlando asked him to do something or he's busy in his new lab on the other side of the estate. He was a little on edge after he returned from arranging things with Samantha, and I wasn't much better because of...fuck.

Even thinking about my dad pisses me off. And I feel guilty as hell that I haven't told my guys. Austin looked like he needed a million cuddles and some normalcy, so we spent the remainder of the night swimming and joking around. I didn't want to ruin our first official date out of the Blood Match Program to tell him that everything we've been through was a result from my dad's crazy ass idea about where I belong in the world.

Quietly closing the door, I sneak the rest of the way to my room with Kingston and slip inside. I expect to find him in a seductive pose, waiting for me, but his form hides under the burgundy comforter in the dark room. No light filters in from the window at all, but the soft glow of his tablet programed to play music through the surround sound illuminates the place enough to see my way to the bed.

Tugging my too big T-shirt over my head, I abandon it on the floor and creep across the room, focusing on Kingston's rhythmic breathing through the slow melody of the music. I hold my breath and carefully crawl under the covers next to him, trying my best not to startle him awake. Kingston's usually pretty good at orienting himself immediately as to not go into attack mode, but it's best to still be careful. Only someone madly in love with a vampire would chance it.

Kingston doesn't move, his heartbeat and breathing remaining even as he sleeps. I roll into him and press my lips to his shoulder while snaking my hand under his arm and lower to feel his taut muscles, his skin warm from the blankets.

I glide my hand down the length of his body, grazing my fingers over every curve as I map his skin, stopping short.

"Lower," he whispers, taking my hand to guide me to exactly where he wants.

I nuzzle my nose to his throat and kiss him. "You were fake sleeping."

He moans and reaches behind him to slide his hand over my hip, but I don't let him move and instead explore the excitement of his body awakening to my touch. "Diego told me you'd be coming my way."

"Of course he did," I say, kissing his shoulder.

"He also said you might be hungry." His voice comes out all deep and raspy, sexy as hell.

"If I were hungry, I would have gone to Austin," I murmur.

"You did stop there."

I continue to work my hand over Kingston, trying to distract him enough to change the subject from Austin and eating to focus on solely me. He tries to shift, but I press into him and hold him against me so he can't easily move without using his vampire strength.

He tips his head back, stretching his neck to kiss my cheek. "But don't worry. I'm not jealous."

"Good. You shouldn't be. I've missed you, you know. The extra day in between our nights—"

"Really fucking sucks," he says, finishing my thought.

"Mmmhmm," I murmur, grazing my teeth gently across Kingston's sweet skin. "So, I want to enjoy this extra moment with you."

Kingston moans again and breaks free of me to flip around so we can face each other. He tugs me close, his hands quick and desperate to curl me around him. Rolling me onto my back, he rests between my legs and kisses me deeply, sucking my lip in between his before slipping his tongue into my mouth. The hardness of his excitement teases me, testing me, but Kingston doesn't rush. He glides his tongue over my jaw and down to kiss my breasts, shimmying lower to see how far I'll let him go.

"Kingston," I whisper, my desire sparking something deep-seated inside me, threatening to consume me.

"No fangs, promise," he murmurs, kissing down my stomach at an incredibly slow pace.

I arch into him, my body humming with anticipation and need. My breathing quickens as he eases my legs open more to accommodate his broad shoulders. I squirm, reaching down to comb my fingers through his hair.

Tilting his head up, he meets my gaze. "Is this okay? You can tell me to stop."

I swallow my nerves and nod. "I want this."

The second the words escape my mouth, Kingston accidentally extends his fangs and swears under his breath.

He quickly composes himself. "I'm sorry, Jewel."

"It's okay. I trust you to be careful," I say, my chest rising and falling, my body tingling, yearning, wanting nothing more than to continue with Kingston.

He releases a small breath. "It's not that. It's just—your eyes. I'm not supposed to test your control. I need to feed you."

"I'm fine," I say.

Kingston runs his hands back up my body to lie on top of me. "I know you are...but just in case."

I bob my head and kiss him. "Thanks for always taking care of me."

"It's all I want from our eternity."

I smile and watch him bite his arm before bringing it to my mouth. He gazes at me intently, his own eyes flashing silver, and I drink his blood until he eases his arm away to see if I'll let go. My body relents, and I bring my mouth to his neck and kiss my way down to his shoulder, sucking hard enough without biting, leaving a trail of marks in my wake. He moans and shifts to align our bodies, desire making him pant.

Amazing pressure builds between my legs, and I gasp and

dig my fingers into his back, our bodies coming together exactly how we crave. Kingston kisses me again, his thrusting rhythm in perfect sync with my body. He whispers my name, his soft voice tickling my ear. His love and longing crash over me in wave after wave, so palpable I can feel it in every single one of his kisses, every moan and breath, every thump of his heart beating wildly against mine.

I enjoy every second of our lovemaking as Kingston builds electrifying sensations over my body. His fingers glide over my skin, touching every inch of me with a desperation that teases my desire. He smiles and adjusts my leg a bit higher until he thrusts deeper, harder, faster. I gasp and moan, my muscles clenching from the crazy-amazing tingles that turn my panting into a loud ass moan.

Humming in his throat, Kingston captures the noise with his mouth, smiling against my lips, enjoying how I can't control my reaction to our passion together. How I arch forward and dig my fingers into his back and press my mouth to his shoulder without biting but just sucking his skin to leave the marks he loves.

Kingston releases a soft moan and kisses me again, slowing down as he finishes until the only movement comes from our pounding hearts and rising and falling chests. He smiles at me in the soft glowing light from his tablet, searching my face for a moment, happier and more relaxed than I have seen him in the last few weeks.

He rests his elbows beside my head. "How about I run us

a bath and feed you some more?"

"Or how about a quick shower and snuggling until I fall asleep instead?"

Kingston kisses my forehead and eases away from me. "You got it. I'm going to cuddle the hell out of you and assure you have the best dream about us."

I reach out and squeeze his butt as he rolls out of bed. Hooking his fingers to my wrist, he ends up tugging me with him, lifting me off my feet to kiss me all the way to the bathroom. The room fills with steam from the shower, and I join him inside, letting the hot water soak my hair. Kingston hums as he meticulously soaps me up with his hands, taking extra care to massage my shoulders and down my breasts.

"Kingston," I whisper, spinning in his arms, knowing he's about to sweep me away on another wave of our desire.

He licks his lips. "I love when you say my name like that."

I flush, my warm skin heating more at his words. "Are you hungry?"

"I'm always starved for you."

I sweep my hair from my shoulder. "Okay, but then we cuddle and sleep. It's technically not your day, and I don't want to be too tired for my date with Diego."

Kingston inhales a sharp breath and purrs deep in his throat, his eyes flashing silver. "Maybe he'll trade with me."

I narrow my eyes at him. "Don't you dare ask again. I don't want Orlando to think he can trade too."

"I'd never."

He's probably right, but I can't help the thought from sneaking into my mind. Because I think under these current circumstances, none of my guys want to shake things up. I've never seen Kingston behave so much. He only calls Orlando names once or twice a night instead of treating him like his name really is asshole.

"I just—"

He closes the space to me and kisses the words from my mouth. "I get it. I won't ask."

I bob my head. "Thank you. I'm still getting used to the arrangement. I need all the time I can to prepare myself for the excruciatingly awkward nights with him."

Kingston frowns, turning pouty as hell, his bottom lip puckering out.

Before he can say anything, I kiss him again. "It's okay, Kingston. Here is better than anywhere else at the moment."

"You shouldn't have to settle for this if—"

I cover his mouth with my hand. "I'm not settling. I am happy. I feel safe with you three here, the world doesn't feel like it'll explode at any second...and I get to be with my cousins. You seem to like it too."

"Hate it," he says.

I raise an eyebrow. "Seriously?"

He blows a breath between his lips. "No, I just hate that I *do* like it here. I hate that I can't provide this lifestyle for you without help or how much of my life I feel like I wasted serving Mitchell and the Divine name."

"The universe doesn't make it easy," I say. "I mean, come the hell on with my blood hunger."

Kingston chuckles. "Right? You're insatiable."

I slide my arms around his body and pull him closer. "You like it."

A loud crash comes from somewhere in the hallway, and Kingston quickly shuts off the water and wraps a towel around his waist. He throws me my robe from the door and motions for me to stay where I am, but I get dressed and follow behind him in time to watch him thrust his bedroom door open.

"Babe, it's fine. Stay there. I'll handle this," he says, waving at me to listen to him.

Two forms blur past the door, and Kingston jerks his arm out and grabs onto someone, dragging the two people apart. Cyprus lands with a thud on the middle of the carpet, and Brayla comes charging at the door, but Kingston blocks her way with his arm.

"What the fuck is going on?" Kingston asks, flashing his fangs at Cyprus and then Brayla.

"I caught him sneaking around," Brayla says.

Cyprus jerks upright, scrambling to his feet. "I wasn't sneaking anywhere."

Brayla flares her nostrils. "You were in Orlando's study."

"I got lost."

"Liar!" she yells.

Cyprus scowls. "Am not."

Brayla breaks past Kingston and charges into the room. She picks up Cyprus off the floor and holds him in front of her. "Yeah, sure. If that were true, you'd look at me."

"Brayla," I say, drawing her attention to me. "Is that necessary?"

Kingston grabs Cyprus away and slams him against the wall. "Totally necessary, babe. But it's not going to be Brayla asking the questions. It's going to be me."

DISTRACTION

CYPRUS STRUGGLES IN KINGSTON'S ARMS, and I rush across the room. Fear slithers through me, my body reacting to both Kingston and Brayla's predatory nature. Risking getting yelled at, I press my chest to Kingston's back and cover his eyes with my hands, stopping him from locking Cyprus in a stare that'll open his mind to be manipulated.

"Babe, what do you think you're doing?" Kingston asks, wagging his head back and forth in an attempt to get me to let him go without having to release Cyprus. "This isn't the kind of naughty I like...I mean, while I'm preoccupied."

I try not to react, though his comment makes me want to laugh. He picks the worst times to joke. Ignoring half of his comment, I lean into him and whisper, "I'm stopping you from performing something incredibly invasive on our guest. Not cool, dude."

He releases a soft growl at me. "You never had a problem before."

I draw him closer to me and hug him from behind, getting him to release his death grip on Cyprus. "Those people were out to hurt us, and the others gave you permission. Cyprus falls into neither of those categories."

"That you know of." Kingston swivels to narrow his eyes at me.

I glare right back at him but trail my gaze lower, drinking in his still damp skin, the sharp curves of his hips, the line of hair that disappears into his towel. He makes it incredibly hard to stay focused and to take him seriously when he's practically naked. His lips twitch up in the corner, and he has the nerve to reach up and run his thumb over my bottom lip, pretending to wipe drool from my mouth. He knows I'm getting distracted and uses it to tease me.

"Please, babe. Let me find out," he pleads, his voice lowering.

I flick his chest, making him release another playful growl. Tugging his hand, I pull him to me but spin the both of us so that I'm between Cyprus and Kingston. "Nice try, but no. Not happening." I stand tall, squaring my shoulders to create a bigger barrier with my body to stop him and Brayla from attempting anything crazy before I have a chance to figure out what the hell is really going on. "You're going to let me do the asking. He's my responsibility and under my protection."

Kingston sighs but doesn't argue. "You're lucky I enjoy you talking to me like this."

I pat his cheek. "You can't always be in charge, dude."

"Wanna bet?"

"Do you?"

"Fuck, hurry up with this shit. I need to be alone with you to find out." Kingston turns me to face Cyprus and rests his hands on my shoulders, obviously standing tall and puffing out his chest in an attempt to silently threaten the guy behind my back. I don't even have to look at Kingston to know. I can practically feel his intimidation burning against me.

Brayla steps closer, now more in control. She wants to know as much as Kingston, but after yesterday, I don't think she'll do anything to piss me off. We still haven't talked about the whole thing. I need a moment to figure it out. But later.

Because Cyprus fidgets, crossing and uncrossing his arms. Straightening his shirt, he messes with the hem, clearly uncomfortable that the three of us stare at him. He drops his gaze to the floor and rubs his hand up his face and into his hair. "I'm really sorry for this, Jewel. I didn't mean to cause any trouble or interrupt your shower."

I wish he didn't point that out. "It is what it is, but before these two decide to overrule my decision to do things the donor way, I need you to be honest with me."

His jaw tightens, and he nods.

"Why did you leave your room during daylight hours? You've been with the Vaduvas long enough to get on a vampiric schedule," I say, shifting on my feet, nearly certain I look a friggin' mess with my still dripping hair.

"Couldn't sleep. Was bored as hell." Cyprus flicks his gaze to look up at me for a second.

I tilt my head, studying him, trying to read him the best I can. I don't know him well enough to tell whether or not he's bullshitting me. "So you went into Orlando's office? You're lucky it was Brayla who found you in there, you know."

"Yeah, the rest of us would've ripped your fucking head off," Kingston whispers under his breath too low for Cyprus to hear. "Samantha would deserve having to console her sobbing Blood Match after everything she—"

I step on Kingston's foot, and he has the bravado to press his hips into my ass, poking me with his still prominent boner. I nearly lose my steely façade.

"Not sure if that was lucky," Cyprus says, drawing my focus from Kingston's bulge.

"Oh, it was," Kingston says, his voice low and unintentionally sexy as all get-out. He presses harder into me, trying to get me to step closer for him to get a better look at Cyprus from behind me, but I resist, pushing back a bit.

I shift in his arms, the movement making him dig his fingers into my shoulders as he totally tries to distract me in an attempt to let him have his way. "He's r-right." Stupid mouth. Kingston's going to be in so much trouble. "If Orlando caught you—"

"He'd have drained me," Cyprus says, finishing for me. It's the first thing I'd think of if I were in his position.

I shrug. "Doubt it, but you'd have probably been thrown out." I haven't seen Orlando hurt a single human yet, so I don't know. I never asked him. The only time I've seen him drink straight from a source was with Hayden...and my dad. He has a way of manipulating people into providing blood to him though he could easily take it. Everything I thought I knew about Orlando is now in question. But still, it doesn't change everything he's done. He's still an asshole and creep. Just more tolerable. Mitchell really lowered my standards after his craziness.

Cyprus doesn't respond, allowing awkward silence to fall between us. I can't tell if he's purposely trying to trip me up or if he's taking advantage of me to get his story straight in his head.

Obviously, Kingston thinks the latter, because he says, "Instead of trying to change the direction of the conversation, why don't you tell us why the fuck you were snooping around? Boredom doesn't cut it. You have plenty of entertainment in your room. You could've asked Liz to keep you company. You could've even knocked on one of our doors. I would've given you a thousand things to do to cure your supposed boredom."

Cyprus inhales a few deep breaths, his composure faltering under Kingston's scrutiny. "Okay, fine. You're right.

That's not why Brayla found me there."

She flies at us, but Kingston intercepts her before she tries anything. "I knew it!" she yells, jabbing her finger at Cyprus.

He bumps his back against the wall. "But I wasn't snooping. I swear."

"You better have a good reason then," Kingston says, the familiar click of him extending his fangs sounding in my ear. "Because if you don't, I'll have no choice but to hand you to Brayla to do as she sees fit. It is her household. And fair warning, if you think the Vaduvas are man-eaters..."

I whack Kingston. "Be nice."

"Not until this guy gets the hell out of our room so I can properly snuggle you like you requested," Kingston says.

Brayla offers me a small smile, because it's probably the first time I've stood up for her since our arrival. I keep my face expressionless toward her. We still have a lot to discuss but haven't had the chance to do so.

"Brayla isn't like the Vaduvas," I tell Cyprus.

Kingston grumbles in my ear. "She's worse."

"Kingston."

"He's right, Jewel. I am worse. I won't send him off during a good time, so he better have a valid reason." Brayla inches closer, placing her hands on her hips. "Now tell me. Did Samantha put you up to this?"

"Viorica?" Kingston adds.

Cyprus doesn't respond to either of them, creating even more tension. Most donors would be shouting a million different things to assure they don't find themselves on the receiving end of a vampire's anger, but Cyprus isn't like most donors. He once told me he wasn't afraid of vampires and not in the same way a Blood Rebel isn't afraid of vampires. He wants to be one.

I sigh and glance to Cyprus. "You gotta give them something, Cyprus. Right now, you look guilty."

"Because he is, babe," Kingston says, lifting me off my feet to move me aside to get closer to Cyprus. "Now, I'm doing things my way. He had his chance."

I crinkle my nose. "Cyprus, please. You don't have to be afraid of the Vaduvas. If it were them, we'll protect you."

Cyprus groans and rubs his hand on his neck. "It wasn't them. One of the staff asked to meet me there. Said they snuck some alcohol and that we could party since Orlando was gone. Please, don't throw me out. I don't want anyone getting in trouble."

I frown and side-glance Kingston who looks right back at me. "Alcohol? A party? Orlando doesn't care what the staff does around here during daylight hours as long as they don't hurt anyone or cause trouble."

Cyprus shrugs. "I didn't know. It's just what he told me. He said to meet him in the study, and we'd head out. I never had alcohol and was bored and curious, so I agreed."

Brayla huffs and crosses her arms. "Who was it?"

"I don't want to say," Cyprus says. "You look ready to murder someone."

I turn my attention to Brayla. She kind of does. Reaching out, I touch Brayla's arm before she blows up. "Brayla won't hurt anyone, but you have to tell us who it was. They obviously wanted to set you up."

Cyprus lifts and drops his shoulders. "Aiden or something. We only talked for a minute. He was in a rush."

"You mean *Hayden*?" I ask, my brows shooting up on my forehead. Of-friggin'-course it was Hayden. He and Orlando have a weird ass arrangement. Hayden exchanges his blood for time with Ramona. He might hate vampires, but he obviously understands how things work. My dad did the same thing with me.

"Yeah, that's his name. Hayden. He seemed pretty cool," Cyprus says, bobbing his head.

Brayla releases a scary ass growl and fists her hands. "That asshole. He set you up and took advantage of Orlando's absence."

Kingston surprises me by tipping his head back and laughing. Now that he knows it wasn't another vampire, he couldn't care less. "Looks like someone wanted to sneak off to visit with your sister for a little sexy ti—"

I cover Kingston's mouth with my hand. "Knock it off. That's the last thing I want to think about." I don't even like to imagine Hayden in the same room as my sister, probably filling her head with stories about how well taken care of I am while she remains imprisoned here, though I know Orlando wouldn't consider using her as a blood source, not if he ever wants me to stop hating him. I think he does it to keep Hayden in line, to be honest.

"What? Can't blame him. If that were you and me, you bet I'd—"

Before Kingston finishes the words, Brayla vanishes from our room. I blink with wide eyes, shifting to Kingston. He purses his lips, knowing exactly what's going through my mind. I want him to follow Brayla.

Kingston shakes his head. "No fucking way, babe. Don't you even ask. It's none of our business. Brayla has it under control."

I cross my arms. "Come on. You're not even a little curious as to why Hayden went through the trouble? It can't possibly be just about sex."

He flares his nostrils. "Hell yeah it can, and that's not something I want to interrupt, especially because I want to enjoy the rest of these unexpected hours with you."

"Kingston. I think you're wrong. Please, just take me."

"Why?" he asks, touching my cheek to peer into my eyes. His hard features soften the longer I lock my gaze to his. "You saw how she was last time you saw her. And Hayden's a dick. Let Brayla handle whatever the two of them are plotting."

His words ignite a blip of uncertainty in me. Plotting? Yeah, they totally are. Hayden knows that my dad is alive. He was there in the forest. He also knows that I rejected my dad. What if Ramona knows, and Hayden will tell her to keep her against me? What if this ensures that Ramona will forever consider me an enemy? Coming here, seeing for myself that Orlando was good on his word, and also now knowing that I didn't ensure a lifetime blood debt for my sister, I had hoped that we could mend things one day...even if it takes until she's old and gray.

I puff out my bottom lip. "I just...please, Kingston?"

Sighing, Kingston points from Cyprus to the door. I nearly forgot the guy was standing there. "Go to your room and don't come out until someone gets you. Got it?"

"Yes, Dad," Cyprus mutters and pushes past us.

Kingston growls and snaps his teeth but doesn't follow him. Slamming the door behind him, Kingston turns back to me and drops his towel to the floor, showing off his raging boner in a last ditch attempt to get me to change my mind.

I slowly drink him in, breaking his stern expression in the process. "Seriously?"

He nods. "Super serious. I'm dying for you again."

Sucking my bottom lip between my teeth, I close the space to him but dart around him to the closet. I throw him a pair of pants, and he lets them land on his head. "Then you better hurry and get dressed."

He groans. "I hate when you say shit like this. So not sexy."

I turn my back on him and drop my robe to the floor, smiling to myself at his intake of breath. Grabbing a dress, I slip it over my head without putting on any undergarments. "That's too bad. I was planning on making it up to you after, but since you're—"

Kingston hooks his hands around my waist and lifts me off my feet. "Fucking A. Let's make this quick."

"I don't see the big fucking deal, Brayla," Hayden yells, his voice echoing into the hall from the open door. "I pay my dues. Orlando isn't here."

"You should've asked," she says.

"Don't be a bitch, Brayla," Ramona says.

Brayla releases a growl and something crashes. "Don't you friggin' talk to me. It's your fault I nearly lost Jewel. She is finally coming around, and I won't have you two messing it up. I know you, Hayden. If I find out you said something you weren't supposed to, I'll assure you never see Ramona again."

"I'd like to see you try," he says.

Two figures crash into the hallway in front of us, and Kingston spins me around and shields me as plaster and debris rain through the room. Brayla hisses, extending her fangs, and shoves Hayden deeper into the crater their bodies created in the wall.

"You'll be lucky if you ever see Ramona again. You know the deal," she says, looking scary as hell with her flashing silver eyes and snarl. I half expect her to bite him.

"You tell 'em, Brayla," Kingston says, twisting one side of his mouth up in the cockiest of all cockiest grins that ever bestowed his handsome face. And he looks friggin' hot, especially ly since it's not directed at me.

Brayla startles and releases Hayden so fast that he doesn't have time to catch himself and lands hard on his knees. "As head of this household, this is my business, Kingston. Take Jewel back to your wing. I have things in control."

"You sure?" Kingston asks, peeking at me. "Looks to me like we were about to find two bodies, one of which, my match annoyingly still might have a slight attachment to no matter how infuriated it makes me."

I nudge him with my fist. "She's my sister."

Kingston grabs my hand and holds it between both of his so that I can't take more than a step forward without him. "She's the bane of my existence. *Our* existence."

"I think I can name a few people who qualify for that title, and Ramona doesn't. I would even consider Hayden more so than her," I say, looking from Hayden, who finally manages to push himself off the floor, to Ramona. She burns a glare at me from the doorway to her room. The intensity of her glower digs into me in a bad way, and I can't help turning my head away from her.

Brayla dusts her hands off. "You two are going to be the bane of my existence if you don't just leave and let me handle it." She turns to Kingston. "I never thought you were one to waste hours alone with Jewel."

He groans and squeezes my hand. "I can't believe you put me in a position to agree with Brayla."

"I'll make up for it," I say, smirking. "But, you have to let me go and give me a second with Ramona."

From the look he gives me, scrunched nose, lined eyes, and tight mouth, I'd think I just asked him to let me walk Starlight Row after dark without vampire blood in my system. Kingston tightens his fingers through mine and spins me away a few feet to press my back into the wall. Holding our hands between us, he leans into me, bowing his head next to mine to bring his mouth to my ear.

"Babe, please reconsider what you're asking. Whatever it is, it's not worth it. You're putting me in a position that requires me to disappoint you, and that's the last thing I want to do. It's unfair." Kingston breathes a soft breath into my hair.

"Unfair?" Annoyance washes over me. "You think asking for a moment to talk to my sister is unfair to you?"

He stiffens. "Fuck. See, you're already mad."

"I am not," I argue. "I just think you're being overprotective."

"With good reason. She tried to stake you. She tried to ruin our Blood Match. She is not worthy of even an ounce of your compassion and devotion. If your positions were switched, she'd have never even tried to take care of you. She's selfish. Ungrateful."

"Kingston," I say.

He rests his head on my shoulder. "Nu-uh. Don't you *Kingston* me. Ramona is out of her mind crazy and hostile, and she'll hurt you if given the chance."

"Can you blame her for being angry?" I ask.

"Yeah, I fucking can. She's angry at the wrong person.

She should be pissed off at your dad. He's the one who put you two into this position. He should've—" Kingston shuts his mouth and pulls away, linking his fingers behind his head, stopping himself from saying what's on his mind.

"He should've what?" I ask, touching his shoulders. "You know you can speak your mind with me. I'm used to it. It won't hurt my feelings."

Kingston turns back to me and engulfs me in a hug, lifting me off my feet to nuzzle his neck to my throat. "He should've listened to Orlando, but it doesn't matter. I hate to think this, but I'm glad your dad pulled this dick move. If he hadn't, I—I don't want to think about it. No point. We're here now, together, safe. And you can get everything you need. You deserve to be happy, Jewel. We deserve to be happy. Ramona doesn't make you happy, so be pissed at me or mad that I don't want you to give her any time. I don't care. I'd rather you be angry than crying your eyes out because you care for people you shouldn't."

Kingston sets me on my feet to look at me, and I stand in surprise. His words resonate within me, snuffing out my ability to be angry. I couldn't be. Not at him. Not for how much he loves and cares about me. Not for his need to protect more than my body but also my heart.

I feel the heavy gazes of everyone looking at us, though only Brayla could hear the conversation between me and Kingston.

"Let's just go, babe," Kingston says, reaching out to take

my hand.

I lock our fingers together and pull him back into me, jumping up into his arms to embrace him. His tense muscles relax, his thrashing heartbeat slowing. I don't think he was expecting me to react like this, and he happily devours my affection.

"Yeah, just go, Jewel," Ramona says, drawing my attention to her. "Listen to your master."

Kingston loses his hold on me and swears. No one has a chance to stop me as I rush Ramona and knock her off her feet.

We both scream.

SECRETS

"GET OFF OF ME!" RAMONA shoves her hands into my chest in an attempt to fight back.

"No. Not until you friggin' answer my questions." I straddle her, pinning her down under my weight. Hayden yells from outside the room, but Brayla blocks his entrance.

"Fuck off," Ramona says, flailing her legs, but she's not a match for me. I've been training in combat against vampires while she's been sitting in this room and gobbling up all of the lies Hayden fills her head with.

"How could you be like this to me?" I ask her. "I did everything I could to get us out of The Boxes. I entered the Blood Match Program for you."

Ramona grinds her teeth, her face turning red. "You act

like it was some kind of sacrifice."

"I almost matched with the psycho who used to own this place. His plans for my future with him were—" I shake my head and push the thoughts away. "Kingston, Diego, and Austin saved me from a terrible fate. You should've been happy that I wasn't chained to some table to be fed upon over and over until I died. You know, his coven sister tried to kill me after that? You have no friggin' clue what I've been through."

"Sounds so awful," she mutters, glaring at me. "Poor, poor, Jewel. So defenseless and so needy and desperate that she'd do anything with a vampire to feel loved."

Kingston growls. "Say one more thing, Ramona. Go on."

"You won't hurt me," she says, smiling. "Jewel doesn't have it in her to let you. I've heard that she demands you don't drink from anyone other than her. Disgusting how much she likes it."

Kingston disappears from behind me, and Hayden yells out. Ramona freezes beneath me, her hard features shifting with fear. A shadow falls next to me, and I shift and peer up at Kingston holding Hayden, bending his neck while flashing his fangs.

"Stop it!" Ramona finally manages to say. "Jewel, make him stop."

I don't move.

"I'll never forgive you if you let that monster hurt Hayden," she says, composing herself.

"You already won't," I say.

Ramona bucks, trying to break her hold on me. "Brayla! Don't let them. Orlando will be mad at you. You know he likes Hayden. He's the only one who can give him the information he needs."

Kingston growls deep in his throat, sending both Ramona and Hayden's hearts racing. "Don't worry. He'll still be able to when I'm through."

"Jewel!" she screams, her shrill voice making me wince.

I close my eyes, sucking in a long breath. "Kingston, it's okay. You can put him down."

"But, babe," he argues. "They deserve it."

"I know they do," I say. "But this isn't going to change things or make me feel better."

He squeezes Hayden harder, making him heave for air. "It will for me. You should give Ramona a real reason to hate you since she's dead-set on doing so despite it being all your dad's fault."

"You mean Orlando's," Ramona says, still trying to break free of me.

"No, he means Dad's," I say. "He's responsible for all of this. He never cared about us."

"Liar!" Ramona screams. "He did everything for us. He would be so disappointed in you, Jewel."

I lick my lips. "You're right. He would be, but not because of what you think."

She glowers. "Then why?"

Glancing over my shoulder, I look to the others as silence

fills the room. Kingston even lets go of Hayden to pay attention to my conversation with Ramona.

"Jewel," Brayla warns. "Don't."

Kingston's eyebrows pinch together. "Don't what?"

Brayla ignores him and glides closer. "I mean it."

I swallow the burning in my throat. Ramona should know. She should hear it for herself that our dad is alive and well. That he set us up with Orlando. She should know that the only reason she's stuck in his debt is because Dad assured it. I want her to see how wrong she is about our dad. I want her to know that he is truly responsible for this mess.

Kingston grabs Brayla, stopping her from flying at me. The two of them break out in a fight, matching in strength, though Kingston's fighting skills are far more superior than Brayla's from his experience.

"Jewel, don't," she calls, trying to get past Kingston. "Kingston, don't let her."

He holds her. "Let her what?"

Brayla closes her mouth. "I—I can't tell you."

Leaning down, I bring my mouth to Ramona's ear, making her stiffen. "You want to know how I know Dad doesn't care?"

Ramona waits for me to answer my own question.

"Jewel!" Brayla screeches.

"Dad is alive," I whisper softly into Ramona's ear. "He faked his death to pass on the blood debt. So no, he doesn't care about us. All he cares about is himself."

"You're lying," Ramona says.

I pull away and get to my feet. "Ask your boyfriend. He knows."

Ramona darts her gaze to Hayden, who confirms it without even having to say anything. Brayla manages to break free of Kingston and rushes toward us. Kingston pulls her away and intercepts, dragging me off Ramona. But Brayla doesn't come after me. She lands on top of Ramona and cups her face in her hands, trapping her in her intense stare.

"Forget what Jewel told you," Brayla says. "You will not remember us being here at all."

Ramona slackens under Brayla without a word.

"Brayla, please," Hayden says from the door. "Don't do this. She deserves to know."

Flashing her fangs, Brayla glowers at Hayden. He takes an automatic step back, but he's not quick enough. Brayla launches to her feet and charges him, slamming his back into the wall. Veins pulse in Hayden's neck, his jaw clenched, his body stiff with anticipation.

"Do not speak a word of this. Get out of here and never disobey me again. Ramona is off limits to you without permission. Understand?"

Hayden relaxes under Brayla's mind manipulation. "I understand."

"Now apologize to Jewel and return to your quarters," Brayla says.

Hayden looks at me with glassy eyes. "I'm sorry, Jewel."

Without another word, Hayden disappears from the room, leaving the three of us with Ramona. She remains on the floor, staring at the ceiling. Brayla motions for Kingston to take me from the room, and the world blurs as he relocates me into the hallway. I listen to Brayla instruct Ramona to forget we were there once more before commanding her to sleep.

"Jewel," Kingston says, running his knuckles along my jaw. "What did you tell Ramona?"

I press my lips together. I knew he'd ask me, and I don't know if he'll buy any of my answers except for the truth.

Brayla materializes next to us. "Jewel and I are allowed to have secrets, you know."

Kingston tilts his head and searches my face, my expression surely giving away the fact that I am keeping something from him.

"And to be honest, it would be shitty of you to get mad at her for it, all things considered," Brayla adds.

Kingston's jaw twitches, but he doesn't respond to her. "Can I take you back to our room?" he asks instead of prying for more information.

I nod my head, a mixture of emotions burning through me.

Brayla touches my shoulder before Kingston can take off with me. "Jewel, you really don't have to tell them everything. They keep so much from you."

Slowly, I meet Brayla's brown eyes. "They do it to protect me."

Brayla squeezes my shoulder. "And that's exactly what I'm trying to do. Just think about it, okay? Once you tell them, you can never take it back."

A light tap on Kingston's door draws my attention from his as we lie on the bed, our hands entwined, our lips close enough to meet if one of us would lean just an inch forward. I thought for sure the second we returned to our room that Kingston would corner me and demand answers or freeze me out for not spilling my heart yet, but he did neither of those things. Instead, he set me on the bed, pulled the blankets around us, and hugged me. And we've been in each other's arms since.

"Hey, beautiful. I'm back," Diego says through the door. "Can I come in?"

Kingston subtly nods his head a moment before bringing his lips to mine for a feather-light kiss.

"Yeah, it's fine," I say without moving away from Kingston.

The door creaks open and two sets of footsteps enter the room. Neither Kingston nor I get up or move, just continuing to stare at each other. A thousand questions swirl through his midnight depths, but he doesn't ask. I think Brayla's words got to him about secrets. I know they got to me.

"We brought breakfast," Diego says, pausing.

The door to the room clicks closed. "You okay, Jewel?" Austin asks.

A cool body slides into the bed behind me, and Diego's

big hands wrap around my waist. "Did you keep her up all night, bro?" he asks Kingston while leaning to kiss me on the throat.

"Not in the way I prefer," Kingston says. "But it's fine. We're just having a staring contest."

"I hope you're winning, beautiful," Diego says. He puts a little bit of pressure on my stomach, trying to coax me to roll over to face him without pulling me away from Kingston. It's Diego's night, but we're still in Kingston's room. At least they don't yell at each other as often when they break their rules. Like now. Kingston lets Diego lie with us on his bed.

I ease my fingers from Kingston's and roll over to face Diego. Kingston closes the space to mold against my back, surprising me with the lack of his boner poking into me. Looks like I managed to actually kill it tonight. At least he doesn't tell me that I did.

"I think me and Kingston tied," I murmur, hugging Diego for a moment, snuggling my face into his chest to breathe in his sweet scent.

"You guys okay?" Austin asks, setting down the tray of food on the night stand.

I lean up to peer at him and raise my hand. "I don't know, really."

Austin frowns, taking my extended hand to kiss. He turns his gaze to his brother. "Kingston?"

"What she said," he responds, burying his face in my hair to kiss between my shoulder blades.

"Okay…"

Instead of answering Austin and Diego's silent question about what the hell is up with us, I jerk Austin forward, sending him sprawling on top of us. He doesn't put up much resistance and lands on top of me without putting weight down, just bracing above us on his arms. His muscles bulge, and I stretch up and hook my arms around his neck until he does a one handed push up to hug me back.

I release a laugh. "Don't be afraid to smother me, Austin."

"Just be afraid of smothering us," Kingston says.

I nudge Kingston with my elbow, and he groans and rolls onto his back. Austin drops down on me and brushes his lips to mine for a second before getting back to his feet. Diego slides his arms around me before Kingston has a chance to shift back to me and stands up.

"Come on, beautiful," Diego says, scooping me into his arms, letting me wrap my legs around him. He takes the tray of food and manages to carry me and it. "Let's do breakfast in our room. I have some catching up to do with you. Austin and Kingston can hang out with your cousins."

I rest my head on his shoulder without protest.

"Maybe you can then tell me what's going on. I can practically see the thoughts on your mind swirling through your stunning aqua eyes."

"You better not, babe," Kingston says.

Diego spins us around, making me cling onto him. "Is it

between you and Jewel?"

"Yes," Kingston says the same time I say, "No."

"Jewel."

"Kingston."

Austin swings his head to look to each of us, and Diego adjusts me in his arms again. The tension between Kingston and me is so palpable that no one can ignore it. I press my lips together in an attempt to remain expressionless. I knew I couldn't pretend that what happened with my sister was nothing for much longer, but I was hoping to at least make it through breakfast.

"I've been trying not to pressure you and give you time to sort through your thoughts, but I swear you better not tell Diego first." Kingston fists his hands. "I was the one there. I know you guys have a connection and he's easier to talk to than I am, but...I'm trying my best. I want you to know that you can tell me anything too."

Ah, hell.

"Jewel knows that, Kingston," Austin says quietly.

Diego tightens his hold on me. "And you need to take a breath and chill out."

"Chill out?" Kingston throws his hands up and spins around to face the wall. "Something's up between our girl and Brayla."

"Who fucking cares," Diego says. "I will not allow you to make Jewel feel bad for not wanting to tell you what's on her mind. If she chooses to tell you, great. If she wants to come to me instead, she shouldn't feel guilty. I was her first personality match."

"Yeah, Kingston," Austin says, positioning himself between us and Kingston. "And that's something you wanted to deny. You can't pull this shit."

Kingston looks at me. "Jewel."

"Watch it, bro," Diego says.

I pat Diego's cheek. "It's okay, you two. Kingston's fine. He's just upset."

"Damn straight I'm upset. I thought you could trust me." Kingston's eyes flash silver, his fangs peeking out from beneath his pouty mouth.

I sigh and wiggle until Diego sets me down. Turning to him, I say, "I'll meet you in our room. You too, Austin."

Diego and Austin hesitate, drinking me in to see if they should listen to me and go or try to stay to help calm Kingston down. But Kingston slumps his shoulders and returns to our bed to sit on the edge.

"Just five minutes, okay?" I tell them again, shifting on my feet.

"Okay, beautiful. Call us if you need us."

I watch Diego and Austin leave the room, taking my breakfast with them. Kingston remains on the edge of the bed, ever so pouty. I can't resist pouting myself as I stroll to him and plop beside him. He automatically takes my hand and holds it up to his chest, letting me feel this heart thump under my palm.

"As cute as you are sulking, I hate it," I say.

"Killing your lady boner, I hope," he murmurs without looking at me, but I can feel his attention and focus on every inch of me regardless.

I release a breathless laugh and shake my head. "I can't tell. I'm torn between wanting to attack you with my mouth or cuddle you until you beg me for space."

He finally looks at me. "I'd never."

I pat his knee. "I know. And I'm sorry if it came off as me not wanting to talk to you about the Brayla thing."

"So it's just a thing?"

I sigh. "Apparently not."

"As long as you recognize it as a massive ordeal."

"I never thought it wasn't. I know it kills you that I haven't told you what it was about and what Brayla blew up over and manipulated Ramona's mind to stop her from remembering." I lean into him, hugging my arms around him. "And I'm sorry. It's not that I don't want to tell you. I'm just not sure how. It's...going to piss you the hell off."

He groans and rubs the heels of his hands in his eyes. "So you *are* afraid to tell me."

"Kingston, no. I don't know what I am. Not afraid. Confused, maybe. Nervous."

"Now you're really killing me." He rests his head to my shoulder.

"What I have to say might."

"If this has to do with Orlando..."

I scoot closer, pressing my leg to his. "No."

"I was just going to say we'd get through it."

Sliding into his lap, I sit on him to face him, taking his face in my hands. I meet my lips to his, kissing him tenderly without getting carried away. Kingston relaxes in my arms and rests his face on the crook of my neck, softly caressing his lips to my sensitive skin.

"We can get through anything, you know," he adds.

I kiss him again. "I know, especially together."

"I guess we should meet my brothers then, huh?" He eases back and smiles at me. "Unless you want to take a couple more minutes."

"They're probably listening," I murmur through another kiss.

"I don't care."

I giggle and push against his chest to get him to give me enough space to talk without mumbling into his mouth. I know if I don't, he'll take the opportunity to deepen our kiss, and I might just let him.

"I'll make up for it later. I mean, if..." I let my voice trail off. "If you can forgive me for keeping something from you."

Kingston stands up, carrying me with him to the door. "I'd be a total hypocrite if I didn't, Jewel. I get it. More than you know. I'm sure you have your reasons. But I want to make it so that we never have to worry. Mitchell ingrained such secrecy and strategy into my mind that it's taking me a while to open up to you the way I know you want."

"We'll get to that place."

"Hopefully now. Because you're freaking me out, in all honesty. I mean, a secret with Brayla? I can only assume the fucking worst with her."

"I...I didn't plan it. I technically didn't have a choice."

Kingston growls, tightening his hold on me. His eyes flash silver, and he tilts his head back to look at me. "You better not mean—"

I don't respond, keeping my face expressionless. "I'll tell you everything, but your brothers need to know too."

Kingston rushes to open the door, speeding at a vampire's pace to my room with Diego. He thrusts open the door only to slam it shut and lock it. Austin and Diego watch the two of us from their spots in the sitting area, leaning close like they were trying to figure things out before I even tell them.

"Brayla manipulated Jewel's mind." He looks at his brothers. "I hope you guys are prepared to leave, because I'm going to kill her."

I squish his face in my hands. "You are not. It's not what you think."

Kingston sets me down and grabs a scary ass sword from the display case on Diego's wall. "Doesn't matter. She crossed the line."

"Kingston," I say.

He doesn't look at me. "Who's backing me up?"

Diego gets to his feet and holds up his hands. "Let's talk about this first."

"We'll talk after," Kingston says. "Austin, you backing me up?"

He glances at me. "Yeah."

My eyes widen. "You guys."

"No, Jewel. You are not going to stand here and excuse her behavior. I don't give a flying fuck if you have history. She betrayed you as much as Ramona did. You're too damn nice. You care too much."

Tears burn my eyes, but I don't let them fall. "Maybe I do."

"And we love that about you, beautiful," Diego says, coming up beside me. "You wouldn't be you if you didn't care, even if they're undeserving."

Kingston moves past me too fast to grab onto. "But we're your matches. We made a vow to you. I can't just stand here and watch you get hurt over and over again."

Austin joins him. "Pack us a bag," he says to Diego.

I groan. "No."

"Don't let her out of your sight," Kingston adds.

Tugging away from Diego, I race across the room. Kingston and Austin both tense, but neither of them moves. I grab onto the front of Kingston's shirt and stare into his round, midnight eyes as they flash silver.

"Jewel," he whispers. "Let me do this."

I shake my head and pull him away from the door. "No. You need to let me explain myself first."

"But I need to find Brayla."

I clutch him tighter. "Kingston, listen to me. It wasn't Brayla's idea. She's being used."

"Orlando?" Austin asks.

"No, he doesn't know."

All three of my guys frown, finally settling down enough that I know they won't abandon me to do something crazy like murder Brayla and go against the Ortega name. The only reason they'd jeopardize their chance to join Orlando's coven would be on my behalf, and it's the last thing I want. They already do too much for me.

"Mitchell?"

I crinkle my nose. "That might be less of a surprise, but no. My dad."

Confusion pinches Austin's face. "Your dad? I don't understand."

Kingston growls and punches the wall. "Are you kidding me?"

"I wish I were," I whisper. "But no. My dad is alive, and he wants me to help the Blood Rebels."

NEW EXPERIENCES

"HE'S A DEAD MAN." KINGSTON paces in a circle too fast for me to focus on. "The only good thing about this shit show situation is I get the satisfaction of ripping him apart."

"He's her father, Kingston," Austin says.

"He lost the ability to say that the moment he left her. I bet he's the type to say that we should thank him." Stopping in place, Kingston turns to me. "You know I'm right, babe."

I lift and drop my shoulders without arguing. I can't blame Kingston for being angry. I'm friggin' pissed. But Austin's also right. He's my dad. He made the decision he thought was best, even if it did put us in an awful position.

"Instead of killing him, why don't we hunt him down and bring him back? It will help with the tension between

Jewel and Ramona," Diego says, stepping closer to me. "Think about it. We'd possibly gain an ally in Hayden. Never hurts to have rebels on our side."

I wring my hands together. "Hayden knows. He was there with my dad."

"Of-fucking-course." Kingston materializes in front of me. "You know we have to do something, right? If we don't, it'll put you at risk. I know you, babe. The second someone threatens any of us, you'll jump up and try to save the day...like in Haven Springs. From what we've learned from Orlando, the rebels are far more organized and widespread than we realized. I can only imagine them deciding not to give you a choice in the matter of whether or not you help. We must take action while we have the upper hand."

Diego hooks his arm around me. "I have to agree with Kingston. We no longer have Donor Life Corp to back us. Because of Orlando's ties to your family, they'll test him. You remember what he said about your ancestor."

How could I forget? She died protecting her blood source.

I turn my attention to Austin. "Do you feel the same?"

Austin stares at his brothers for a long moment as they converse with their eyes. After a silent minute, he focuses on me and nods his head. "I do. I know you don't feel like you are, but you're a predator. You stand the best chance against fighting vampires."

"You're the real man-eater," Kingston says, his voice

lightening. "I'm nearly certain every vampire would bow down and let you drain them."

Diego chuckles. "I'd die happy for sure."

I twist my lips to the side. "Now's not the time."

Kingston nudges my arm. "It's either tease you or go on a murdering spree."

I pout my bottom lip out.

"Actually, I thought of a third option. But you gotta lose the clothes." Kingston grins at me, his sharp features relaxing at his suggestion. I wish it were that easy for me to switch my mindset.

Austin links his fingers through mine, ignoring Kingston. "You know, it almost makes sense that the mutation would be symptomatic with you as a female considering there are far fewer women in the world. Kingston makes a point."

Kingston leans in, sandwiching me between his brothers, not giving me any space. He kisses my forehead. "Fortunately for the male vampire population, it's you and not your sister."

"I'm pretty sure her attitude was exactly what my dad was hoping for in me." I bounce on my feet to shake out the rest of my tension, my nerves settling now that Kingston finally chilled the hell out.

The three of them remain crowding me in the best way possible, each of them touching me like it's what they need the most in this moment. I could use it too.

Diego shifts behind me to massage my shoulders. "That's much better. I thought Kingston might set you off."

Austin squeezes my hand. "He'd have deserved to be devoured."

I smirk at him. "You wouldn't have let that happen."

"Maybe just a bite," Austin says with a laugh.

Heat floods my face, and I release a tiny breath. My whole body buzzes at the thought. I can't help it nor can I tell whether it's me or my deep-seated nature. My guys notice my reaction at Austin's comment, their faces lighting with all sorts of amusement.

"Damn," Diego whispers, putting a bit more pressure on my shoulders. "She totally wants to, Kingston."

I playfully elbow him in the stomach. "Do not."

"You so do," Kingston teases, risking touching my chin. "And you know what? After all this shit, I'm going to let you."

My eyes widen, my heart picking up speed. Fuck me. I can't hide the fact that the idea of doing something new with Kingston excites me. "Really?"

Kingston swears and says something I can't understand. "Damn it, bro. You were right."

Austin laughs and shoves Kingston toward me. "Won't be long. You can't resist her forever."

"Show our girl how brave you are," Diego adds, roaring a laugh while hugging his arms around both me and Kingston, pinning him to me.

Kingston straightens his shoulders and tilts his neck just a bit. "She knows I'm brave and fully prepared to satiate her every desire."

I kiss Kingston's throat, making him tense for just a second. Shimmying my body, I manage to break free. "You guys, knock it off," I say, playfully swatting Diego and Austin as they try to grab onto Kingston.

Kingston dodges them to embrace me, spinning me away from his brothers. "Yeah, you're embarrassing our girl."

"That's never bothered you before," Diego says, lifting an eyebrow.

Austin attempts to snatch me from Kingston, initiating a game of keep away. "And so you know, Mr. Personality Match, you're reading Jewel wrong. She's far from embarrassed."

I giggle and kiss Kingston's neck, grazing my teeth just enough to make him release a breath. And then I suck harder, tasting his sweetness without breaking his skin. The sexiest noise ever escapes his mouth, and I land with a thump on the bed. All three of my guys stand around me, staring at me with amusement.

"Uh-oh," Kingston whispers. "She has that look in her eyes."

Diego flashes his fangs at me. "My favorite."

Austin slowly reaches out and brushes my hair behind my ear. "So incredibly sexy."

"Fuck," I whisper, the intensity of their gazes burning over me as longing, hunger, and desire light up their faces. "You guys..."

"It's okay to give in to your needs, Jewel," Austin says, his voice deepening.

What started out as a playful game between the four of us morphs into something more serious. I shift under their sudden intensity, their need. My own desire. Linking my fingers to the comforter, I twist the blanket in my hands, inhaling a few breaths. My body continues to buzz the longer they stand there watching me.

Kingston gently kicks my bare foot with his socked one as I sit on the edge of the bed. "Looks like you could seriously use some food and hugs. I don't know about you, but after that info bomb you set off, I want some together time. Even if it means a damn group hug."

I smile at him, biting my lip. I can't stop myself from squirming and rubbing my legs together at his suggestion. Nothing has ever sounded so good. "I am sorry for not telling you guys right away. I know how bad secrets feel." My voice comes out soft, breathless.

"I'm over it. I can't be mad, babe," Kingston says, his voice just as low.

"I never was," Austin adds, drawing my attention to him. He closes the space more and gently rubs his fingers over my shoulder to push back my hair. I shiver.

"Same." Diego sits down next to me and pulls me into his lap but keeps me facing out toward his brothers. His lips brush against my collar where Austin exposed a bit of my skin. "And I'd love nothing more than to let you drink from me if you want to," Diego murmurs, sliding his fingers over my middle.

The prominent extent of his lust awakens under my ass, making me squirm just a little. Neither of us reacts, remaining expressionless though my sudden quick breathing totally gives me away.

Austin and Kingston settle in next to us, one on each side, and they link their hands with mine.

Kingston kisses my hand. "Yeah, babe. Devour me too."

Austin shifts closer. "Mmmhmm."

I tilt my head back to rest it against Diego. "How can I resist?"

"You can't." Diego bites his arm and holds it up to me, his sweet, syrupy flavored blood tantalizing me to draw his offering to my mouth. "Why try anyway? We want nothing more than to take care of you, beautiful."

He's right about my inability to resist, but not only because my body begs me to give in. I know how much my guys love giving me what I need just like I do for them. And it's been too long since we shared a moment together like this. They seem like they need it as a confirmation that no matter what kind of shit life throws at us, that we're going to be okay.

I wiggle a bit, smiling to myself as I work Diego up for a moment before bringing his arm to my mouth. The familiar click of his fangs extending sounds in my ear. I moan softly and taste his sugary blood, tingles rushing over my whole body as the side effect of drinking solely from him awakens everything good inside me, dragging it out.

Tilting my head, I let my hair fall from my neck and expose my shoulder to him. Diego nudges the fabric away and kisses my skin tenderly, grazing his fangs slightly, building anticipation inside me. I hum and nod my head, giving him silent permission to bite me. His mouth builds pressure on my shoulder until his fangs pierce my skin.

I release Austin's hand and dig my fingers into his leg. He covers my hand and guides it until I feel his bulge of excitement. I rub my fingers over his pants, stroking along the length of his hardness, teasingly exploring it. A million thoughts cross my mind, tangling into a jumbled mess. This wasn't how I expected to start my night, but as it turns out, I'm more than okay with the direction this heads.

Diego eases away from my shoulder and kisses my throat, running his cool fingers over my heated skin to staunch the bleeding. I continue to drink from him, sucking harder and harder, my body zinging with electricity aroused from the bliss ignited through me from all of their presences.

"Can I feed you now, babe?" Kingston whispers breathlessly, his voice deep with desire.

I don't let go of Diego, struggling to pull myself away. Kingston leans in and brushes my hair from my other shoulder to expose my throat and kisses my warm skin.

"Whenever you want," he adds, sliding his fingers over my leg to sneak up under the hem of my long shirt and between my thighs, making me gasp. I'm pretty friggin' sure I wouldn't have let go of Diego otherwise, but none of them were going to ask me to.

Diego runs his tongue up my neck and takes my earlobe between his teeth. "I'm going to move you onto the bed. Is that okay, beautiful?"

I bob my head, panting, unable to even squeak a word out. Diego shifts me between him and Kingston, and Kingston tugs me up onto the bed until I rest my head on his lap. He bites his arm and offers it to me, letting me drink from him while combing his fingers through my hair. Diego rubs my hands between his, caressing up my arm over and over again until I trail it over his legs to touch him in a way I know he craves.

Kingston's eye contact breaks from mine for a second to map down my body. He releases a soft murmur in his throat, extending his fangs, his eyes flashing silver. And then I feel Austin's hands trail up my legs, and he gets between them to kiss me on my thigh. Austin makes me moan so friggin' loud against Kingston's arm that I pull away only to grab Kingston by his shirt to yank him down to kiss my lips. He shifts to lie beside me and tugs my shirt up to expose my body to the three of them before drawing his lips down to explore the curves of my breasts.

I continue to rub my fingers over Diego, my attention pulled in three directions, but I don't feel torn. I feel better than ever. So hot and sexy. Loved.

The thrill and excitement of this moment leaves me on the edge of an imaginary cliff, fully prepared to jump with my guys ready and waiting to catch me. Their desire and need for me heats me up from my core. I had no idea I could ever feel so good, just being with them, taking a brand new step together. It fills me up with hope and love and certainty that this is more than real. Being with them comes as natural as breathing and being and existing.

I comb my fingers through Austin's hair, my body shuddering with passion and ecstasy, and he smiles at me as he bites his arm to give me his blood next. I wiggle and shift, silently holding my arm up to Austin to bite. Kingston works over my chest and gently pierces the top of my breast to drink. Diego lies back on his elbows enjoying my touch until the need within me subsides, and I release Austin's arm without having to be pried away.

I lick my lips, smiling, taking a moment to give my attention to each of them. Kingston kisses me sweetly, shaking his head with a small laugh. "The things I do for you."

I caress my fingers over his cheek. "Was it weird?"

He smiles with his fangs. "Fuck no. You're our girl. Nothing weird about taking care of you."

"You make us all feel loved," Austin says.

Diego settles in beside me. "And wanted."

Kingston reaches over and punches Austin's shoulder. "Only slightly jealous as hell. I mean, shit. That moan."

Austin chuckles. "Every single time. So hot."

Diego touches my blushing cheek. "Tell me about it."

I shake my head and smile, opening my arms to hug the

three of them together. Austin kisses me softly, squeezing my hand, and then he pushes up to get off the bed. He strolls across the room to the seating area and grabs the tray of breakfast he made me.

"I wish I didn't have things to do," Kingston says. "I want to stay and soak in our girl's beautiful smile."

I grip his hand, stopping him from getting up. "If it's a murderous rampage, you better stay."

"That can wait a few hours," he says.

I sigh.

"He's kidding, Jewel," Austin says. "We won't do anything rash until we've had a bit more time to discuss our options."

"But it will have to be dealt with," Kingston adds. "Maybe tomorrow."

"On your night?" I twist my lips.

"That's how important it is."

I get to my feet with Diego following behind me. "Promise me you won't confront Brayla or tell Orlando yet. Let me be the one."

"With us present," Diego says. "In case."

"Definitely." I stroll away from him and close the space to Austin to hug him. "I'm tougher with my backup."

"Not true, but it at least makes us feel better." Austin brings his lips to mine. "Now have fun with Diego. Kingston and I are going to Midnight Valley for a bit tonight to see if we can use our budding alliance with the Vaduvas in our favor to find Liz's grandson."

"Really?" I ask.

"We promised her, and now that the threat against us is inactive, we want to fulfill it," Kingston says, tugging me from Austin and into a hug. "So if you need anything...call Orlando."

I groan.

Diego wraps his arms around the both of us. "We won't need anything. It's all good."

Kingston and Austin each kiss me once more before leaving the room. I stroll to flop on the bed to bury myself under the covers, but Diego catches me midair and slings me onto his shoulder. I screech and laugh, patting my hands to his back.

"Nope. No going back to bed," he says.

I turn placid and just hang from my waist on his shoulder. "That's fine. I can sleep anywhere. Here's perfect."

He chuckles.

"You're surprisingly comfortable," I add, grazing my fingers over his back. "Despite these rock-hard muscles. That are totally kissable. Lickable. Bitable."

Diego flips me off him and engulfs me into a hug, lifting me off my feet for a second. "Still not satisfied, huh?" he teases.

I snap my teeth at him. "Insatiable."

He beams me a brilliant smile and guides me toward our closet. "Plenty of time for that in a bit but let me take you where I planned on first."

"And where's that?" I ask, picking out a dress and sliding it over my head.

"It's a surprise."

Diego pulls my favorite pair of slip-on flats from their spot on the shelf and sets them on the floor for me to step into. He grabs a hoodie and tugs it over his head and then hands me a sweater.

"Let me guess—"

He holds his finger to my mouth. "Nope. No using your irresistible charm to make me tell you."

My smile widens, and I nip his finger. "You need to work on your restraint."

He wags his eyebrows at me. "Maybe later. Right now, take it easy on me."

"Just this once."

Voices sound from somewhere in the hall, and we both look up. "We better hurry before someone stops us."

"What do you mean?"

He hides a weapon in a concealed sheath on his black pants. "We're sneaking out."

DATE NIGHT

DIEGO PULLS THE VEHICLE TO the curb in the middle of the small abandoned community of Ombre Noire and shuts off the engine. Without electricity, the dark town contains an eerie feel that sends a tiny bit of fear through me.

Exiting first, Diego strolls around the hood of the truck, watching me watch him with his gorgeous smile. It helps loosen the tension in my muscles. Opening my door, he offers me his hand and helps me step down from the monstrous truck. Where Diego used to drive sleek, high-performance cars as a Divine, he's now taken to vehicles better suited for battle with unbreakable glass and more room. It helps that the truck is also raised too far off the ground to be harassed by shadow dwellers.

"Where are we going?" I ask, peering around. Glancing up, I take in the glittering stars above us. Without the light of the city, the dark expanse of night sky sparkles brighter than I've ever seen it.

"Do you remember what we told you about Ombre Noire?" Diego asks, clicking on the flashlight he pulls out from under the seat.

"That it could have been a vampire's paradise had the local shadow dwellers not ravaged the human population?"

"That's right." Grabbing a backpack, he slings it onto his shoulder and shuts the door. "And because of that, most of this place remained untouched, even under Roger Caruthers' rule. His previous staff lived on the estate."

Diego pulls me along a broken sidewalk, pointing out any deep cracks I could trip on with the flashlight. I'm surprised he doesn't just pick me up and run us where we need to go, but I think showing me the town is all part of the adventure.

"You're not worried that someone will bother us here?" I finally ask, stopping to peer into a still intact window of a shop. Old clothes hang on various racks, untouched for who knows how long.

"Nah. Orlando and I swept the area last night and sent anyone looking for residency to the far north side to an old apartment complex. Even if they did explore, they'd leave us alone." Diego holds the flashlight up to illuminate the dark building. Old faded posters decorate one wall with dirty mirrors on the opposing wall. Various signage dangles from the ceiling, declaring some sort of sale. The place looks ancient.

I tap my finger on the glass. "Unless they were batshit starved."

Diego whacks the glass door with the heavy flashlight, surprising me. "It's a good thing I got the most badass match in existence to save my ass."

I laugh and shake my head, stepping back so that Diego can clear the rest of the glass to allow us into the building. "Is this the surprise?"

"Nope, just a detour. You look curious."

Taking my hand, Diego helps me climb inside and shines the light again around the small store. He strolls through the narrow aisle, running his hand across a row of hanging clothes, sending a dust cloud into the air.

I sneeze. "This place hasn't been touched in a while."

"I'm guessing since The Divide or shortly after. Most of this place remains undisturbed." Diego takes a couple of steps away from me and tugs out a shirt with an unfamiliar logo printed across the front. He chuckles and holds it out to me, imagining what I'd look like with it on. "Yup, this is the logo of a band that Kingston likes."

My eyes widen. "Really?"

He offers it for me to take. "You should wear it for him later."

I smile and twirl my finger to get him to turn around so that I can put it in his backpack. "What about for you and Austin?"

Diego shines the flashlight through the room and taps his finger to his chin. He runs his hand over another rack and pulls an off-the-shoulder sweater from a hanger. I lift an eyebrow at the slogan across the front, and he laughs. "What?"

"Hottie?" I shake my head. "Was this a vampire's way of labeling people."

He chuckles and hands me another top with the word *Goddess* across the front in glittery sequins. "Just the fashion of the time. But I don't mind labeling you appropriately."

Taking off my sweater, I hand it to Diego and shrug into the *Hottie* sweater, adjusting my dress and bra straps to hide beneath the fabric. Diego smiles, biting his bottom lip, and slowly drinks me in, beaming the flashlight from my feet to my shoulders. I sweep my hair back and show him the bite mark he left on me.

"What do you think?" I ask, bouncing on my feet.

Diego closes the space and bends down to brush his lips over my sensitive skin. "Perfect."

I spin from his arms before he can get carried away and pluck a few more shirts from the rack. I find one that says *Book Nerd* on the front, and Diego howls a laugh when I mention it's to wear for Austin. He moves to the wall and pulls a pair of glasses from an old display case and puts them in the backpack.

"To go with the shirt," he says, grinning.

I crinkle my nose, whipping my hair back and forth. "You're ridiculous...and incredibly sweet. I'll make sure your brothers thank you for the effort you put into wrapping me up for them."

He chuckles. "Maybe I'll get the next free morning."

I grab his hand and pull him toward the door. "I think that can be arranged."

Diego and I stroll hand-in-hand through the small town, taking our time to peek into every storefront we can. He points out an old bookstore and tells me that I should save the adventure for Austin and then we pass by a music store with old instruments in the window.

"I bet you could get Kingston to play something for you," Diego says. "It's been a long time since I've heard him."

"He never told me. I just thought he was obsessed with music and dancing." I cup my hands to the window. "What does he play?"

He waves his hand. "Everything. It was more of a human hobby of his. You bet he'll probably try to throat punch me for telling you."

"I bet he'll say he doesn't remember." I turn and glance at Diego.

"Just use that pouty mouth against him."

I laugh. "Let's stop by here on the way back. I have an idea for later."

"Whatever you want, beautiful."

Diego slides his arm over my shoulder, pulling me close. He bends slightly to walk with me, and I hug my arms around him, stretching to kiss him every few feet. His face lights with a smile, and I savor every bit of his happiness. Whatever my guys settled with Donor Life Corp has really lifted whatever worry that has been stealing their smiles from me the last two weeks. I'm so thankful to have it back.

Diego guides me along and motions to a store across the street at the end of the block. "And here we are."

Only remnants of an old, unreadable sign stick above the front window. I narrow my eyes, trying to get a better look as we approach, but a metal gate blocks the entrance like the store attendant closed down for the night and never returned.

"What is this place?" I ask, gripping onto the cold gate.

Diego motions for me to step back, and he locks his fingers to it and bends a section of it enough to allow him to break open the door. He smacks his hands together and then rubs them on the front of his shirt, smiling at me the whole time.

I sniff the stale air. "This is...interesting."

"Sorry I didn't get the chance to come inside earlier, but what's the fun in that if I already got to experience the adventure?" He steps inside the building first and waves the light around. "Shit, we might have to convince Kingston and Austin to come exploring. They'd get a kick out of this place. Very back-world."

"Are these movies?" I ask, stepping through the broken door.

"Uh-huh. Probably one of the last rental places in existence. This town is so small that they were already behind in technology at the time of the uprising and someone managed to preserve a little piece of history when the Duchanne Region won this area in the lottery."

"The what?"

Diego runs his finger over a few DVD cases just like the ones I inherited from my grandfather. "It's how territories were agreed upon during the divisions."

"Oh."

"But let's not talk about that. I want to see if there's anything here to add to our collection." Diego grasps my hand and tugs me along toward a long wall with shelf after shelf of DVDs. He picks up a few and holds them up to me to inspect.

"You know I'll watch anything with you," I say, smiling. I pop open the case. "But probably not this. It's empty."

Diego frowns for a second. "Empty?" The second the word escapes his mouth, he holds up a finger to me. "If I remember correctly, these are displays. They keep the actual disks behind the counter. I'll be right back. Why don't you pull out the blanket?"

Shrugging out of the backpack, Diego hands it to me. I unzip it and tug on the edge of a thick flannel blanket and pull it out. Beneath it, I spot a small container with the breakfast Diego packed to-go because he couldn't wait another moment to leave the estate. He hasn't said anything, but I think knowing that Austin and Kingston are out, leaving just Orlando and Brayla behind with us makes him nervous. Especially after what Brayla did.

My stomach rumbles at the sight, and I can't resist popping the lid off of the yogurt and fruit mix. I swipe my finger into it and suck on it, closing my eyes as the sweet berry flavor explodes across my tongue.

"I'm sorry, beautiful. I should've saved the tour of the town until after you ate," Diego says, returning to my side with a basket filled to the top with clear cased DVDs. He sets them on the floor and takes the blanket.

"It's fine. I didn't realize I was starving for food until I saw the container," I say, scooping up another glob with my finger.

"And watching you do that is making me incredibly hungry. But for you."

I laugh and slowly suck my finger back into my mouth with my eyes closed and release a purposeful moan.

Diego snatches my hand and draws me to him, bringing my finger to his mouth. I poke it on his fang and let a drop of blood splash onto his lip. His tongue glides across it ever so slowly, making my plan to tease him backfire, because I find myself leaning closer.

He smiles and brushes his lips to mine only long enough to make me crave more.

"Tease," I murmur, nudging him with my knuckles.

"Not for long."

Diego spreads out the blanket right in the middle of the floor and plops onto it. Digging into the backpack, he pulls out a spoon and motions for me to sit down with him. I nestle between his legs and let him feed me a few bites.

"Good?" he asks, using his thumb to wipe a glob he got on my chin.

"Mmmhmm. This is perfect. Thank you for going through all this trouble." I shift to face him. "You're so good to me."

"You deserve it." Leaning forward, he kisses me lovingly, pulling me closer until my legs rest over his and we completely face each other. "I know things haven't been exactly great lately."

"How are you handling everything? You don't have to keep it all bottled up. I want to be here for you." While Kingston's more vocal about his displeasure and Austin always speaks from his heart, Diego would much prefer to focus on me so that I don't worry about him. I can't help it though.

"Surprisingly, it's not as bad as I thought," he says. "I wouldn't say life is perfect or that Orlando is suddenly a good guy, but I don't feel the same pressure to be the perfect heir any longer. He does things differently than Mitchell."

"And how do you feel about the arrangement?" Because none of my guys have said much. I know they react to my feelings and want me to be happy, but I learned a long time ago that sometimes that's not always possible. Not for me anyway.

Diego tightens his jaw, pressing his lips together. "Which arrangement? Mine or yours?"

"Mine."

He remains expressionless, not giving anything away. "My thoughts about it don't matter."

Reaching out, I touch his cheek, and he tilts his face into my hand like he needs to feel the weight of my fingers against his skin. "Of course they do, Diego. You're important to me. If you hate it, I want to know."

Diego closes his eyes and breaks my gaze on him, a dozen emotions crossing his face. He doesn't respond to me for what feels like an incredibly long and painful moment. Arching forward, he bows into me and rests his head on my shoulder.

"What's wrong, Diego?" I ask. "Why don't you want to tell me?"

He clears his throat. "Because I feel like an asshole."

"You could never be."

He releases a small, slightly strangled chuckle. "You give me too much credit, Jewel. I'm just not as vocal as Kingston."

I slide my arms around him and hug him, letting him continue to bury his face into the crook of my neck. "Please, tell me. I won't get mad. If you don't like the arrangement, maybe we can work something else out."

Diego finally relents and pulls away from me, taking my hands between his. His gray eyes search my face, staring at me with such intensity that I feel like Diego can peer through my skin to see my soul.

"That's the thing, Jewel. The arrangement bothers me far less than I thought it would," he admits, his brows puckering and creating lines on his forehead.

"Oh." Well, that was unexpected. I don't even know how to respond.

He groans and leans into me again so that I stop staring at him. "See? I'm a complete asshole. I shouldn't be okay with this. I should hate it. But..." His words trail off, and he huffs a breath into my neck.

"But what?"

"You show me so much love and affection that I don't feel like Orlando's taking anything from us."

"Because he's not."

"Don't get me wrong. I hate that he put you in this position. I can't forgive him for all that he put you through, but I just think about the alternatives and how everything can be so much worse—Orlando doesn't seem so bad."

I think over his words for a moment. I can't blame Diego for feeling this way—hell, I kind of feel this way after witnessing the monstrosities that Mitchell is capable of. I just wish we both didn't feel so bad for feeling this way.

"I understand and see your point," I say.

He pulls back and tilts his head. "You do?"

I release a small laugh. "Is that hard to believe?"

He crinkles his nose. "No, but it caught me off guard a little. I sometimes forget how empathetic you are."

"I also don't think it makes you an asshole. It makes you hum—well, I guess not human. I don't know. Real?" I laugh again, fumbling over my words.

Diego slides his hands under my ass and pulls me closer so that I'm straddling him. He kisses me so deeply, brushing his tongue to mine, tangling his fingers through my hair and not allowing any space between us. I sink into him, devouring the taste of his sweet mouth and how desperate his hands feel roaming over my body.

Easing away, he meets my eyes again. "I didn't think it was possible to love you more."

"You're not the only one who can be careful with a heart," I say, kissing him again. "And if you're okay with the arrangement we have with Orlando..."

"You'd be open to staying?" he asks, blinking in surprise.

I shrug. "Maybe. There are a few things I need to deal with first."

He pushes my hair behind my ear. "Brayla?"

I embrace him, snuggling my face into his shoulder for a moment, trying to stop my racing heart set off by both his touch and the new thoughts swirling through my mind. "And the whole memory thing. I'm really friggin' nervous about it."

"We're here for you, Jewel," Diego says. "We'll get through it."

He makes it so easy to believe him. If only a huge part of me didn't want to doubt it so much. I'm afraid things will change. I'm afraid that I'll suddenly find myself more out of control than ever.

I open my mouth to tell him my fears when something crashes at the back of the store. Diego jumps to his feet with me in his arms and quickly flips me onto his back before I can even orient myself to what the hell is happening.

He clicks off the flashlight and unsheathes his dagger. "Do you sense anything?"

I frown. "Huh?"

"Your fear cues. You're not afraid."

"Because I'm not."

He hums under his breath. "I don't think it's vampires. I don't hear them."

"Humans?" I ask.

He shakes his head. "Probably an animal. Let's go check to make sure. I don't want to end our date if we don't have to."

"Your brothers will try to kill you if they find out that we decided to check on a noise instead of leave," I tease.

He holds a finger to his lips. "It'll be our secret."

"You bet."

Diego quietly strolls across the dark room and opens up a door that leads to the back room of the building. He kicks some trash aside and turns his flashlight on. I cover my mouth with my hand, my eyes widening.

"Close your eyes, beautiful," Diego says.

But it's too late. I don't think I'll ever get the sight of the human remains from my brain. Old ones. The bones are all that's left of the guy besides his clothes.

"What do you think happened?" I ask, scanning the room.

I notice the backdoor was once reinforced with wood, but part of it now lies on the floor with a gaping hole that leads to a back alley. That's when I see them—two green flashing eyes peering right at us.

"Hard to say, but it wasn't recent. I'm sorry, beautiful. I didn't know this guy was here."

I reach my arm over Diego's shoulder and point at the door. "Look," I say, not responding to his comment. "Is that a cat?"

Diego shuffles forward. "Looks like it."

"Can you catch it? It looks hungry."

Diego sets me on my feet. "It's feral. It might not want to be caught."

I squat down in front of Diego and click my tongue. "Come here, baby. You hungry? I'll feed you."

"Damn, I never thought I'd be jealous of a cat," Diego says, crouching next to me.

I laugh and whack Diego on the knee. "Look, it's coming over."

"I don't think anyone in the world could resist that kind of offer from you."

The orange and white cat saunters into the dirty room and meows, cautiously heading in my direction. I hold out my hand, and it pads closer and sniffs the tips of my fingers. I risk getting scratched and rub it under the chin, and it nudges harder into me.

"I think it likes you," Diego muses.

"Can we take it back?"

He shrugs. "I don't see why not."

Sudden gunshots ring through the air, startling the cat, and it darts away from me. Diego swears and scoops me up, allowing me to hook my legs around his waist and face him. He rushes to the main room and stops short, peering through the caged entrance at the street.

Another pop resonates through the air, and I cover my ears. "What the hell?" I ask Diego.

"It's Hayden," he says.

I twist in Diego's arms to watch as Hayden fires his gun at a figure slowly creeping his way closer to him. The vampire could easily close the space, but he looks like he's having more fun dodging bullets and stalking Hayden.

"I should intervene," Diego says, setting me on my feet. "Why don't you gather our things and wait here?"

"Just let him handle it," I say, surprising myself.

Diego chuckles. "I'll let him panic for a moment longer, but he has a deal with our coven."

Our coven. I don't mention the fact that he made it sound like this is a sure thing, but the words make me frown a little.

"How 'bout two moments?" I ask.

Diego smiles wider. "I'll make it three."

I return to our spot in the center of the room and gather our belongings, shoving as many of the old movies into the backpack as possible. Diego waits in the doorway for Hayden to have to reload his weapon before running out. I hustle to the door to watch everything unfold. Hayden waves his arms around, and Diego steps between him and the vampire. I can't make out their words through the ringing in my ears.

The vampire nods his head stiffly to Diego and turns his back on him. I slide my way through the broken door and onto the sidewalk. The backpack catches, and I give it a good tug, rattling the metal gate.

"Jewel, watch out!" Diego calls.

But I'm not fast enough. A cool hand locks onto my wrist and yanks me off my feet. Diego roars.

HEART IN HAND

"BEAUTIFUL, IT'S OKAY," DIEGO WHISPERS, stopping a few feet away from me.

I stand in shock, staring at the squishy heart in my hand. Blood drips from my mouth and onto the front of my shirt, my body still humming despite my best efforts to chill the hell out. My fingers sink deeper into the warm organ until it slips from my hand and splats next to the dead body of the vampire at my feet.

Turning my hand back and forth, I inspect the dark blood staining my skin and sleeve, hiding the weird scratches from breaking through bone with my bare hand. I try my best not to shove my fingers into my mouth for another taste.

"Jewel," Diego says, shuffling a slow step closer. "Are you

hurt?"

I don't respond to him right away. I can't. I'm afraid to speak. I'm scared of tasting the blood on my lips. Blood I devoured straight from the vampire who thought he could get away with coming within even a foot of me.

"I wouldn't get too close," Hayden comments from his spot in the middle of the street. "She might go after you next."

Diego squares his shoulders. "She'd never hurt me." Striding forward, he closes the space to wrap me in an embrace, attempting to prove his point.

I hold my hand up before he can. "Please, Diego. Stay back. What if he's right? I couldn't live with myself if I hurt you."

"You won't," he repeats, directing his words to me this time. The certainty in his voice lessens the panic raging through me like a hoard of starving shadow dwellers.

"You sure? Look at him. I wasn't even hungry. I didn't feel out of control. But the second he came after me...something in me snapped. It was like I was watching myself from the outside." Spinning on my toes, I walk a few feet away to plop down on the sidewalk. I cover my face with my hands and freeze at the strangely appealing blood still warm on my fingers.

Diego steps closer again, and I jerk up and hold my palms out to him, making him hesitate.

"If your boyfriend wants to risk his demise, let him. One less vampire to wor—"

I surprise Hayden by launching from the ground at him. Diego hooks his arm around my waist and intercepts me from midair to cradle against him. Hayden doesn't catch Diego's movement right away and scrambles back and hits the ground with a thud. Murmuring voices sound through the air from somewhere in the distance, and Diego stiffens.

"Better run for it, asshole," Diego says. "You shouldn't be out here past dark."

Hayden pushes himself up and dusts off his pants. "Curfews don't apply to me."

"Neither does good sense." Diego motions down the street, and I spot a few figures lurking. "What are you doing out here, anyway? This isn't an official territory yet and those vampires interested risk no real punishment except being denied residency. Humans who venture here unescorted are considered trespassers. If they catch you, they'll most certainly keep you."

"They could try, but they'd be sorry. I have ways of assuring safe passage."

"Care to elaborate?" Diego asks.

Hayden lifts and drops his shoulders, his cocky ass smirk getting under my skin. "I'm sure you'll eventually find out. Tonight's been a real eye opener."

A few growls sound from somewhere in the distance, and Diego peers over his shoulder. I squeeze him tighter, burying my face into his hoodie. Hayden's words get to me worse than his smile. I want to ask him what he means, but another part of me wants nothing more than to go home, because I'm scared—not of the figures gathering. I'm more scared of me.

Diego searches my face for a moment before looking at Hayden. "I'm going to let this go for now because I want to get Jewel home but don't think we're finished. This asshole attitude of yours will guarantee that I get Orlando to void his arrangement with you. Do anything stupid, and I promise you won't see Ramona anymore. Understand?"

Hayden clenches his jaw and nods, fury morphing the smug smile from his face. Turning around, he stomps away while reloading his gun, not even bothering to look at us behind him.

Diego clears his throat. "That donor is under the protection of the Ortega Coven. If he doesn't make it back to the estate unharmed in the next few minutes, no one here will be granted residency." His words float through the air, trickling to those still lingering to watch us.

"You should let them have him," I whisper, my voice threatening to betray how shaken I really am.

"You bet I want to, but...unfortunately, Hayden might have information we want," Diego whispers with a sigh.

"About my dad?" I meet his stormy eyes, catching a dozen emotions flickering through his gaze before he has a chance to compose himself.

"It's not like we can trust Brayla to give us the answers."

I rest my head against him. "You're right. Now, can we please go home? I want to get this blood off me."

Diego picks up the backpack, hugs me close and takes off, leaving the body of the vampire behind. The world blurs, and I squeeze my eyes shut as the wind tries to turn my burning gaze into real tears. I promised myself I wouldn't cry. The guy was an idiot who thought he could attack me. But holy shit balls. I ripped out someone's heart...and tasted it. Fuck. Me.

The ride back to the estate flies by in just as dizzying a blur. Diego pushes the vehicle to its limits and risks driving with me on his lap. I listen to his beating heart, thumping much slower than mine to calm down.

When we reach the line of palm trees that leads to a trickling fountain, Diego parks and sets me on my feet the second we get out. Light glows through the crystal windows in bursts of rainbow prisms across the expansive porch. We hesitate in the soft glow, looking at each other.

"Looks like you've had quite the night," Orlando says from a chair where he sips blood from a glass.

Shit. From the startled expression crossing Diego's face, even he didn't hear Orlando. "Were you waiting for us?" I ask, placing my hands on my hips. "That's creepy as hell."

Orlando stretches his legs out without getting up. "Actually, no. But I would be lying if I said it wasn't a pleasant surprise to see you so delectable."

I hold out my hand to him. "If you say so. You're welcome to a taste. It's not as good as my matches, but it's not disgusting either. Maybe comparable to the best gen. pop. you can find."

His eyes flash silver, and he cocks his head, catching my sarcasm immediately. "I suppose there is some truth to your words."

Diego chuckles from next to me and clears his throat. "If you will please excuse us, brother, we need to get cleaned up before dinner."

I shift on my feet and peer at my blood-soaked shirt. "If you haven't noticed, I haven't exactly mastered the vampire art of clean eating."

Both he and Diego laugh.

Orlando raises his glass up. "Perhaps we can work on that, if you're even still hungry."

Before I can react, Diego nudges me past Orlando. Brayla materializes from the stairs and stops in her tracks. Her eyes widen at the sight of me, and she brings her hand to her mouth. Neither of us says anything to her as we push past to take the elevator up to our wing of the estate. I think she whispers my name, but then I hear Orlando call hers and the front door clicks closed.

Diego offers me a small smile, neither of us saying much, but I don't even know what I'm supposed to say. I mean, apologizing for him being in love with an uncontrollable hot mess doesn't exactly feel right in this moment.

"Bath or shower?" Diego asks, tugging me along to keep up with his quick stride.

"Do I look like I want to bathe in the blood of an idiotic jerk?" I ask, smirking at him.

He swings his head back and forth. "What about a shower first and then a soak...with me."

"You'd actually take a bath with me? Can you even fit in the tub?"

Tipping his head back, he laughs. "We can make it work. I want nothing more than to rub every last bunched muscle from your body."

I suck in my bottom lip between my teeth. "I'd like that. We wouldn't want your brothers to—"

"To interrupt? Too late, babe." Kingston's voice trickles through the door to my room with Diego.

"We won't be long, Jewel. Just need to catch Diego up on tonight," Austin adds.

"Sounds like you need to catch us up too."

The door swings inward, and Diego rushes Kingston and surprises him by pinning him to the wall. I quickly slam the door, and Austin materializes in front of me, his green eyes searching every inch of me for a wound that isn't there.

"Don't say a damn word about Jewel's appearance," Diego says, holding Kingston in place. "I'm warning you."

Kingston's mouth drops open at the sight of me, and I frown and tip my chin to rest on my chest so that I look at the floor instead of any of them.

Diego releases Kingston and turns to us. "Austin, give her some space. She's not hurt, but she's wound up and in a little shock."

"And bloody as fuck," Kingston says. "Is that yours, bro?"

Diego swings out at Kingston, but he's quick to move closer. Austin intervenes to keep me out of the middle of a brawl between his brothers.

"I mean, damn. I thought she got enough to eat," Kingston says, picking up and dropping a clump of my sticky hair.

"I did," I say.

Kingston raises his eyebrows. "Shit, babe. You and Diego are freaky as fuck. I mean—"

Austin slides out of Diego's way, and Kingston spins around to dodge another punch from his brother. The two of them square off, flashing their fangs. While I'm kind of used to Kingston pointing out stuff in my relationships with his brothers, they still try not to let him get away with saying stuff that might embarrass me. Maybe them too.

"It's not Diego's blood," I say, hugging my arms around myself.

Kingston's frown deepens. "What do you mean it's not Diego's?"

Uh-oh. I think I just made it worse. Because now Kingston knows that another vampire was within reach of me.

Austin holds up his hand to Kingston. "Orlando's?"

Kingston stiffens at the possibility, but he manages to get his scowl under control until his face evens out. But in his midnight eyes, I can see that the thought bothers him just as much. Kingston struggles the most with his possessiveness, and most definitely in regards to Orlando.

Diego and I glance to each other, having a silent conversation. Not telling his brothers about me tearing a guy's heart out will prevent any fighting between them, but I don't exactly want them to think of all the scenarios that could have gotten Orlando's blood on me in Diego's care. They will both surely think of something way out there.

"Up to you, beautiful," Diego says, putting the decision on me.

I scrunch my face and turn to Kingston and Austin. "We have some things to discuss, but first..."

Hooking my fingers to the hem of the bloody sweater, now so stained that I can't see the *Hottie* label on front, I yank it over my head and drop it to the floor. I shimmy out of the dress next and stand before the three of them in my undergarments.

My skin heats under the sudden shift in all their gazes. Diego closes the space between us and wraps me in his arms. "But first, our girl wants a shower."

"And then a bath," I murmur.

Kingston groans and laces his hands behind his head. "This is going to take forever."

"You're welcome to help, dude," I tease and then immediately regret it because Kingston raises an eyebrow. "Whatever gets this blood off of me the fastest."

Diego rests his chin on my shoulder. "But once she's clean, you guys leave."

I smile at him. "Yeah, we still have plans for the rest of the night."

"You're telling me you ripped a guy's heart out?" Kingston asks for the second time.

I glance at him standing a few feet away in the shower steam. I totally did not expect him to literally join us to help, but here he is. "Yup."

"With your bare hand?"

Diego nods. "It was fucking awesome."

Austin gently scrapes his fingernail under mine to clean out the blood. I hadn't realized how much more meticulous he was compared to his brothers, taking the whole clean every inch of me seriously. "She has organ tissue under her nails."

"Because she squeezed the hell out of it," Diego says with a chuckle.

I flick water at him. "So not funny."

He comes closer and runs his fingers through my hair, pulling it off my back. "You're right. I'm sorry, beautiful." Scooping up the bottle of shampoo, he squeezes some into his hand to lather into my long tresses. "At the time, it was rather shocking."

"I can't imagine," Austin says, moving to grab a sponge to scrub my arms.

"Oh, I can," Kingston says, inching his way closer.

It takes everything in me to pretend this group activity is normal, but the closer they all move to me, the harder my heart pounds. This wasn't the direction I had expected my night with Diego to head. I can tell they're all probably thinking the same thing.

Austin brings the sponge up to my face and gently washes the blood from my skin. "You're right, Kingston." He holds my gaze, smiling at me. "You're a total badass. Especially these last few weeks."

"And this time I completely agree. You've managed to control most of those boner-killing tears," Kingston says, finally closing the space to me.

He grabs the shower sprayer and starts rinsing me off. The three of them go quiet, busying themselves with the task at hand. The sudden lack of talking makes me shift on my feet, no longer distracted by their conversation.

I clear my throat. "I think I'm good. You've all tested my restraint enough. You don't want me to accidentally rip one of your hearts out testing my self-control this long."

Kingston has the nerve to aim the shower spray in such a way that makes me jump and fall back into Diego.

Diego roars a laugh. "You think this is hard for you?"

"Obviously you're hard for me," I tease.

"Fuck. I gotta get out of here," Kingston says, squirting me with the shower sprayer again. "Do not ask me to stay."

I smile and nudge his glistening shoulder with my knuckles. "I wasn't planning on it. This is torturous enough. I don't think my body could handle such an adventure." I bite my lip between my teeth.

"I could assure it," Austin says, his voice turning low.

Silence draws between the four of us, and I look at each

of them, my heart ricocheting around my chest in an attempt to escape. Goosebumps tingle over my skin. I shiver despite the holy friggin' hotness of my guys and the steam from the shower.

Then the three of them laugh.

I take a breath.

Kingston slides his arms around me and kisses the tip of my nose. "Teasing you never gets old."

Austin links his fingers through mine and spins me to him, pressing his body into mine. "Maybe we'll discuss this another time. Kingston would need some clear-cut ground rules."

OhmyeffingGod. "Um, I..."

He touches my flushing cheeks. "Or not. You're cute when you're flustered, Jewel. Incredibly kissable."

"More than kissable. Which means we gotta go," Kingston says. "We definitely don't have time to get into this with a body to dispose of and gathering vampires who might have seen something."

"They didn't," Diego says. "It happened so fast. I was already holding him, so if someone did see, it looked like it could've been me."

"That's not what I had imagined when you told Austin you'd handfeed Jewel to guarantee she eats, but I guess it's acceptable," Kingston says.

Austin chuckles. "What he means is good. The less attention, the better. Unless it's ours on Jewel."

A soft moan escapes my lips.

Kingston groans. "Get all that freaky shit out of your system, babe. My time is coming soon." Glancing at Diego, he adds, "Try not to exhaust her. That's my responsibility."

Kingston and Austin disappear before either of us can comment, and Diego grins at me, turning off the shower. Without a word, he draws me to him and lifts me off my feet to carry me from the shower and to the tub.

He kisses me while blindly trying to turn on the water, and I grab his arm to stop him. I slide my hands up his back, feeling his muscles rippling under my touch. He sits me on the edge of the sink, standing between my legs, fully ready to give in to the desire sizzling through me.

"I've wanted this all night," Diego says, working his lips to my throat.

"I'm sorry for inviting your brothers to stay." I drag my hands down his body and lace my fingers around him in a way that makes him moan breathlessly.

"No need to apologize. They wouldn't have left until we told them what happened." His fingers tighten on my shoulder as he lets me stroke the length of his excitement, working him up the way he likes. "Plus, I love seeing you blush like crazy."

I giggle with a moan as Diego's hands leave my shoulders to travel down my body in desperate exploration to touch every inch of me. I shift on the sink, completely opening up for him, and he kisses me again while aligning my body with his, wasting no more time. Crazy pressure builds between my legs for a moment before we both moan as he sinks into me, making me gasp.

He starts slowly, savoring every sensation that explodes between us. His hands hold me securely in place while mine roam over his broad back, drawing lower, mapping every sharp curve of his muscles.

My whole body hums with need and desire, and I stretch up trying to meet my lips to his. He lifts me from the sink and carries me from the bathroom, but we don't make it farther than the couch closest to our bathroom. Diego falls back onto it with me on top of him, and I bend down and kiss him, caressing my tongue to his. He pants into my mouth, helping me keep the rhythm he likes by squeezing my hips and rocking me on him until my muscles clench and release, electricity zinging through me. I throw myself forward to rest my head on his shoulder to enjoy his motions and the pleasure he ignites through me with his passion.

Not long after, he moans so sexily into my ear and kisses me again. I lay on top of him, snuggling in his arms. Our chests press together with every deep breath, our hearts pounding louder than my breathing. Pulling a blanket from the end of the couch, he covers the both of us, and we stay together without talking, just soaking in our love and desire, until a soft knock sounds on the door.

"Jewel, Diego. May I come in?" It's Brayla.

Neither of us responds to her.

"I thought long and hard about everything going on, and I really need to talk to you," she continues. "Please. I don't mean to interrupt your time together, but it's important."

I pull back from Diego and frown. "I don't know."

"We should wait for my brothers to return," Diego says, calling out to Brayla.

She hums her agreement. "I've already asked them to meet. They're waiting in the basement."

"The basement?" I ask.

"Yeah, it's the only place Orlando doesn't go."

DADDY ISSUES

"WE DON'T HAVE TIME FOR this bullshit, Brayla," Kingston mutters from his spot on the concrete steps of the freezing basement. "Give me one good reason why I shouldn't kill you and tell Jewel you mysteriously disa—fuck." Spinning, Kingston meets my gaze, his eyes flashing silver. He probably expected me and Diego to come through the entrance by the atrium, but we took the long way to check on my cousins. "Can you blame me, babe?"

I lift and drop my shoulders, not giving a verbal response.

"I wouldn't," Austin says.

Diego squeezes my hand. "You know I'd help."

Brayla heaves a huge sigh. "If I didn't think that it really takes all of you to protect Jewel's life, I'd put you to the test.

You're not the only one transitioned into power."

Kingston flashes his fangs. "You have decades of catching up to do, so I'd love to see you try."

It's my turn to sigh. "If this is going to turn into something other than an apology from you, Brayla, then we're leaving."

She dodges past Kingston and materializes in front of me. All three of my guys growl when she takes my hand, but it's more instinctual and derived from their very nature. They react like this to mostly everyone.

"I'm sorry, Jewel," Brayla says. "I'm sorry to all of you. I know I've done some things that you disapproved of—"

"You put Jewel's life in danger. You messed with her head when we entrusted her wellbeing to you. If Orlando found out, you know he could send you to the shadows," Austin says, surprising me. I expected the intense reaction from Kingston.

Kingston steps closer to Brayla and cuts between me and her so that she has to look at him. "Now you better give us a damn good reason why we shouldn't tell him. This goes far beyond a small infraction to your vow to him. What you did—that's treason."

She swallows, shifting on her feet. "It wasn't my intent. You don't understand. I had no idea the truth about Jewel. Noah lied to me. He used my need to protect Jewel against me. It wasn't until our last visit that I realized what he was doing."

"And what exactly is he doing?" Diego asks. "This obviously isn't about getting his family back considering it was his fault that they were separated in the first place."

"You're right. It's not," I say.

Brayla frowns. "He wants Jewel to use as a weapon against our kind. He threatened that if I don't get her to see things his way soon that he'd kill me."

Kingston punches the wall. "Empty fucking threats, Brayla. You're an Ortega. If you're afraid of a little Blood Rebel, you have bigger problems."

"You have no idea of his reach. I bet you didn't know that he's the reason Orlando picked me to try to Blood Match with in the first place." Brayla rubs her cheeks and then runs her fingers through her blond hair.

"Orlando was trying to use you to get to Jewel," Diego says.

Brayla shakes her head. "He's never needed me to get to Jewel. He could already get to her. *Noah* wanted to use me to get to Jewel, and he used Orlando to do so."

"And now you just had a change of heart?" Austin asks, stepping next to me.

I realize that my guys create a wall between me and Brayla, stopping her from even looking at me now.

"No," she says, making Kingston growl. "My heart has always been on Jewel's side. Don't you see? She's my best friend. I've always wanted to do what was best for her. I didn't want her being used."

"But we weren't fucking using her, Brayla!" Kingston shouts. I grab onto his shoulders and pull him into me, doing my best to keep him from attacking. Because in this moment, I'm not sure he won't try.

"I know that now, and I'm sorry. That's why I came to you. Noah thinks that I'm going to bring Jewel back to him before sunrise. He said that he'd create a distraction to give me the chance."

Diego straightens his shoulders. "What kind of distraction?"

"I don't know."

"Then what good are you?" Kingston spins to face me. "We gotta go, babe. This place isn't secure like the Divinity Estate was."

"I'll inform Orlando," Austin says.

"No, wait." Brayla locks her fingers to his arm, stopping him in place. "I have a plan. You might think I'm some naïve girl from The Boxes who has no idea what's going on, but I've been fighting to survive all my life right alongside Jewel. I didn't meet here just to warn you. I know where Noah is staying. We can get to him first."

My guys turn to have a silent conversation with each other. They all sneak looks at me, their pouty mouths not disguising that whatever they plan to come up with might be something I won't agree with.

"If we bring him back here, Orlando will know you betrayed him, Brayla," Austin says quietly, but he looks at me the whole time.

"But it's an easily solved problem," Kingston adds. "If Jewel allows it."

My mouth dries at his insinuation. "I—I can't make that kind of decision."

"And it would be unfair for us to ask you to," Diego says, speaking up. "So, I think we'll put it into Brayla's hands, beautiful."

I frown. "What?"

"I'm going to be straight with you, babe. In your dad's shitty words, we sometimes have to do things we don't want to. I know he's your dad and you're naturally opposed to ending the threat he poses—"

"You mean ending his life," I say.

Kingston growls at me, narrowing his eyes. "Babe, he's a fucking worthless piece of shit and doesn't deserve your mercy. Think about everything he's done to you."

"I know, it's just—"

"He had Orlando mess with your head." Kingston slaps a finger to his palm. "He kept your whole existence a secret from you." He smacks two fingers to his palm.

"He abandoned her, forcing her to take care of three minors," Diego adds.

Kingston holds up three fingers.

"Betrothed her without even telling her," Austin says.

"What?" I ask. "He did not."

Raising an eyebrow, Kingston gives me a pointed look.

"Why do you think Orlando tried to claim you? You weren't wrong about your dad changing his arrangement."

I purse my lips. "So, he did trade me for passage." It's not a question. I've known for a while that something changed after my mom died and Dad had to figure out how to care for us. But I also know he wasn't planning to go through with it.

"Yes. And he broke his agreement. Orlando took your dad to stop him from attempting to take you to the Blood Rebels. He knew what kind of fate was in store for you, Jewel."

"You make him sound like a good guy," I murmur.

"We all have our opinions, and we can discuss more of everything later, but if Brayla is right, we need to get going," Diego says, knowing me well enough that I'm on the verge of planting my ass to the steps and demanding everyone tell me every single detail they know. My head has been messed with so much that I struggle to accept things I don't remember personally.

"Promise?" I ask.

"Promise," all three of my guys say.

Kingston glances between me and Brayla. "Now about your dad."

I tighten my mouth, a dozen thoughts spinning through my head. "I can't let him manipulate my life anymore."

"Damn straight."

Diego turns to Brayla. "Looks like the ultimate decision is up to you."

She turns to me. "Jewel, I hope you can forgive me."

"You're staying here with Austin," Kingston says, blocking my way. "It could be dangerous. Maybe a trap. You know I can't put my trust in Brayla no matter what story she spins."

"I want to see him one last time," I argue.

"He doesn't deserve it."

I grip the front of his shirt in my hands. "Please, Kingston. I know you want to protect me, but I need this. Do you know how hard it was before without the closure?"

"I think we could safely get her in and out as long as we have the advantage of surprising him," Diego says, wrapping his arm around my shoulders.

Austin eases me from Kingston and takes one of my hands. "I'm sorry, Jewel. I have to agree with Kingston. It's not worth the risk."

"I'll go in first," Brayla says. "If there's a threat, I'll tell you. You can get Jewel out of there."

"You don't think it'll raise suspicions?" Kingston asks.

She shrugs. "It might, but I'll say I got an unexpected opportunity. Only Noah and my dad stay in the cabin. The rest of the rebels stay somewhere else. They won't tell me."

Kingston unhooks a hidden holster from under his jacket and situates it on me. "Obviously. You're a threat to them, Brayla. At some point, you won't feel the same bond to your family as you once had. And as for your unexpected opportunity? You will tell them that Jewel came by her own free will because she doesn't want anything to happen to us."

Diego hugs me. "That does sound exactly like our girl. Selfless."

"More like infuriating. Definitely stubborn." Kingston flicks my shoulder. "A pain in my balls."

"Yet extremely lovable," Austin adds, handing me another weapon to carry in my hoodie pocket.

I smirk. "So, does this mean I get to go?"

"If you get even a scratch, I'm slaughtering them all, including Brayla. Do you understand?" Kingston asks.

I lock my eyes with his midnight darkness. "Yeah, okay."

"I'm serious, Jewel."

"So am I."

He spins and drops a few back-world words under his breath. I grab the back of his jacket and pull him into me, hugging him from behind. He tries to turn to face me, but I squeeze him, holding him in place.

Standing on my tiptoes, I stretch to caress my lips to his ear. "If you can manage to control your desire to destroy the universe, I have something for you when we get back."

"What?"

"A surprise." I slide my tongue over his earlobe and suck it gently into my mouth, making him release a deep purr on the verge of a growl from his throat. "So try to be good and let Brayla handle it, okay?"

"You're lucky I love you."

"The luckiest."

Turning to his brothers, he says, "Dibs on carrying our

girl."

"Actually, I should," Brayla says. "In case."

Kingston breaks my hold on him and spins me to the wall to whisper in my ear. "If she tries anything, fucking devour her, babe."

I meet his pouty mouth for a kiss. "Got it."

"Really?"

I pat his cheek. "I'll rip her heart out too."

"Murder is sexy on you."

Diego groans. "And you say *we're* into freaky shit?"

Austin presses his lips together in an attempt not to laugh but doesn't say anything.

Brayla comes up next to me and takes my hand. "Come on. We have to go."

Austin hoists me onto Brayla's back, and I lock my arms around her neck. Diego takes the front, Kingston beside me and fully prepared to rip me from Brayla, and Austin protects my back.

The five of us quietly leave the estate from the useless second story door that drops into the front yard. Diego breaks into a quick sprint ahead to check the grounds, but it's as empty as usual. Orlando would be in his study right about now accepting blood from Hayden. As long as we make it back for dinner, he won't bother us when it's not his night.

Brayla slows the deeper we head into the forest. "It's not far from here. Straight down this path through the trees."

"I'll do a quick sweep," Diego says.

He disappears into the trees, and I lose sight of him. Kingston rubs smooth circles on my back, assuring that my heart doesn't start banging around like crazy from nerves. I close my eyes and listen for any noise I can pick up.

And then I hear the voices.

I frown and reach out and tap Austin's shoulder. "Is that...?"

He clenches his jaw, his green eyes flashing silver. "Orlando's here."

Diego materializes in front of us, startling me. He silences any oncoming screech from me with a kiss over Brayla's shoulder and then locks his fingers under my arms and flips me off her and into the air. I cover my mouth with my hand to stop my body from reacting, and Austin catches me in his arms.

"We have to go," Diego says.

"But—"

Gunshots ring out through the night, and Orlando roars. Austin tenses, holding me tighter. Brayla's mouth drops open, and she dashes in the direction of the cabin. Kingston tackles her, the two of them skidding across the dirt. He presses her face down and restrains her arms behind her with his strength.

"I knew you fucking set us up," he growls, flashing his fangs.

She struggles beneath him. "I didn't. I swear. Please, we have to go to Orlando."

More shots ring out and someone yells. Kingston jerks up

to look at us, and Diego and Austin slowly nod. Kingston vaults off Brayla and comes to our side. Austin hands me over to Kingston, and I hold onto his back.

"She's *my* daughter. I will not take no for an answer." It's Dad. His deep voice hums through the air.

"She belongs to *me*," Orlando says.

Lights cut through the trees, and something booms, sending the whole ground shaking. Kingston ducks near a tree, flipping me around to protectively shield me from whatever the hell that was.

"Go," Kingston tells Diego.

Dozens of more pops sound through the air, and I cover my ears. Kingston pulls us to our feet and lifts me back into his arms. Austin stands in front of us while Brayla takes the back. Diego leads the way through the trees, surprising me by heading in the direction of the noise.

"Stop," Orlando calls. "Don't pursue them, not with Jewel."

I realize he's talking to my guys. He knows we're here.

"Brayla, return to the estate and prepare a room in Austin's lab for me. I've been injured."

"Injured?" I ask.

Orlando groans. "Jewel, it's nothing to concern yourself over. I'll survive just fine."

Kingston follows his brothers forward while Brayla vanishes. Through the trees, I catch sight of the glowing cabin. Orlando sits on the porch with a body in his arms.

The second our gazes meet, he drops the man aside and holds up his hand. "Keep her back."

"Is that?" My chest clenches as I peer around. It's not just one body. There are several.

Austin jogs forward to Orlando and offers out his hand. "Let me help you."

A strange noise ticks through the air, drawing our attention to the cabin. Diego rushes forward and helps Austin drag Orlando up.

"Run!" Diego yells. "Hurry."

Kingston spins with me in his arms and bolts away. The loudest noise I've ever heard booms through the air, sending my ears ringing. The world blurs, my head spinning. I hit my back on the ground and blink through my hazy vision at a strange cloud crawling across the glittering sky.

I black out.

REPERCUSSIONS

"YOU ARE QUITE THE FIGHTER, you know," Orlando says, sitting next to me on the curb.

The shadow of the building stretches out a few feet in front of us, and if he tried to extend his legs, his dress shoes would hit the direct sunlight.

I shift and stick out my tongue at him. "You scared me."

"My apologies, precious Jewel. Your father has not made such visits easy for us. Where is the old rebel now? Surely trying to scrounge up something pitiful to feed you." Reaching out, Orlando brushes my hair from my shoulder, but I don't look at him. I know better than to get lost in his gaze. He'll take everything I know in this moment and hide it away from me.

"He does his best," I say, leaning forward to rest my chin on my knees.

"For himself. Things could be so much easier. You'd never be hungry. You wouldn't have to subject yourself to the shame of general population donations. No one deserves to taste how exquisite your blood is."

My face warms. "You don't know that my blood is exquisite, and it's not like...can you taste differences in blood from Donor Life Corp?"

"I couldn't tell you. I've never had it. I've heard it referred to as bland and unimpressive." Orlando nudges my shoulder with his. "And I know your blood is decadent without having to experience even a single drop. Because you're ravishing. Spectacular."

"And you're going to kill me if you utter another compliment." I turn my head and meet his gaze for a second. "I know what you're doing. It won't work."

"What if I shower you with gifts?" Reaching into his pocket, he pulls out an orange and holds it out to me. "Your favorite."

"My cousins will be so excited," I say, trying to reach for it.

He stretches his arm away from me. "Not so fast. This gift is for you."

"And I'd be happier to give it to my cousins than experiencing it for myself."

"Perhaps I can bring you another for them. But please, let

me enjoy this." He slowly peels the orange and offers me a piece.

The burst of sweet tanginess explodes across my tongue, reminding me of the time I had gotten an orange as a present from my mom. I moan and lick the juice from my fingers.

Orlando offers me a handsome smile. "I look forward to the day when you accept my official proposal and allow me to remove you from this horrid lifestyle your father thinks will mold you into his perfect, rebel daughter. Fear and isolation. Naivety. A world so unworthy to have been graced by your presence."

I break his stare and glance at the shifting shadow, inching its way closer as the sun crawls across the sky. "Orlando..."

"The donor life is short and bleak at best. I'm offering you forever. No one can take care of you like I can." He gently touches my knee. "Just imagine. I could make you happy. Satisfy your every need."

I try not to react to his comments. Every time I remember Orlando, all of our stolen moments sneak up on me. He's the most charming man. And so handsome. Nothing like the boys I grew up around. "Orlando, I'd love to think about it, but I'm afraid of the disappointment. The reality of my life...I can't. Ramona needs me. Dana and Fallon—"

"Are not your responsibility. Your dear Ramona will come of age soon enough. She can manage your share of donations. Your family will be fine. You, on the other hand, will not be."

I sigh. "What you're offering...why? What do you get out of it?"

"Isn't it obvious, Jewel? You're remarkable. Beyond your beauty and blood. I've grown quite fond of you over the last year. These moments are no longer enough for me."

"But they have to do. You know how my dad is. How can I trust that he would properly care for my family? He is more concerned with the fight."

"My point exactly. He cares so little for you, when I..." His voice trails off, and he brushes his fingers through his hair.

"When you what?"

Orlando rises to his feet and offers his hand out to me. "Maybe some other time. The shadows are moving, and you must be off before Noah suspects you've taken a detour. I'd hate for you to be kept home."

I let him help me to my feet. "Give me time to think about what you've said? I might consider such a thing when Ramona turns eighteen."

"I find great hope in your words, but unfortunately, now is not the time to consider such futures." Orlando closes the space to me and cups my face in his hands. "May I leave you with a kiss? Perhaps part of me will linger with you."

"You want to kiss me?" I swallow, warmth rising through me at the thought.

He smirks. "Always."

I slowly nod my head, my heart picking up pace. Orlando caresses my cheek with his fingers, searching my eyes before *closing his to lean down to me. I lick my lips and stretch up to meet him, but something clatters nearby, stopping our lips from touching. Orlando spins me and presses my back to the wall, and I stare with wide eyes as another vampire appears a few feet away only to disappear just as quickly.*

"My apologies, Jewel. You must go."

I try to pull away from him. "Please, let me remember so I can think about it. Just this once. I won't tell anyone."

Orlando tightens his mouth. "I can't. It's far too danger-ous to leave your mind open, especially now."

My brows furrow. "But I hate it."

"I'm sorry, Jewel. I am. You know the only way I can al-low such a thing." Leaning in, he brushes his lips to my cheek so lightly it feels like a cool winter breeze. "I'll see you again. I promise. You'll come this way next week."

My body slackens in his arms. "But until then, you'll for-get me. Go straight home and avoid the shadows."

"Orlando..."

Something shakes me, tugging me from sleep. Confusion washes over me, my mind trying to catch me up with the present.

"Jewel? Try to sit up. I need to assess your condition."

"Orlando?" I blink the shadows from my eyes and stare up at the ceiling instead of the sun in the sky like I was expecting.

"Damn it," Kingston says, his voice pushing away the dream completely. "Did she really just ask about him first?"

I groan and try to sit up, my head pounding with a splitting headache. "What the hell are you talking about, dude? What happened?"

Kingston slips his hands under me and slides onto the bed to prop me against his chest. "You called out for Orlando in your state of confusion. I'm so fucking jealous you were dreaming about him instead of me."

I puff out my bottom lip and turn to look at him. "Dream me apologizes. It wasn't exactly in my control. Plus, I save you for my fantasies."

His pouty face softens, and he smiles at me before planting a soft kiss to my temple. "Damn straight."

"Don't be an asshat, Kingston." Austin draws my attention to him. "Jewel consumed Orlando's blood, which is now wearing off. It's only natural for her to have some side effects as it works through her system."

"I consumed his blood? How long have I been out? Please don't tell me I—"

Diego comes up beside Austin. "You didn't attack him."

"I only wish you had." Kingston nestles his chin into the crook of my neck.

"We needed to make sure that you woke up satiated in case. What happened tonight—sorry, Jewel. We have a lot to talk about with Orlando and Brayla." Austin sits on the edge of the bed to look at me. Touching my face, he turns my head from side to side for a moment and then tucks my hair behind my ear. "Any pain?"

I shake my head.

"Dizziness?"

"Not anymore."

He offers me a small smile filled with relief. "Well, if you're up to it, we can go to them now."

I lean away from Kingston and into Austin, kissing him sweetly. "Whatever you guys want."

They all look at each other with dozens of silent thoughts splashed across their faces. They're usually more unreadable than this.

"What?" I ask after a long moment full of so much brooding, I can barely handle it.

"Orlando wants to unlock your mind now. He needs to make sure you're okay and that Brayla didn't do any-thing...more regrettable." Diego stands close and takes my hand. "But you won't be alone. Promise."

My heart races at the thought. I knew the time would come, since it was part of our agreement to let Cyprus stay as a guest in our household, but after that weird ass dream? I'm freaking the hell out. What if it was a memory?

Who am I kidding? It *was* a memory. It had to be. I've been experiencing more and more in my dreams, which makes it sometimes hard to tell what really happened in my life or not. And I hate it. I despise that I can't rely on myself for an-swers.

"Oh."

"We still have time to kick Cyprus out and deny Orlando, babe," Kingston says.

Austin reaches around me and punches him back onto the bed. "We discussed this. We were not to influence Jewel's decision."

Kingston sighs. "The choice is completely yours, Jewel."

I flick my gaze to my hands and study the sapphire and diamond bracelet I never take off. "I think I'm ready for this."

"You sure?" Austin asks.

I nod my head. "I just want to get it over with."

The three of them wrap their arms around me in the best, sexiest vampire sandwich ever, and I savor the strength that radiates from them. Austin kisses me first, just softly enough to remind me that he's here. Diego gathers me to him next, resting his head to mine, our breaths sweet and mingling, and then he molds his lips to mine in a kiss that makes me ache in the best way possible.

I shift to face Kingston, and he runs his fingers along my cheek, just gently stroking above my jawline while capturing me with his midnight dark eyes. "No matter what, we're good. Okay? Better than good. Amazing."

I bob my head, my mouth quivering. "I'm scared."

Austin tightens his fingers through mine. "Of what, Jewel? We're not leaving you."

"What if...what if I *like* him? Forgive him? What if I change?" I purse my lips, my eyes squinting with a frown.

Diego kisses my shoulder. "Orlando might have locked away pieces of your memory, but you're still you. And if you like him? So what. You're the most loving and caring being in the universe. We're not threatened by a shift in your feelings toward him."

"I love you guys. More than I ever imagined. I just want to make sure you're always happy," I say.

"You forgot satisfied," Kingston teases.

"Definitely that."

He flashes his fangs. "Then let's go."

I hesitate outside the double doors to Orlando's bedroom. Yellow and orange flames dance in the grand fireplace of his study, and I take a moment to absorb the warmth of the room into my bones. Diego kneads his fingers into my shoulders, doing his best to loosen my bunched muscles. Kingston and Austin each hold my hands.

"Precious Jewel, you do not have to wait for an invitation to enter my quarters." Orlando's voice trickles through the door, sending a shiver through me. Not a bad one, but a weird feeling none-the-less.

"What about my matches?" I ask, shifting on my feet, narrowing my eyes like if I glare hard enough, I could see through the door.

"My brothers may always join you at your request," he says.

Austin moves forward first and opens the door for me, swinging it inward to glance around before tugging me inside with him. Kingston follows along, and Diego trails behind to close the door. I stop in the middle of the room and catch sight of Brayla sitting in a chair next to the bed. Mascara runs down her cheeks, her nose red. I don't think I've seen her look so sad since...I can't remember.

"You may be excused, Brayla," Orlando says. "Do not wander far."

Brayla takes his hand as she stands. "Call me if you need me."

"That will depend on Jewel." Orlando trains his blue eyes on mine, drinking in the sight of me while ignoring Brayla as she releases his hand and crosses the room in my direction.

Kingston cuts her off, stopping her from closing the space.

"Jewel, you're my best friend," she says from over his shoulder. "Whatever you decide, I'll understand. I just hope you can eventually forgive me."

I sneak around Kingston to meet her gaze. "I hope so too."

She offers me a quivering smile and disappears from the room, shutting the door behind her. I turn and stare even though I can't see her, but I can't help it. My eyes want to glance everywhere instead of at Orlando lying on his bed.

"Jewel," Orlando says, his smooth voice soft, gentle almost, like he knows I'll run from the room if he speaks any louder. "How are you feeling?"

I turn away from the door to finally look at him. "As good as to be expected finding you in the woods with my dad."

"I meant physically. The blast of his hostile attack knocked you unconscious." Orlando pushes himself higher up on his bed, and the sheet drops to reveal his horribly ravaged chest. He catches my reaction and frowns before pulling the bedding up enough to conceal most of his wounds from bullet holes.

"Shit balls," I whisper. "That's not from the explosion."

"Your father seems to hold an unparalleled hatred and animosity toward me," he says. "Quite unfounded, to be honest. I've done nothing but aid the Jordans. Protected you. I've done everything he asked of me out of respect and kindness. And then he does this." Orlando waves his hand over his body.

"Not to mention using Brayla," I murmur. "Though you should've never promised her a Blood Vow to get to me."

"That's where you're wrong. Inviting Brayla into my coven was not to get to you. Brayla's devotion toward you is a rather appealing aspect. I knew she'd make a great ally and would hopefully help ease your transition away from the Divine name."

"What a great ally she was," Kingston mutters sarcastically.

"Brother, I know you're upset, but can you blame Brayla for what she did? She does not have the same life and world experiences as you. And ultimately, I knew she'd do the right thing. Sometimes you must face the consequences of your actions before realizing the gravity of your mistakes. To gain perspective." Orlando gives each of my guys a look. It sounds like he might not be talking completely about Brayla.

"Wait, what do you mean you knew she would do the right thing?" I ask as his words sink in.

Orlando's frown deepens. "Jewel, if you think Brayla could sneak something as critical as your father being alive by me, then you highly underestimate my power."

His words strike through me, setting off fiery anger in my core. "Wait, you *knew*?"

"Let me explain."

"Hell yeah, you better explain." Striding across the room, I stop next to Orlando's bed and glower at him. "How long did you know for?"

Orlando pats the edge of the bed, inviting me to sit down. "I know you're angry."

I ignore his hand. "Of course I am. Now answer my question. How long?"

"The moment I tasted the blood in his cell. Because it wasn't his. Brayla claimed that she lost control and then incinerated his body in a moment of panic. She then proceeded to ask when I could collect you. It was rather uncharacteristic of her, considering she knew I had a plan."

"Are you kidding me?" Austin yells, flying toward Orlando. He lands on top of him and punches him square in the face, sending his head snapping sideways. "You bastard!"

Orlando growls but doesn't fight back through another

hit. It takes both Kingston and Diego to pull Austin off, and another look at me for him to gain his composure. He slides his arm around my waist, pulling me to him to rest his head on my shoulder like I'm what he needs to keep cool.

"Brother, please. You must imagine being in my place. I was presented an opportunity, and I took it. Wouldn't you have done the same knowing what you know now? I could not have anticipated that your loyalty would shift to Jewel or that you wouldn't react negatively toward her dietary needs. All I knew was that you were enamored with her and proposed a Blood Vow. In my eyes, her life was in jeopardy. I knew she couldn't transition, and I promised her that I'd protect her." Orlando sighs and slumps forward. "Now, I must deal with the repercussions of my actions."

"What repercussions? You have Jewel here," Austin says. "I think you've gotten what you wanted all along."

Orlando lifts his chin to glance at me, his blue eyes flashing silver. "Hardly. Jewel is the last person in the world I want to despise me, but this is a compromise I must accept."

"Maybe you should have never stalked her," Kingston says, interjecting.

Diego stands taller next to me. "Tormented her."

Austin releases a small growl. "Allowed Katherine Duchanne to scheme against us and get within a foot of her."

Orlando sighs. "Though she was quite useful to me in establishing my presence in this territory, I'll give you Katherine, seeing as I underestimated her actions. As for the other things...Jewel must decide for herself."

I scrunch my nose. "I'm pretty friggin' sure I have to agree with my guys."

Orlando motions me to come closer again. "Maybe not. Once I unlock your mind, you'll see things rather differently."

I rock on my feet. "Doesn't mean a good different."

He shrugs. "I guess we'll have to wait and see."

UNLOCKING MEMORIES

ORLANDO'S BED DOESN'T SEEM SO big with all five of us sitting on it. Austin works on removing any remaining bullets from Orlando's body even though they'd have popped out as he healed. Vampires might be regenerative, but if the wounds are serious enough, it takes a bit longer. The last thing I wanted from my night was to participate in this weird ass group activity, but Orlando asked for help before he proceeds with unlocking my mind. It also gives my body a chance to work through any remaining vampire blood in my system.

"Babe, you're looking at that tray like you're going to pop those fragments in your mouth and suck on them." Kingston picks up Austin's medical tray with the bloody bullets and relocates it farther from me.

I shake my head and stick my tongue out at him. "Careful, dude. I'm feeling extremely bitey." Leaning closer to him, I purposefully press my nose into his shoulder and sniff. "You smell amazing."

He snaps his teeth at me. "I can't wait to hear how good I taste."

"You're testing my restraint," I tease.

Leaning in, he kisses me softly. "You're not the only one starving, but I'll wait until you can have something too."

Orlando watches and listens to our playful banter in silence, and I try my best not to keep glancing at him. For one, I've never seen him without a shirt, and now that he's healing, I can't stop my stupid body from appreciating the definition of his muscles.

"Here, beautiful. Eat this," Diego says, handing me a plate with a giant blueberry muffin. "It'll help take the edge off until we can satiate your blood hunger."

I groan and shove a piece in my mouth, trying to ignore the excitement his words stir in me. When he says it like that...

"Almost done, Jewel," Austin says. "But Orlando could use some blood to quicken the process."

Ah, hell. He means me. I shouldn't be surprised. Giving Orlando my blood is part of our arrangement. It just seems far more intimate to be feeding him in his bed instead of while sitting around the table, pretending that everything is normal. Well, I guess it kind of is now.

"Oh, yeah. Of course," I say, trying to keep my voice even.

"Should we be worried that she'll suddenly turn into a bitey, powerful, uncontrollable, extremely sexy savage?" Kingston asks, sliding his arm under me to scoop me into his lap. He hooks his arm across my chest and playfully pins me to him. "Because I don't mind holding onto her in case."

I shift on his lap, rubbing my ass against him until I feel his arousal. "Can you survive my wiggling?"

He embraces me tighter and flexes his prominent excitement, making me giggle and blush and totally regret teasing him. My move backfires as desire sneaks up on me. "All day, every day."

"Careful, bro. She's hungrier than she's letting on," Diego says, holding up a piece of the muffin to my mouth.

I make a point to slowly take the piece without using my teeth, sucking the tips of Diego's fingers in the process. "I'm fine."

"I'm not," Kingston complains. "That was fucking hot and now I'm jealous as hell. Let me feed our girl."

"No way." Diego keeps the muffin out of his reach. He breaks off another piece and offers it to me.

I tease Kingston by taking it even slower and darting out my tongue to lick off the crumbs from Diego's fingers. Diego chuckles and beams his brilliant smile at me, loving the gesture as much as Kingston's jealousy over it.

It's then that I realize Austin watches me just as intently.

He doesn't mention it, but he's totally jealous too. Probably even more so considering how much he friggin' loves hand-feeding me. And then I catch Orlando's gaze, and my face explodes in imaginary flames. It wasn't my intent to allow him to witness the playful behavior I share with my guys. The longing on Orlando's face is so evident that I have to shift my eyes away.

"Ready for a blood draw?" Austin's voice cuts through the sudden intensity of everyone gazing at me.

I bob my head. "Yup. You can draw for yourselves too."

"No need for me," Kingston says. "Like I said, I'm waiting for our girl."

"I can too," Diego says. "If you want Jewel."

I shake my head. "It's cool, Diego. I'm nearly certain Kingston has all sorts of plans for our time together."

Kingston kisses my throat, grazing his fangs along my skin. "You bet I do."

Austin comes to my side, and Kingston only loosens his hold enough to let me free my arm. He continues to graze his lips over my neck, distracting me from the blood draw that I don't even feel the pinch this time.

Diego clears his throat. "You might want to slow down, Kingston. You're poking at Jewel's instincts."

"Damn right am I poking them. Exactly how she likes."

I laugh and bite my lip. "Can't deny that."

"Yeah, but her eyes are changing like crazy. Unless you want to be devoured—"

"All done," Austin says, patting the top of my hand. He carefully stretches my arm and kisses my palm. "Eat a bit more of your muffin, Jewel."

"When you're ready, we'll begin." Orlando's words draw my attention to him, and I trail my gaze over his chest, the wounds no longer bleeding but only bruised. He sets his empty glass on the nightstand beside him. "It's been a long night. I'm sure we could all use some rest."

My heartbeat thrums faster in my chest, knowing that I've put this off long enough. Nodding my head, I hand Diego my plate and wait for Kingston to shift me off his lap.

"How do you want me?" The second the words come out of my mouth, warmth crawls up my chest and to my collarbone. I didn't intend for my voice to come out all breathy and inviting, and I definitely didn't mean to make it sound like I'm implying anything other than preparing for him to unlock my mind.

"Sitting is fine. Just come a bit closer," he says, patting the spot in front of him.

I shift and glance at my guys. Austin says, "We're right here."

"I'll hold you if that'll make you more comfortable, babe," Kingston says.

Orlando shares a look with him, but I can't see Kingston's expression from my position.

"Actually, yeah. I'd like that. All three of you, if that's okay?" I turn my attention to Orlando with my question.

"As long as no one interferes, it's fine by me. This will take a little longer than the previous times I've had you remember me. I'm going to remove the block completely. Your mind might take a bit of time to orient itself, but you'll have access to everything we've ever had between us." Orlando remains expressionless. "Fair warning. It could be intense and overwhelming."

That does nothing for the panic rising through me. "Okay."

Kingston massages my shoulders. "We'll help you through it, Jewel. Promise."

Nudging me forward, Kingston gets my body to move despite my mind screaming at me to stay where I am. Orlando sits up straighter and rests his back against the headboard, adjusting his legs to the side so there is a spot for me to sit close without getting onto his lap or sitting between his legs. Kingston settles in behind me so that I can rest my back against him. Austin and Diego sit close enough to hold my hands. No one complains that we're all practically sitting on each other. Treating this situation like it's not a big deal helps with my nerves.

"A little closer, Jewel," Orlando says.

I scoot forward until Orlando can comfortably cup my face in his hands. He gently combs my dark tresses behind my ears and tilts his head slightly, his eyes searching mine, drinking me in.

"I've waited a long time to be able to do this. And I'm

sorry for how my actions affected you. I hope you'll forgive me one day. That maybe there was enough good between us that you'll let me back into your heart." Orlando's eyes flash silver, and he stretches closer.

I don't respond to his comment. I can't. My body slackens under his stare as he locks his blue eyes to mine. I concentrate on my guys' even breathing, their heartbeats calm compared to my rapid one, and just knowing how relaxed they are eases the panic and slows my vitals.

"Jewel," Orlando whispers, closing the space to me even more. "Remember me."

Something clicks in my mind, and a wave of confusion pours through me before realization. It's the strangest thing. It's like everything I thought I knew about my life, all the memories I hold from growing up suddenly shift and change. Even memories from my time at the Divinity Estate.

"Remember all of our times together. Remember your father in the moments he wanted you to forget. Remember the forgotten moments of your mother. You will see your life as you lived it and not as I made you believe you did."

Dozens of memories swell through me, fragments of hundreds, if not thousands, of times spent in the shadows. I remember the very first time I met Orlando in person instead of only seeing him in the shadows, when the blood my dad took from him in a container wasn't enough and Orlando suggested I drink as much as I needed.

That same moment was the first time I saw my dad

afraid. But not because of Orlando. He was scared by my first reaction toward Orlando being a huge ass smile. How I told Dad that Orlando looked nothing like the shadow dwellers he warned me about. I also remember how much of a fight I put up when Dad denied my request to let me remember Orlando. And why he manipulated my mind to fear the shadows. Even though I couldn't remember him, I felt something different about the shadows. I wandered into them. Now, I remember my first moment alone with him.

Orlando breaks his stare, tipping his head back to glance at the ceiling. My chest heaves, my body gasping for air that doesn't want to come. Kingston wraps his arms around me and embraces me, smoothing his hand over the length of my back over and over again. Austin and Diego both join Kingston in hugging me, and I inhale deep breaths like as long as I'm breathing in their closeness, everything will be okay.

"Jewel," Orlando whispers, his low voice tugging at a dozen memories that leave me feeling out of control. "Are you okay?"

"I—" My voice catches, and I clear my throat. "I don't know."

Orlando touches the top of my foot. "I hope you can find it in you to forgive me. You know this isn't how I imagined things would turn out."

"Everything you did..." I let my words trail off for a moment. I can barely focus, my head spinning.

"Was in your best interest."

"You should've listened to me. You should've given me a choice," I say, anger burning through me. "I trusted you."

"I know."

"*You* should've trusted *me.*" I finally manage to pull myself together and slide from Kingston's arms only to link my fingers with his. "I—I need some time to process. I'm sorry. I have to go."

I motion for Austin and Diego to join me, and they do so without question. We cross the room in silence, and Kingston opens the door for us. I don't get a chance to leave before Orlando materializes in his study and stands in our path.

He surprises me by taking my hand. I think my guys are just as stunned by his action that none of them moves or says anything. Kingston doesn't even growl.

"If you're going to take some time to think about our past, I want you to also think about our futures." He looks at my guys. "All of you."

I bob my head.

"It is more important than ever that we come to a permanent agreement and arrangement. I know I said I'd give you an entire month, but things are changing, Jewel. Your father's recent actions are quite concerning. You must decide quickly."

I turn my attention to my guys for a second before turning back to Orlando. "You'll have my answer soon."

THE FUTURE

I LISTEN TO THE SOUND of Kingston's heart drumming rhythmically against my ear. Austin breathes softly into my hair, his arm hugging my waist. My arm stretches across Kingston's chest, and Diego holds my hand between his. Diego and Austin were going to leave once I fell asleep, but my mind keeps swirling with thoughts. My guys clonked out a few hours ago, and I didn't have it in me to wake them up, so I just savor this moment of peace that helps me see things clearly.

Because I want moments like this all the time. I want them so badly that I'll do anything for them. To be able to cuddle and be with Diego, Kingston, and Austin without having to worry about Mitchell, about what happens if the world finds out that I'm madly in love with all of them and we choose to be together. Without having to worry about what threats hide in the shadows. I need this to be permanent. I can see how content my guys are. They need it too.

But then there's Orlando.

Shaking my head, I push my thoughts of him away before they consume me. The movement jostles Kingston, and he opens his eyes, shifting to look at me. I gently ease my hand from Diego's and glide my fingers up Kingston's shirt to rest my palm on his heart.

"What time is it?" Kingston whispers, resting his hand on top of mine. "Have you slept at all?"

I carefully roll from under Austin's arm and onto Kingston, letting him engulf me in a hug. "No. I can't."

Kingston rubs the length of my back with his hands. "You hungry?"

Tilting my chin up, I meet his gaze. "I don't want to wake up your brothers."

"They won't mind, babe."

"In a second. I just..." I shimmy up a bit more, straddling Kingston to meet him for a kiss. He hums softly in his throat, his hands continuing to explore my back until his fingers find the hem of my shirt and slide under to touch my skin.

He deepens our kiss, slipping his tongue into my mouth to awaken my desire. I react by pressing my weight into him, feeling his body harden against me with his excitement. The soft click of his fangs sounds through the air, and he gently bites his own lip, sending drops of his sweet blood across my tongue.

I suck his lip into my mouth, releasing a moan at the tingling sensation blossoming from my mouth to travel through the rest of my body.

"Damn," Diego whispers.

Inhaling a soft breath, I ease myself away from Kingston. "I'm sorry."

"For what?" Austin asks, shifting up on his elbow.

"Um…"

"Beautiful, we're good," Diego says, smirking at me.

"And we can go," Austin adds.

I look at Kingston, and he raises an eyebrow at me. His fangs peek out from beneath his top lip, and a tinge of his blood stains his swollen skin from my kiss.

"I think our girl wants you to stay for a while longer," Kingston finally says. "She hasn't even slept yet."

"I'm a bit hungry, too," I murmur. "Everything's kind of taken the energy from me, but my mind won't stop."

"She's completely tense as well," Kingston says, puffing his bottom lip out.

I lean in and suck it between my teeth again. "He's right. I might need a full body massage."

Silence draws between us, and I push myself up and away from Kingston to see if my request might have been too much. But the three of them grin at me, sending a wave of warmth crashing around my chest.

"How full bodied are we talking about?" Kingston asks.

I lick my lips, his sultry gaze smoldering over me. "I don't know. I guess I'll let you know. Or you'll tell me."

Diego looks at his brothers. "I'm good with whatever."

"Me too," Austin says. He looks at Kingston. "Kingston, what about you?"

Kingston rubs his chin, smirking. "Fuck yeah. I just want our girl to be happy."

I laugh and cover my face for a moment, trying to calm down the sudden excitement zinging through me. "I want you guys to be happy too."

Diego steals my hands from my face. "I'm plenty happy."

"Especially seeing you like this," Austin says, grinning. "Your anticipation is sexy."

"You know what would make me even happier?" Kingston says, giving me a hot once-over.

"Hmm?" I ask, scooting a little closer.

Kingston rubs his lips together. "If you lost the shirt."

Before Austin has a chance to open his mouth, I hook my fingers to the hem of my shirt and tug it over my head. I throw it at Kingston, and he lets it land on his face with a laugh. Austin holds his hand out for me, but I don't take it. I wag my finger at Diego when he tries to inch closer.

"It's only fair if you lose the shirts too," I say, smiling wider.

Kingston tears his shirt right off. He tosses it at me, and it lands on my head, making me crack up. Strong fingers lock around my ankles and pull me closer. I screech and laugh harder as Kingston lifts me up to try to kiss me. I stretch and arch my back to lean away, teasing him with the gesture, and he buries his face between my breasts.

Diego takes the opportunity to kiss me, and I moan against his mouth, my laughter trailing off as desire blossoms through me. Kingston sets me down, his own smile fading as the four of us turn serious. I squirm in place, unsure if I should do something. I have no idea what I'm getting myself into, but whatever it is will surely be as amazing as my guys.

"Come here, Jewel," Austin says, reaching out for me. "Don't be nervous. Why don't you eat first?"

He surprises me by taking the initiative and biting his arm. I don't hesitate and lock my fingers around his wrist to glide my tongue over his tangy blood. I suck harder, my body buzzing as I react to our closeness.

Diego eases his hands under me and lays me down on my stomach in a way that allows me to continue getting what I need from Austin. Kingston moves to the other side of me, and I moan at the feeling of Diego and Kingston working their fingers over my body, massaging my knotted muscles.

It's nearly impossible to keep my hands to myself, my fingers taking on a mind of their own to trail over Austin's leg. He combs his fingers through my hair, playing with the strands. I slowly break away from his arm and shift to look at him. His green eyes crinkle in the corners with his smile.

"You can have more," he says, his voice low and husky.

"I'd like that." I trail my fingers across his lap. "Is this okay?"

"Definitely."

I bring my lips to his arm and suck until his blood pools in my mouth. Stroking my hand over his lap, I tease him for a moment before slipping my fingers into the hem of his pajama pants. Austin exhales a breathless moan, and I draw my mouth away from his arm to look up at him again. He gently touches my cheek, and I shift up to kiss him.

Cool fingers rub along my back, drawing my attention from Austin. I stretch and capture Diego's lips next. Kingston traces his fingers up my legs, and I gasp at the sudden burst of electrifying sensation that explodes through me as he teases me.

I pull my hair away from my shoulder. "Austin, come here."

Austin settles behind me, pulling me closer to him. He kisses my bare shoulder while trailing his hands around me to caress the sensitive curves of my breasts. I bend my neck more, silently inviting him to bite me. Pressure builds on my shoulder for a second before Austin's tongue trails over me, and he sucks harder. I moan at the sensation, at his hands caressing my chest, and reach for Kingston, drawing him to me for a kiss that he breaks away from to blaze kisses in a scorching trail down my stomach.

"Diego," I whisper. "Can I bite you?"

He runs his fingers across my cheek and crawls to me.

"I'd love that."

I squirm in Austin's arms, feeling his teeth graze my shoulder again, my body aching for him to continue. Diego nestles in close enough to bring his arm up to my mouth, but I only use it to draw his body to mine with no space between us until I can comfortably reach his shoulder and explore the length of his prominent arousal.

"Jewel, is this okay?" Kingston asks, playing with the hem of my lacey shorts. "I promise no fangs."

"Mmmhmm," I hum, pressing my mouth into Diego's shoulder.

"Relax," Austin whispers into my ear, taking extra care to memorize every inch of my breasts.

Kingston undresses me completely, and the intensity of all three of them drinking in the sight of me sends goosebumps across my skin. I slow my exploration of Diego's body in anticipation as Kingston lowers himself to the bed between my legs and bends my knees.

A loud ass moan escapes me, and I press my mouth into Diego's shoulder to silence the noise. The sweet scent and taste of his skin sends my already buzzing body into full-on ecstasy, and I bite him hard enough to draw blood, making him grunt and moan, his hand tightening around mine to direct me with what he wants.

I lose myself to the pleasure and love and attention the three of them give me until I reach the point of release. I knock Austin back and land on top of him, nearly kicking

Kingston. If Diego wasn't quick to catch my leg, Kingston would've ended up on the floor. I laugh in embarrassment, covering my face with my hands. Austin doesn't let me hide for long, and he and Diego grin at me like they enjoyed my reactions as much as I enjoyed the sensation of my body exploding in the best friggin' way possible.

"Ah-fucking-mazing," Kingston says, plopping down next to me and Austin. He pulls me closer to him and cuddles me in his arms. "That was even better than I imagined."

My chest heaves as I attempt to catch my breath. Kingston slides his hand between my legs, and I moan and sink back onto the bed.

All three of them chuckle.

"That was..." I shift in his arms to face him, and his smile widens as he searches my face. I kiss him softly and wrap my arms around Austin and Diego too. "I don't even know how to explain it. I feel so happy right now. Incredible. So loved."

"Because you are," Diego says, leaning over to kiss me. He plays with my hair, moving it so that it doesn't fall in my face.

"We'd obviously do anything for you," Kingston says, poking my bottom lip.

He looks proud as all get-out, and I bet if his arms weren't around me, he'd totally try to high-five or fist bump his brothers. Ever since we arrived, they've been even more loyal and loving toward each other. They don't bicker about my relationship with each of them unless it's something serious. Deep down, I know it's because they can relax. Because they're free from Mitchell and his expectations. They've been under his rule for so long, that even though they had a life of wealth and power, they weren't free. Not like now.

"And love the fuck out of it," he adds. His teasing words ignite more warmth in my cheeks.

Austin slides his hand up and down my back. "You're our girl, Jewel."

"You're my guys," I say. "I love you all so much. You have no idea how grateful I am to have you with me, especially after everything. I want to assure you're content and happy. That you're okay."

"Better than okay," Austin says. "Nothing has ever felt more right."

"Same here, beautiful," Diego says. "I know life with us hasn't always been great, and you've been through a lot, but I'm more confident than ever that we're strong enough to deal with anything that comes our way. This life we have is more than I imagined or expected."

"Yes to all that, but I *could* be a little happier," Kingston says, grabbing my hand. He guides it lower on his body until I cop a feel of his still raging boner.

I hum and caress him until he snatches my hand and holds it between his. Kingston hugs my arm tightly, his chest rising and falling in his attempt to get himself under control.

"Babe," he whispers, his words practically purring. "You're killing me. It's taking all my restraint to behave, and you know how hard that is for me."

"Or how hard *that* is for me," I say, eyeing his pants while sucking my bottom lip between my teeth to playfully smile at him.

"Damn," Diego says, exhaling a small breath. He groans and buries his head to my shoulder, gently sliding his fingers up my side. "I didn't think it was possible for our girl to get even hotter." He kisses me. "I'll let you assure anything you want."

I giggle and roll into him more for a hug and a teasing stroke.

"Shit. I thought she was teasing," Kingston says.

Austin shifts to let me fall between him and Diego and slides his hand across my stomach. "Count me in."

Shit balls, does their sudden eagerness elicit all sorts of tingling sensations across my body. I prop up on my elbows and stare at each of them for a moment.

Diego stretches to caress my burning cheek. "Maybe some other time."

"When you're completely ready." My sudden nerves must be giving my thoughts away. Because I'm not sure I could handle such an adventure just yet. Not until I know for sure the direction our lives are heading.

Kingston chuckles. "So glad it's my night."

I laugh and shake my head. "We'll definitely talk more about it."

"Now's good," Kingston says, giving me a serious once-over until he breaks into another laugh. "God, I fucking love seeing your reaction. I'm only teasing you, babe."

Easing myself away, I sit up before the three of them put me to the test on my word. I grin and blush at the thought again, wagging both my index fingers at them. "Technically, I was only teasing you too. Sort of. But that's not what I meant about assuring your happiness."

Kingston grabs my foot and tugs me closer until I crawl into his lap and sprawl my legs across Austin and Diego. "I'm dying to know what you meant, babe."

"Is this about what Orlando said?" Diego asks. "About the arrangements?" It felt so long since we talked about it, but I already know his answer.

I rest my head to Kingston's chest. "Yeah."

"We told you that we'd do whatever you wanted," Austin says.

I shake my head. "But that's not what I want. I need this to be our decision. I need to make sure that you'll be happy with what happens next."

Kingston snuggles his nose to my bare shoulder. "I know I complain a lot, Jewel, and I don't mean to, but I think that staying here and joining Orlando's coven is our best option at creating the life we want together. While I'll never forget what an asshole he was, I think if you can move past it, I can move past it."

I touch Austin's hand. "What about you?"

Austin stares at our interlocked fingers. "One of the few

things that scares me the most in the world apart from losing you is losing control. And I'm afraid the risk is far greater without a powerful coven."

"But are you happy?"

He nods and kisses my hand. "Very. Things are different here. I feel like it's possible to strive for change in our world. We're not bowing to Mitchell. We're pushing back."

"Hell yeah, we are. And you know my answer, beautiful," Diego says. "I think we've found a place where we belong that works for us as long as it works for you."

I smile at them. "You know, I'm still trying to process everything with Orlando, and I don't know what to expect from this whole thing, but I'm fine with the agreement. If you all feel like this works, then I guess this is going to be our permanent home."

"Yeah?" Kingston asks, smiling at me.

"Yeah." I pull them to me for a hug.

Diego sneaks a kiss to my lips. "I guess it's settled."

Austin bares his bottom teeth at me in a nervous smile. "Looks like we're going to be the Ortegas."

I crinkle my nose. "I'm never going to get used to that."

"Fucking A. Maybe in a century."

I poke Kingston's lip. "I guess we'll find out."

IMPATIENT

"YOU GAVE ME YOUR WORD." Liz's voice trickles in from the hallway, drawing my attention away from the journal Austin gave me this evening to replace the one I left behind in Haven Springs. He thought it'd help me sort through all of the memories still sneaking up on me if I let them.

"We're working as hard as we can," Diego says, trying to keep his voice low. "Things grew complicated. If we just go into the Aku Region and attempt to break Turner's contract, we could start a possible war. The program is in revision, which could turn his contract over to the Rosenburg Coven. Things must be handled discreetly."

"That's unacceptable, Diego. You know the risk to his life each day brings," Liz says, her voice raising.

Kingston whistles softly, drawing my attention away from the blank page of my journal to focus on the argument occurring between Diego and Liz. He stands in the doorway to our bathroom with a towel slung over his hips, his damp hair sticking to his forehead and steam still glistening across his chest.

I drop my pen and trail my gaze from his dark eyes down the rest of him. "What's with the towel?"

He chuckles and lets it drop to the floor. "Thought I heard Diego."

I point my thumb toward the door over my shoulder. "He's in the hall with Liz. She's angry that you guys haven't figured out how to get her grandson yet." I twist my lips to the side. "Though I can't blame her. I thought you and Austin were taking care of it?"

Kingston sighs and wiggles his fingers to get me to saunter across the room to him. He stops short of the closet and turns to me, pulling me close to feel the heat of the shower still warming his body. "There was a complication."

I tilt my head back to look at him. "What kind?"

His jaw tightens. "The kind you shouldn't worry about while I'm trying to seduce you."

Narrowing my eyes, I purse my lips and crinkle my nose at him. "Not gonna work, Kingston."

He has the nerve to poke me, and not with his hands. "It did earlier."

I fail to hold a straight face, my big ass smile taking over my frown at the thought. I playfully jab my finger to his rock-hard chest and stop him from getting any closer. "Well, not this time."

"You sure?"

Something crashes in the hallway, and Kingston growls under his breath and throws his clothes on while I stride across the room. He still manages to beat me and blocks my path, cracking the door open only wide enough for him to see. I tickle his sides, catching him off guard, and he steps back enough that I dodge past him and into the hallway.

Diego picks up shiny pieces of glass from a broken vase full of roses now spilled across the floor. A door slams, and I jerk my attention to Liz's room, recognizing the familiar clomping of her boots.

Kingston bends down and starts collecting the flowers. "You were supposed to let me handle her," he says to Diego.

"She cornered me on the way over here," he says, flicking his attention to me. "I couldn't avoid it."

"I'll go talk to her," Kingston says. "Maybe once she hears my plan, she will calm the hell down."

Diego sets the broken glass next to the roses on the table. "I tried to, but she thinks we're going back on our word. I doubt she'll listen to you either, bro."

Kingston nudges me to Diego. "Take Jewel. I'll meet you guys in Orlando's room. I'm going to still try. The last thing we need is another pissed off human on our hands."

I stiffen in place. "Why don't I talk to her?"

Kingston raises his eyebrow at me. "Because she's angry. Unpredictable." He waves at the broken vase. "Violent."

"And I'm tough enough to handle her," I argue.

Diego rubs the back of his neck. "Jewel has a point. Maybe Liz will listen to her instead."

"Fucking fine, but I'm coming with," Kingston says, extending his hand out to me.

I cross my arms. "As long as you wait outside."

"No."

I offer my hand to Diego. "Then you meet us at Orlando's."

Kingston flashes his fangs at me, narrowing his eyes, and then he slumps his shoulders and pouts his lip. "Fine, I'll wait outside, bossy babe."

I laugh and take his hand too. "You like it."

He raises an eyebrow. "Sometimes. But I get a turn at telling you what to do later."

"Sure, dude," I say. "Whatever you want."

Diego swings our arms. "Careful, beautiful. He'll take full advantage."

I bump Kingston's shoulder. "I count on it."

Kingston can't stop his smile and tugs me and Diego along the short distance to Liz's room. I hear her murmur something under her breath before she turns the music on. Raising my hand, I knock on the thick wood and try to listen past the noise. Liz doesn't respond.

"Maybe we should just come back later," Diego says, narrowing his eyes at the door like if he looks long enough, he could see through it.

"Liz!" I call, banging my fist harder on the wood. "It's me. Can you open up?"

She still doesn't respond, and I turn the doorknob, but it doesn't budge. I knock a few more times and wait. Diego and Kingston look ready to scoop me up to take me away to try again later, but one look from me has Kingston staring at the ceiling.

"Liz! Come on. How are we going to work this out if you ignore me? I'm trying to help you."

"Sometimes people don't actually want to be helped." I startle at Cyprus's voice next to me. "They only want you to fuck up to prove true whatever damn thoughts they had about you."

Kingston and Diego shift so that I can peer past them at his still closed door next door. No wonder I didn't hear him until he said something.

"Eavesdropping is rude, you know," Kingston mutters as Cyprus cracks open the door.

"Only if you're caught, right?" he asks, rubbing the top of his cropped hair. "Because I know vampires have super hearing."

Kingston remains surprisingly expressionless toward Cyprus' comment, though I can tell his sarcasm is dying to burst out at any second. "Is that so?"

"It only seems fair us donors get to do it when we can."

"*You* donors? If I remember correctly, it's my girl who is donating her blood. Not you." Scowling, Kingston breaks his steely façade. I squeeze his hand and pull him closer until he slides his arm around my back and hugs me. Diego steps slightly forward, his tall frame towering over Cyprus enough to intimidate him without even glaring.

Cyprus turns his attention to me, curling his fingers into fists at his sides, taking my guys' scary ass vampire presences in stride. "Fair point. I'm just used to thinking of myself as such. Jewel would understand."

Eek. I know Kingston gets all possessive over me when it comes to others, but I didn't expect Diego to release a soft growl. He steps closer to me and hangs his arm over my shoulders. I glance up at him and smirk, totally and unexpectedly loving every second of this.

"I do," I say, turning back to Cyprus. "And it's fine. But if you'll excuse us, I do need to talk to Liz."

"What if I come with you? It's probably better if an exempt like myself be there. You can assure her that her grandson isn't in as much danger as she thinks, and I'll show her empathy and make her feel like we relate since Evora is with the Vaduvas."

Damn it, if his idea isn't perfect. "That's actually a pretty good idea," I say, flicking my attention to my guys for their reactions.

Kingston obviously hates that Cyprus did make a great suggestion. "Only slightly. You still have to get the old woman to open the door."

Cyprus slides around Kingston and steps in front of Liz's door. Looking over his shoulder at me, he smiles and raises his hand to knock. "Maybe you guys should step a few feet away. She's not going to want to talk if she sees you."

I turn to Diego and Kingston expectantly, and Diego drapes his arm over Kingston's shoulders and hauls him with him until they stand ten feet away and out of view of the door. They whisper to each other, glancing at me, but I can't make out their complaints with the pulsing bass thudding through the air from Liz's music.

Cyprus leans into me. "You know, I was wrong about you. I thought you might've gotten your way occasionally because of the blood source thing, but it looks like they treat you more like an equal because that's how they see you."

I inch my body back a bit so that he can't try to whisper anymore. "You're lucky they do. In any other coven, you'd probably get locked away or transferred out or something for the way you act."

He curls the corner of his mouth in a half smile. "Good thing I'm not, huh? I guess Evora was right about her being the better one for the Blood Match Program."

I shrug. "I don't know. You would probably catch on real quick."

"We don't have all night," Kingston says loud enough for Cyprus to hear.

Cyprus ignores him but doesn't continue our conversation and instead raps his fist on the door and says, "Hey, Liz. Can you turn down your music?"

The music clicks off a second before the door swings open. "I'm sorry, Cy—" Liz straightens her shoulders at the sight of me by his side.

"Can we come in?" Cyprus asks, leaning his hand on the doorframe to stop her from slamming it in our faces. "Just for a minute?"

Blowing out a breath, Liz steps back and waves her arm to invite us in. I peer around the quaint room with slate gray walls that match the bedding, a black painted desk, small closet with only a tenth of the new clothes I have, and a TV and entertainment console on a dresser.

Liz motions to the desk chair, but I remain in my spot. Cyprus takes her up on her offer and plops down. She perches on the edge of her bed and covers her face with her hands. Releasing a small groan, she composes herself and finally looks toward me, her silver hair shining in the soft light.

"I assume you're here on behalf of your matches," Liz says.

I shake my head. "They didn't want me to come here."

"Damn straight," Kingston whispers through the door but only low enough so that I can hear him.

"Of course they didn't," she says, sighing. "So why did you?"

I shift on my feet. "To let you know that we're doing everything we can to extract your grandson from the Aku Region."

"Everything? I highly doubt that's the case. You know, I trusted that you'd follow through with your promise, but I guess I shouldn't have put so much faith into vampires. That's your fault, Jewel."

"*My* fault?" Uh-oh. I'm nearly certain that my guys were right about me coming here. Because instead of helping Liz, I only want to scream at her.

"The relationship she shares with her matches is quite impressive," Cyprus says, speaking up. "Seeing her faith in them makes it easy to believe that they'll help."

"Because we will," I say. "And I'm sorry it has taken longer than expected. When my guys agreed to help you, they had the Divine name. Now, we're covenless...at least until we make things official."

"And when will that happen? I've heard your griping every time you must visit with Mr. Ortega." Liz rubs her hands on her jeans. "My Turner doesn't have forever to wait unlike them. He could be killed at any moment. He could be so miserable that he wishes he was. I—I can't stand it. He should have never been allowed to be put into that position. Our life was fine."

Tears gloss her eyes, but Liz blinks a few times without continuing. I get my legs to move and cross the room to sit beside her. Cyprus rolls the chair closer and puts his hand over hers, comforting her in such a human manner. The action was nearly lost on me, because vampires are cautious about whom they touch, and the staff wouldn't dare. The simple gesture reminds me that I might be different, but I can empathize with Liz. I always worry about my family. It's why I matched in the first place.

"I don't know if you remember, but I wanted to enter the program so my sister didn't have to. It almost feels like a waste now considering..." Cyprus's words trail off as he loses himself to his own thoughts.

I'm so engrossed in what he's saying that I don't realize I'm leaning too far forward and have to plant my feet to the carpet to stop from falling over.

"The rest of your family didn't make it to Haven Springs?" Liz asks, now switching roles with Cyprus to comfort him. I'm glad she asked, because I wanted to know.

He shakes his head. "It is what it is. Evora seems pretty happy even as a Blood Match. At least that makes one of us."

Liz's brows furrow. "Happy?"

"Very. Going from living in a shithole apartment in Dark Terrace Ranch to a mansion with servants, all the food you can eat, doing whatever you want while hanging out with hot vam—she's fine. Feels really connected to Sammy."

"If it makes you feel any better, it's rarer than you think to be harshly mistreated by a match. Sure, there are some horrible vampires—like the one who originally owned this place—but the cost of the program wouldn't make it worth it to go through donors. It's meant to be a partnership of sorts." I rest my elbows on my knees. I don't know exactly how accurate my words are, but of the few other donor matches I've met, they seemed fine.

She groans. "I don't know. I just have this terrible feeling. Turner hasn't even contacted his mom in months."

Probably because a lot of people in Haven Springs obviously just assume the worst. I'll never forget Liz's first reaction to me, thinking I had been abused and mistreated during the duration of my contract.

"Tell her that we can fix that. We'll put her in contact with him," Diego whispers.

"Do you know how hard that will be? We're not associated with a coven yet. We have no access to Donor Life Corp's files," Kingston argues, keeping his voice low.

"As a board member, Orlando—"

"He'll never go for it. Who is Liz to him?"

I clear my throat and turn my attention away from the door. "What if we arranged a call?" I ask her. "Show you he's okay? Will you worry less until we can get things in order?"

Kingston softly growls. "Damn it, Jewel. Orlando won't. She's just going to get more pissed off and try something stupid."

"You'd arrange that for me? Really?" Liz asks, her eyes lighting up.

I bob my head. "I'll speak to Orlando right away. He kind of owes me."

Liz frowns. "Owes you?"

Cyprus looks just as curious.

I shrug. "Long story, but I don't want to get into it. I can get him to do this."

"Okay, thank you, Jewel," Liz says, patting my hand. "And I was thinking...if it's going to take a while to fulfill your promise, I'd like you to retrieve the rest of my family from Haven Springs."

Ah, hell.

ONE CONDITION

ORLANDO SITS ON THE PLUSH loveseat near the fireplace in his study. Crystal goblets sparkle on pretty, floral-print placemats on the coffee table in front of him. Ruby red candles flicker from silver candelabra at the center, and a vase full of the prettiest bouquet of flowers of all colors glitter in a multifaceted glass vase. On the floor, three giant pillows make extra seating, and on the part of the table next to Orlando rests a covered tray that I'm sure has food on it for me.

"Precious Jewel, it's so nice to see you," Orlando says, standing up from his place.

"Can you not call me that anymore?" I ask him, suppressing the hundreds of times he's used the pet name out of affection. "Your mind games ruined it for me."

He blinks a few times in consideration. "Okay, I suppose I deserve that."

I bite my tongue to stop my rebel mouth from telling him that of course he deserves it. But I know my sarcasm and anger might be better kept locked away, especially since we're here to inform him of our decision to join the Ortega Coven.

Appearing from the bedroom, Austin distracts me enough that I break my gaze from Orlando. Austin rolls out his medical table with his blood draw equipment. He keeps everything he needs to extract my blood in several places throughout the estate along with supplies in case of injury. Usually, Austin draws my blood in the dining room when we're all together, but Orlando asked to eat in here away from my little cousins and other human guests.

Orlando beckons me forward. "I do hope you slept well, Jewel."

"She didn't," Kingston says, sliding his hand around my waist to guide me into the room when my feet refuse to move right away. "Took her until an hour before sunset to even close her eyes."

I dig my fingers into his side at his comment. We both know that his words are only true because he kept me up a while longer after his brothers went back to their rooms.

Orlando remains expressionless.

"She slept half the night, though," he adds. "Might be extra bitey because we missed lunch."

Yeah, because I nearly drank a whole day's worth of his

blood while he skipped out on mine. He managed to bite his own shoulder in an attempt to try something new, and it turned out rather successful.

"I'm only a little hungry," I murmur, the memory of our night flitting through my mind.

Kingston gives me a little squeeze and winks, smirking. "Except your eyes flashed at the thought. You can't deny your blood lust."

"Whatever. Can we just eat before I devour the lot of you?" I smile at Kingston. "You'll be first."

He flashes his fangs. "I'm ready, babe."

Brayla's soft footsteps draw my attention from Kingston, and we both turn to look over our shoulders to watch her stroll down the hall at a human's pace. I haven't seen her since after the explosion, but she smiles at me like her usual self.

"Hey, Jewel. Jewel's boy toys." She gives Orlando her attention. "How are you feeling, Orlando?"

"Much better." Orlando flicks his blue gaze from her to me. "Like a weight has been lifted from my soul."

"In which you dropped on mine," I say under my breath but loud enough for everyone to hear.

Orlando's mouth twitches, a thousand thoughts hardening his features as he tries to figure out exactly what's on my mind. I try my best not to give anything away. He should be left as frustrated and confused as I am. He might be excellent at mind manipulation, but I can play my own mind games if I want to. And right now? I totally want to. Call me the leader of the petty as fuck club.

Austin motions for me to come to him, allowing everyone to ignore the sarcasm threatening to start—or should I say finish—the night off like I've grown used to. Pulling me to him, Austin engulfs me in a hug and lifts me off my feet a few inches. He sets me back down and kisses me softly.

"Remember you're strong enough," he whispers so quietly that only Kingston and Diego hear because they're standing so close. "And if you need help, we're here to help."

I smile against his mouth and kiss him once more. "Thanks. I needed that."

Brayla crosses the room before us and sits on the fluffy pillow across from Orlando. She stretches her leg underneath and touches his shoe with her own, smiling at him when he looks at her. I gawk at the two of them, trying to figure out exactly what their real relationship is like. I know it's none of my business, but a part of me needs to know. The part I want to deny exists.

Austin gets me to move my feet, and I drag them forward, unable to pull my attention from Brayla and Orlando. I'm nearly certain they share a whisper, because Brayla's smile widens, and she shakes her head.

Brayla must feel me watching her. She breaks her gaze, and she and Orlando both look at me. And so do my guys. It seems that unlike everyone else in the room, I can't mask my feelings as well. All I can do is replace one with another, but my curiosity always controls me no matter how hard I try not to let it. I can't help wanting to figure them out. Orlando told me that whatever kind of relationship they have was none of my business because every coven has their own infrastructures and rules, and because I wasn't part of his, he would not discuss it.

And Brayla? I don't really know what is up with her. She told me she didn't love him. They even have their own rooms, but I know it wasn't always the case.

"You look as if you have something to say, Jewel," Orlando says, tilting his head slightly.

I open and close my mouth, trying to think of something that won't give away my suddenly consuming curiosity. "Um…"

"We're going to assume things have been worked out between the two of you," Diego says, knowing me well enough to know that the thought lingers on my mind.

"Obviously, since she hasn't been cast to the shadows." Kingston narrows his eyes but manages to keep the rest of his face in check. "Though your loyalty is still questionable to me, Brayla."

"It's a good thing that where my loyalty lies isn't your concern," she remarks, her eyes flashing silver. Looks like Kingston struck a nerve.

"Oh, but it is." He stands taller, nearly puffing his chest out like he could intimidate Brayla. Maybe at one point he could have, but now? All she does is roll her eyes.

I step in front of Kingston and cover his mouth with my

hand. He glowers even more, but he looks ready to try to burn my clothes off with his intense gaze instead of vaporize me. He doesn't move either, his breathing tickling my hand. "Stop."

He glides his tongue over my palm until I pull back. "I can't resist. I need to see—"

Bringing my hand back up, I cut off his words by holding my index finger to his lips. He extends his fangs under my touch, and I purposely pierce myself to let a drop of blood dribble on his lip to get him to control his need to be smug as hell. "You promised to let me tell them."

"Then spit it out already," he mumbles, sucking the tip of my finger into his mouth.

"Tell us what?" Orlando asks, cutting into our quiet conversation.

I shift on my feet and turn to meet Orlando's gaze. Something strange comes over me, and my hands tremble at the icy sensation dripping down my back. Suddenly, I'm nervous as all get-out, and it makes me doubt whether our decision to join the Ortega Coven is right. If our selfish reasons to maintain a life of power are enough. If I'm ready to commit to a life that permanently includes the two people who betrayed me. Eternity is a long time. I just hope this decision proves to be the best one for me and my guys.

"We're right here," Diego says, massaging my shoulders while gently easing me away from Kingston and Austin to guide me toward Orlando.

I know I'm taking an unnecessarily long amount of time

to settle down, but my need to get things over with vanished the second I realized that this is it. Our lives will change. Things will change. I'm officially allowing Orlando and Brayla to be a part of my life.

Kingston's too slow to get to the couch, and Austin takes a seat and motions for me to sit between him and Orlando where he can easily draw my blood. Glancing from me and then to Diego plopping down next to Brayla, Kingston looks ready to snatch me up to sit with me on his lap. But something makes him hesitate.

I shift and catch Orlando staring at Kingston. He's not glowering or anything, but I still don't like it. "Come here, dude. There's room if we play lapsies. You don't have to sit way over there."

Kingston relents to my playfulness, and I step in front of Orlando to make room for him to sit. Orlando's careful not to touch me, though I'm close enough that he could. Kingston gathers me on his lap, and Orlando leans forward to remove the lid from the tray to show off an amazing looking spinach salad with strawberries and almonds.

"Enjoy," Orlando says, picking up the plate to bring it closer.

"Actually, let me feed you all first, and then I have an announcement to make." I lick my lips and hold out my arm to Austin.

"Sounds like we might share a celebratory toast," Orlando says, searching my face.

I somehow manage not to let my emotions get the best of me. Diego smiles at me from across the table, stretching his leg out to playfully kick my foot to show me that it's going to be okay. Kingston rubs my knee, and Austin traces circles on my wrist. "Don't get ahead of yourself. You don't want to ruin it."

"Of course not," Orlando says, smirking at me.

Austin quickly and painlessly draws my blood, filling glasses for the four of them. Brayla pours her own from a thermos on the table, and I wonder who on the estate is her blood source, considering that I know she has a personal donor.

All three of my guys bite their arms, and Orlando follows suit, filling up the last empty glass for me. It takes everything in me not to stare at the bite marks on everyone's arms. My body buzzes, the sweet scent of their blood wafting through the air, now smelling stronger as my needs kick in.

Orlando holds the goblet to me and smiles, reading my reaction as if I scream it out for every vampire in the nearby vicinity to hear. Kingston has the nerve to chuckle and slide his arm over my lap to press me into him—or should I say hold me still.

"Better hurry up, babe," he says, taking my glass from me with his free hand to stop it from spilling over the both of us.

I clear my throat and turn to Orlando. "The four of us have decided what we want for our futures."

Orlando leans closer. "And?"

"We accept your invitation to join the Ortega Coven, but I have some conditions."

My words wipe the smile off everyone's faces. I hadn't talked about any conditions with my guys, but only because I didn't think about them until this moment, seeing Orlando's eyes light up and hearing Brayla's breath of relief.

"The conditions are already set," Orlando says, keeping his voice even. "Unless this has to do with Brayla. If you feel like you can no longer trust her—"

I shake my head. "It's not that."

"Then what?"

"My sister."

Orlando's eyes flash silver as he jumps to the conclusion I expect him to. "Brayla, please go retrieve Ramona."

Brayla gets to her feet and disappears without waiting.

"You have my word that I'll file the proper paperwork to assure the cancellation of the Jordan blood debt in regards to her, Jewel. Ramona will be free to go come sunrise." He raises his glass of my blood up. "Now, shall we toast to our unity?"

"No, wait. That's not the condition," I say.

Orlando lowers his glass.

"I want you to transfer the Jordan blood debt to Austin," I say.

"Austin?" Both Diego and Kingston say while Austin says, "Me?"

I bob my head. "I can't transfer it to all of you, and Austin would be the least likely to murder my sister."

Kingston groans. "Damn it. You're so right, but...you sure you want to deal with this? Maybe your dad might see it as a peace offering or whatever and leave us alone. I'm sure he would love you to help free Ramona."

"Kingston makes a valid point, and it should be one we seriously consider," Orlando says, surprising the hell out of me. I never in a million years thought that the two of them would ever agree on something.

"I agree too," Austin says. "It'll be one less thing to worry about."

"What?" I ask.

"Hayden will also be absolved of his arrangement, correct?" Diego asks Orlando.

Orlando nods. "It's tied to Ramona, so yes."

"Then I agree. I think it's time to reassess our position and cut out any ties we have to the Blood Rebels. Not only do any prior connections weaken our stance and position on the board, it'll leave less room for another attack." Diego stretches his arm across the table to touch my knee. "Jewel, I know what you're thinking, but this new alliance we're creating must be strong from the start. The other regions need to respect us if we're to pull their allegiances away from Mitchell."

"I—" Footsteps draw my attention from Diego, and I catch sight of Brayla escorting Ramona down the hallway in our direction.

Orlando sets his glass down and stands up to meet the two of them, but I scramble off of Kingston's lap and grab

Orlando by the hand. He automatically stops and glances down at my fingers around his. I don't let go. If I do, he'll turn his attention to Ramona and Brayla. Right now, I need him to look at me.

"Orlando." His name sounds so softly on my lips that his features relax. I swallow and meet his gaze. "That's my condition. If you cancel her contract, I will pack my bags."

"Jewel," Diego says, coming up next to me. "We never discussed this."

Kingston and Austin join his side, and Kingston says, "You can't just throw in new terms."

"And don't you think it's better to just let her go?" Austin asks. "You never wanted her here. We could return her to Haven Springs. Maybe your cousins could go back as well. Don't you think that would be safer anyway?"

"We can make Liz return instead of bringing her family here," Kingston adds. "She can watch them."

I shake my head. "No."

Diego touches my shoulder. "You entered the Blood Match Program to assure your family got a normal life with other humans. Things have settled in Haven Springs. The people were only a threat to us. They're not a threat to your family."

I think about his words. He's right. I did enter the Blood Match Program out of desperation. Out of the need to see that my family had a future outside of the general donor population. The whole time I was forced to stay in Haven

Springs, I kept thinking over and over again how it should be Ramona with my cousins instead of me. But, things changed. I'm not Jewel Jordan from The Boxes. I'm not even Jewel Divine. I'm soon-to-be Jewel Ortega of Ombre Noire, and all I can think about now is how the last thing I want is to expose my family to a life where they despise vampires—despise me for loving them. For being half.

If I allow Orlando to cancel Ramona's contract, I'd be handing her over to my dad. He's officially the last person in the universe I want to entrust my family's future to. Not after he gave up his right to have a say in our lives.

I straighten my shoulders. "My condition is still the same. Transfer Ramona's contract to Austin or I will not join your coven."

Orlando meets my intensity with his own. "Does that also go for your matches?"

"No," Kingston says, speaking up.

I jerk my attention to look at him.

"We're sorry, beautiful," Diego says. "I know you worry about your family, but this is our future together."

"And we promised you forever. We promised to protect you," Austin says. "This is how."

My heart aches for the first time ever at their words. Taking a step away, I put a foot of space between us. Pain clenches my chest, and I hug myself, trying to wrap my mind around everything.

"You wouldn't stay without me," I say, barely able to see

through the shadows sneaking in to crowd my vision.

"We're not going to play these games, Jewel. Not for Ramona," Kingston says. "Not after everything she did. So come here and let me hug you. I know you're upset."

My insides twist and turn, heartache and panic stealing my breath away. Tears burn my eyes, but I blink through them. This isn't about getting what I want. It's more than that. It's about Ramona and what will happen to her if we let her go. Any chance of reconciling will be gone. The Blood Rebels will take her in. My dad will twist everything about me even more. She'll turn into him. I can't allow it. I could never forgive myself.

"I'm not playing a game," I say, my voice shaking. "I'm not staying."

Turning on my feet, I stride toward the door. Diego cuts me off and blocks my way, standing between me and where Brayla holds onto Ramona. Neither of them says anything, just watching me start to lose my shit.

"You're not leaving, Jewel," Orlando says from behind me. "It's not safe."

I meet Diego's eyes. "I can't stay. You have to understand. He'll destroy her."

I don't have to mention my dad for Diego to know who I'm talking about. His face falls, his steely expression turning sullen. Austin appears beside me and takes my hand. Kingston comes up behind me. They enclose me between their strong bodies, trying to smother the hurt and turmoil out of me. And usually, finding myself between them helps me breathe. But not right now. I can barely inhale. I'm suffocating.

"You guys lied to m-me." I can't stop my voice from breaking.

"Babe, that's not fair," Kingston says. "You threw this shit out of nowhere."

I try to push between them. "You said that it was my choice."

Kingston's eyes flash silver. "It was and you made the decision."

"And I'm changing my mind."

"Jewel." The depth of his voice sends a shudder through me.

Inhaling a deep breath, I clench my fists, trying to compose myself. Something in my expression makes the three of them step back to widen their circle, and I push my way out of it. I glance from Orlando and to Brayla in the hall. My heart screams for me just to let this go. To keep my shit together.

"You lied to me," I repeat, turning my gaze toward the rug.

"How the fuck so?" Kingston practically shouts.

Austin touches his shoulder, getting him to look away from me. They share a few whispered words that I can't hear. Kingston glides forward, closing the space back to me. He cups my face in his hands and searches my eyes for a moment.

"I'm sorry, babe. I didn't mean to snap. But I'm trying to

understand," he says.

"You told Jewel that if she wanted to leave, she could," Brayla says, speaking up.

Kingston growls at her.

Brayla extends her fangs at him, not letting him threaten her. "You said you'd follow her."

"Whose side are you on?" he snaps.

"Jewel's," she says. "Now calm down. I was only trying to help."

"Beautiful," Diego says.

I turn to look at him.

He rubs the back of his neck. "I'm sorry. I know you're hurt, and you're angry, but we're not going to let you do something rash. We're staying, and you are too."

I release a small breath that sounds more like a whimper. "Was it ever really my choice?" I ask. "If I didn't want to add a condition and just wanted to leave, would you have agreed?"

"We'd have convinced you to stay," Kingston says, crossing his arms.

Austin smacks him.

"I guess I was right."

I close my eyes for a second, shutting out the world the best I can. No one says anything. No one attempts to come closer. No one stops me when I turn to leave. Each step away from my guys turns more painful than the next, but I need a moment alone. It's one of the few times I've felt like I needed one.

Brayla pulls Ramona out of my way, and I stop in front of my sister. She tightens her mouth, looking ready to yell at me, but one glance toward Orlando's study stops her. I can feel the weight of my guys' stares on my back, but I let them burn me, setting my heart ablaze.

"Ramona," I say, hugging myself. "I'm sorry for the way things turned out. All I ever wanted was to give us all a life better than what we were provided. I hope you always remember that, okay?"

Her eyes gloss over, but she doesn't say anything.

"I want you to remember that it was my guys who fought for your freedom...against me. Just remember the reason you were here in the first place. Dad will try to tell you otherwise, but he's why. He used us. When you see him, don't let him continue to do so. I'm leaving it up to you to remind him that it's more than about the fight. It's what Mom would've wanted."

"I don't understand," Ramona says. "Dad?"

"He's alive. I'm sure Hayden will take you to him. Now, take care of yourself. I love you." I turn and stride toward the stairs, leaving my sister in confusion and everyone else in utter silence.

My whole body aches, my heart screaming at me for putting it through this torture. Chiming laughter draws my attention to my cousins' room, and I find myself standing in front of their door.

Cracking it open, I peek inside to find them both sitting

on the bed, smiling at each other while talking to someone on their phone. They catch sight of me, and Dana holds up the phone so that I can see Berto and Raul on the screen.

"Do you think it'll be okay if they come over tomorrow?" Fallon asks.

I frown, trying my best not to react. "Can we talk about it?"

Dana turns the phone to her. "We'll call you back in a bit."

She hangs up the line, and I enter the room and shut the door behind me. Leaning my back on the cool wood, I take another deep breath to compose myself.

"Is something wrong?" Fallon asks, getting to her feet.

Dana follows behind her, and a moment later, they both tackle me in the best hug I could have ever asked for from them. Neither of them bugs me with questions, just embracing me until I finally find the nerve to pull away.

"I have a couple of things to tell you two," I say, motioning for them to join me on the bed.

"What's up?" Fallon asks. "Is everything okay?"

I shrug my shoulders in response. I'm afraid my voice will betray me if I try to utter anything other than what my heart feels. "I'll let you decide."

They both stare at me intently, waiting for me to continue.

I clear my throat. "We're officially joining the Ortega Coven."

"That's good, I guess," Dana says.

"Orlando's canceling the Jordan blood debt," I add.

Their eyes light up.

"And they're returning Ramona to Haven Springs. They want you to go."

"What?" they both ask. "But—"

I shake my head, cutting them off. "It's okay. If you don't want to go, I won't make you. Not yet at least until we manage to get Liz's grandson. I want nothing more than you guys to live here, but things are changing. It's not safe."

"What do you mean?" Fallon asks.

I take both of their hands. "I didn't want to tell you like this, but my dad's alive."

Dana's eyes widen. "Uncle Noah?"

I nod. "He's going to try to come for me, and I can't put you guys in the middle anymore."

Fallon's lip quivers. "But Jewel."

"I'm sorry," I say. "None of us really has a choice."

THE PROMISE

"ORLANDO, YOU SHOULDN'T BE HERE," I say, sur-prise washing over me. His familiarity sinks in, and I close my eyes for a second while my mind catches up to remind me that I know him. I used to be excited to see him, but now I'm wor-ried about his arrival. "I'm angry with you for trying to make me miss my appointment."

Orlando leans on the door of my new bedroom, taking in the dresses I've sprawled across the king-sized bed. "You're preparing for a date?" He ignores my comment.

"Yes, my first," I say, running my fingers over a pretty gray dress that matches Diego's eyes.

"The results of your matching were quite unexpected. How are the Divines treating you?" He reaches up and combs

a few stray strands of hair behind my ear.

"Amazing. Look at this place." I wave my hand around the room. "Everything is fine. You don't have to worry about me anymore. They're nothing like I imagined. As caring as you've always been. Now please, you need to leave. If someone catches you—"

"No one will catch me."

I swivel away from Orlando and head back to the bed to look over the dresses the seamstress tailored to fit me. "You're wasting your time. I've already made my decision to see this through. I signed the contracts. My family is in Haven Springs and happy. You and my dad were wrong about the Blood Match Program. I get to pick my final match, you know."

"Don't be fooled by their charm. Whatever this is, it isn't good. They'd never truly put a choice such as this in a donor's hands." He glances at the door to the balcony. Rushing across the room, he swings it open, letting in bright sunshine to light up the door to the hallway. Any vampire who dares enter will be blasted in the face. "They know you're special."

"I'm not special," I say.

"Precious Jewel, don't be silly."

I roll my eyes. "I'm sorry if you're unhappy with my decision, but I'm asking you to go. This life you had planned doesn't work for me. Being here, Blood Matched to the Divines, it's the best thing to happen to me."

"You'll change your mind."

"I won't."

"Jewel."

I turn my gaze to the floor, so I don't have to witness the hurt crossing his face. He might have envisioned a future between us, but I haven't. I couldn't even if I wanted to. He hasn't allowed me to remember him. "Orlando, you need to leave. This is over."

"How will you survive?"

"I'll figure it out. I always do."

Orlando rushes me and spins me into the wall, caging me against it. Any normal time before, I wouldn't be intimidated, but his blue eyes flash silver, and he bares his sharp fangs at me, sending my heart racing.

"You're stubborn."

"Why? Because I wanted to assure my family's safety? You should understand because you obviously think you need to assure mine. I mean, look where you are. And you say I'm the stubborn one." I glare at him, daring him to deny it, but he doesn't. All he does is lean in so close that our lips nearly touch.

"Don't think I'm giving up so easily, precious Jewel. We have an arrangement. I'll let you see this through the trial period, but don't think you're safe from danger. You're still a donor in their eyes."

My body slackens under his words as he locks me in his gaze. "Orlando, don't do this."

"You leave me no choice. I can already see your growing infatuation with the heirs. They seem nice now but just wait.

Things will change when you're forced to choose, and none of them are worthy of you. Not like me. You're mine."

I try to resist his hold on my mind. "You can't claim me."

"In the eyes of Donor Life Corp, I can. All it would take is something unfortunate to happen to your father. He signed the blood debt contract."

Anger washes over me. Jerking out my hand, I slap him. "What has gotten into you?"

His jaw tightens, and a dozen thoughts mar his usually handsome face. He doesn't respond to my question but continues to lock his gaze to mine. "You're mine, precious Jewel. You'll understand one day."

"Stop."

"A fighter like your father. Just as stubborn. But don't worry. I'll be around and assure you get what you need."

"Please don't."

His eyes flash silver. "Jewel, I'll leave now, but I must warn you. If you're insistent on being difficult and remaining with the Divines, we can't meet like this again. I'll not risk exposure until I'm ready. I'll not ask you to remember me again. Not while you're unwilling to leave."

"What?" I ask. "But if I see you, I'll be afraid. You really want to do that to me?"

"It's the only way."

"What are you talking about?"

"If I'm ever to try to collect on the Jordan blood debt, you can't know. They must not be able to extract that infor-

mation. If they suspect you entered the program to avoid it, you'll be punished. You went through all this trouble to assure your family enters Haven Springs that I won't ruin that for you, but I also won't ruin this for me."

"You can't be serious. You're going to try to collect on the stupid debt? But my dad—"

"I'll do what I have to if things come down to it."

"You know the program protects me. They would go after Ramona," I say.

He smirks. "I'll be interested to see what you do."

"Orlando."

"Forget me," he whispers.

I frown. "You know how much I hate this. I won't forgive you next time."

Orlando meets my frown with his own. "I will not risk them finding out about you. About me. Not if they get into your head."

"They promised they wouldn't."

"I'm sorry. You will forget me. You will forget the arrangement. As far as you know, your father abandoned you."

I try with everything in me to break my eye contact, but I can't. My mouth refuses to speak.

"Be wary, Jewel. The Divines have many enemies. They might not protect you like I do." He bites his arm and holds it to my lips. "Now drink. Drink and forget me. Lock our memories up tight. You'll never tell. It'll hurt too much."

I can't stop my body from accepting his blood. My mind

spins under his words.

The communication line to my room rings, and a picture of Ramona flashes on the wall. "When you answer the phone, you'll ask Ramona to help you pick out a dress. You'll act normal. Leave the door open, too."

"Orlando..." I whisper. "Please don't. I need to remember."

"I have to. Forget me."

The strange whine of squeaky hinges tugs me from sleep, and I roll over on the empty bed and grab a pillow to bury my face in. The night catches up to me in a whirlwind of emotions that forces me to curl my knees to my chest and suck in a few deep breaths.

"Guys?" I ask, sitting up in bed.

No one responds, and I toss the blankets off me and pad my way across the room to peer into the hallway.

"Are you ready to talk?" Orlando materializes in front of me.

I glare at him and try to shut the door, but he stops it with his hand.

"What about accepting something to eat?"

I shoulder the door, forcing him to move his arm or risk it getting smashed before I lock it. I'm actually surprised he doesn't come in or that my guys haven't shown up yet. I don't know if I'm relieved or disappointed. I expected them to come bursting in to try to work things out, but they've kept their distance. I haven't even heard Kingston's usual groans or pacing, and I'm nearly certain he hasn't returned to our wing.

Austin's soft voice filters in through the door, but he and Orlando speak too low for me to hear. I sigh and return back to my bed and flop down, burying myself in the covers. The voices fall silent, and I listen to the faint breathing of Austin and Orlando hovering.

"Jewel, may I come in?" Austin asks after a few minutes, tapping his finger to the door. "I've brought you something to eat."

I flip over and stare at the wall without responding. A shadow catches my attention from my closet, and I stare at the doorway without moving.

"Now is not the time to go on a hunger strike," Orlando says, pulling my attention away.

"You're not helping. She's highly reactive when she doesn't get her way..." Austin groans, letting his voice trail off. I sit up and peer around, looking for a camera or something. It's like he could see the grimace crossing my face. Or he just knows me. "Jewel, I didn't mean it like that."

Taking a breath, I roll off the bed again, pulling the blanket with me. I wrap it around my shoulders and head to the door. A long shadow casts across the floor next to me, and I stop short. I guess I was wrong about Kingston not coming back to our wing. It looks like he snuck in here while I slept.

A hand slides across my stomach, and a strange scent hits my nose. I open my mouth to yell, but another hand covers my lips. The world blurs, and I hit my chest to the wall as someone crushes me against it.

"If you make any noise, I'll sink my teeth into your neck," a raspy voice whispers. "I'm here to take you back to where you belong."

I swallow the burning in my throat, feeling the scratch of sharp fangs against my neck. There's no possible way for me to scream out and not get bit. Fear assures that my body complies with the unfamiliar vampire's demands, and I bob my head.

"Jewel," Austin says, tapping on my bedroom door again. "Please let us in."

I realize the vampire and I are only in the closet.

"Tell them to go away," the guy whispers, his cool breath making me shiver.

I clear my throat. "Go away."

"Let me give you your breakfast, and then I'll give you your space. You have to be hungry. It's not safe to risk waiting this long," Austin says.

"Demand he leaves or I'll bite you," the vampire says.

"He's not—"

The vampire pricks my neck with his fangs, cutting off my argument. Anger rushes through me even though he didn't bite down, but it's enough to kick my ass into motion. I swing my elbow back and slam it into his stomach. He growls, shoving me hard, and I hit my back to the wall.

"Help!" I yell, finding my voice.

The vampire laces his fingers around my neck, cutting off

my words. He leans in and tries to capture me with his stare, but I don't look. "You belong to Mitchell Divine. You will return to him."

Shadows edge my vision as the vampire crushes my airway, sending panic rushing through me. The door to my bedroom crashes open, and the vampire snarls and jerks his head toward me. I scream out and shove my hands against him so hard that he stumbles back and smashes into the wall. Blood pours from him, and I stare in shock as Austin rushes into the closet and yanks the vampire out.

The vampire hits the floor with a thud, and Orlando aims a dagger at him.

But he's dead.

Austin and Orlando jerk their attention to me, and I rub my bloody hands together, my whole body trembling.

Austin takes a step back in surprise, but Orlando doesn't move, meeting me with a serious expression. I give him a once-over, taking in his casual attire and how his shirt stretches across his broad chest.

The memory of my dream comes back to haunt me, stealing my ability to even think straight. It's so strange, replaying a moment I know I lived through differently than what I thought. That was one of the first times Ramona vocalized how wrong she thought splitting my time with my guys was. She hated all of the dresses I had picked out too for my first date with Diego. It was also the first time I had met Laurel after she burst into my room.

I close my eyes, my head pounding, both versions of that night coming together. I haven't thought about Laurel in forever, and now that I do, it makes my mood even worse.

"Are you okay?" Orlando asks.

I shake my head. "Do I look okay? This guy got into my room. He was trying to take me to Mitchell, said that I belonged to him." My voice sounds hoarse, the words aching as they escape my lips. "How could this happen?"

Austin and Orlando glance to each other. "We've been outside your room the whole time," Austin says, stepping closer, inching his way to me like any sudden movements might set me off.

Orlando disappears into my closet. "It seems he got in through here. A trap door."

"What?" I ask. "I friggin' hate this house."

Austin stops beside me but doesn't touch me. "Take a breath, Jewel. You don't look well."

"I feel like shit and just want to go back to bed." I turn away from him and stroll to the bed and sit on the edge, trying to keep my bloody hands from touching anything.

"Jewel, that's going to have to wait. We have a few things we need to discuss," Orlando says.

I stare at the body of the guy. "Don't you think you should be scouring the premises for more threats? This guy was in *my* room. He must have gotten a lesson from you."

"Jewel—"

"Jewel's right. Take the guy and tell Kingston and Diego.

Give me a few minutes with Jewel," Austin whispers to Orlando. "I'll call for you."

Orlando remains expressionless as he drags the body out of the room. The door slams, startling me, but I stay still in my spot. Austin retrieves a few towels from the bathroom and sits beside me, shifting the bed. He cleans off all traces of the intruder's blood from my hands and sets the towels on the ground.

"You know, I hate this house too," he murmurs.

"You're not going to mention the fact that I killed that guy?"

He holds my trembling hands between his. "Remind me not to make you so angry when you're hungry."

I groan and bow into him since he won't let me hide my face. "This is so messed up. First my dad and the whole Ramona thing and now this with Mitchell. What the actual fuck? Can't the universe get that I already belong to you? It's like the universe is against me."

Austin rests his hand on my shoulder, just gently rubbing his fingers in circular motions. "It's not. It's just figuring things out. And whatever claim Mitchell thinks he has is unfounded. He's testing us. I don't know how this happened, but I'm sorry if we've failed you, Jewel. We'll take care of everything."

"You didn't fail me. The guy is dead," I say.

He slumps his shoulders. "I'm not talking about that." He doesn't attempt to say anything more or move closer, but his silence speaks volumes to me. It hurts him as much as it does me that we've found ourselves in this position.

I finally give in and shift closer to him. "You probably think I'm ridiculous for feeling this way."

He smirks, though his eyes don't light up. "That would be Kingston."

I rub the heels of my hands into my eyes. "I can hear him calling me a brat now. But you know what? So is he."

Austin doesn't respond to my words. Instead, he twists the lid off the thermos on the tray of food and offers it to me. "Before you say anything else, I want you to drink. You'll feel better if you do."

I take the thermos from him and look at the dark liquid. "Are you afraid I'm going to attack you like I did that guy? Is that why Kingston stayed away?"

"You did threaten you'd devour him first." He chuckles while he says it and reaches out to touch my knee.

"Honestly, it would have probably been you or Diego," I say, bringing the thermos to my lips to sip it. I automatically pull it away and stare at the contents again.

Austin clears his throat. "It's only Orlando's."

I crinkle my nose. "Am I being punished?"

"Of course not. It's just that you haven't eaten since..." His voice trails off as he thinks about our little adventure with Kingston and Diego. "Orlando's blood is more powerful, and you need less. We just weren't sure of how you'd react to the three of us coming in here. I know you're upset."

"It is what it is," I say quietly while I set the thermos of Orlando's blood down. "I know you all think I'm being unreasonable, and nothing I say will change that. I just—" I flop back down and turn away from him.

"We should've been honest with you, Jewel." Austin molds his body to mine and slides his hand around my waist to pull me closer to him. "I'm sorry that you're disappointed. It was never my intent to hurt you or break our promise to leave if you decided you didn't want to stay. We were just so certain that you would agree."

"I did agree," I say. "I just—everything with Ramona. It doesn't feel right. And suggesting that I send my cousins to Haven Springs? I just got them back."

"I know. I wish things were different, but the truth is you're dangerous to be around, Jewel. Not because you might hurt your family, but because you're a target. Look what happened the second you were alone? People don't know how strong or incredible you are, but they know something must be different if we were willing to give up the Divine name for you. Regions will try to test our power, especially because our coven is new. Most don't know Orlando and will test his place."

I sigh and roll over to face him. "You forgot the Blood Rebels."

"Which is why it's important to give in and show them we're trying to right some things. Ramona being here does nothing to benefit us."

Leaning forward, I rest my head to his shoulder. "Handing her to my dad will cement her fate. She will die for their cause."

"Maybe not. I think your words might have resonated with her."

"I can only hope."

Austin touches my cheek, running his finger along my jawline as his green eyes search my face. I want nothing more than to see him smile. I know he feels just as deeply as me, and it's hard for him to see me hurting.

"Jewel, can I kiss you?" he whispers, drawing his gaze to my mouth.

I lean closer. "You don't have to ask. You know how much I enjoy your affection."

"I *am* sorry, Jewel. This was not how I envisioned everything to turn out tonight." Austin rubs his lips together and searches my eyes.

"It's okay, Austin. I don't think any of us envisioned it like this."

He gently squeezes my waist, sliding his legs between mine to entangle our bodies. "Let me make it up to you."

"You already have. I think *I* need to make it up to you. I know how relieved and excited you were about officially accepting a place in the Ortega Coven, and I ruined it," I say, trying not to pout. So instead, I hug him tighter.

"We sometimes forget you haven't had decades to work on your emotional control. Though, even decades haven't worked for Kingston."

I laugh, the sudden gesture like a breath I've been dying to take. "We can't help that we're fiercely passionate."

Austin smiles, his green eyes lighting up like he can finally breathe too. "Which I love...mostly."

Austin closes the space to my mouth and brushes his lips to mine softly at first, just tasting and testing me. I sink into him, my hand roaming over his side and to his back to get as close as possible. His sweet kiss turns fervent, his lips wandering away from mine to kiss down my throat while his hands put pressure on my hips to pull mine into his so that I can feel him completely.

His scent tugs at something inside me, and I push him onto his back and get on top of him. Bending forward, I pin his hands over his head, interlocking our fingers and making him smile. He gazes up at me, his green eyes turning silver with hunger and desire. I kiss him again, sliding my tongue into his mouth, brushing it against his until I have to ease back to breathe.

Pulling him up slightly, I yank off his shirt and graze my lips to his shoulder before drawing my tongue across the taut muscles of his skin. He moans into my hair, sending tingles through me, and I grind against him, feeling how hard I make him.

"Jewel," he whispers, my name sounding so incredibly sexy like he's begging me to continue.

"I want you," I say, straightening my back to touch my

fingers to the button on Austin's pants.

"I want you too," he says, reaching for my hands. "So damn much."

I pause for a moment. "But?"

He releases a small puff of air. "Orlando's waiting."

"So?" I say, leaning back down to kiss him.

He arches his pelvis up and between my legs, and I shift and move, rubbing my body against his through the fabric of our clothes. Moaning, he runs his hands up my hips and to my ass, holding me to him.

"You're testing my control," he says, panting, his fangs now peeking through his lips. "I want nothing more than to give into you."

"Then do it," I say, tugging my shirt over my head. "You know how I am when I don't get what I want."

I meant my words to be playful to joke about his earlier comment, but Austin frowns and sits up, hugging me to him to rest his head on my shoulder.

"I was only kidding," I say, cupping his face to get him to look at me.

He rubs his lips together. "I know, Jewel. But we really should stop before you realize that you more than just desire me."

I tilt my head.

"I'd gladly let you bite me," he adds. "But when you're making a conscious decision and not losing control."

"I'm not—" I slide off Austin and onto the bed. He's

right. Being with him like this made me ignore the hunger pulling at my stomach. I sigh. "Okay, fine. You're right. How did you know? Are my eyes flashing like crazy?"

He props up on his elbow. "I'm in tune to your needs as much as you're in tune to mine."

"Oh."

"And your eyes aren't flashing silver. They're solid silver. Have been since we found you."

I blink a few times and sit up to look at the mirror on my vanity table. "Shit. Give me the thermos. I could go after you at any second."

He chuckles. "Possibly, but I'd be okay. This is a good sign. It means you're getting better control."

"Or maybe my body is patient, knowing that you'll give me what I need. I'm not injured or feeling threatened by you."

He pokes my lip with a smile. "Which means you're less of a savage than Kingston thought."

I playfully snap my teeth at him. "Careful, Austin. I don't have decades of experience in restraint."

"Then you better let me feed you. The others will be coming to check in at any moment." Austin scoops me off the bed and cradles me against him, propping his back on the pillows.

I laugh and rest my head against him. "You could just call them and tell them we're fine."

"Your laughter already has them heading our way." He picks up the thermos off the nightstand and hands it to me. "I know you would prefer something else, but we don't have a lot of time to satiate you completely. If you hurry, I'll give you some of mine to chase it down with."

I bring the thermos of Orlando's blood to my lips and take a small sip. It's strangely familiar, sending tingles across my tongue and down my throat. Austin trails his fingers up and down the side of my leg but doesn't watch me as I start to gulp.

I drain the thermos and hand it back to him to set down. "Your turn."

Austin chuckles and brings his lips to my shoulder, grazing his fangs to my skin. "Okay."

I shiver. "Don't tease me."

"Never." He shifts me on his lap to face him, bending his neck slightly. "But you first."

My body shudders with excitement at his invitation. "Are you sure?"

"More than anything."

Austin embraces me, drawing me closer until I kiss the smooth skin of his neck. I start slow by just sucking gently, grazing my tongue and then my teeth until he shifts with desire under me. His fingers dig into my hips as he guides my body to move against his the way he likes.

"Ready?" I whisper, my own desire setting me off.

"Mmmhmm."

I bite Austin, and he releases the sexiest moan in my ear, enjoying the action as much as I do. His tangy, citrusy blood coats my tongue, igniting an electric sensation from my core to the rest of me. I suck hard, letting my body take control. Austin surprises me by really getting into it, reaching up to graze his hands into my lacy bra to play with my sensitive skin.

Easing away from his shoulder, I meet him for a tender kiss, letting my gasping breath blend with his. He envelops me in his arms, holding me close, running his hands up and down my back. He smooths out the goosebumps prickling my skin, and I comb my hair away from my neck to expose my skin to him.

"They're coming," Austin whispers, caressing his lips to my skin without biting.

"Then you better hurry," I murmur.

He releases a small breath of a moan and pierces my neck with his fangs. I shift on his lap, rubbing my fingers across the planes of his chest, mapping my way across his hard nipples and to his rippling abs.

Voices murmur from somewhere down the hall, not calling my name or anything, just Diego and Kingston talking loud enough so that we can hear their arrival.

"Jewel and Austin need a few more minutes," Orlando says, his voice humming right through the door.

Austin pulls away from me and presses his cool fingers to his bite mark to staunch the bleeding. "Just one." Reaching over, he grabs my shirt and dresses me, taking a second to kiss my forehead, then the tip of my nose, and finally my lips.

Nerves tighten my muscles hearing Orlando whispering something I can't fully hear, but he says both mine and Austin's names, and possibly the word blood lust. It's now that I realize Orlando didn't even leave for that long and probably tossed the body in some closet or something to deal with later. He's just been standing outside the door.

Austin must sense my sudden annoyance, because he cups my face to get me to look at him. "He was only nearby in case you lost control, not because he was eavesdropping. Promise."

"How do you know?" I ask, my lips uncontrollably pouting.

"Just trust me, okay?"

I sigh. "You know I always do. Orlando, on the other hand, doesn't deserve my trust." I say the words loud enough for everyone to hear.

"I hope to someday earn it again," Orlando responds. "Now, if you'll allow it, we'd like to come in."

"Only if you all come in with smiles," I say, smirking at Austin. "No pouting, glowering, rolling eyes, or growling allowed."

Austin chuckles and shifts me onto the bed next to him.

"And shirts are optional," I add.

The door swings open and Orlando enters first, smirking at me with way more amusement that I expected from him considering he's always on the serious side. Or maybe because I am usually the serious one with him.

Diego strolls in after him and turns his attention directly

to me, offering me his most swoon-worthy smile. I scoot to the edge of the bed and hold out my arms. He lifts me off my feet and holds me against him instead of joining me on the bed.

"I'm so jealous right now," he whispers into my ear quietly enough for only me to hear. "I wanted to be here for you. I'm so sorry."

"You're here now," I say, giving him a peck on the lips that he turns into a kiss so full of love and longing that he's the one who has to pull away first.

I tip my head back to look for Kingston, but he's not here. "You better be out in the hall undressing, Kingston."

"I'm not," he says. "But you guys go ahead and start."

I wiggle in Diego's arms until he sets me down and strolls to the door. Kingston stands with his back toward me and doesn't even turn when I approach him. Reaching up, I place my hand on his shoulder and try to get him to turn around.

"What the hell, dude?"

"Permission to enter your room was based on something I'm currently incapable of," he says, holding strong against my attempt to spin him again. "So I'm not going in."

I try to dodge around him to glimpse his face, but he turns again. "Are you friggin' kidding me?"

"No, I'm super serious."

"Come on, Kingston," Diego says. "Enough with the games. Just get your ass in here. Jewel was just attacked. Mitchell has started a war over her. You know we have something time-sensitive to discuss."

Shit. A war? What the hell?

I shift and peer at Diego standing in the doorway with Austin still on the bed and Orlando sitting in the chair at the vanity table. "What are you talking about?"

"We agreed to join the Ortega Coven," Austin says, speaking up. "With everything that has happened, to ensure the strength of our union, we must act quickly and perform the vows in front of the board of Donor Life Corp. This will permit us to act on behalf of Orlando and also put a stop to whatever Mitchell thinks he can get away with."

"It'll also give us the access and influence we need to strengthen our region before someone tries to threaten us more than the Blood Rebels already have," Diego adds.

"So why involve me?" I ask. "I technically can't join your coven. This is all you."

"She's not going to go for it," Kingston says. "I know our girl, and she'd rather be a pain in the nuts than be reasonable."

I snap my head to look at him. "Wow, okay."

"Kingston," Diego warns.

Kingston spins and flashes his fangs. "What? I have every right to prove that I've been nothing but honest. You all call me out on my bullshit, so I'm calling her out too."

Austin gets to his feet. "It's called being tactful. You've had decades to learn."

"I don't care. I'm angry, okay? This was supposed to be a good thing, and now I feel like a fucking dick because I don't agree with Jewel and what she wants. I'm not going to just stand here and act like everything is fine." He turns back around and faces the wall.

"Kingston—"

I hold up my hands. "It's fine, Diego."

"Jewel and Kingston can deal with their personal matters another time," Orlando says. "We need to be leaving shortly if we're going to accomplish everything we need to by tomorrow evening."

"You guys are leaving tonight?" I turn my attention away from broody as hell Kingston to Orlando. He meets my gaze, his face as expressionless as ever. Leaning forward, he rests his elbows on his knees and props his head on his hands.

"As are you. Under these unpredictable circumstances, we cannot allow another moment for someone to come in and take advantage of the situation. Brayla is part of our coven and must join us. You staying alone under the protection of humans is not an option. You'll need to pack a bag. We will be staying through the day in Dark Terrace Ranch."

"Oh, okay." I swivel and glare at the back of Kingston's head. "That's fine."

"Good," Orlando says.

"Don't sound so smug, babe. That's not what I was talking about," Kingston mutters under his breath.

I frown. "Huh?"

Orlando clears his throat. "While we're meeting with the board, I'd like to re-file for your Blood Vow to assure your position in our coven."

"But I can't transform. They will find out about me," I say.

"We'll figure it out. It does not have to be a grand affair. We'll limit your exposure to other vampires. Protect you. You have my word." Orlando gets to his feet and crosses the room to me. "This is our best option considering that Mitchell still argues that you carry the Divine name even though he renounced his heirs."

My mouth dries at his words. "What?"

"That's what the threat with the intruder was about." Orlando takes my trembling hand. "Your Blood Vow application is supposed to transfer to the coven that arranged it."

I don't pull away but allow him to hold my hand. I'm afraid I'll lose my shit if I let go. I might be pissed off and angry with Orlando, but I can't stop my body from accepting his familiarity. "So how will re-filing help?"

"We can transfer it. I have the resources to do so," he says.

"Okay. Do it. I don't want to get caught in the middle of some contract feud. I promised Blood Vows to Kingston, Diego, and Austin, and I intend to keep them."

I gaze toward my guys, finally catching Kingston looking at me. And holy shit balls do I regret it. Their pouty faces speak a million words, and I know something is wrong without them having to tell me.

"Which we can do privately," Orlando says. "But unfortunately, as a human, only one vampire can promise you a Blood Vow. There is no way around it, especially after the fiasco your Blood Matching turned into."

"Oh, um." The words stick in my throat. We've been over this a dozen times. Choosing one of them? Putting me in this position kind of started this whole mess. But it was Donor Life Corp, not them. Now? Fuck me.

"Beautiful, don't panic just yet," Diego says from behind Orlando. "We're not putting you in the position to pick who you will vow on paper."

I laugh nervously. "Thank friggin' God. You know how I feel about that."

Kingston audibly groans.

I frown. "I'm guessing you lost Rock-Paper-Scissors?" I attempt to turn toward him, but Orlando doesn't let go of my hand.

Before Kingston can respond, Orlando reaches into his jacket and pulls out an intricately engraved metal box. Onyx stones and rubies stud the swirled vine design, glittering in the soft light overhead.

"Jewel, I know how you feel about my brothers, and I want you to know that I respect your decision to share your love with them. They're admirably protective of you, attentive to your needs, and I grossly underestimated the place they picked for you in their lives." He pops the box open with one hand and smiles at the sparkling necklace inside.

I gawk from the box to him and then to Diego, Austin,

and Kingston who stand frozen behind Orlando completely expressionless. They just stare at me, making me all sorts of nervous. They tend not to react when they're trying to be strong for me. And if they're hiding their feelings this must be...

"With saying that, I vow to always assure your wellbeing in this world. To devote myself to you and our coven. I promise if you accept my vow of forever, you will no longer fear or worry about your life. You will hold a place in my coven as an equal. All I ask is that you wear my crest and show me the same loyalty as you do your matches."

I cover my mouth with my hand, shock freezing my insides. Is this really happening? "*You're* proposing?"

Orlando pricks his finger on his fang and drips blood into the tiny teardrop vial that screws into the onyx pendant shaped like a bird with a golden beak. He smirks up at me, something strange in his blue eyes that I can't decipher. It leaves my mind and body at war, battling it out so hard that I'll probably die before either side of me wins. "I thought it was rather obvious. I know this might come as a surprise to you, but I hope that you realize this comes from not only a place of strategy but also loyalty. I do not expect more than what I've asked for in return."

Darting my eyes away, I turn my attention to my guys. I don't even know how to respond to Orlando. I know from our past that we once had shared similar feelings but nothing grew past the possibility of creating a life together because of my dad and the circumstances we faced. But even so, that past life has long since ended. It never really started.

Clearing my throat, and instead of telling Orlando how I feel or how confused and weird this all makes me, I frown at my guys and say, "You guys suck at Rock-Paper-Scissors."

My comment gets a laugh from Kingston, but then he groans and rubs his face. "You fucking bet I would've won if we had played. But we couldn't ask you to choose one of us. We know how you feel, and to be honest, it makes us a little nervous to pick between us because we all want the formality with you." And the two who don't get it would be crushed. That's what I was afraid of. We might make this work, but a vampire's innate nature makes them possessive. Everything has finally settled in my relationship with them that this could upset our balance.

But to formally accept a Blood Vow from Orlando? He was never part of my plan.

I tilt my head, trying to stay calm despite my racing heart. I know they had good intentions and would never purposely try to upset me, but a little warning would have better prepared me for this. "Wait, so you guys just decided to offer the chance to *him*? Without discussing it with me?"

"Fucking A," Kingston says, turning to Diego and Austin. "I told you she wouldn't go for this."

"You were so upset that we didn't want to add to it. And I'm sorry. We're in a difficult position," Diego says.

Austin rubs his face. "One human to one vampire. I

know that things haven't gone according to our promises or plans, and I understand your hesitation, but can you please try to trust us?"

"I do trust you, Austin." I wave my hand at Orlando. "But him? No."

"Jewel," Orlando says, closing the distance and silencing my guys with one look. "It must be one of us. Your matches did not want to have to make the decision, so I took it upon myself to do it for them. It's only a little application with our names on it. You can't be that repulsed by the idea. I know you're angry with me, but you must know that I do care. This is all for you."

I inhale a few quick breaths through my nose, trying my best to keep my cool. "For *me*. You're full of shit. This is for you."

He shrugs. "I won't lie about my fondness of the idea."

I slide past Orlando to face my guys. "How do you know he's not going to use this against you? That this isn't going to come and bite us in the ass?"

The three of them silently look at each other, but it's Kingston who says, "We're vowing ourselves to the Ortega Coven. You'll be promised a spot regardless."

"But I promised a Blood Vow to you three," I say.

"We promised you the same, but we don't have a choice, beautiful," Diego says. "We cannot let Mitchell think for one second he's going to use your current vow against us. It doesn't matter whose name is on the paper. Nothing's going to change."

A knock sounds on the door, drawing my attention to it. "Orlando, I have everything ready to go. I know Jewel would want to say goodbye to her cousins before I head out to drop off Ramona and get Liz's family."

"They're going with you?" I ask.

The door cracks open, and Brayla peeks in. "The less time in Dark Terrace Ranch, the better. You know that. But don't worry. They'll be completely safe with me."

Our gazes meet, and Brayla looks from Orlando holding the Blood Vow necklace to me on the verge of a meltdown. She scrunches her face and comes in, closing the door behind her.

"I'm sorry if I interrupted this moment, but I'm glad I didn't miss this," she says, sauntering closer. Her focus draws away from her plans with my cousins to me. "Isn't the necklace pretty, Jewel? I helped pick it out. It looks similar to the one I got with my Blood Vow."

"You picked it out, Brayla?" I ask.

She nods. "You are my best friend. I wanted it to be perfect. I helped with the ring, too." Turning to glance at Orlando, she purses her lips. "You haven't showed her yet."

Orlando rubs the box between his palms. "Jewel has doubts about my proposal."

Brayla's eyes widen. "Oh. Well, maybe once you see the ring, Jewel." She takes the box from Orlando and pops it open to show a black band with aquamarine stones that match my eyes. "Beautiful, right?"

I carefully take the ring in my hand and inspect it. "You like it?"

"Of course I like it," she says. "You should totally let me take you to pick out something for your boy toys too. Orlando did tell you that we'd hold something privately, right?"

I tighten my jaw. "He did."

She tugs on my hand and pulls me away from everyone to speak with me. "So why do you have doubts? Don't you know how lucky you are to have Orlando willing to give you what you want?"

"Not without an agenda or conditions."

"I thought it was fair." She places her hands on my shoulders. "And I'll be here. Your boy toys are here. This will assure you remain with the Ortega Coven."

I think over her words for a moment, searching her brown eyes.

"And you know what? I can't wait. You're my best friend and will officially be my family. I know that things aren't exactly like they used to be between us, but I care about you and want to assure your safety and wellbeing as much as everyone here," she adds.

"You promise?" I ask her, knowing she speaks the truth, but I want to hear it out loud.

"Yeah. I promise. Forever."

Reaching out, I take her hand in mine. "Awesome, because I'm promising a Blood Vow to you."

Her eyes widen. "Me?"

I look at my guys, their serious expression morphing into full-blown surprise. Austin's mouth opens slightly, and Kingston and Diego look to each other.

I bare my bottom teeth in a cross between a smile and a grimace. "I can do that, right?"

Kingston pinches his chin in his hand. "Shit. I guess you could. Brayla *is* an Ortega."

"Are you sure, Jewel?" Austin asks, wringing his hands together.

Diego crosses his arms. "Brayla is—"

"Perfect. This way I don't have to choose any of you."

THE PROPOSAL

"I WANT TO GO," I say, standing outside the van my cousins climb into with Ramona and Brayla.

"That will put you in unnecessary danger, Jewel." Austin slides his arms around my waist. "They'll be fine with Brayla. She'll meet us in Dark Terrace Ranch in time for our vows tomorrow evening."

I pout my bottom lip. "But—"

The world spins, and Kingston covers my mouth with his hand, stopping me from screeching out in surprise. He sets me on my feet inside a closet-sized bathroom off the foyer of the estate.

I place my hands on his chest, feeling the thrum of his heartbeat on my palms. "What are you doing?"

Kingston peers down at me, his eyes capturing mine in his never-ending intensity. "I want to talk."

"Now?" I ask. "My cousins are leaving."

"Yes, now. If we don't, I might not get the chance at another moment alone with you for days."

I suck in my bottom lip between my teeth. "Okay. Go on. Tell me how infuriated you are with me over everything."

He narrows his eyes at me. "Damn straight I am. That bullshit you pulled about Ramona pissed me the hell off. It made me feel like complete crap too. You know how I feel about her, and yet you decided to go ahead and go against a decision we made together on her behalf."

"I'm sorry, Kingston. I just—she's my sister. All I could think about was how she'd end up back with the Blood Rebels. How they'd completely ruin her."

"Forcing her to stay here would ruin her, Jewel," Kingston says. "She already hates us. It would just make things worse. You get angry when we make decisions for you, but you did the same thing. Not only for us but for Ramona."

I sigh. "I know, Kingston. I'm sorry. I didn't mean to make you feel like I was disregarding you, but you didn't help. I mean, you promised that we could leave if I wanted to."

"And I'm sorry for that. I should've been honest with you. It's just—I hate this."

"Hate what?"

"Hate that I can't give you everything you want. That you have to settle for a life unlike the one we imagined. If

Mitchell—" He snaps his mouth shut and shakes his head.

I touch his cheek, locking my gaze to his so he doesn't try to glance at the floor. "I wasn't lying about being happy here with you. It might not be how we imagined, but it's okay. I'm excited about our vows and having a home together. That we get to build our region how we want."

"To an extent," he murmurs, leaning into my hand, feeling the weight of my fingers on his cheek.

I smile. "It's going to be amazing."

Bending down, he brushes his lips to mine. "As long as you don't accidentally devour me in a fit of rage."

"What about in a fit of desire?" I tease, pulling his lip into my mouth to suck on it hard enough to make him press my back into the sink.

"That, I could accept."

"Too bad we don't have time," I say, playing with his belt. "Four days is forever before I can make it up to you for being a pain."

"You don't need to make anything up to me. You wouldn't be you if you didn't occasionally make me want to...spank you."

I burst out laughing and pat his chest. "Would that make you feel better? I could turn around and—"

Kingston kisses me so passionately that my laughter turns into a gasp that has me rushing to unbuckle his belt. I slide his pants down and wrap my fingers around his raging boner, stroking him while he unzips my dress, letting it drop to the floor. He drinks me in for only a moment before he lifts me off my feet to set me on the counter.

Kingston wastes no time, tugging my satin and lace underwear off to touch me in a way that sends me arching back to rest my head against the mirror. He adjusts my legs up onto his shoulders and builds a crazy amount of good pressure as he moves in a rhythm faster than usual. He watches me watch him with so much desire lighting his face that my whole body tingles, my rebel mouth unable to remain shut as I release a moan that turns into a scream of pleasure I'm certain everyone can hear.

Kingston caresses his lips to mine to feel the vibration of my voice against his skin. His body slaps against me in a way that makes me clutch him tighter. He leans in, twining his fingers through mine, his midnight eyes locking to me as he thrusts over and over again that I'm certain the mirror will crack at any second. And then another explosion of tingles ignites through me, and I squirm and drop Kingston's hands to grab onto counter with another moan.

"Damn." Diego's soft voice trickles through the air, making me slap my hand over my mouth.

"I'm officially a little jealous of your guys' relationships," Brayla says.

Kingston grins at me and links his fingers through mine again as he hums his moan deep in his throat and starts to slow down. His chest rises and falls as fast as mine as we catch our breaths. We remain together, holding hands, just breathing and smiling at each other until he eases away and helps me sit upright to wrap me in an embrace that I sink into.

"I really want to take you back to our room to cuddle the hell out of you," he whispers.

"If only."

After we clean up and re-dress, Kingston strolls with me back to where Brayla leans against the van. Ramona sits in the front seat and stares at the dark night ahead of her without glancing up, but my cousins wave to me from their window.

"Everyone ready to go?" Orlando asks, coming out of the house behind us.

Two of the human staff members carry our bags to the sleek blue car silently idling behind the van to store them in the trunk. Austin takes his medical bag from them and puts it behind the seat and glances at me with a smile that makes me blush.

"No," I say.

Kingston squeezes my hand. "Jewel's worried about the safety of her family."

Orlando tightens his jaw. "I see."

"I thought I could escort them with Brayla," he adds. "It wouldn't hurt to be cautious, especially if Liz's family is returning with her for the time being."

"They are plenty capable of assisting if something were to happen. Vampires are the least of my worries," Orlando says.

I clear my throat. "Please, Orlando."

He turns to my guys. "I nearly forgot how difficult it was

to tell her no."

"So don't," I say.

"Does this mean you trust me to protect you in my brother's place?"

I raise an eyebrow at him. "I wouldn't go so far to say that. My safety is the least of my worries."

Orlando smirks. "Good, that's one thing you shouldn't worry about."

Ugh. Twisting my words. I want so badly to argue that just because it's not a priority doesn't mean that I trust him to protect me, but I don't. He should know that I just don't worry about the danger involved in traveling to Dark Terrace Ranch. Not anymore. The danger lies within the city's walls and not outside it.

"Now, someone gather the old woman and the Vaduva match's heir. I'd prefer to settle in early and be able to enjoy my night with Jewel."

Brayla disappears and brings Liz and Cyprus from wherever they were on the side of the house. Liz touches my shoulder as she passes and tells me that she'll look after my cousins like her own. Cyprus breaks away to sit in the middle of the backseat in the spot I usually take.

Austin and Diego join him, surprising me, and I try not to react to having to sit up front with Orlando. Technically, it is his night.

Kingston pulls me in for a hug. "Keep my brothers safe, all right? Rip the hearts out of all our enemies if they try to test you. And take pictures. I hate that I missed that shit."

I shake my head with a smile and kiss him. "Be careful, okay? I miss you already."

He combs my hair behind my ear. "Miss you more."

I walk Kingston to the van and hug my cousins one more time. "You guys be good for Kingston and Brayla, okay?" I turn to Ramona, though she doesn't look at me. "Take care of yourself, Ramona-babona. I wish you the best in life. If you ever change your mind or need my help, don't be afraid to reach out."

She doesn't respond, so I peck Kingston's cheek and squeeze Brayla's hand before jogging back to the car where Orlando stands with the passenger's door open.

He stops me from getting in and rests his hand on my shoulder. "She, nor your father, deserves to ever have had your love, Jewel. They'll regret all that they put you through. One day, they'll wish they had done right by you. I know I do."

"Thank you," I whisper to stop my voice from shaking.

I never thought I'd think this, but I hope Orlando is right.

"Take a breath, beautiful," Diego says as Orlando pulls the car to the front of the Blood Match Center. "We will not let anyone hurt you or set you off."

"But, I need to do something before we go," Austin says, leaning between the seats. "As soon as Sammy comes for Cyprus."

"There she is now," Diego says. He flings open the door and hops out, pulling Cyprus to his feet.

I watch from the front as he meets Samantha, Evora, and Gabriella halfway to the door. Gabriella clutches Cyprus's face in her hands and plants a kiss right to his lips. I'm not the only one who gapes in surprise. So does Cyprus. He's quick to smile, letting the gorgeous vampire take his hand and tug him along.

"No wonder he was bitter about having to leave Midnight Valley," I muse.

"I've met very few humans who could resist their charm," Austin says, drawing my attention away from the window.

Diego returns, and Orlando joins him outside the car, leaving me with Austin. Austin takes my hand and helps me into the backseat. I expect him to hand me a glass of blood, but he digs a tiny container out of his bag and pops it open to reveal some sort of liquid.

"What's that?" I ask.

"We worry about your body's reaction to stressful situations, so I'm going to insert contacts into your eyes to combat any chance of them turning silver. They're going to be uncomfortable, but it'll only be until we get to the suites."

"I didn't think they made those anymore," I say, motioning at the container. "The medical center always fixed a donor's poor eyesight unless they aged out of making donations."

"Because good eyesight is important with mind manipulation. And contacts are rare. I had to come up with something myself last minute, which is why they'll be uncomfortable."

I frown. "Okay."

"I'll be quick."

Austin gently holds my eyelid with one finger and manages to insert the tiny, nearly invisible circular silicone disk onto my eyeball before I can blink. My eye stings and waters, and I raise my hand to rub it, but Austin stops me.

"Try not to touch it. You could pop it out," he says.

"I can't see with it on. Everything is blurry as hell."

"Hold still while I get the other one in, and I'll run you inside as fast as I can." Austin gently pries my other eyelid open, because my body doesn't willingly want to experience another round of torture, and he sticks the contact in place.

Cool air engulfs me as he jumps out of the car with me and dashes toward the entrance to the Blood Match Center. I blink a dozen times, feeling the contacts move, causing more than discomfort. They annoy me a hundred times more than having someone apply makeup to my lashes.

"Mr. Ortega," a familiar, deep voice erupts through the room, igniting panic in my heart.

I shift in Austin's arms, trying to figure out which blurry form is Mitchell, but Orlando steps in front of me to block me from view. Diego takes his place at Austin's side and links his fingers with my trembling ones.

"You're exactly the man I wanted to speak to. I see you've brought Jewel back. Are you done playing games and ready to return what belongs to me seeing as I no longer have heirs and must uphold her Blood Vow myself," Mitchell says.

I open my mouth to tell him to fuck off, but Austin covers my lips to stop me.

"Seeing as you sent someone into my region to steal my precious Jewel during her transition from the Divine Coven to the Ortega Coven, I assume you must have forgotten that your former heirs have the ability to transfer the application upon approval from the board."

Mitchell releases a threatening growl. "Which will certainly be denied."

Panic rises through me.

Orlando stands taller. "I suppose we shall find out after tomorrow's ceremony. Until the final decision about Jewel is made, she will remain in my possession."

Austin jumps back, spinning me protectively away as Mitchell launches himself at Orlando. I blink my eyes, trying to get a glimpse of the fight unfolding in front of me. Diego stands protectively, guarding both me and Austin, but Orlando prevents Mitchell from getting within even a dozen feet of me.

"Mr. Divine. Mr. Ortega," Viorica's sharp voice cuts through the lobby of the Blood Match Center. "Must I remind you that we have appearances to maintain? Any feuds you have should be handled discreetly outside of these premises. This building belongs to Donor Life Corp. It is considered neutral territory."

Neutral territory? I guess that makes sense considering this is where the board meets to discuss...whatever it is they discuss. Region disputes, stipend distributions, the program. Whatever keeps the peace, I guess. I never thought much about it.

"I'd rather enjoy relocating our...discussion," Mitchell says.

"Unfortunately Mitchell, that will have to wait. I have important matters that take precedence over your personal problems or have you forgotten?" Viorica taps her heel on the tile floor in annoyance. Even with blurry vision, I can sense her gaze on me, and I try my best to read into her. A part of me thinks she's intervening for our sake and not her own. From what I know from the things my guys have told me the last few weeks, the alliance between the Divine Region and the Vaduva Region has been weakened. Covens choose to align based on power, and I guess my guys were right about the ability to sway things in our favor.

Mitchell releases a low growl, the noise sending the hairs on my arms up as a chill travels down my spine to make me shudder in Austin's arms. He disappears without another word, and Viorica steps closer to Orlando, proffering her hand.

"Please accept my apology, Mr. Ortega. You must understand the fragility of the situation. It has been decades since our territory had such a rapid shift in power. Actually, funny enough, it involved the former Divine Heirs as well." Viorica leans to peer at Diego and Austin around Orlando. "I always knew Mitchell couldn't keep his reign over you forever, and I rather enjoy seeing a young woman being the reason. It's still a shame to not have you, Jewel, but I suppose a female held above instead of beneath a male is second best to complete control of them."

Her coven isn't nicknamed the Widows without good reason. Viorica has an interesting way of ruling Midnight Valley, to say the least.

"Does that mean we have your vote for the transfer of Jewel's Blood Vow?" Diego asks.

Viorica hums under her breath. "Perhaps. I'd like to see how the rest of the board decides."

I frown and open my mouth to tell her that we're doing her a favor by keeping Cyprus for Sammy, but Austin squeezes my sides, stopping me.

"I'm certain it'll go in our favor, Ms. Vaduva," Orlando says. "Be warned. Getting caught up in a personal vendetta does nothing to strengthen your position on the board. You've never struck me as the type to appease a man throwing a tantrum because he's far too concerned with his ego to let things go."

Viorica surprises me by releasing a small laugh. "No warning needed. I'm rather confident that the outcome will be favorable for me either way. Now, if you'll excuse me. I'm sure Diego and Austin can show you to your floor."

After Viorica disappears, Diego leads the way to the elevator with Orlando strolling next to me. He rests his hand on Austin's back, acting as a barrier to anyone who might attempt to get to me. While the lobby is unusually empty, I can still hear the subtle noises of vampires moving throughout the building.

"I know you have a lot to say," Orlando whispers into my ear on the elevator. "But please refrain from speaking until we're in the safety of my quarters."

I groan and bury my face into Austin's neck, distracting myself with the sweetness of his skin until the world blurs under his sudden speed. I find myself in the middle of a grand apartment with a view of the sprawling city glowing with twinkling lights.

I steady my body between Austin and Diego, trying to orient myself to my surroundings. Orlando motions toward a gray sectional couch. A round table with a vase of fresh flowers rests in front of it. He sits down before me, and I take my place on the opposite end. Neither Diego nor Austin sits, waiting in their places near the door.

"Why don't you two go grab our belongings and put in a dinner request for Jewel?" Orlando says, scooting across the wide cushion to close the space to me. "I need a moment to talk to Jewel."

I try not to pout and just nod my head. "Will you call Kingston for me too?"

"Sure thing, beautiful," Diego says. "We won't take long."

I motion for them to come to me and give each a kiss on the lips without getting up from my spot. Austin touches my cheek and smiles, silently assuring me that everything will be okay without having to speak the words out loud. Orlando's gaze bores into the side of my face as I watch them go.

And then he gently touches my hand. "Jewel, I don't want you to worry about the application, okay?"

I stiffen and finally meet his gaze. "You said it would be transferred."

"And it will be."

"*If* the board approves." My eyes burn, and I rub them in an attempt to get the uncomfortable contacts out.

Orlando grasps my chin. "Here, let me help you."

If they weren't friggin' bugging the hell out of me, I'd bat his hand away. Instead, I relent to his gentle touch. My vision clears a moment later, and I stare into Orlando's blue eyes. He sits close enough that all he'd have to do is bow his head a few inches, and he could kiss me. His eyes even shift toward my mouth as he drinks in my face.

"The board will approve the transfer, okay?" he says, the softness of his breath caressing my skin. "Mitchell was trying to get to you. To us."

"Well, it worked." I lean back and cover my eyes, inhaling a few soft breaths. "I hate this. I hate all of this. You know, back in The Boxes, I never felt like such a possession. Like I had no control over anything. And it's getting worse."

Orlando rests his hand on my back, just lightly testing me

to see if I'll move, but I don't. "It won't be like this for much longer."

"You say that, but you treat me no differently," I say, shifting away.

His fingers play with my hair, moving it from my back so that he can rub his fingers into my tight muscles. "I'm sorry, Jewel. I'm trying to do better."

I rest my elbows on my knees. "You should have told me about the vote."

"I know."

"You should've talked to me about the proposal, about your plans."

He sighs. "You don't make it easy."

Shifting, I turn to face him. "And you think you do? You hurt me yet you expect me just to accept things as they are. I deserve better than this. I deserve to get to decide if I want to share my blood with you or my time."

His eyes flash silver. "You wouldn't give me the chance otherwise."

I shake my head, grimacing, a million thoughts rushing through my head. "How do you even know?"

"Because I know you, Jewel. You've made your feelings quite clear."

"I don't even know how I feel. I'm just—everything is so confusing. I haven't even had the chance to process anything. I'm still trying to sort through what's real or what you've created," I say, my voice growing quiet.

"Let me help you. Please." His voice comes out just as soft as mine.

"I don't know."

He reaches up and brushes my hair from my face to keep me from veiling myself from him. "What are you afraid of?"

"Us. What it all meant. I love my matches, Orlando," I say. "And they love me."

His mouth twitches in the corner. "I know. I've accepted that."

I dig my nails into the palms of my hands, trying my best not to blow up. "You haven't. Not really. If you had, you wouldn't want a moment of my time. You would respect my decision."

He sighs. "You're right. But can you blame me?"

I swallow my nerves and shrug.

"The last thing I wanted to do was hurt you. I never wanted to mess with your mind in the first place. You know I'm madly and deeply in love with you, Jewel," he says. "I promised you forever and you promised me."

I frown. "I didn't."

"You did."

COMPLICATIONS

I SIT IN THE MIDDLE of the sunny street, staring up at The Boxes. Tears burn my cheeks, my chest aching. Grief clings to my soul, and I'm not sure if I'll ever recover from this mess. First Aunt Dottie and now Mom. Dad doesn't even know yet. Neither does Ramona. It was just my mom and I holding each other, waiting for someone from the human health clinic to arrive. They never did. It was someone from the lab instead to take Mom's final donation.

And she wasn't the only one on our floor. I saw twenty-seven phlebotomists on my way outside. I didn't believe Dad when he told me the possibility, but I knew he was right the second I opened the door for the man in full protective gear. He even swabbed me for the flu virus. Had I tested positive for it, I'd—I can't even think about it.

"Precious Jewel," a soft voice whispers. "Come to me."

Fear replaces the ache in my heart, and I get to my feet and spin around to find a blond vampire with vibrant blue eyes gawking at me from the shadow of the building. He offers me a closed lip smile, surprising me. I've never had a shadow dweller respond in such a way. Most growl or hiss. Taunt me. How does this guy even know my name? I don't have my donor bracelet yet. I don't have to go for another few weeks now that Mom...

I take a few steps back without a word, clenching my fingers into fists. As long as I stay in the sunlight, he won't bother me much.

"Don't be afraid. I'm not going to hurt you," he says, toeing the line between the shade and sun. "I just want to talk. You can stand in the sun if you want, but I need you to come a bit closer."

I hug myself. "I...can't."

"Your mother passed away, didn't she?" he asks, his sharp features softening with a frown.

I've never seen such an expression on a vampire before. Something about it makes him seem less threatening. Handsome even. He's well dressed, unlike any of the shadow dwellers that hang out on Starlight Row.

My throat burns from crying, and it takes everything in me to get my mouth to work. "How d-did you k-know?" It would be one thing to assume a family member, but to men-

tion my mom specifically? Who is this guy?

He waves to me. "Come closer, Jewel. I need to get a good look at you."

I don't move. I can't. My dad has told me a thousand times to stay away from the shadows. It's so ingrained in my mind that my body won't even allow it.

Shrugging out of his jacket, the vampire covers his head and squares his shoulders. He's going to brave the sunlight. I've heard rumors of it happening if you walk too close to the shade, but he's ready to jump straight into the sun. Holy shit balls.

Panic pushes my body to move, and I scramble back. The vampire rushes right at me into the sunlight faster than I've seen any shadow dweller move. My world blurs, and I scream out, feeling the weight of his fingers dig into my sides. I squeeze my eyes shut, my red eyelids turning dark as we enter the shade of another building. My back hits a cool wall, and the vampire touches my cheek, grazing his fingers along the sticky trail of tears I can't stop crying.

"Don't bite me, please. I'm not of donation age yet." I lift my shoulders in an attempt to protect my neck. I'm close enough that it probably wouldn't matter.

"Look at me, Jewel," he whispers, leaning in so close that I can feel the coolness of his breath on my lips. "I will not hurt you or bite you without your consent. I know you're not ready for such an experience just yet."

I shiver, my body reacting to his words. He makes it

sound like something I want. "I'm pretty friggin' sure I'll never be ready for that freaky ass experience."

He chuckles, the breathlessness of his voice somehow managing to suppress the fear in me. "Nothing could ever be anything less than pleasurable between us. Just a few days ago you asked what it was like."

What the eff? I slowly flutter my eyes open, my heart crashing around my chest in an attempt to escape. The vampire presses harder into me until his heart thrums against my rising and falling chest. His blue eyes flash silver, and my body slackens in his arms.

I release a small breath. I should be terrified, but I'm not. "What do you mean a few days ago?"

"Remember me, Jewel," he says.

Recognition flits through my mind, and I throw my arms around Orlando's neck, nearly sending us both back into the sun. He hugs me close, scooping me up to hold me in his arms while letting me bury my face into the crook of his neck.

"You're here," I whisper. "I'm so glad."

"I'm not going anywhere. I was worried about you when you didn't walk your family to school this morning." Orlando squeezes me tighter, trying to smother the trembles from my body.

"Mom got worse, and Dad couldn't miss work. They— they didn't even try to save her, Orlando. A phlebotomist came in and—" I choke up at the memory, still fresh and as painful as ever in my mind.

"I'm so sorry, Jewel. Donor Life Corp issued a cleanse to stop the spread of the virus. The board won't risk it spreading. It's speculated to have come from another territory, and the city is now under quarantine."

"What? Oh, shit. Dad's going to lose it. He doesn't even know she's gone. I don't have the authorization to send him a message yet. Only Mom—" I sob a cry, my heart breaking all over again. "What are we going to do? My dad can't donate blood to support all of us."

"He won't have to. I'll take care of everything." Orlando leans back to look into my eyes. "I'll make the arrangements and cover the expenses until Ramona comes of age. You'll never have to donate, my precious Jewel. Your family will have a happy life, and we'll have our forever."

Hope rises in my chest, and I bob my head. We've talked about this a dozen times before, but Orlando warned me that Dad would fight against it. He hates vampires so much that he'd rather risk my life in the city than just let me go. But now? What choice will he have? My need for vampire blood grows stronger. Dad doesn't even know the extent of it. He's lucky Orlando doesn't ask for his blood every time, considering he's not registered with Donor Life Corp and needs a personal blood source. Dad could never maintain it. It's why we sneak around. Orlando has always been kind enough not to make my mom pitch in. "Would that mean my dad will no longer have to give you his blood?"

"There will be no need. We won't be in the city any longer."

I sniffle a few times, composing myself. "Where else would we go?"

"Anywhere. Our life will be magnificent. You'll never have to worry again. We can contently survive on each other. Protect each other."

My heart picks up speed as I try to imagine such a life outside of the city. It never felt like a possibility, but he sounds so certain. "Promise?"

"I vow to it. These last few months...I can't wait for the rest of forever."

"What about my family?"

"They're going to be fine. Safer. Your father won't have to worry so much about you. Just think about it. Imagine what would happen if you accidentally lost control one day? I can't follow you in the shadows everywhere. Your father thinks keeping you isolated will stop such a thing, but that kind of life is only manageable for so long. Your mother would want this. You know she didn't agree with your father. She hated seeing you so sick when you were withheld from what you need."

"You're right. She asked me to remind my father that life isn't always about the fight," I say.

"And this fight isn't yours regardless of what your father thinks."

I rub my lips together. "If only he could see you like I do."

Orlando leans into me, pressing a kiss to my cheek despite the saltiness of my tears. I hug him close, letting him hold me. We say nothing for a few minutes, just listening to the sounds of the city around us.

"I love you, Jewel," he whispers. "I hope you know that. I'd have taken you sooner if it wasn't for your father. I'm a man of my word and am obligated to do as he asks for now. I owe it to the Jordan family. For Jade's sacrifice."

A smile curls my lips for the first time today. "My dad's always been wrong about you. No other vampire would let him boss them around like this."

He hums in his throat. "He gets that from your great-great grandmother. You carry the same trait inside you. Such fighters."

"You like it." I bring my mouth to his to kiss him, to taste the sweetness of his lips for the first time. It's all I want to think about in this moment as I agree to give into him. To see what life outside Dark Terrace Ranch could be like. He manages to ease the ache in my chest and comfort me. The world doesn't seem so bleak and short in his embrace.

"Orlando, you son of a bitch! Jewel, get away from him!"

Orlando sets me on my feet next to him and turns to glower at my dad. Dad strides in our direction and reaches for his work belt, pulling a screwdriver free. Only my dad is brave enough to threaten a vampire, one as powerful as Orlando at that.

I step in front of Orlando, stopping my dad in his tracks.

"*Stop. Don't do anything crazy, Dad. We were just talking.*"

"*He's in your head. You can't believe anything he says. Now, get over here, Jewel.*" *Dad's voice bellows through the air, the deep anger scaring me more than Orlando ever could.*

"*The only reason he ever gets into my head is because of you,*" *I say, trying to keep my voice even.*

Dad charges closer, and Orlando links his fingers through mine and tugs me back a foot. I can tell it's taking him a lot of restraint not to do something rash.

"*I'm going to kill you, Orlando! You turned her against me,*" *Dad says.*

I hold my palm out. "*Stop it! He didn't. I'm not against you, Dad. I just—you don't understand. He's trying to help. Something's happ—*"

"*Help? Seducing you isn't helping. I see it all over his face. I'll not allow such a disgraceful occurrence. You are not to be with Orlando. He only wants to see you caged.*" *Standing taller, Dad waves his screwdriver at Orlando.* "*And you! We had a deal. Jewel was not to know you away from me. You're jeopardizing her.*"

"*Dad, please. Orlando's going to help us,*" *I repeat, trying my best to keep Dad from starting a fight he can't win.*

"*We don't need his damn help. You're getting stronger. As soon as the quarantine is removed—*"

"*You knew about the quarantine?*" *I ask, my mouth hanging open slightly.*

"*What do you think I've been doing all day? I've been*

sealing every exit except the main entrance to the city." Dad doesn't look at me as he says the words.

"It's worse than I thought. We need to move quickly," Orlando says, glancing at me. "It'll be harder to leave if we wait."

Dad scowls. "You are not taking her. Jewel, honey. Get over here. I mean it. Don't let him scare you. This is temporary. Your mother will be heartbroken if you fall for his charm."

My chest tightens at his words, and I look at Orlando. "I need a moment with him. Meet me later?"

Dad braves the shadow to rush to me. "Absolutely not."

"Dad, please. Donor Life Corp sent—"

Dad grabs my arm, trying to pull me away from Orlando. "I know what Donor Life Corp did. I had been expecting it."

"You knew? Why weren't you here? Why did you make me stay alone?"

"You had to see what vampires do. They don't care about us. All they care about is assuring their food source. That's what we are to them."

"That's not true," I say, trying to free myself from Dad's strong grip.

"It is. Now, the deal, Orlando. Do it. Make her forget. Everything. If I find you trying to meet with her again, you'll regret it. You might be powerful, but I have my own resources too."

"Dad, please," I beg. "You're being unreasonable."

"Do it," Dad repeats.

I shift and peer at Orlando. "Please, no. I hate this. I can't just forget you. How will I manage now?"

He touches my cheek. "Precious Jewel, I'll figure this out, okay? He can't keep you from me. He'll see once things are set into place by Donor Life Corp. Now, Jewel. Go with your father."

"No!"

"Damn, is our girl okay?" Kingston's voice drags me from my dream.

I curl in on myself, reaching out for something to hold onto. "Come here, dude. I need your cuddles. That was—fuck. Donor Life Corp cleansed the city after the flu outbreak?"

Kingston doesn't respond to me. He's not quick to hold me either.

"Kingston?" I sit up in bed and peer around.

"Fuck. Call Austin or Diego, Orlando. She needs a serious hug, and I doubt she'll accept one from you."

I groan and sit up, spotting Kingston's projection on the wall. Orlando sits on the couch exactly where I left him after he admitted he loved me for the first time since he took the block off my memories. And now I'm as confused as all get-out. That dream I had—the memory—it was intense. I barely remember the day my mom died, and what I do remember was nothing like what I know really happened. My dad had Orlando steal the last moments I had with my mom away from me. He asked him to suppress my grief.

I'm so angry at him for that—my dad. How could he?

Clearing my throat, I meet Kingston's worried eyes and say, "It's okay, Kingston. Just more memories coming back to me."

"Your mother's death?" Orlando asks quietly, drawing my attention to him. "I heard you whispering in your sleep."

I don't have to confirm it for him to know he's right. He looks at me exactly how he did the moment he found me sitting in the sun, staring up at the clouds, trying to figure out what would happen with the rest of my life.

"Fuck," Kingston repeats. "Babe, I'm coming now. I just called to tell you that everything is good."

"Yup, great," Brayla says, turning the phone.

My cousins wave at me from next to Liz. "We'll see you soon, Jewel!"

Kingston appears back on screen. "Orlando, get Diego and Austin. I mean it." He frowns at me. "I'll be there soon."

His projection disappears as the line disconnects, and I flop back on the bed and stare at the ceiling. "I thought he'd be back."

"Unexpected delays, but all is fine," Orlando says. "Why don't you try to go back to sleep?"

I shift onto my side and meet his blue eyes. "Can't."

"Are you hungry?"

I inhale a small breath through my nose. Before I can respond, Orlando gets up from his spot and walks across the room to the quaint kitchenette. He blurs around the kitchen for a moment and comes to my side carrying a plate with some banana bread and cut up fruit in one hand and my thermos in the other.

"I can call the chef if this isn't something you want," he says, handing me the plate.

"It's fine. I think I just want the thermos."

I set the plate on the side table and unscrew the lid of the thermos, bringing it to my mouth. Orlando stares at me, and I raise an eyebrow and quickly chug the whole thing down, feeling the warmth tingling in my stomach.

"What?" I ask, licking my lips.

"Your heart's still racing."

"Well, yeah. I just remembered what you—what my dad made you do. You know, I've always felt so guilty that I didn't mourn my mom the way I had expected to. How could you give into that specific request? You messed with more than my mind. You messed with my emotions. What kind of excuse do you have? You can't blame Katherine this time. You had no one to make appearances for." Katherine was his excuse for his monstrous behavior before as he was using her to gain status in the Donor Life Corp territory. Still angers me every time I think about her.

He sighs. "I've made a lot of regretful decisions, but that one was on you, remember?"

I pull my legs to me and rest my chin on my knees, searching my memory for the moment he speaks of. "Outside the market," I whisper. "I'm sorry. I forgot. I'm still struggling with getting everything straight. Things blur together unless I know exactly what I want to remember."

Orlando takes a seat on the edge of the bed. "You always had a way to test my power as a vampire, Jewel. I never wanted to take away that part of you, but I felt so hopeless in my attempt to comfort you."

"You think you felt hopeless?" I ask.

He turns toward me, sitting cross-legged beside me. "I'm sorry, I didn't mean—"

"No, I'm sorry," I say, interrupting him. "It's just a lot to take in. This is all so hard. It's like every time I make plans for my life, they change. Someone or something comes along and shoves me in the opposite direction. And now it's so fucked up to see my dad unlike I've ever seen him. Why did you do it?"

Orlando leans back on the headboard and stretches his legs in front of him. "You know it's always been complicated. The deal I had with your father—"

"I'm asking why you allowed me to think he was a good man." I twist my neck to meet his gaze. "Why did you allow him such authority over me? You could have just kidnapped me and been done with it."

The corner of his mouth twitches up. "I thought about it a dozen times, but I had made a promise to your mother that as long as you were safe, I wouldn't. The deal with your father only extended until you hit maturity, but by then, your mother had passed and you wouldn't leave your family. Your mother's death made your father worse. He became obsessed with his self-imposed mission. Without your mother, he grew absent. You know this."

He's right. I do. That's when he started talking about leaving Dark Terrace Ranch and moving to The Orchards. At the time, I had no idea what it meant. I had no idea that he was more than just a conspiracy theorist.

"The quarantine didn't help. It made things quite difficult. You registering as a donor put you in the system as well. When I offered your father a way out, a way that the two of us could be together, he took it. But then…" He lets his voice trail off.

"He turned against you," I say. "So you made good on the blood debt."

"I thought it was the best way. I never imagined that—never mind. It doesn't matter now." He falls silent and stares at the blank wall in front of us for a long moment.

"You're right," I say, finally finding my voice. "It doesn't matter. And I don't blame you."

He shifts in his spot, turning more toward me. "You don't?"

I knock my knuckles into his leg. "I understand that a vampire is only as powerful as his coven. That's why loyalty was so important to Mitchell."

"He's probably already in search of new heirs."

I shift to look at him again. "But still. You could've been

less of an asshole about everything."

Placing his hand next to mine, he grazes his fingers along my pinkie, just testing me for a reaction. I don't automatically recoil, and he slowly slides his hand on top of mine. "Perhaps. Maybe you wouldn't have fallen so hard for my brothers had I managed to deal with Katherine accordingly."

I smirk at him. "Doubt it. Have you seen them? They ripped a creep vampire apart on my behalf the first day I met them."

"That probably pokes right at your nature," he teases. "I feel fortunate to have had the power and strength to gain such an alliance in your matches."

I scrunch my nose. "You're just saying that because we're a packaged deal. Don't think I've forgotten your possessiveness. Sharing goes against your nature."

"You would think so. But Jewel, you underestimate the effect you have on us. I don't know if it's something you were born with or just who you are, but you've gotten to me so much so that I'm willing to compromise. Your allure...I want to protect you. I *need* to protect you. Your matches feel it too."

Linking his fingers through mine, he brings my hand up and holds it to his chest, making me lean closer to him. Our eyes meet again, sending my heart racing at a much quicker pace than his. "Orlando..."

He smiles, shifting closer, and runs his fingers up my jaw to push my hair behind my ears. "You know, they remind me a lot of my coven brothers from before The Divide. I've been alone for so long now that I forgot what it felt like to have such a bond. I know they're still unsure of me, and I doubt Kingston will ever more than tolerate me, but things have fallen into place better than I had imagined."

I try to search my memory for what happened to his coven, but it's not there. It's something Orlando never shared with me, and now I'm curious. "What happened to them exactly? Your coven brothers?"

"The uprising was a tumultuous time, and not just for humans. Covens fought covens. Humans with each other. Fear took over and caused a lack of order. The governing bodies disintegrated world-wide. My brother, Phoenix, perished during the first attacks in an attempt to control the rapid spread of transformations caused by Donor Life Corp."

"Mitchell said you were responsible for the uprising. Said covens were torn on whether to go back into hiding after culling the population." I know now that Mitchell spewed utter bullshit, but I still can't help saying the words to see Orlando's reaction. To see some sort of truth.

He releases a soft groan of a laugh. "Of course he would. He's a Divine. The savior of humanity."

I twist my mouth. "I knew he was lying."

"The rest of my brothers were caught up in his madness during the divisions. It wasn't only humans divided. The strongest had to take reign over the newly turned. The out of control. None of us were truly prepared for The Divide. After

I lost Antoine and Rowan, I withdrew from society. There is a lot of uninhabited world out there. Pockets of rebels escaped from the cities. Some in hiding since the uprising. It's rather easy to come to a mutual arrangement. Rebels hate us, but they still need vampires like me. Vampires who never agreed with the uprising and who saw that the world needed to unite and not destroy everything."

His words leave me burning with questions. All my life, all I've known was Dark Terrace Ranch. I didn't even know other cities still existed until Diego showed me a map. And now this? I can't even truly imagine.

I run my free hand through my hair. "Yet here we are stuck in Dark Terrace Ranch about to face the board and trust that they'll give us what we want."

"It has nothing to do with trust, Jewel," he says. "It has to do with power. Control. Compromise. What benefits who. It would be in the board's best interest to give you to the Ortega Coven."

I sigh. "This is still a lot to deal with."

"I know."

A knock on the door draws our attention away from each other. "Orlando, sorry to interrupt but there's a problem."

"A problem?" Orlando asks.

Diego opens the door, followed by Austin, and the two of them turn their attention to us sitting together on the bed. Neither of them reacts, though they both stare at Orlando's hand entwined with mine.

"You're awake," Austin says.

Orlando eyes me. "She relived the memory of her mother's death in her dreams."

Diego closes the door behind him and strolls in our direction. "That must've been difficult. Are you okay?"

"I could use a hug," I say, tugging my hand from Orlando's to hold my arms up. "From both of you."

Austin breaks his serious expression and smiles, catching up to Diego to meet me at the edge of the bed. I pull the two of them hard enough to make them climb on the bed to give me a proper hug where I'm sandwiched between them. I can feel the weight of Orlando's gaze on us, but I don't let it stop me. The tension and uncertainty swirling between everyone makes me shift and bury my face into Diego's neck where I brush my lips to his sweet skin.

"Is this awkward?" I ask, pulling myself away to meet everyone's gazes.

"Hell yeah it's awkward." Kingston's voice resonates through the air. "I'm not there."

Diego chuckles and runs his knuckles over my cheek. "What Kingston means is that it's new and different for us."

"You can admit it's awkward," I say, leaning in to kiss him.

"Just a little."

I look at Orlando. "For me too. We have a lot to talk about after tonight."

Austin slides his arms around me. "You know we're good

with whatever you decide, Jewel."

I shake my head. "No. That's not how I want things to be. We're committing to a life together. All of us."

Kingston groans. "Damn it. Why am I not there again?"

I spot Austin's com device glowing on the bed with Kingston smirking at me with a raised eyebrow. Picking it up, I cradle it in my hands and stick my tongue out at him. "Just wait until you are. I have big plans as a thank you for taking care of my cousins."

He pops out his bottom lip, his face shifting from playful to brooding. "About that."

Ice slides down my back, the edges of my vision shadowing. "What happened?"

Diego pulls me onto his lap and engulfs me in a hug. "It's a small snag in our plans, but it's going to be okay. We'll take care of it."

"Did Blood Rebels—" I snap my mouth shut and exhale a long breath through my nose. "Did they come after you? Is anyone hurt? Where's Brayla? Liz's family?"

Austin rubs my back. "Take a breath, Jewel. No one is hurt, but we have to go. Our arrangement with Liz must be fulfilled now or...things will get complicated."

"And murdery," Kingston adds. "Which if you'd let me, I could handle everything myself and still make it to Dark Terrace Ranch. But it would have to be without Brayla."

"What?" I frown at his words. "Kingston, you can't do that."

"The murder or returning without Brayla?"

I puff a breath of air. "Both."

He sighs and rubs his hands on his face. "What do you want me to do, Orlando? I can't handle this on my own."

Orlando leans closer to peer at Kingston. "Even if you returned, we cannot establish our coven without Brayla unless I file to outcast her from our region."

"She wouldn't be able to return for a minimum of a year," Kingston says. "She could possibly join another coven in the meantime, but then she couldn't uphold a Blood Vow to Jewel. And who knows what kind of stipulations a new coven would require. Viorica required Samantha to join permanently. Going against her coven is an automatic death sentence."

"I think most others would do the same to take advantage of the situation. Brayla knows too much," Diego says.

"Do you think she could manage without a coven?" Kingston asks.

Disbelief drops my mouth open. "Are you kidding me? Why is this a thing?"

Diego rubs his big hand on my back, massaging the tension building in my muscles. "It's to prevent power plays. We're responsible for a region. We can't just come and go as we please. It would cause disorder and weaken alliances."

I sink in on myself, pulling my knees to my chest. "We can't just outcast her to the shadows. Wouldn't you guys have to tattoo her or something? She'll turn into..."

"She's already a lunatic, babe," Kingston says.

"Not helping." Austin releases a small growl. "As much as I dislike Brayla, I agree with Jewel. Brayla is part of our coven. You wouldn't want us to deem you an outcast, would you?"

"That's different," Kingston argues.

"How so?" Austin and I both say.

Austin takes my hand. "We're family. Jewel loves Brayla enough to choose to Blood Vow to her. They have a mortal bond despite things. She may have fucked up, but she did what she thought was helping Jewel, and I can't fault her for that."

Orlando sits straighter. "You two go and see if you can handle the situation with Kingston. I'll stay here with Jewel and stall for as long as I can."

I grimace. "I'm not staying here."

"The hell you're tagging along, babe," Kingston says.

Diego sinks into me and rests his head on my shoulder. "I know this isn't ideal, but we can't focus like we should while our attention is split to assure your safety."

"Can't Orlando go and one of you stay?" I ask.

"Sorry, beautiful. We're not established as part of the Ortega Coven yet."

"Not to mention that Mitchell would take advantage of the situation," Austin says.

Orlando reaches out and touches my knee. "Don't worry, Jewel. Your matches are as capable of handling the situation as I am at taking care of you."

I squeeze my eyes shut. "Okay, fine. But you guys better hurry up and get back here so we can get this over with and then celebrate."

"Damn straight," Kingston says. "It'll be a night we'll all remember."

A NIGHT TO REMEMBER

"WHERE ARE THEY?" I ASK, pacing around the room for the tenth time.

Orlando stops in front of me. "They'll be here."

No matter how calm Orlando acts, I can't stop worry from gripping my chest. "Why aren't they answering their phones?"

"Could be a number of reasons," he says, placing his hands on my shoulders. "But I assure you. Everything will be okay. Now, get dressed. We have to appear in front of the board."

"Without them?"

"To stall the board, we must be present." He spins me toward the wardrobe where a white dress hangs on the wall.

"Will you please just trust me? I will keep you safe."

I sigh. "I'm trying to. I am. I just—this sucks. None of this would've happened had you let me transfer Ramona's debt to Austin. Brayla would've never had to take her."

"Don't be so sure. The old woman grew impatient enough to request help from a Blood Rebel. She was probably partly responsible for the explosion. It's those less vocal that must be watched accordingly," he says.

"Is that why you let Hayden hang around? This was probably all him," I mutter.

Orlando beats me to the wardrobe and holds out the white dress to me. "No, I don't think so. I've been keeping a close eye on Hayden as well as your father. It was neither of them. Hayden's one of the few who knows their capabilities and thinks beyond what lies in front of him. It's what makes him a good leader to his people. He understands the world enough to survive. Just like your father. It's not a wonder Ramona grew infatuated with him."

Ugh. "I don't want to think about that."

"Good, because you need a clear head. You must remain in control. If you do not, you risk exposing yourself. I might not be the only one who has dealt with dhampirs. I'd rather keep your secret safe."

I cross my arms. "Well, yeah. Me too."

"Good. Now get dressed."

Orlando remains outside while I enter into the small changing area sparse of clothes unlike I'm used to. Kingston had always assured every place I stayed had hundreds of options to choose from. Now? I guess it's not so important. I don't plan to return to Dark Terrace Ranch again if I don't have to.

I quickly strip from my clothes and step into the dress to pull it up around me. A sweet scent wafts through the air, drawing my attention toward the room. My stomach growls, my deep-seated hunger demanding that I give in and take care of it.

"Orlando, really? Did you just bite your arm?" I ask.

He hums under his breath. "Your senses are rather strong when you're starved. My brothers were right about you being insatiable."

I attempt to zip up the back of the dress and fail. "I'm not starved."

Gathering the fabric, I stroll from the wardrobe to find Orlando filling up a glass of blood. He jerks his attention up, his eyes flashing silver in his intensity. I uncontrollably avert my gaze to his bleeding arm, while he practically devours me in my dress with his eyes.

"Ravishing," he whispers to himself.

His compliment stirs warmth in my chest. "Maybe not for long if you don't take care of that bite mark. You should be afraid that I might attack you and get blood everywhere."

He laughs, the sound strange yet familiar. "You're the last person I'm afraid of, Jewel. If it makes you feel better, I'll excuse your needs based on your lack of control if you want."

I tighten my jaw. "Orlando."

"You don't have to be afraid of yourself. Never with me."

"Please," I whisper, turning my gaze to the floor. "I know this isn't a big deal for you, but I'm not there yet anymore."

His smile falters, and he quickly staunches the bleeding on his arm, taking care to roll down his sleeve to hide it from me. "My apologies. I mistook our moment earlier as being more than what it was to you. I had assumed since you want to discuss our futures, you were open to the possibility of—" He shuts his mouth without finishing his words and steps closer. "Never mind. Here, drink this."

I take the glass from him and stare at it. "Is there no more of Diego and Austin's blood to mix with it?"

He shakes his head. "I think your nerves are making you exceptionally hungry. You've consumed twice as much as usual."

Crinkling my nose, I stare at the dark red liquid, wishing with everything in me that my stomach would shut up already. Doesn't my body realize it's making this all sorts of friggin' awkward for me?

"Not that your dietary needs are bad. You shouldn't be embarrassed."

"That sounds like something Austin would say," I murmur, finally bringing the glass to my lips.

Orlando closes the space to me and tilts his head to gaze at me with a smile. "He does understand that aspect more than anyone."

"He told you about his control issues?" I ask, licking my lips, holding my dress up with one hand while clutching the glass with the other.

Twirling his finger, he motions for me to spin around. I twist on my feet and stand utterly still as he sweeps my hair over my shoulder. He gently grasps my hip with one hand while he tugs up the zipper for me and hooks it in place. "Yes, of course. I know it might seem weird to you, but we've gotten to know each other. We've spent time together the last few weeks establishing our relationships as coven brothers on the nights we're apart from you."

"I knew that," I say. And I did. I just didn't think about the fact that they would share personal details or try to find some sort of commonalities outside me. Now I feel like crap by how selfish I've been not even thinking about what it means for my guys to join Orlando's coven.

He rests his hands on my shoulders and nudges me to turn back around so that we face each other. "You still seem surprised."

"And I feel bad. No wonder they were upset about the Ramona thing." I thought it was more about my safety. About me. But it wasn't. It was about them, too. They not only wanted to join Orlando's coven for my benefit. They want to because they like it. "Why didn't they tell me?"

"I can't answer for them but try not to get too upset."

"You're standing up for them?" I'm not mad or anything, but I can't stop my curiosity from getting the best of me.

"Why?"

"Experiencing your disdain and fury is far worse a punishment than what I imagine an eternity of damnation to be like."

I raise my eyebrows.

He chuckles. "I'm kidding. But if I have to hear Kingston pace and complain another night, I—"

I press my finger to his mouth. "You better get used to it. We're fiercely passionate."

"That is something we can all agree on."

Orlando's com device chimes from the bedside table, and I dash across the room in an attempt to beat him to it. He lets me win, and I scoop the thing up and jab my finger to the screen to accept the call from Diego.

"Where are you...holy shit balls!" I nearly drop the phone at the sight of his double black eyes.

"Beautiful, I need to talk to Orlando."

Orlando doesn't give me the chance to argue and ask what the hell happened. Instead, he steals the phone, hits a few buttons, and abandons me to hide in the bathroom. I startle at the door slamming and dash across the room.

"Speak quietly. She's listening," Orlando says.

I twist the doorknob, but it doesn't budge. "Orlando, you asshole! Open up!"

He turns on the shower, trying to drown out the noise. "Not good...soon...no...I'll keep...safe."

His words cut in and out as I shove my ear against the

door.

"...trust you," Diego says.

The water shuts off, and Orlando swings the door open. I fall forward, nearly eating shit on the tiles. He catches me, narrowing his eyes, though amusement lights up the rest of his face.

"Damn it, babe. Can't you behave for five minutes," Kingston says.

I huff. "Not without your threats to spank me."

He releases a funny as hell cross between a purr and a moan and a gasp, taken by surprise by my comment. "Give her the phone, Orlando. I need to see her. Just for a second."

Orlando releases his hold on my arm to grab the com device. "Don't be alarmed by his appearance."

I scrunch my brows and take the phone from him. "Fuck, dude. What the hell?"

Kingston runs his tongue over his split lip. "You look so hot. How dare you tease me when I can't be there to rip that dress off you." Glancing next to him, he says, "Look at our girl. I can't believe we're missing this."

I spot Diego and Austin sitting next to Kingston with their backs against a cement wall. Light glows from somewhere above them, creating dark shadows across their bruised faces, making them look even worse.

"You look stunning, Jewel," Austin says.

"Incredible," Diego adds.

I pop out my bottom lip. "You guys...thanks. But seriously, answer my question. What the hell happened? Why aren't you going to be here?"

Kingston brings the phone to his face so that I can't use my pouty face to convince either of his brothers to tell me. "It's complicated, Jewel."

"That's not an answer," I say, curling my lips.

Kingston's eyes flash silver, and he glances at Austin and Diego again. "Did she just growl at me?"

"You bet I did."

Orlando touches my shoulder, getting me to turn my focus to him. "Jewel."

My eyes widen at just the sound of my name. "Oh shit. He's dead, isn't he? Liz's grandson is dead."

"Actually...he seems to rather enjoy his new life here in the Aku Region," Kingston says, answering for Orlando. "He's not willing to come, and his match's coven put up one helluva fight. The only way we can get Turner is to either kill them all and take him against his will or figure something else out."

My mouth forms an O. "So, now what? Are you coming back?"

Kingston flashes his fangs, but not at me. He looks at something else by him. It's then that I hear the growl of another vampire. "You're going to be coming to us."

I blink a few times. "But the meeting."

Diego takes the phone from Kingston. "You'll be going with Orlando as planned. Please listen to him."

"Don't forget your contacts, Jewel," Austin adds.

Kingston leans back into view. "We want you out of there safely without incident, so don't be a pain in the balls. Orlando's going to have to request to postpone things, and the board gets rather annoyed by inconveniences."

I scrub my hands over my face. "Whatever, okay. Try not to get into more trouble."

He smirks. "Back at you. Love you, babe."

"Love you, Jewel," Austin and Diego add.

The line clicks off, and I face Orlando. He straightens his tie and squares his shoulders, looking ready to face whatever comes our way. His confidence eases the panic sneaking up on me. I never thought I'd have to be in this position—of relying solely on Orlando to get me through things—but I should know by now that the universe loves to test my resolve.

"We should get going," Orlando says, reaching up to comb his fingers through my hair, fixing it on my shoulders. He proffers his hand to me. "May I pick you up?"

I nod my head, and he scoops me up, cradling me against him without making me attempt to straddle him in a dress.

"Hold on tight," he says, his breath whispering against my ear.

Sliding my arms around his neck, I link my fingers together and rest my head on his shoulder. "Okay, I'm ready. I trust you to get me through this."

"I'll prove to you that we can get through anything, Jewel," he whispers.

Looks like it's not only the universe testing my resolve.

"Jewel, you're alone," Samantha says, standing outside the boardroom with both Evora and Cyprus.

"Um." I glance at Orlando. "You don't have the power of invisibility, do you? I mean, you're sneaky as all get-out, but I'm pretty sure you can't hide in plain sight."

Gabriella materializes next to Cyprus and flashes her fangs at him in a smile that I can only describe as starving. "Damn, Sammy. I'm pretty certain Jewel's never going to forgive you. I don't know why you bother being nice."

"Because she needs Jewel. Why else be nice to someone?" Merrick appears on the other side of Evora and smirks but not at me, at Orlando. "Am I right, Mr. Ortega? Can't beat them so join them and all that jazz. It was a rather smart move. I love a man who can strategize and see beyond what he has to take in front of him. You have Mitchell seething."

Samantha reaches over and smacks Merrick on the shoulder. "Shut up. He could be around here somewhere. You know Mother specifically told you to mind your mouth."

Merrick shrugs. "I just thought I'd warn him seeing as Jewel looks well-adjusted to yet another fiercely powerful, sexy man." She reaches out and touches Orlando's shoulder. "Does she provide everything you need?"

"Merrick!" Samantha hisses.

Merrick beams a fake ass smile in my direction. "What? Why can't I ask? If she's not, I wanted to invite him to celebrate the union of his coven. I'm sure Jewel didn't even plan anything special. She wouldn't know how big of a deal a moment like this would be."

"I thought he was with Brayla," Gabriella says. "They did agree to a Blood Vow."

Merrick flashes her fangs. "A vow to elevate status not one to fulfill one's needs."

I furrow my brows. "It's not like that between them." I regret the second the words leave my mouth because everyone, including Orlando, looks at me. I should've just kept my mouth shut. It's not like any of this matters.

Merrick tips her head back and laughs. She glances at Gabriella with an amused smile like my words were the funniest thing she's ever heard. "Rather unfair, don't you think? You make them share you."

"You should take my sister up on her offer, Mr. Ortega," Gabriella says, chiming in. "I'm sure your brothers can vouch for her. Or maybe one of them is free. Whose night is it? Where are the disgraced heirs anyway? I never thought they'd leave Jewel's side."

Orlando sets me on my feet and drapes his arm around my shoulders. I stand straight, not letting him pull as close as he obviously wants to while I'm under the scrutiny of practically everyone. Even the two board members who have arrived early stare at me from their seats. "As enchanting as that sounds, tonight isn't a good night. Possibly another time, Ms. Vaduva."

"Seriously?" I mutter to myself, covering my mouth in

the process.

Merrick's ruby lips split into a dazzling smile, and she steps closer and touches Orlando's arm. "You know how to reach me."

"Of course. Now, if you'd excuse us, we need to take our seats. I'm sure the other board members are waiting for our arrival before joining us."

Orlando drops his hand to the small of my back and guides me forward. I clench my teeth to stop from glowering. I don't know what has gotten into me, but damn it. I should not be jealous of Merrick or annoyed that Orlando gave her hope for a future...what Kingston would describe as a booty call.

I shudder at the thought and trail next to Orlando, training my gaze to the floor. The last time I was in this boardroom was when the board sentenced me to a life in Haven Springs after Mitchell staked his claim on me as a Divine Heir to stop Orlando from going through with the Jordan blood debt.

I'm pretty friggin' sure if Orlando took his hand from me that one of the other board members would try to kill me so they wouldn't have to deal with what seems like a game of who gets Jewel. Or they'll try to take me for themselves to see what the big deal is. It's not the first time someone questioned why everyone wants me.

"Mr. Ortega, it's so nice to see you." Zara, the only other female vampire on the board besides Viorica, materializes in the doorway. She saunters forward, her plum lips complementing her golden skin and wide brown eyes lined in charcoal shadow. "Congratulations on your union with such exquisite heirs. You know I always thought Austin, Diego, and Kingston were never utilized to their full capabilities under Mitchell."

Orlando stops in front of the woman and kisses her cheeks. "Ms. Aku, you've met Jewel." Aku? That's the region Liz's grandson matched into.

Zara turns her attention to me but only nods. "How could I forget the donor who must taste so earth-shattering to unite a coven practically on her behalf?"

"I find it rather interesting that someone of your stature would go to the extent of stealing from Mitchell all for...her," a man with a shaved head says. "Dear Katherine was rather enamored as well. It's unfortunate what happened. I had warned her to just reapply for a new donor."

Orlando slides his fingers through mine, squeezing them lightly to get me to look at him. His eyes flash silver, and he reaches out and touches my cheek. "I am truly sorry for your loss, Mr. Duchanne. Katherine had an unhealthy obsession with my precious Jewel ever since I let her in on my arrangement with the Jordans. She crossed a line."

"Might I suggest that the obsession was probably with you," Zara says, running her finger over his shoulder.

"Funny what revelations come to light with shifts in power." The man, Mr. Duchanne, turns his attention to me. "It's not often I've heard of a donor surviving the wrath of my sister. You must be something fierce, Ms. Divine."

"Jewel no longer goes by that last name, Ademar. Be respectful," Zara says.

"You may call her Ms. Ortega," Orlando says.

Mr. Duchanne lifts and drops his eyebrows. "I suppose we shall see."

The tapping of heels draws everyone's attention to the door where Viorica appears with Mitchell right behind her. His eyes automatically narrow on me, and I shift closer to Orlando and drop my gaze to the floor with what feels like my heart and stomach. The rest of me would follow if Orlando wasn't suddenly holding me by the waist.

"Mr. Ortega," Viorica says, sashaying into the room, the hem of her knee-length skirt flowing with her movements. "Where is the rest of your coven? You cannot go through vows alone."

"And some of us don't have all night," Mitchell snaps. "I'd like to finish this and take back what is mine."

I jerk my head up to glare at him, and he meets me with a leer that screams how much he anticipates the opportunity to drain me until I'm on the verge of death only to keep me alive. At this point, I doubt he'd kill me. He'd take way too much pleasure in parading me around like a trophy or some shit.

Orlando stands taller, gripping onto me tighter. "Unfortunately, I need to postpone the ceremony. My brothers were called away on business and can't make it tonight."

Half the board sighs. Mitchell's smile widens. Viorica watches with her usual bored expression.

Mitchell steps closer, linking his fingers together in front of him. "Because my former heirs find themselves too preoccupied to bother showing up to such an important ceremony, I'd like to motion to have Mr. Ortega return Ms. Divine into my care considering she can no longer transfer her Blood Vow application."

"That seems reasonable enough," the last male vampire board member, who I don't think I've ever heard his name, says. "The donor is not worth my time. To prolong the transfer does no one any favors."

What the fuck? It most definitely does me a huge favor.

"I'm sorry, Mr. Ortega," Zara says. "I think I have to agree. Mitchell has invested a great deal into Ms. Divine. Sometimes compromises must be made for civility. You've already persuaded his former heirs to join you."

Orlando releases a low growl. "Grant me time and I'll assure it's worth your while. Perhaps a generous allocation of my region's share of blood donations will do?"

Zara turns her attention to me. "Or maybe a sample of your best blood source."

Orlando squeezes my hand again as my face loses all control. I'm quick to compose myself but not before Zara notices and wiggles her fingers at me.

"I'd gladly lie on that table if it meant I wouldn't have to return to Mitchell," I whisper to Orlando, still loud enough for all the vampires to hear.

Zara hums in her throat. "What do you think, Mr. Bellamy? It might be our only chance to discover what it is about this donor that has started a blood feud."

Mr. Bellamy leans his elbows on the sleek table. "I'll pass. My vote stands as is. Let's get on with it."

Shit.

Orlando rests his hand on the table, leaning closer to the board. Only he and Mitchell remain standing, though Mitchell glowers from a few feet away. "Might I remind you that anything Mr. Divine invested in Jewel was on behalf of his former heirs, for whom he chose to renounce after decades of obedience and servitude under his name. But with saying that, Jewel has chosen to accept a Blood Vow from Ms. Brayla Ortega instead. Seeing as she is an established member of my coven, I'd like to transfer Jewel's application on her behalf. She was a contender as a Blood Match."

"If she was here to claim her, then I'd consider it," Mr. Bellamy responds. "As it is now? No."

Zara rests her hands on the table. "With hearing that, I vote no as well. I find the sudden change in proposal unsettling considering the accusations of Ms. Ortega breaching her contract."

"That does sound rather suspicious. A donor should not have such capabilities to entice not only one vampire but an entire coven. I believe such antics pose a threat which you can't discern, Mr. Ortega. I vote no."

The edges of my vision shadow. I can't believe this just happened. If three of the six board members just voted against my transfer, that only leaves Viorica, Mitchell, and Orlando. Majority rules.

"Please," I say, stepping closer. "You can't do this."

"Oh, they can," Mitchell says, baring his teeth at me. "And if they didn't, I could use my authority to overrule."

I swallow hard, the lump in my throat refusing to go down. It wouldn't be the first time that Mitchell used his authority to overrule a vote cast by the board. I just didn't think he would risk doing it again.

Orlando slams his hand on the table, startling me. "This is unacceptable! I have an agreement going back generations through the Jordan bloodline passed to me by my deceased coven brother that guarantees Jewel be mine. I will not allow my future coven member to be a Divine. She has and always will be an Ortega. Do not test my power."

Silence falls over the board as Orlando's words sink in. Mr. Duchanne and Zara glance at each other. Mr. Bellamy trains his eyes on the table, not giving his thoughts away. Mitchell clenches his hands at his sides, his lips twisted, his eyes flashing silver.

"I vote yes to the transfer," Viorica says, standing up.

"Yes?" Mitchell asks, his voice growling with the word. "You'd dare to test our alliance, Vi?"

"If what Mr. Ortega says is true, then yes. But I'll only

agree that the Blood Vow be transferred to his name." Viorica turns her attention to me, waiting for my reaction.

"That seems rather unfair," Mr. Bellamy says. "The donor looks like such an act is torture, especially if she accepted a Blood Vow to someone else. I still hold my vote to return her to Mitchell. He'd at least show her mercy if he chose not to uphold the Divine vow to bring her into his coven. He'd use her as the blood source she was intended to be."

I realize I must be seriously frowning, because everyone turns their attention to me. "I—I—that's not true. The idea of accepting a Blood Vow from Orlando isn't the worst thing in the world."

I rub my hands into my eyes, accidentally pushing out one of the annoying contacts. Orlando notices immediately, his blue eyes widening. He doesn't even have to tell me that the board's words set me off enough to unleash the predator inside me that would love nothing more than to throw itself at Mr. Bellamy, who sits closest, to punch his heart out for even suggesting that returning me to Mitchell would be some sort of mercy.

"That doesn't sound very satisfactory," Zara says, speaking up. I keep my gaze locked on the floor in fear of anyone noticing the silver flashing in my eyes. "A Blood Vow should be beneficial to the vampire proposing, whether it be love, loyalty, or an advancement of status and power. Obviously, your loyalty lies with another since you accepted a vow from Ms. Ortega, who has done rather well in her promise to Mr.

Ortega to help him build a position and coven in this territory. Now, if Orlando found Ms. Ortega's vow unsatisfactory, he could part ways with her and invite you into the position of running his estate..."

Orlando tightens his jaw. "That won't be necessary. My vow to Brayla stands."

"Well, she obviously cannot advance his status," Mr. Duchanne quips. "What else is there for her to offer?"

"Her love," Orlando says, drawing my attention from the floor to him.

Mitchell's laughter echoes through the air, sending panic through me. Orlando ignores him and turns me to face him so that no one else in the room can see the expression crossing my face. My lip trembles, my heart racing. Orlando's intensity burns through me, reminding me of a dozen times before.

"He's right," I whisper so lowly that I'm not sure anyone can hear me. "I don't have much to offer in a Blood Vow, but my love is one thing I will freely give."

"She's just saying that," Mitchell snaps.

I'm pretty certain I'd agree to anything at this point to guarantee that I don't remain a Divine, but it's more than that. I might have mixed and hurt feelings toward Orlando and where he stands in my life. I most definitely would prefer to be standing here with Austin, Diego, and Kingston, professing my love to them and promising them forever. But what I just admitted is true.

Deep down in the part of me that I try to suppress hides

Jewel Jordan, the girl from Dark Terrace Ranch I thought I gave up long ago to be Jewel Divine. But I didn't fully give up that part of myself. I just locked her away and now she is pushing to break free. I'm still the same girl who met Orlando in the shadows and planned a future with him before my dad tried to steal it away. But I'm better. Stronger. Willing to do what I want for myself and for those who are willing to fight for me.

And now, I still want to plan my future with Orlando, with my guys, with Brayla, with the people who care about me most in the world. This isn't about some power play or some game against Donor Life Corp. This isn't me doing something I don't like in life just because I have to. This is me, Jewel Jordan, ready to embrace the change in my circumstances. To be the change in my life.

But it's clear that Mitchell is angry enough that the board wouldn't accept a half-assed agreement. They need proof.

"Then you don't know precious Jewel like I do," Orlando says, running his fingers along my jaw. "She means every word she says."

"This isn't a power play or a trick," I say.

Orlando nods and smiles. "I know. And I promise to keep my word. My vows. You are ours."

Leaning down, Orlando slowly, almost painfully, closes the distance to me. My heart crashes into his, a hurricane of emotions raining through my body, my soul, every inch of me as he grazes his lips to mine to seal his promise.

I stand frozen, unable to move, my lungs refusing to even let me breathe.

"I vote yes to transfer Jewel's Blood Vow to Orlando Ortega," Zara says.

"Agree," both Mr. Duchanne and Mr. Bellamy say in unison.

Viorica hums softly. "As do I. Congratulations, Mr. Ortega. We approve your Blood Vow to Jewel."

"Denied!"

Mitchell flies at Orlando and me so fast that my mind can't process what's happening. The world blurs, and my back hits the nearest wall as Orlando sandwiches me against it. He roars, drawing a scary ass blade from inside his jacket, but Mitchell pulls out two and attempts to rush him.

A figure blurs in front of us, knocking Mitchell off his path and into the massive table. The board members scatter, leaving their seats, doing nothing as Viorica lands on Mitchell and tries to restrain him.

"Our alliance is done," Mitchell yells.

Mitchell jerks his head up and rams it into Viorica's, knocking her back. Just as quickly, he shoves her with all his strength, sending her into the wall. It sinks under the force, and she huffs and tries to pull herself from the debris. Mitchell doesn't give her the chance and charges at her, daggers drawn and ready. She covers her face with her hands, bracing herself for what's to come.

Someone screams, and a few figures fly into the room inhumanly fast. Mr. Bellamy and Mr. Duchanne vanish seemingly into thin air as they exit through the open doors. I catch sight of Merrick locking her hands around Mitchell, dragging him back a few feet. Gabriella and Samantha join her, each trying to restrain Mitchell.

Viorica manages to get back to her feet and unsheathes her own dagger. "Mitchell, this is enough!"

"You cost me an heir!" he shouts.

Viorica snarls. "You were going to waste her."

"And none of that concerns you." Breaking free of the Vaduva sisters, Mitchell blurs so fast that my eyes can't keep up.

Orlando locks his hands on me and lifts me off my feet, preparing to head to the exit. I hold on tight, keeping my eyes locked on the fight unfolding. Mitchell's too fast for the Widows to catch again, so they form a protective wall around Viorica.

"Mitchell, enough," Zara says from her position near the exit. "If you harm Viorica, it'll be an act of war."

Mitchell stops in his tracks and looks at the elegant woman.

"I assure you that I'm not bluffing," she adds.

Mitchell releases a growl that steals every bit of warmth left inside me. Blurring again, he rushes toward the Vaduvas with his daggers glinting in the overhead light. He grabs Gabriella by her long, black hair and pulls her away, spinning her to restrain her against his chest.

"You cost me an heir," Mitchell repeats, holding a blade to Gabriella's throat.

"Mitchell, be reasonable," Viorica says, stepping closer. "Let her go. We can discuss—"

Mitchell's eyes flash silver, and he jerks Gabriella away enough to swipe the dagger cleanly through her neck. Screams pierce the air, not only the Vaduvas' but also my own, and blood spills across the floor with the dropping of Gabriella's body.

Orlando covers my eyes, trying to block the scene before us, but it does nothing to stop the fury rising inside me.

A small thud sounds in my ears, and I cringe knowing exactly what caused the noise. Viorica releases a scary as hell growl of her own, but no one moves.

"An heir for an heir," Mitchell says, his icy voice striking me through the heart. "I'll call this even."

"You bastard!" Merrick yells.

Viorica intervenes and pulls her daughter back. Samantha drops to her knees and pulls Gabriella's body to her. The scent of her blood trickles through the air, making me tense.

Mitchell wipes his daggers on his pants and looks in our direction. "Blame Mr. Ortega. Had he relented to give me Jewel, none of this would've happened."

"Stay calm, Jewel," Orlando whispers, turning my head so that Mitchell can't get a good look at me.

"He killed her," I say. I might not have liked Gabriella, but she didn't deserve that fate, especially not at my fault.

"I know, but please. You have to stay in control. They'll know. Tension is too high."

"He needs to die."

"That's not so simple."

"It is. I've seen you fight. I can help you."

Orlando shifts me. "We have other priorities. I must catch Zara before she leaves."

"But Orlando."

"I'm sorry, Jewel. No."

NIGHTSHADE PARK

ZARA WAITS BY THE ELEVATOR with her arms crossed over her chest. She remains expressionless as Orlando approaches, still carrying me in his arms.

"Jewel, Orlando, wait." Samantha runs at a human's pace in our direction, tugging along both Evora and Cyprus by their hands.

I frown at her from over Orlando's shoulder. "I'm so sorry, Samantha."

"Apologizing would make you seem at fault to some," Orlando whispers in my ear.

His soft breath makes me shudder, and I grip the lapels on his jacket, tightening my hold on him. Shifting me away, he turns in Samantha's direction, giving her a once-over, probably judging to see whether or not he should worry about any threat she might pose.

"What Jewel means is that what happened to Gabriella was a cruel and unjust shame. Tell Viorica that she has my support in regards to however she decides to proceed," Orlando says.

Samantha bobs her head. Her silver flashing eyes gloss over, making them glow brighter, but she keeps herself composed. "Thank you. I'll let her know." She shifts on her feet, glancing at Zara, who listens intently instead of entering the now open elevator. "I was also hoping that our arrangement is still in order in regards to my match's heir."

"Sammy, don't you think it'd be safer for him to stay with us?" Evora asks.

Samantha shakes her head. "Not while we mourn."

Cyprus reaches around Samantha and touches his sister's shoulder. "I'll be fine, sis. It's not so bad in Ombre Noire."

Orlando sweeps his hand toward Cyprus to motion him onto the elevator. Cyprus hugs his sister and steps on, moving to the back corner. Zara enters next, and Samantha holds her hand in the door like she's afraid it'll shut before Orlando and I can step on it.

"Your generosity will be repaid," Samantha says.

Orlando steps onto the elevator with me in tow. "No need, Ms. Vaduva. Your mother's vote to ensure Jewel's Blood Vow is suitable enough. I do hope we can come to form an alliance."

I wiggle a bit, trying to peer at Samantha. "Are you sure taking Cyprus right now is a good idea, Orlando? We're—"

Orlando leans in close like he's going to try to interrupt me with a kiss, and I pull back and snap my mouth shut. Kissing him nearly caused my undoing, not to mention it got Gabriella killed in the process. Not gonna happen again.

"Going to be fine, Jewel," he says, turning his gaze to my mouth. "Cyprus handles himself well."

Orlando nods to Samantha and hits the button to close the elevator door, trapping us inside with Zara. She stands close to Cyprus, showing him more attention than she should, but Cyprus manages to remain calm. His heartbeat thrums steadily while mine crashes about. I can't tell if it's because this whole situation leaves me tense or because of Orlando's burning gaze still locks on me. Either way, I can't wait to get out of this box.

"I suppose you would like me to grant you access to the Aku Region to retrieve your brothers," Zara says, finally breaking the silence building between us.

"You knew?" I ask, frowning at her.

"Of course I knew, dear Jewel. I've known all day. I couldn't wait to see how Mr. Ortega handled the situation." Her gaze narrows on Orlando, who breaks his stare on me to glance at the woman. "And I must say, I'm rather impressed. With the both of you."

Orlando's lips twitch in a smirk. "Which part impressed you the most?"

"I didn't think you had it in you to test Mitchell the way you had." She turns to me. "And Jewel, accepting a Blood Vow from Mr. Ortega when everyone knows how much his brothers vie for you. Risking a feud within your soon-to-be coven before it's aligned is quite brave and bold. If I didn't know better, I'd say you were better intended as a Vaduva."

"Sorry to disappoint you, Ms. Aku, but there will be no repercussions or feuds involved in Jewel's decision to formally accept my Blood Vow."

She hums softly. "Time will tell. It's unfortunate Jewel's clever plan to attempt a vow with Ms. Ortega fell through. A vow built for loyalty allows for love elsewhere. No wonder you chose Brayla for neither love nor loyalty, Orlando. Too many get caught up in mortal emotions, but donors sometimes have a way of reminding us of...other times."

I try to wrap my mind around everything she says. I had no idea that Blood Vows came with some sort of stipulation.

"Indeed," Orlando says. "Now about my coven brothers."

"I'll grant you access now...as long as you follow through with a taste from your best blood source." She smiles at me, extending her fangs.

"You can't be seriously asking to bite—"

"We'll head to the lab now." Orlando shifts me onto his shoulder, cutting off my argument with pressure to my stomach. I swing my arm out to smack him, making him jump in surprise, totally not expecting me to slap his ass, but it was all I could reach.

"Lovely," Zara says. "Perhaps you'd consider an alliance with the Aku Region as well."

"I guess we'll see."

"Guys!" I yell despite my good senses the second I spot Austin, Kingston, and Diego sitting on the couch in the grand living room of the Fire Crest Estate. Zara's mansion sits nestled high on a mountainside, overlooking the glittering city of Nightshade Park below.

The three of them stand up and let me come to them instead of rushing in my direction. Something dark prods at my heart, and I frown. I was expecting a helluva lot better welcome than three serious faces still lightly roughed up with bruises.

"First one to hug me can bite me on the car ride home," I whisper as I approach.

That gets a much better reaction, and the three of them sandwich me so quickly that I don't even know who got to me first. I laugh and kiss Austin's neck because it's the only thing I can reach.

I wiggle in their hold and stretch to kiss Kingston's chest. "Jeez, you guys must be starving. Did they not offer you anything?"

"Something substandard," Kingston says, tilting his chin down to kiss the top of my head.

Diego nuzzles his nose to my shoulder and kisses me there since I can't shift to reach him, and none of them loosen their hold on me. I reach behind me and rub my hand over the back of his head, ruffling his brown hair.

"You look stunning. I'm so glad you didn't change out of that dress," Diego says, sliding his big hands around my stomach.

"But whose blood spatter? That wasn't from drinking," Austin asks.

Kingston touches my bodice where a few blood drops stain the fabric. "Yeah, you're way messier than that."

I stiffen, my whole body reacting to the question. Opening and closing my mouth, I attempt to whisper Gabriella's name, but I know if I try to say anything, it'll come out too loudly and everyone in the vicinity will hear. It is customary for a coven to announce the death of a member on their terms. Sometimes they never do because it can cause others to test power, at least, according to Orlando.

"It's so nice to see such affection even after the donor you're fond of promised her love to another." Zara's sultry voice hums through the air with her entrance. "I expect marvelous things to come from the union of the Ortega Coven."

"Love?" Austin asks softly.

They break apart from me and search my face.

Zara sucks in air through her teeth. "Oh, have you not told them yet?"

"We just got here," I mutter, turning to glare at her.

Orlando steps between me and Zara. His protectiveness doesn't go unnoticed considering my guys haven't moved. I can't tell if it's the sudden shock of hearing about Orlando's promise of a Blood Vow to me or if it's some sort of vampire custom that stops them from reacting, but either way, I despise how much I can't read them in this moment. No one, not even Kingston, gives anything away.

Orlando touches my shoulder, drawing my attention from my guys to him. "Jewel, please allow my brothers to escort you to the car. I need to handle a couple things, and we shouldn't keep Cyprus waiting long. Now would not be the time to test the Vaduvas." Turning his head, he looks to Kingston. "If you don't mind."

"Of course not," Diego says, stepping closer.

I attempt to take his hand, but he disregards it to place his hand gently on my lower back. I grimace, staring at the side of his face, but he doesn't look at me. Austin takes the lead while Kingston follows, and we stroll in awkward as hell silence through the glass, metal, and marble mansion to the wide, arched tinted colored glass doors.

Cool air engulfs me, chilling the sudden perspiration beading along my hairline. I step closer to Diego and snuggle into his side to slide my icy fingers under the back of his hoodie. It's not until we're twenty feet down the driveway where the car idles that Diego tightens his hand around me to rub up and down my side.

"What the hell is wrong?" I ask, keeping my voice low enough so no lurking vampires on the premises can hear. "You guys are treating me weird."

Diego tips his head toward mine. "Wait until we get to the car, beautiful."

Two figures stand outside our car, one leaning his hands on the doorframe and peering into the open window in the backseat. The taller of the two figures turns their attention in our direction, and I tense at the sight of the guy's silver eyes.

"Get away from our car!" I scream, dashing around Austin too fast for any of my guys to catch. If Diego had a better hold on me, I would've never escaped them, but my deep-seated nature stirred with my fear for Cyprus kicks me into motion, not giving me a chance to think things through.

I don't make it far. Austin snatches the back of my dress, yanking me hard enough to pull my feet right out from under me. He catches me in his arms, stopping me from crashing to the dark asphalt. Kingston and Diego rush forward to the car. The vampire grabs hold of the other person and spins him behind him.

The back door swings open and Cyprus hops out, waving his hands. "I'm fine, Jewel. We're just talking."

Kingston shoves his hand into Cyprus's chest, knocking him back on the seat. "Do you have a death wish? You never open the window in a foreign territory."

Cyprus scowls. "Chill out, man. These guys are cool. I was just talking to Turner about the program."

"Turner? As in Turner Matthias," I ask. "I mean, Turner Rosenburg?"

"You must be the coveted Jewel," the vampire says, giving

me a slow once-over. "How charming it is to meet the donor responsible for nearly ruining Turner's future. You were rather lucky that at least one of these dickheads had the intellect to ask Turner if he actually wanted to have his contract breached. Things could have ended badly otherwise."

I look at Austin, who presses his lips together, giving it away that it was him who asked the question.

"Yet you still beat them up, Mr. Rosenburg?" I ask.

He wags his eyebrows at me. "It was a fair trade. And call me Roswell. Ros for short."

I gape at him. "Fair?"

Kingston steps closer to me and finally meets my gaze. "He's right, babe. You know what would happen if someone tried to do this to you."

They'd tear them apart. They have ripped vampires apart on my behalf.

"It was also fortunate that alliances wear thin. Mother Aku asked that we refrain from doing anything drastic to upset the donor who has her pretty little fingers wrapped around...possibly more than you anticipated. You must taste as incredible as you are beautiful. I can see the appeal. It's hard not to get lost in your ocean eyes." Turning to Turner, he smiles at him. "Don't you agree?"

Turner darts his gaze over me. "I'm not going to comment."

"That's probably a smart decision," Diego says.

Ros grins. "My match did rate high for intelligence. He

comes from a long line of health keepers. That's how we met, you know. It's been great to have him around for the daytime household. Even my one female has taken a liking to him, so the potential of procreat..."

Turner reaches out and knocks Ros in the arm. "Shut the hell up."

My eyes widen. "So *that's* the reason you don't want to go? But I thought..."

Ros flashes his fangs at me in a smile. "Not everything is about sex, love, or loyalty, Jewel."

I blush, my face warming. "I know."

"People also don't always do things for selfless reasons," Austin adds. "Turner chose to enter the Blood Match Program because it was the only way to transfer out of Dark Terrace Ranch."

Kingston glances between the two of them. "The Rosenburg Coven jumped through probably every fucking loophole Donor Life Corp has to offer to assure his match to Ros."

Diego slides his fingers through mine. "The whole thing was probably a huge shock to his family. They were pretty well off in the city."

"So, are you two...?"

"He's my almost perfect match. Ninety-two percent," Ros says, winking at Turner. "That's all you need to know. Now, if you'll excuse us, we need to take our leave. Tonight's made me appreciate the effort I put into acquiring Turner."

Ros motions for Turner to join him. Turner gives me one

last long look, preparing himself to be relocated at a vampire's pace to wherever Ros plans to take him. A dozen emotions cross through me, seeing the two together. A sense of relief, for the fact that Turner didn't join the Blood Match Program out of desperation, washes through me. But the relief battles with the sudden sense of dread coiling around my insides. If we don't bring Turner back or breach his contract, where does that leave us? My own family is at stake.

Before Turner can leave, I surprise him by reaching out and grabbing his hand. Ros releases the scariest noise ever, sending my whole body into panic mode. Diego immediately towers next to me, flashing his fangs at Ros, and Turner gently tugs his hand from mine.

I reach for him again. "Wait, please. I know I'm probably the last person you'd want to help, but I'm begging you. Your grandmother has my family. She took one of our coven members. She won't return them unless we bring you with us."

Turner turns his attention to Ros. "That sounds like something Nan would do."

"There are plenty of ways to take care of their personal problems without dragging you into this. To give that much power to a group of donors honestly makes me question the infatuation Mother Aku has. She'd be interested to—"

Anger and annoyance collide over me, kicking my body into action. I launch myself at Ros, surprising the hell out of everyone. I don't get the chance to touch him because Diego locks his fingers to my hips and drags me back, but Kingston and Austin fly forward and each take one of Ros's arms to assure he doesn't attack me.

"Don't threaten us!" I yell, my voice resonating through the air. "I wanted to do this without hurting anyone." Jerking my attention from Ros, I glare at Turner. "Is that what you want? If we do this any other way, they're dead. Your family is no longer in Haven Springs. They're with Blood Rebels."

Turner pales, his eyes widen at my words. "What?"

I throw my hands out. "What did you expect to happen? You haven't contacted her. She was desperate, thinking you were living some horrible life."

"Maybe I could call her," Turner says, looking toward Ros.

Ros's eyes flash silver. "Absolutely not. If she's as unhinged as they say she is, I'll not allow them to have access to you. The last thing my coven needs is to deal with Blood Rebels." He looks at me. "I'm sorry, Jewel. I must do what's best for Turner. If your coven knew what was best, they'd handle your situation accordingly."

"Please," I say again. I'm not beyond groveling. "Just one call. You don't have to tell her anything. Just show her you're okay, and..." My eyes widen, my mouth breaking into a smile as an idea hits me.

"Uh-oh," Kingston mutters. "I know that look."

I whack him in the shoulder. "Shut up. I have an idea. A good one."

Ros removes his hand from Turner to cross his arms over

his chest. "Go on."

"Can we use your match just for a moment? We can show Liz that he's fine...and that we have him."

Kingston scoops me off my feet and snuggles me against him. "Fuck, that's a brilliant idea. If we can arrange a meeting, we can plan accordingly. Minimize casualties." He tosses me over his shoulder, dangling me upside down and spins to face Ros. "Do this for us, and I can guarantee an alliance between our regions."

Ros remains silent and expressionless for a moment. "I suppose that is satisfactory."

I just hope it works.

SOUL BARING

THE DRIVE HOME WAS UTTERLY silent. After the performance Turner put on for Liz, I was nearly certain she'd agree to drop her demands. But something is up. I think the Blood Rebels got into her head. Or the vampire life. Either way, I don't think I'd agree to doing anything for the old woman now. She was perfectly content doing exactly what Donor Life Corp did to me by ripping me away from my perfect life with my matches only to throw me into a community that thinks I'm better off dead.

"Want me to call my brothers to assist in giving you another full body massage?" Austin asks from next to me.

I roll over to face him and reach up to push strands of his blond hair off his forehead. "That's tempting, but..."

"You have a lot on your mind. I understand." He pulls me close and brushes his lips to my temple. "Though I'd sure love to distract you. I've missed you, Jewel."

I can't resist his soft voice and roll on top of him, straddling his body while pressing my chest to his to meet him for a kiss. It sets off everything good inside me and steals my breath away, sending my heart ramming against Austin's.

"Jewel." The sound of my name on his lips, his breath mingling with mine, ignites my desire in such a way that I rush to undress, stripping my shirt off to throw on the floor. Austin reacts to my fervent passion, flipping me off of him to hook his fingers to the thin fabric of my underwear to tug them off me.

I lay exposed beneath him, my chest rising and falling, my desire heating my skin to warm Austin. He drinks me in, memorizing every inch of me with his intense gaze, lit with fire that smolders me to my very soul.

I reach out, linking my fingers to the soft material of his boxers before I burn up and disappear under the weight of his desire. All I want to do is show him that whatever strange turns our lives take, that no matter what, I love him. What we have together is special. Perfect.

"You're torturing me," I whisper. "My body aches so badly for you."

He smiles. "I just love to enjoy every inch of you. Will you let me?"

I nod my head, shifting and moving beneath him, running my hands across the hard muscles rippling and flexing under my touch.

He brings his mouth to mine, kissing me as feather soft as his fingers explore the curves of my body. Breaking away, he glides his tongue across my jaw and down my throat, stopping every few inches to nip and suck my skin in a way that leaves my whole body humming.

"Get back here!" Kingston's voice sounds through the wall, drawing my attention away from Austin for a second. "You can't just waltz in there. She's probably sleeping."

"Well, we don't have all day." It's Cyprus. "Orlando said—"

"Orlando probably didn't expect you to come charging up here to disturb our girl." The way he says it almost makes it sound like I'm also Orlando's. I might have agreed to a Blood Vow, but none of us discussed any of this. With Cyprus in the car, and having to tell them about Gabriella's death, it just didn't feel like the right time.

Austin grasps my chin and brings his mouth to mine. "Let Kingston handle whatever is going on."

I slide my fingers through Austin's messy hair, pulling him in close for another kiss. The familiar click of his fangs extending pulls a wave of desire from me, and I throw caution to the floor with the rest of his clothes.

Sucking his bottom lip between mine, I nip him just hard enough to have him sinking into me with a moan that vibrates across my mouth. His fangs graze my tongue, and a hint of sweetness floods my mouth as he gently bites his own lip to tease me and get me to kiss him harder.

A loud thud crashes into our door, shaking it on the hinges. "You did not seriously just try to dodge past me," Kingston snaps.

"What are you going to do about it? Bite me?" Cyprus asks.

Kingston growls.

"Fuck," I whisper.

"It's all right, babe," Kingston says through the door. "I have it under control. Let Austin take care of you."

Austin carefully leans over and turns on some music, and I release a small laugh that he immediately steals away to replace with a moan. My whole body tingles under his weight. His slow movements gradually build up until I'm gasping with the pleasure he arouses in me.

"Fucking A!" Kingston yells. "Diego, grab him. I'm going to kill him otherwise. He's getting on my damn nerves."

Kingston's voice sounds over the music, and someone starts banging on our door. Austin releases a small breath that I'm pretty sure is actually a swear word before he slows down and eases away from me. Grabbing the comforter, he wraps it around him and leaves me lying in surprise on the bed. I snatch the sheet and chase after him, grabbing onto him as he yanks the door open.

I slide in front of him and meet Cyprus's wide eyes. Kingston stands frozen with his fist hovering midair and ready to punch the guy.

Kingston drops his hand. "Go back to banging Austin, babe. I got this."

His words ignite my face with heat so intense I'm sure I'll burn up at any second. "OhmyeffingGod, dude. Did you have to say that in front of him?"

Kingston shakes Cyprus by the front of his shirt. "Your needs are nothing to be ashamed of."

"Doesn't mean you have to announce them." I purse my lips, attempting to keep a straight face. "Just fulfill them."

Kingston releases the sexiest noise, giving me a once-over. And then he friggin' turns to Austin and says, "You okay with that invitation?"

My mouth falls agape.

"I mean, Diego can handle this bullshit."

Diego chuckles. "I can join you all after."

I step back and sneak under Austin's arm. "I think Austin's got it covered today. I'll gladly accept some cuddles later though."

Cyprus chooses now to try to swing at Kingston. Huge friggin' mistake. Kingston grabs him and shoves him against the wall, capturing him in his gaze. Cyprus slackens in his hold, unable to break away under Kingston's mind manipulation.

"Go to your room and wait to be called upon. Write an apology letter to Jewel about interrupting her day because you're too damn impatient."

Kingston releases Cyprus, and he blinks a few times, looks at me without a word, and turns on his feet to stride back to his room. He slams the door and clicks on his own music loud enough that I'm sure the vampires lurking on the outskirts of town could hear it.

My eyebrows pinch together. "What the hell was all of this about?"

"The fuckhead squeezed his damn eyes shut the whole way here and used your need for me not to murder anyone against me. The guy is crazy, Jewel," Kingston says. "The vampire population dodged a bullet when Evora beat him to apply to the Blood Match Program."

"Maybe not," Diego says. "You heard Orlando."

I frown at the fact that neither of them answers my question.

"It's a good thing Austin was working on putting our girl in a good mood. She's less stubborn when she's—"

I swat Kingston's arm. "Okay, dude. I get it. Can we not discuss my mood?"

"But it's so fun."

"Especially being the reason behind said good mood," Austin murmurs, hooking his fingers around my waist. "Which I want to assure remains as such. I wasn't kidding about distracting you."

"Considering what you've been through, I have to agree, beautiful," Diego says.

I laugh and shake my head. "You guys were the ones who

were forced to miss your coven vows, got your asses kicked, had to find out about the shit Donor Life Corp pulled with the whole Blood Vow thing, and then you had to endure a way too long, awkward as hell car ride. I'm rather surprised you haven't even asked me about it."

"Quick, Austin. Take her back to bed and ravish the hell out of her before I do," Kingston says, pointing at the room.

The world spins, and I squeal, hitting my back on the bed. Austin buries his face in the crook of my neck, kissing my skin while propping himself up on his elbows.

I stretch up and kiss him. "Why does it feel like you guys might be the ones who actually need distracting? You know, all you have to do is say so."

"What gave it away?" Austin asks, still trailing his lips over my skin.

"Kingston hasn't complained or claimed to be jealous once."

"Because I have no reason to be anymore." Kingston's voice murmurs through the wall. "I don't want you to worry about that."

I raise an eyebrow at Austin, and he shakes his head, smirking. "I wasn't, but why do you think I'd worry?"

Austin relaxes against me and rests his head on my shoulder. "Kingston, why don't you just come in here and talk to our girl? You too, Diego."

I frown. "I'm sorry. I didn't mean—"

He interrupts me with the best kiss ever. "No apology

needed. I have a lot on my mind as well."

"Okay, but since this feels like it's about to be a bare our souls type of moment, I expect you to bare at least half your bodies upon entrance," I say, smirking at Austin.

Coming into the room, Kingston fake glares at me. "You enjoy teasing us way too much." He turns to Austin. "Bro, I'm sorry, but I'll always take our girl's bait. OG body match and shit."

Kingston throws his shirt at me, hitting me in the face, and I laugh so loudly that he loses his pants, cracking me up. I clap my hands and motion him to come over, grinning like a maniac. I can't help it.

"I was kidding, dude," I say, patting the spot next to me.

"You were not."

Diego closes the door behind him, drawing my attention away from Kingston, and I screech out and fall back to the bed, laughing hysterically while covering my face.

"Fuck, Diego," Kingston says. "She said half."

"She said *at least* half, and you know I'm all in to give our girl what she wants."

Kingston slides onto the bed next to me and sweeps my hair from my shoulder. "Drop the sheet and show me your tits, babe. Please, I'm begging you."

I knew my guys were seriously and unashamedly all in love with me as much as I'm crazily, fearlessly, all-consuming in love with them, but this feels like a huge relationship grow-ing moment, even if it's just us learning to be completely comfortable butt-ass naked. It's not like we haven't seen each other. I mean, I'm nearly certain everyone has seen Kingston, but to be able to carelessly play and joke and tease...these feelings are what I crave from my life with them. This is a very us-against-the-world moment, like in the end, when it comes down to it, we're in this life together.

I run my tongue over my teeth, my face burning so hotly but not from embarrassment. I'm amused as all get-out. "I'll show you mine if you show me yours."

Kingston shifts the sheet away and proceeds to poke my leg with his rising desire, surprising the hell out of me. I laugh even harder, my eyes watering as I basically start cackling like a friggin' maniac. I wave my hands in front of my face, unable to control my reaction. And then I start to hiccup, making Diego bellow a laugh.

"I don't think Jewel understands how prepared we are to see to it that she gets what she wants as much as possible," Diego says.

Austin touches my flushing cheek. "I think she knows now."

"You guys," I say, my chest heaving with my out of control heart. "I love you. I hope you can always feel it, no matter what. I can't wait for our Blood Vows. I wish I could shout it to the world. More than anything."

Both Austin and Kingston slide their fingers through mine, and Diego rubs his hands up and down my shins, sprawling my legs across him. None of them says anything, though I can see dozens of thoughts flicker in their eyes as they gaze from me to one another.

"Okay, soul baring time," I say, drawing their attention to me. "What's up? None of you mentioned anything about basically anything since we left Nightshade Park. I know you guys didn't expect the whole Blood Vow thing between Orlando and me to happen since I asked Brayla, but it's really not that big a deal...right? You guys were on board to let him."

More silence.

"It does bother you." I pull away from Austin and Kingston and cover my eyes with my hands and groan.

Austin drapes his arm over my shoulders, pulling me close. "It's not that, Jewel."

"Well, it kind of is for me. It's going to be hard as fuck keeping my hands off you in public," Kingston says, sinking into me. "But you know what? It's whatever. I'll just keep you home. In bed. However you want."

I lean back a bit. "Huh?"

"Don't worry. We can throw in some other activities too."

I turn to Diego. "What does he mean by that?"

Diego side-glances his brothers. "Orlando didn't tell you?"

"Um, Gabriella was murdered after we proved that my acceptance of Orlando's vow was sincere enough to stop the board from denying the request. They were brutal, Diego. They all wanted to just hand me to Mitchell."

Austin releases a growl. "What?"

I bob my head. "I—I wasn't going to let him take me. They'd only postpone your union and not the transfer of my application. Orlando brought up our past, the agreement he made with my family, basically everything he had that didn't require him to fight."

I continue on, finally telling them everything that happened at the meeting. They listen in silence, scooting closer, not even fazed by the fact that we're all still naked under the covers. My heart betrays me as I tell them about the kiss I shared with Orlando, stopping me from saying it meant nothing.

"The truth is, I'm confused," I finally say. "I hope you know that this doesn't change anything for me. I love you all."

"Do you think he knew?" Austin asks.

I bring his hand up and press it into my cheek. "Knew what?"

Kingston stretches his arms in front of him and groans. "Knew that the board would only accept a Blood Vow based on love instead of loyalty or status."

Diego releases a soft breath. "Sending Austin and me away to assist you would have made it convenient. If we were there, Jewel would've had a choice in the matter."

I straighten my shoulders. "Wait, you think he set us up to claim me?"

"Blood Vows based on love require the both of you to be exclusive, Jewel. We had agreed on a formal Blood Vow based on loyalty. Most vampires stick to that type to avoid the trouble of having to cancel an agreement if things don't work out," Austin says. "Forever is a long time."

Ice blossoms in my middle to grow up to freeze my heart. "I had no idea. You guys never told me that there were different kinds of stipulations. I thought it was whatever we promised in exchange to be transformed. I thought love would be involved."

"For us," Austin says. "But I guess you might want to extend the same to him."

"It doesn't matter," Diego says. "We're going to be fine. Hiding our affection will just make moments like this even better."

Kingston sneaks his hand under the covers and trails his fingers over my thigh. "He's right about that."

"But I don't want to hide my love for you. We shouldn't have to. And if Orlando set me up—" I snap my mouth shut and groan.

"You could always devour him, babe. I can't always be the one willing to sacrifice myself first for your needs." His light-hearted voice almost makes me smile. He turns to Austin. "Look at our girl. She fucking loves the sound of that."

I bump my shoulder into Kingston's. "Dude. I'm just hella friggin' annoyed."

"Mmm. Keep talking back-world to me."

"You're handling this well, you know. All of you." I reach out and touch Diego's knee through the blanket. "Is it because you're all in a vulnerable position? I expected some swearing. Threats to destroy the universe. A confrontation with Orlando."

Kingston thrusts the sheet off all of us, exposing us to each other. "The last thing I feel is vulnerable."

I give him a long look, trailing my eyes from his you-know-you-want-to smile down the rest of him. "Obviously." I give Diego and Austin the same attention. Austin leans back, totally unfazed. Diego gives me his own intense look, devouring me with his eyes. I shiver and squirm, trying not to dive back under the blankets before his smolder has me throwing myself at him.

"Nude bonding experience aside, which by the way, isn't a big deal if you're trained in selective vision, I'm handling it well because a formal agreement doesn't mean shit to me when you've already vowed your love and forever to me," Kingston says.

"He might also be acting calm for your benefit," Austin says. "You seem to react toward each other's passion, and I don't know about Kingston and Diego, but the last thing I want today is to see you worked up over something that only causes us a slight inconvenience in public. You're still our girl."

"We love you, beautiful, and like we've told you since the first day here, we know you love us."

"Yeah, babe. If you're going to be worked up over something, it'll be me...possibly them." Kingston tilts his head toward his brothers. "In the best way possible."

I full-on giggle and pat his chest. "How about we start with a blanket fort, some breakfast in bed, and then a hot shower?"

"Possibly a full body massage?" Austin says, kissing my shoulder.

"That sounds like the perfect activity to make this into the best day with you before whatever shit show is to come. What was the whole Cyprus thing about anyway?" I ask flouncing back on the fluffy pillows between Kingston and Austin.

Diego slides his hands up my legs to rest on top of me in a hug that makes my skin buzz. "Nothing to worry about now, beautiful. It can wait. I just want to give you whatever you want."

I smirk and kiss him. "Is that so?"

Diego doesn't get a chance to respond.

Someone screams.

LOVE AND LOYALTY

"I SHOULD TEAR YOUR THROAT out for coming back here." Orlando's deep, threatening voice hums through the air.

"That would be a huge mistake." Hayden's familiar voice sets off my heart in an excruciating way.

"How so?"

Hayden releases a strangled noise and gasps. "Get your brothers."

"We'll meet you in your office," Kingston says loud enough for Orlando to be able to hear from where he stands somewhere out in the hall.

I rush to find my clothes. Austin slips my shirt over my head, and Diego holds out a pair of cotton shorts for me to step into. Kingston wraps my robe around me before quickly dressing himself. I expect him to grab me to pick me off my feet, but Austin scoops me up, cradling me against him.

The world blurs as Austin darts through the estate behind his brothers, running us to Orlando's study in his private wing. Diego and Kingston bolt ahead of us and stop in the doorway. I spot Orlando holding Hayden by his shoulders, his fangs extended, his handsome face snarling.

"You asshole!" The words fly from my mouth before I have a chance to think about it. "You better have a damn good reason for returning."

Orlando shoves Hayden, and he stumbles back and falls onto the coffee table. Instead of scrambling to his feet, Hayden sits upright and holds his palms up to us in surrender. His gaze darts from Orlando to my guys, and then he turns his attention to me.

"I've come to warn you that you're being set up. The Blood Rebels have no intention of returning your family or Brayla," Hayden says.

I blink a few times, processing his words.

"Do you think I'm an idiot, Mr. Andrei?" Orlando asks.

Hayden clenches his jaw. "No, but—"

Orlando rushes Hayden again and grabs him by the front of the shirt to slam him onto the floor. "Your warning comes with no use to me. I had never expected the rebels to hold up their end of the bargain considering Liz is not one of them yet a mere pawn to play with."

I wiggle in Austin's arms until he sets me on my feet. "Wait, if you've known that then what exactly were you planning to do?"

Orlando turns his gaze to me. "Our plan is no longer a concern."

I frown. "You were going to just attack, weren't you? Show them we can't be messed with? God, that sounds like something Mitchell would do."

All three of my guys growl as Orlando snatches me away and sets me down in a corner to cage me in with his body. I press my hands into his chest and push him back, but he holds strong. And then he has the nerve to cup my face.

His eyes flash silver. "I thought you knew me better than to jump to conclusions and compare me to him."

"And I thought that you knew me better than to keep things from me." My words lace with anger as I think about not only the Blood Rebels but also the type of Blood Vow I unknowingly got myself into with him.

Austin, Kingston, and Diego come up behind Orlando. Diego risks putting his hands on Orlando's shoulders and tugs him back a few feet. I expect all hell to break loose, but Orlando releases a breath and remains in control.

"I'm sorry, Jewel. I didn't mean to overreact. It was never my intent to keep anything from you but rather choose an appropriate time to get into things." Orlando extends his hand to me, and I look to my guys to help me decide what to do. None of them react, leaving the decision up to me.

I relent and take Orlando's hand, letting him guide me to the loveseat. Hayden stands and moves to lean against the wall. I can't stop myself from flicking my gaze to him in an attempt to assess the situation.

"Why are you even here?" I ask, unable to keep the question to myself despite Orlando looking like he has something more to say to me.

Hayden presses his lips together and looks to Orlando without a word.

"Go on and answer her," Orlando says, taking a seat beside me.

Austin nestles down on my other side and slides his fingers through mine, squeezing them gently to stop my nails from biting my palms from my tight fists.

"Because despite what Noah thinks, maintaining an alliance to a coven is important. He thinks eliminating those who seek to control—"

"Protect," I say, interrupting him.

"*Protect* you," he repeats, spitting the words out. He shifts his jaw and continues. "He thinks killing your matches will benefit our goals. I, on the other hand, don't agree."

Kingston crosses his arms, sitting on the coffee table in front of me. "Interesting. Sounds like a power struggle."

Hayden shrugs his shoulders. "Noah can't get over his personal vendettas to see reason."

"So why come here? Why help us?" I ask, leaning forward to get a better look at him.

"He's not helping us, beautiful," Diego says from behind me. He leans over and kneads his fingers into my tense shoulders.

I frown.

"I'm helping my people," Hayden says. "We still haven't recovered from your ambush or the re-evaluation of Haven Springs."

I open my mouth to snap at him that he was the one who ambushed us after kidnapping my cousins from Haven Springs. Kingston nudges me with his foot and shakes his head when I look at him. As much as it burns me to keep the thought to myself, I relent to him. Calling Hayden out is pointless. It won't change anything.

"If you're aware of what Noah plans to attempt, you can properly prepare. I'll give you Brayla's location," Hayden adds. "In return, I expect you to leave my people alone and let me handle them. The novelty of Noah's sudden resurrection will wear off soon enough."

"I have to give Mr. Jordan credit. He is a lot like his father. Strategic. Cunning. The perfect leader. You will struggle to regain your following, Mr. Andrei."

"I don't fucking care about power. I care about Mona and keeping her safe. What Noah intends to do will get us all slaughtered or worse."

The sudden softness in his voice extinguishes the rising anger inside me at the mention of my dad. "Oh," is all I can manage to say.

"Damn it." Kingston takes my hand, drawing my attention away from Hayden. "Babe, we can't be certain that he isn't full of shit. He could be using Ramona to manipulate the situation since you still somehow infuriatingly hold her dear to you."

Austin leans closer to me to rest his chin on my shoulder. "Kingston's right, Jewel. People like him will do anything for their cause. Noah's setting a trap, but Hayden could be doing the same thing."

"Especially if there is a sudden power struggle," Diego adds, keeping his voice low so that Hayden can't hear him.

Orlando squeezes my hand. "I've worked with Mr. Andrei for quite a while, and I do believe he's being sincere."

I raise my eyebrows. "You do?"

"Are you willing to risk a fight on that possibility?" Kingston asks.

"Yes," I say at the same time as Orlando.

Kingston scrubs his face with his hands. "Fuck."

"I don't think we should risk it," Austin says.

"I have to agree with Austin." Diego kneels and hugs me from behind. "I know you think you'd be helping Ramona, but that might not be the case. I think we should stick to our original plan and bait them."

"Bait them with what?" I ask.

"Cyprus," Kingston says.

I swing my head to look at Orlando. "That's what he was shouting about this morning? What did you plan to do? You know you can't just use Evora's brother because he's staying here. He's under my protection."

"He offered his assistance. I told him if you agreed, then we'd work something out. It wasn't a bad idea. He'd have begged the rebels to take him back with them, where we could track their location," Orlando says.

"They would kill him if they found out he was working for us." I wave my hand up and down at myself. "Hello, I'm living proof with my traitor against humanity self and all."

"He thought it was worth it," Kingston says.

"Worth what?"

Orlando heaves a sigh. "None of that matters now. You obviously won't agree. Stubborn as always."

I whack him on the knee, making him chuckle. "You better watch it."

"I'd listen to Jewel. She was already considering devouring you," Kingston says.

Hayden releases a strange noise from his throat, drawing all of our attention to him. He leans his back on the wall, shoving his hands into his pockets. His heartbeat picks up speed, his fear cues going wild under the scrutiny of my powerful vampires.

"So does this mean you'll accept my offer to lead you to Brayla or what?" Hayden manages to say.

Everyone looks at me. "Um, well we're not using Cyprus."

Orlando stands up and crosses the room to Hayden.

"We'll consider under one condition, Mr. Andrei."

Hayden curls his lips, glowering. "And what's that?"

"You must first allow me access to your mind."

Hayden scowls. "Fine, but hurry up."

Orlando locks Hayden in his gaze faster than I have time even to blink, and I push from the couch and stroll a few feet in their direction. Orlando doesn't react to my closeness, and I study the silver flashing in his eyes.

"Why don't we go get some breakfast?" Austin asks.

I shake my head. "No. I want to stay."

"It's fine," Orlando says, still holding Hayden in his gaze. "You don't mind if Jewel stays, right Mr. Andrei?"

"I want her to stay," Hayden says, his voice sounding strange, automatic.

"Good. Now relax. Slow your heartbeat. There is no reason to be afraid. I won't hurt you."

The familiarity of seeing Hayden in this state strikes a hot nerve inside me, and I shift on my feet, rubbing my now sweaty palms on my robe. Hayden's heart rate slows, but mine picks up even more, pounding so hard I can feel it in my head.

Orlando leans closer to Hayden, blocking my view of his face. I can't decide if it's to protect me or to protect him, since he knows my feelings about mind manipulation. "Now, Mr. Andrei, tell me. Why are you really here?"

Hayden's hands hang lifelessly at his sides. "To tell you about Noah's plan to strike."

"And what is your reason for that?"

"I don't want my people getting hurt," Hayden says.

Orlando pauses for a moment, considering his next words. "You trust us enough not to turn against you?"

"No."

"Then why bother?"

"I trust Jewel." Hayden's admission surprises the hell out of me, considering he has called me a traitor to humanity time and time again.

"Do you really think she cares about you or the rebels enough to save you?" Orlando's voice deepens. I don't like the direction his mind manipulation heads. I'm not sure I want to know the answer.

"Not me."

Orlando tilts his head. "Elaborate."

"I don't think Jewel cares about me, but she cares about humanity. I was wrong about her."

Holy friggin' shit balls. I never thought I'd ever hear him say such a thing. Of course, he probably wouldn't have if it weren't for Orlando manipulating his mind.

"Is that why you were willing to help her in Haven Springs or did you just want to keep her alive to benefit your situation with Ramona?"

"Neither."

"Make him explain," I say, bouncing on my feet.

Orlando straightens his shoulders. "Explain your reason."

"I think Jewel has the potential to make changes I, as a human, cannot. Noah wants to use her against vampires, to take down our enemies, but I know she will eventually die like the other dhampirs we've located."

"Other dhampirs? You know how to find them?" I ask.

Hayden doesn't respond to me. Instead, he says, "Jewel's situation with you is an anomaly. I've never seen someone have such influence on vampires. Noah thinks all vampires are the enemy, but I think some are worse than others."

"Thank you, Mr. Andrei. That's all I needed to hear."

Hayden drops to his knees, his eyes uncontrollably watering. I can't help the pity that grips at my heart, seeing him so vulnerable while trying to pull himself together. I know that Orlando had a good reason to get into Hayden's head to prove that he wasn't setting us up, but the invasiveness of mind manipulation, especially seeing Orlando do it, stirs all sorts of fear, anger, and foreboding inside me though he promised to never get into my mind without my consent again.

Austin spins me around and engulfs me in a hug, rubbing his hands up and down my back. "I wish you would've let me take you back to our room. That couldn't have been easy to witness after everything."

"I had to watch to make sure." I press my nose into the front of his shirt, inhaling a deep breath of his citrusy scent.

"We could've handled that, babe," Kingston says, sandwiching me between him and Austin.

Orlando extends his hand to Hayden and surprisingly helps him to his feet. "Jewel is still learning to trust me, so I preferred she watched regardless." Orlando comes up behind

Austin to get a better look at me. "And as you can see, Hayden's fine."

"Are you sure he wasn't acting?" A part of me can't help questioning, especially because I've acted my way through mind manipulation. I want so desperately to believe that Hayden really isn't out to get us—at least right now—but Orlando isn't the one I struggle to trust. The only ones I trust are Kingston, Diego, and Austin.

"Positive. Your skills have improved my approach." Orlando runs his finger over my forehead to pull the strands of dark hair veiling my face out of the way.

I slide out from between Austin and Kingston but don't make it far before Diego hooks his arm around me. "Not sure you're helping your case."

"You have to admit, his technique was rather ingenious," Kingston says.

Diego nods his approval. "I never thought to test someone by controlling their heartbeat."

Kingston smirks. "I'd have opted to control his bladder."

I grimace. "Ew, dude. That's just wrong."

"A little humiliation wouldn't kill the guy. The asshole shot me, babe. Excuse me if my moral compass breaks in regards to him. Making him piss himself would be letting him off easy." Kingston releases a play growl at me and snaps his teeth, jerking out his hand in an attempt to grab me from Diego.

Diego spins me away. "If I didn't know you were transformed before me, I'd seriously question your age, bro."

Kingston tries to grab me again. "What can I say? Our girl keeps me youthful."

Austin holds his arms out, initiating a game of keep away with me. "Or some people never grow up."

"Diego, don't you dare," I say, clutching the front of his shirt.

I screech as the world blurs around me. Heaving a breath, I land in Austin's arms and brace myself to be thrown again as Kingston charges us. Austin tosses me back toward Diego, but Orlando intercepts and catches me, making all three of them pause. But only for a second. Kingston rushes toward me, and I push away from Orlando hard enough to surprise him. My ass hits the floor, and I scramble back and wave my hands up.

"I'm not a plaything, and you all can't just try to distract me with your games. Shouldn't we be preparing? Someone has to take me to talk to Cyprus to let him know," I say, knowing my guys well enough to know what they're doing.

Kingston stands in front of me and fake pouts, sticking out his incredibly kissable bottom lip. "Come on, babe. You know you love being my sole form of entertainment. We're not even meeting Liz until midnight. The sun hasn't set."

I glare at him. "Seriously, dude?"

"Super serious. But if you prefer I make you scream some other way, I can make it happen," he teases. "Just the way you like."

Grabbing the front of his shirt, I pull him closer and align our mouths but don't meet him for a kiss. "Actually..."

He leans in closer. "Yeah?"

I snap my teeth at him. "I'm a bit hungry. We can talk about this over breakfast."

He sticks his tongue out at me. "Tease."

"You like it."

"Do not."

Austin slides his arm around my stomach and lifts me off my feet. "It's a good thing I love it. Now, let's eat before we test your control too much."

I lean in and nip his earlobe. "Ah, come on, Austin. I want nothing more than to devour him."

"Making me jealous, beautiful," Diego says, joking with me.

"Be careful. I might be in the mood to devour the lot of you."

Austin hums in his throat. "Well, if you're offering..."

My cheeks burn.

"She can start with me first," Orlando says, drawing my attention to him.

The thrum of my heartbeat sounds through the air, and I can't stop my body from warming to the thought even more.

"Damn," Kingston mutters. "I can't decide if her reaction is a good or bad thing."

I clear my throat and kick my leg out to poke him in the stomach with my foot from Austin's arms. "Definitely good."

He gives me a playful once-over. "How so?"

"Because that would assure you survive me."

He flashes his fangs. "And if not, at least I'll die happy."

"I'd prefer you to live happy too."

"Good," he says. "That's exactly what I want for all of us."

MIND BLOCK

"AFTER EVERYTHING I'VE DONE TO help you, you're going to deny me this?" Cyprus's dark gaze narrows on me from his bed.

"Evora would be upset if you got hurt or killed. Since we don't need you to beg the rebels take you with them to find out Brayla's location, we might as well not put you in unnecessary danger." I cross my arms and lean on the doorframe.

"Jewel's right. Great job on coming up with that plan though. I'll make sure someone sends you some cookies." Kingston peeks his head into the room from over my shoulder, meeting Cyprus's glower with a smirk. "Or not. Either way, alliances are fragile, and there is no damn way we're going to test the Widows at the moment."

Cyprus pushes up from his bed. "Fucking asshole. The deal was already made."

My mouth drops open in surprise. "What the hell? What is your problem? Most people would prefer not to test their survival abilities."

Kingston pulls me back before Cyprus can close the distance. Kingston fills the doorway, releasing a low growl from deep in his throat. His threat sends even my arm hairs prickling as he triggers my fear cues. Cyprus halts in place but doesn't stop glaring.

"Liz was right. You guys are a bunch of liars."

"Excuse me?" I ask, hooking my fingers to Kingston's shoulders to get a better look at Cyprus. "Why are you acting like this?"

"Because Orlando said if I helped you he'd—" Cyprus hollers and covers his eyes, bending forward.

I startle and push against Kingston, but he blocks me from entering the room. "Move, dude. Something's wrong."

"Nothing's wrong."

"He's in pain."

"He's getting a little warning about telling you things Orlando doesn't want you to know," Kingston says. Spinning around, he nudges me back until I stand strong and hold my ground.

"Kingston—"

He turns to Cyprus and commands him to sit and calm down. Shutting the door, he turns to face me. "I don't know what their deal involved. He knew I'd tell you if you asked me, so he just kept it to himself. Sorry, babe." Kingston puckers his bottom lip and leans into me to rub his pouty mouth to mine.

I sigh and kiss him, sliding my arms around his neck. "He's so infuriating."

"I know."

"It's making me seriously consider your suggestion," I say against his lips.

He chuckles. "You have to wait until we're officially part of the Ortega Coven and then probably a few more years. After that, we can make it look like an accident. But be prepared. If something happens to Orlando, Brayla gets seniority over us."

I tilt my head. "Seriously?"

"Unless we fail to get her back..."

I groan, and Kingston muffles the noise with his mouth, pressing his body into mine. My back hits the wall, my groan shifting into a breathless noise that makes him slide his hands to my ass to lift me up to feel his growing hardness between my legs.

"You know, if you want to stay here..." Kingston lets his suggestion trail off so I can use my imagination to finish his thought.

I lean back, touching my head to the wall. "O-o-o-oh, you guys are bad."

Kingston smiles and attempts to kiss me again, but I raise

my hand up and cover his mouth.

"Nu-uh. Put me down. I will not be seduced."

Kingston playfully growls at me and relents, setting me on my feet. I wag my finger at him, shaking my head, and all he does is chuckle. Turning away, I stride down the hallway and toward the elevator. The damn thing doesn't come when I call for it, so I head toward the stairs and take two of them at a time.

"We've been caught," Kingston says, calling out without running ahead of me.

I find Austin, Diego, and Orlando strapping on various weapons in Orlando's study. The three of them glance up at me upon my entrance but don't stop what they're doing.

"You're losing your touch, Kingston," Diego says, chucking a knife in his direction. Kingston ducks, and it hits the wall behind him. "I knew it should've been Austin. Hundred percent body match and all."

Kingston yanks the knife free and aims it at Diego. I grab Kingston's arm before he can retaliate, and he freezes and releases a growl instead. Shifting between them, I turn my back on Kingston and place my hands on my hips.

"You guys are in so much trouble," I say, pursing my lips.

Kingston hums.

I swivel and flick his shoulder. "Not the good kind."

Closing the space, he presses against me and points over my shoulder. "Hey, I was just a tool to Orlando's plan. Obeying orders. You can't fault me for that, babe. Punish them, not me...unless it can be reciprocated."

Austin slides a knife into a hidden sheath under his jacket and strolls to me. "We're just looking out for you."

"If you don't want me to go, you should just say so. Do you know how annoyed I'd be had Kingston succeeded to seduce me and I found out you left?"

"Annoyed? Highly doubt it, but okay," Kingston grumbles.

"We don't want you to go," Diego says, squaring his shoulders.

"Uh-oh. I don't even have to see her face to know she's flaring her nostrils. That's not what she wanted to hear, bro. Now you might've just unleashed Brat Babe."

I jerk my arm back to elbow Kingston, but he's too quick to move. "Of course I didn't want to hear it. I want to go."

Kingston locks me within his arms. "So we can hand deliver you to a bunch of rebels? Nope."

"Jewel, I know you are capable of handling yourself, but with you there, our attention would always be on you. It's safer for all of us if you sit this one out." Orlando closes the space to us. His reasoning digs under my skin as his soft voice pleads with me to understand. "Will you please consider staying? If you'd prefer someone else to keep you company, you can tell us." He looks at Kingston. "It won't hurt anyone's feelings."

The hell it won't. Kingston might not react for me to see, but he'd totally be hurt. He's currently all in for a night alone with me, where his sole purpose is to be my personal form of entertainment. Which I love the idea of. But damn it. I don't want to stay here. My chest tightens just thinking about it.

Kingston faces me, cupping my cheeks while staring at me with his midnight eyes. "That's not it. Our girl loves the idea of a night of utter bliss with me. Something else is bothering her." He narrows his eyes, searching my face like if he peers at me long enough, he'll read what's going through my mind. "Spill it, babe."

I twist my lips to the side. "I'd prefer not to."

"It's not about being there for her family either," Diego says from over Kingston's shoulder. Kingston gives him some room to get a better look.

My brows pucker. "Do you guys have mind reading abilities you haven't told me about? Because if that's the case..."

Kingston smirks at me and pokes my bottom lip with his finger to stop my pout. "I wish I could fucking read your mind. It would make shit easier. I'm just guessing."

"He would know as your personality match," Austin says. "So would Diego. And as your body match, I can tell you're not going to let us know until one of us guesses it. You're worried about how we'll react."

I raise my eyebrows. "You guys are kind of freaking me out."

"Then maybe you should work more on controlling your emotions," Kingston says.

Diego brushes my hair off my shoulder. "I don't know about you, but I like that I can read our girl."

I sigh. "You guys…"

Orlando joins our circle between Kingston and Austin, closing me in completely. They don't say anything as he takes a moment to drink me in, searching my face, though I don't look up to meet his gaze. "I think Jewel has reservations about our capabilities."

All three of my guys turn to him with various expressions, but Kingston's raised eyebrow and tilted mouth that scream *what the eff?* makes me break into a smile. "Yeah-fucking-right," he says. "Our girl knows that we can handle our shit."

They all look at me for confirmation.

I shrug. "It's not that I doubt that you guys can handle it, but I'm worried. I don't want to sit around here and just wait to see if everything goes to plan. That was excruciating at the Blood Match Center…and look how that turned out."

I can't help looking up at Orlando.

"You'll be with Kingston," Austin says. "And you don't have to worry about someone coming here or panic about the board. Our security is handled."

"Yeah, but one of you has to go into a friggin' rebel lair or whatever alone. You can't do the swap without someone pretending to be Turner, and since Cyprus is out—"

"Go get him," Orlando tells Kingston.

I snatch the back of Kingston's shirt so fast that he falls into me. Austin jerks me out of the way, and Kingston hits the ground and just lays there with his mouth agape, his big dark eyes focused on me.

"No. He's...pissed off, and I don't trust him now," I say. "Whatever the hell you promised him in exchange for helping us has him flipping his shit. Plus, that would leave whoever does the swap alone."

Orlando runs his fingers through his blond hair and glances to Diego. "You were right. Perhaps I shouldn't have humored such a request."

"What are you talking about?" I ask. "What was in it for him?"

Orlando shakes his head. "Nothing important. He asked to join our coven, and I might have suggested that we'd consider expanding our coven once we were established...if you were okay with the idea."

"Fuck, Orlando," Kingston says, punching him in the shoulder. "That guy is obsessed with transforming into a vampire. You know we're going to have to break whatever agreement we have with the Vaduvas now. He can't stay here."

"I'm aware of that, brother," Orlando says. "I've already made arrangements to send him to Midnight Valley tomorrow night. With the shift of the Vaduva alliance from the Divine Region to ours, Viorica will no longer be obligated to bow to Mitchell's requests."

I hug myself at the mention of Mitchell. "So, this is all really happening?"

Neither Orlando nor my guys give anything away. I don't know much about vampire politics, but I do know that Mitchell and the Divine Region, even without my guys, is still powerful. He'll try to stop any threats that arise by any means necessary. And the Ortega Region isn't even established yet.

"Shit. I'm definitely not staying here now. Plus, if I go, you guys can buddy up. I can just wait in the car," I say, realizing they're not going to answer me.

The four of them turn to each other in consideration.

"Jewel, an immediate threat is unlikely," Austin says. "Our region isn't worth going after at the moment. If anything, Mitchell will continue to test the Vaduvas."

"Unlikely isn't certain. You guys mean everything to me." I give each of my guys a look and then stop on Orlando. "And while I don't know what's up with us, and you piss me off more often than not, my guys respect you and trust that you will do right by us. If they can imagine forever in the Ortega Coven, then I want to assure it."

Orlando's lips twitch, and I can see him struggling not to smile. "You make a valid point."

"I do?"

Diego chuckles and whacks Orlando on the back. "It's hard to say no to her, isn't it?"

Kingston flashes his fangs. "Not for me. So no, babe. We're staying here, and I'm going to ravish you all night and assure the only thing you think about is—"

I spin toward him and slide my arms around his neck, stopping him from finishing his thought. "My shot nerves are making me feel bitey."

Kingston growls at me. "Fuck it, fine."

Diego hugs me from behind, pressing me into Kingston. "I'll stay for that."

"Diego...later. I just want to get this over with and get our family back. You know, I've been known to bite and rip hearts out when I feel threatened," I say with a new lightness in my voice, trying to hide how nervous I am.

Diego stretches to kiss my cheek. "You forgot eat them." God, he still looks proud as eff over the whole situation in town.

I roll my eyes. "I'll pass on the humans, thanks. I just want to grab my cousins and Brayla and get the hell out of there."

"You do realize that the threat still won't be over," Orlando says. "Once they realize what's happening, the rebels will surely come back full force."

I bob my head. "And we'll deal with them accordingly. Humanely."

Orlando breaks away to grab a few more weapons. Turning his back to me, he says, "We'll do our best. If it comes down to them or us, you know where my loyalty lies."

I cross the room and touch his shoulder so that he swivels to meet my gaze straight on. "And you know mine. I will not let them ruin our forever."

His eyes flash silver. "Good."

Commotion sounds out from the grand entrance to the estate, drawing our attention away from each other. Orlando disappears from in front of me, and Kingston hooks his arms around my waist to stop me from chasing after him to see what the hell is going on.

"You lied to me, you son of a bitch!" Cyprus's voice echoes out. I guess I don't have to see with my eyes to know what's going on.

"You're mistaken. I said we'd consider the possibility of expanding our coven," Orlando says.

"I heard your conversation. You can't send me back to Midnight Valley. I'd have no chance there. Viorica doesn't offer vows to males."

I grimace and glance at my guys. "You guys didn't hear him eavesdropping?"

"I thought it was a staff member," Diego says.

Austin nods. "Me too."

"Perhaps you should take it up with Ms. Vaduva." Orlando's voice draws my attention away.

Something crashes, making me tense. "That's bullshit! I bet if you let me talk to Jewel—"

"She already voiced her opinion about you. So no."

Glass shatters, and Kingston pushes forward with me still against his chest, forcing me to shuffle. "I mind manipulated him to stay in his room. Something is up."

"Vampire blood?" Austin asks.

Orlando thrusts Cyprus to the floor and kneels over him, restraining him in place. I try not to react as Diego joins him to help keep Cyprus's eyes open. He struggles under the two of them, fighting like a true Dark Terrace Ranch resident about to face his final donation.

"Did you drink vampire blood?" Orlando asks.

Cyprus relaxes and stops fighting. "No."

"Test him," I say, bringing my arms up to hug Kingston's against my chest.

Orlando stiffens without looking at me, and I tug Kingston forward to stand over Orlando and Diego. Austin hovers nearby, looking ready to launch himself between me and Orlando to block my view of what unfolds before me.

"Slow your heart," Orlando commands.

I close my eyes and focus on pinpointing Cyprus's heartbeat as it slows.

"I don't get it," Kingston says, resting his chin on my shoulder. "I never fail."

Patting his hand, I say, "Maybe you were just too worked—"

Cyprus jerks beneath Orlando, breaking his stare to fight. He grabs a dagger right from a sheath on Orlando's chest and swings his arm to slash it across Orlando's throat. Orlando jerks back, but he's not fast enough, caught off guard. Cyprus's heart slowed. There's no friggin' way he could've calmed it so quickly. Blood spills across the floor, freezing me in place.

"You bastard! You can't do this to me. We had a deal. Jewel will agree. I helped her in Haven Springs. She owes me!" Cyprus's voice strikes me in the chest.

"Get her back," Orlando says, drawing my attention to

him. Blood coats his neck, soaking into the collar of his dark shirt.

I cover my mouth with my hand. "Oh, shit."

Orlando disappears with Cyprus, and I startle at the crash of the display case. Orlando traps Cyprus in the corner, preventing him from coming closer. Austin rushes to Orlando's side and offers him a towel to staunch the bleeding of his wound.

"Jewel!" Cyprus yells. "Jewel, let me talk to you."

Kingston tries to grab my hand to yank me back, but I break free from him. My feet slide across Orlando's slippery blood, and I eat shit and land on my ass. My hands splash the blood, and I sit utterly still, my chest heaving.

"I don't understand. How did this ha-happen?" I ask, bringing my hands up to stare at the blood.

"It seems we underestimated Cyprus," Orlando says. "But don't worry. It's just a flesh wound."

I furrow my brows. "That's not what I'm talking about."

"Jewel," Cyprus says. "Please. Just talk to me. We're on the same side. I want to help you. I'll do whatever you want for the chance to be like them. I know you understand. You don't want to be a donor forever."

His words swirl through my mind. From the first day I met him, I knew that he wanted to transform into a vampire. And after growing up in Dark Terrace Ranch, I can't blame him. But he acts like I can make that decision.

"It doesn't even have to be one of them to transform me.

When you go through your Blood Vow, you can do it. They won't stop you," he continues. "You owe me. I turned against humans for you."

"Not happening," Kingston says, offering his hand to help me to my feet. "Jewel owes you nothing. You did nothing for her."

Cyprus bangs his fists on the case, ramming it hard enough to shake it. "Fuck you! I'm talking to Jewel."

I swivel to look at Orlando, who presses his fingers into his neck. "I can't change you, Cyprus. Ever."

"You can," Cyprus says. "Please. You have to agree. Orlando will rip my head off otherwise. He's already threatened to drink every last drop of me."

He's lying. I don't even have to look at Orlando to know it. And it pisses me off that he would try to manipulate me like this. I might have strange, mixed feelings about Orlando, but I know that he wouldn't jeopardize the slow progress he's made to get me to trust him again.

"I'm sorry if he scared you," I say, keeping my voice even. "We're going to arrange for Samantha to retrieve you tomorrow night."

Cyprus yells and shoves against the display case, tipping it to the floor. He scrambles over it in an attempt to close the space to me, but both Austin and Diego block his way. He tries to dodge around them and risks his limbs to fight, but my matches easily evade his punches. He grabs a piece of broken glass off the floor and swipes it over and over until Kingston grabs him from behind and holds his arms at his sides.

"What the hell is wrong with him?" I ask, peeking over Austin's shoulder. "Is it possible to break through mind manipulation?"

"Offer me a spot in your coven or you'll regret it." Cyprus bucks in Kingston's arms, knocking him in the chin with his head. Kingston could easily hurt him, but I know he's controlling his nature for my sake.

Kingston drops him to the floor, ignoring him like Cyprus ignores my words. "I don't know, babe. It's never happened with me."

"Maybe his eyesight is messed up," Diego says, stepping back as Cyprus crawls on his hands and knees in our direction.

Orlando closes the space to me. "Perhaps something happened in Dark Terrace Ranch. He was in the Vaduva's care. It is possible that a block was put in place powerful enough to override another vampire's manipulation if done carefully." His jaw twitches.

My eyes widen. "Like you did with me."

"Regretfully, yes."

I tighten my jaw to stop from reacting. "He was looking extra close to Gabriella."

"Don't say her name!" Cyprus shouts, sliding across the blood.

Kingston groans deep in his throat. "Ah shit. Babe, you're on to something. It wouldn't be the first time one of the Widows tried to get one of their playthings to be turned. It could be why he fights so fiercely for the opportunity. I don't know. I'll have to contact Viorica."

"There is one way to find out," Orlando says, flicking his gaze to mine. "It'll hurt. It might also cause permanent damage."

I wring my hands together. I know I can't just object. Cyprus is out of his friggin' mind. "Please, try to be careful. This wasn't his fault."

"I'll do my best, Jewel."

Cyprus scrambles away as Orlando stalks him, setting off Cyprus's fear instincts. Diego materializes behind Cyprus to block his path. Cyprus drops to the ground and presses his face into the floor, covering his head.

"Fuck, pick him up," Kingston says. "He's—"

Diego lifts Cyprus to his feet, his mouth covered in Orlando's blood from the floor. "Shit, now he really consumed blood."

Orlando stands in front of Cyprus. "We might have time still. Someone pry his eyes open."

I grimace. "Is that necessary? You can just try in a couple of hours."

"Jewel's right. We don't have time to deal with this." Austin looks at his brothers.

"I don't think it's a good idea to leave him here," Orlando says. "Not with only the human staff around. We can't afford to trust anyone but ourselves."

Kingston mutters something I can't understand under his

breath. "Fucking A. Looks like you get to help us out after all, Cyprus."

I shake my head. "Eff that."

Kingston flashes his fangs at Cyprus, though he keeps his eyes squeezed shut. "Or not. Good thing there's plenty of room in the trunk."

DECOY

HAYDEN LEANS AGAINST AN OLD, rusty car that I can't believe still works. The second we park, Kingston and Diego disappear from the car and into the night to assess our surroundings. Austin sits next to me on the middle seat with a black bag over his head. We were not going to risk being spotted without Turner, so Austin's our decoy.

Orlando swivels in the seat. "Jewel, stay here."

Bobbing my head, I say, "Yup. I don't need the reminder."

I clutch the handle of a dagger, already prepared to use it if I have to. Kingston and Diego return to the car, and Orlando exits, slamming the door behind him. The headlights set the three of them aglow. I shift in my seat and lean forward like if I can get close enough to the windshield, I'd be able to hear the conversation, but everyone keeps their voices exceptionally low.

"Relax and breathe, Jewel," Austin whispers, squeezing my free hand. "We'll be in and out in no time."

I inhale and exhale. "Something feels wrong, Austin."

"How so?"

I twist in the seat and look out the back window. "We're being stalked. I can feel it."

"Diego and Kingston did a sweep. Hayden said the closest lookout point for rebels is a quarter mile down the road, which is halfway to where we're supposed to do the exchange." Austin brings my hand up to his chest to let me feel his rhythmic heartbeat. "If you tap the window, we can get them to look again if you want."

I knock my knuckles to the window, and Kingston, Diego, and Orlando all look in my direction. I wave my hand, and Orlando motions for Diego to return to the car to me. I crack the window without opening the door.

"Everything okay, beautiful?" he asks, leaning his hands on the frame.

I thrash my head, swinging my hair back and forth with the movement. "You guys need to do another sweep of the area."

Diego turns from me to glance at Kingston and Orlando. Hayden looks in our direction, his lips moving in a whisper, but I can't pick up the words. "The area's good. The rebels are exactly where Hayden said they'd be. Kingston and I will follow you guys to the meeting point by foot and then head toward the rebel hideout. It's only about a mile from here in an underground bunker from before the uprising. It's small. We'll be fine."

I bounce my feet and shiver. "Can you please check again? I'm getting seriously freaked out."

"Do it for Jewel, Diego," Austin says. "It can't hurt."

Diego sticks his fingers through the crack in the window, and I set my dagger on my lap to graze my hand to his. He offers me a smile and tilts his head at Kingston, motioning for him to do another sweep of the area. The two of them disappear, and I lean back in my seat, resting my head on the headrest.

Orlando and Hayden stroll in our direction and out of the glowing beams of the headlights. Orlando opens my door and holds his hand out to me. "I'd like you to drive, Jewel. That way you can easily escape if you need to. We can catch up by foot."

Austin lets go of my hand, and I slide out of the car, gripping my dagger for dear life. Hayden steps away from me, putting a few feet of space between us. I only give him a small glance and hop behind the wheel, but I don't strap myself in. Orlando takes his place on the front seat next to me and brings up the map on the dash.

"See this star? That's the supposed exchange point. Noah has men here and here and here. They intend to surround us."

Orlando points at small red dots he programs into the screen. He taps a white star. "This is where the bunker is. Brayla is being held there under her father's supervision. Your cousins and sister are there as well as a few others. Hayden says there are also fifteen people guarding the premises. Five more here, here, and here acting as lookouts."

I reach out and touch a circle. "What's this?"

"That's where you're going to drive us after we handle the situation. We'll meet the others there," he responds.

"Okay."

Orlando reaches across me and grabs my seatbelt restraints and puts them on me before I have a chance to argue. "Any questions?"

"None that I want answers to." Because the one thing we haven't discussed is my dad and what happens to him or what handling the situation means. All I know is that we're using Austin as a decoy and that my dad will call for backup, hopefully drawing rebels away from the bunker to give Kingston and Diego a better chance to get in and out without hurting anyone.

"Jewel, I also wanted to warn you," Orlando says. "We will do what is necessary to handle your father. Our goal is to capture him alive, but..."

"Shit happens," I finish for him.

He reaches out and rests his hand on top of mine that clutches the steering wheel. "You make us want to try our best."

I shiver under his soft touch, feeling the intensity of his stare boring into the side of my face because I can't take my eyes off the road in front of us. Fear prickles over my neck, and I can't shrug the feeling that something's coming. And then I see the silver flash of eyes in the distance ahead of us.

"Orlando." The second his name escapes my lips, Kingston appears in front of the car.

"Everything is clear. We're good to go." Diego taps on my window with his words, startling me, and I tip my head back and suck in another breath of air.

Kingston punches Diego in the arm. "You scared her."

I touch my hand to the glass. "He didn't. I'm already jumpy."

Diego opens the door and leans in, brushing his lips against mine. "Be brave, Jewel. You're our badass and can handle anything. Never doubt that."

"Thanks for the pep talk," I say, hugging his head.

Kingston takes his place and kisses me next. "Behave, babe. I mean it."

"Got it. Be safe and watch each other's backs. I'd like to be able to massage them later." I smile and nuzzle my nose to his for a second.

"You bet."

Kingston shuts the door, and he and Diego go to Hayden. Diego picks up the jerk, and the three of them disappear into the night. I drum my fingers on the steering wheel for a moment and hit the button to adjust the mirror. Austin tugs up the mask for a split second and smiles at me.

"Ready?" I ask.

"Are you?" Austin leans forward in the seat.

"Ready to get this over with."

Orlando taps the dashboard a few times and sets the car on autopilot. The sound of the tires crunching over the rough pavement hums through the air to break the silence of the night. He clicks off the headlights, turning the world dark around us, and I focus on the smattering of glittering stars peeking through tufts of puffy clouds.

"Make sure to keep a clear path in front of the car when you park. Keep it on the road as we don't know the terrain well enough to navigate." Orlando stretches forward in the seat. "Up there, to the left. That's them."

I release a small breath and grip the steering wheel though the car drives itself smoothly down the road. Liz stands with her gun aimed in our direction. The old car she uses as a barrier hums louder than anything, idling in the dark. I spot a few figures inside the car, and a larger figure comes up beside her, but I can't decipher the man's features in the dark.

"Looks like they're trying to bait and switch too," Orlando muses. He shifts in the seat. "I count six, Austin. Four in the car plus Liz and...that's not Noah."

"Is he in the car?" Austin asks.

Orlando taps the dash and turns on the headlights, lighting up the figures. Liz and a strange man shield their eyes, and from the quick glimpse of the car, the driver doesn't have hair and looks bulkier. My dad has always been thin from life in Dark Terrace Ranch.

"No," I say. "I don't think he's here."

"It seems Hayden was misinformed," Orlando says.

"Or he set us up."

A chime rings through the car, startling me, and I jump in my seat. Orlando connects the call on the dashboard, and Kingston's face lights up the screen. Screams echo through the line, sending a chill down my back.

"Get out of there," Kingston says.

"What's going on?" I ask. "I hear screams."

Something pops in the background, and Kingston flashes his fangs. "Get Jewel out of there. Now!"

The line disconnects, and I stiffen in my seat. Austin tugs the bag from his head and releases the driver's seat. I shoot back in surprise and stare up at Austin, and he and Orlando rip at the straps of my restraints, breaking them instead of un-buckling them.

Something collides into the windshield, and Orlando swears. Gunfire rings out, and Austin drags me into the backseat with him while Orlando takes control of the wheel. Austin shields me, stopping me from sitting up to glimpse at what the hell is going on.

"Jewel, the rebels are under attack," Orlando says, jerking the wheel.

A loud thud resonates through the car, and sounds of screams trickle in. A thunk on the back window draws my attention to it, and panic steals my breath. A man lies with his bloody face smooshed to the glass. Another figure lands on the car next to him, and Austin tries to block my view of the vampire, but he's not fast enough. I gasp as the vampire drags the man with him.

"They're outcasts," Austin says to Orlando.

Orlando releases a soft growl. "Think it's a coincidence?"

Austin shifts away from me to peer out the window. "They could've followed us. I don't know."

"We have to do something," I say.

"They were planning to ambush us, Jewel." Orlando spins the wheel, jerking the car hard enough to send me into the door. A yell sounds out from the trunk, and I cringe at Cyprus's voice.

"They'll blame us and try to retaliate," I say. "You know they will."

"And we'll be read—"

Orlando jerks the car again, sending the car skidding off the road and into the rough terrain of the desolate, uninhabited area we've found ourselves in the middle of nowhere. Austin hooks his arms to me, holding me in place, and I grip onto the front seat to stop the both of us from sliding around.

Slamming the brakes, Orlando skids to a stop just inches before the ground drops off into some sort of man-made waterway. Orlando puts the car in reverse, but the tires squeal, spinning without gaining any traction.

Orlando flashes his fangs, glowering at the rear window.

"Austin, take Jewel and head across the river. It's the fastest way to our meeting spot. I'll buy you some time and catch up."

The whole car shakes, several growls sounding out through the air, erupting fear in my heart. Orlando swings the driver's side door open and disappears in a blur. Austin links his hand to mine and thrusts his door open, knocking back an unfamiliar vampire. In one powerful swing, he cuts the vampire's head clean off and kicks his body away from us. Another vampire flies toward us, but instead of attacking Austin, he glides to the trunk of the car and shoves it, sending it rolling.

Austin latches his fingers to the doorframe, fighting against the vampire's shove. "Hurry, Jewel. Get out."

The car bounces and metal scrapes the concrete ledge as the front tires drop off. Cyprus's holler muffles through the air from the trunk, and I stare at Austin with wide eyes. Another vampire attempts to close in on Austin, and I grab Austin's medical kit and chuck it at the vampire, hitting him right in the head.

"Where's the lever to release the trunk? We can't leave Cyprus in there," I say.

"Right behind you next to the headrest. Be careful. It'll bring the seat down, not pop the trunk."

I twist, following his directions, and pull the lever that releases the latch on the seat. The car jolts forward, and Austin grabs me by my wrist and yanks me out. He has no choice but to let go of the car as the two vampires shove it far enough forward to send it teetering on the ledge.

Austin presses my face to his chest and rushes us to the edge of the concrete riverbank with a steep drop to the waterway. He doesn't give me a moment to brace myself as the world rushes out from under us. I bite my lip to stop from screaming, my stomach flying into my throat. Icy water engulfs us, and I panic for a split second until Austin swims us to the surface.

I gasp and cling onto Austin's neck. Austin shakes the water from his face, fighting against the strong current. Peering up, I catch sight of figures blurring in a fight. Orlando knocks Mitchell into the car, sending it over the ledge, but the two vampires that were after us grab onto it and heave it up.

"Cyprus, jump!" I yell, spotting him clutching onto the door, trying to find his footing on the ledge.

My voice draws Mitchell's attention to me and Austin. He races to the car with Orlando right behind him. I stare in horror as Mitchell points at the vampires and then us. Cyprus holds his hands out, and I nearly lose my shit at the sight of Mitchell pulling Cyprus from the car.

But he doesn't attack him or throw him over the ledge. The strange vampires don't go after him either. Instead, Mitchell hands Cyprus a weapon and motions in the direction behind him.

"What the—shit, Austin. Swim. They're going to push the car off."

Austin kicks his legs, swimming us in the opposite direction. Metal screeches on the pavement ledge, and the vampires knock the car off and into the river. Water splashes over our heads, and Austin fights against the shift in the current. Loud pops pierce my ears, echoing over the sound of the rushing water. Growling, Austin jerks and spins, pushing me underwater without warning. He swims us deeper, testing the strength of my lungs in the process. Had he not taught me to swim, I would've panicked and inhaled. But I can't hold my breath much longer.

I dig my fingers into Austin's shoulders, trying my hardest to fight against the burning in my lungs and the dizziness disorienting me. Crisp night air engulfs us, and I heave a breath, spitting and coughing, trying not to flail too much as Austin presses my back into the concrete wall.

"We can't cross," he whispers, covering my mouth to muffle any noise that threatens to escape me. "At least not here. There are rebels shooting. I won't risk you getting hit."

I press my lips together, inhaling deep breaths through my nose. "Did you see Mitchell? He helped Cyprus. Do you think...?"

Austin holds his finger up to his lips, silencing my thoughts. I shift in his arms and realize that he presses me into the wall right next to where the car stands on end, caught on something that prevents it from washing away in the now chest high water. It blocks the current from colliding into us while also shielding us from the shower of bullets the rebels shoot toward the vampires on the ledge above us.

"Jewel," Austin whispers. "I need you to grab my com device from my pocket. I can't let go of the wall."

I rest my head on his shoulder, stretching my arm to feel along his body. He winces and releases a soft groan in my ear. Gently, I slide my fingers into the pocket of his jeans and retrieve the small black box and hold it up.

"You're injured," I whisper. His reaction toward my touch gives it away.

"I'll be fine. Just call my brothers."

I tap my finger to the device, and the screen lights up as I call Kingston. He answers immediately, his eyes widening the second he sees me.

"Shit, babe. We're coming," Kingston says.

"We were ambushed by outcasts working for Mitchell. He's here," I say.

"Us too. Outcasts, not Mitchell."

My heart thrashes at his words. "Oh, no. Where are my cousins?"

Kingston grimaces. "I don't know, babe. I'm sorry. We never made it inside."

Austin dips us underwater, stopping me from screeching out at Kingston to find them. I get my shit together and suck my bottom lip between my teeth, so Austin doesn't have to dunk me under again.

"Jewel, don't panic. We intervened in the threat, but we couldn't stay. The outcasts stole our element of surprise, and the rebels were fighting back full force," Diego says, his soft voice whispering through the line.

"We had to fall back or risk getting hurt." Kingston's eyes flash silver. "Now, where exactly are you? The tracker's bugging out."

"West of the exchange point in the waterway between markers fifteen and sixteen," Austin says, answering for me. "Look for the wrecked car."

"What?" Diego asks.

Kingston flares his nostrils. "Fucking A."

The line disconnects, and I store the device in my bra because there is no way I'm going to attempt to put it back in Austin's pocket. He breathes a soft breath on my neck, hugging me close to him. Closing my eyes, I try to focus on the noise of the fight happening above us. I can hear at least five distinct voices, but none belongs to Mitchell or Orlando.

"I'm going to rip his heart out," I whisper, shivering in Austin's arms. "I'm going to rip it out and step on it even if it's wasteful."

Austin chuckles softly. "I will restrain him for you."

"I just—I don't understand. How did he know?" My question hangs in the air as a few voices grow louder. More gunshots pop through the night, making me wince, and Austin shifts his arm to block one of my ears, so I don't have to let go of him.

A body falls from above and splashes into the water. I yelp and hit my back harder into the wall as a figure swims inhumanly fast in our direction.

Adjusting me to his back, Austin lets go and kicks off the side of the car hard enough that it flips and crashes right on top of the vampire. Austin dives us under, swimming along the shallow side that drops off into a deeper part of the water channel. We resurface, Austin's powerful strokes fighting the current enough to keep us swimming upstream.

"Austin!" Diego's voice rings through the air from above us. "Get ready. Thirty feet until the bridge. Kingston's there. I'm following you guys."

Without responding, Austin pushes himself harder, his muscles rippling against my tight hold.

I keep with his movements, trying my best not to tense every time water splashes my face. A soft whistle sounds through the air, and I stretch my neck to spot Kingston hanging halfway over a small concrete bridge with what looks like a metal pipe.

"Babe! You're going to grab on first, okay?" Kingston stretches his arms farther, holding the rod steady for me.

I squeeze Austin's sides between my thighs and manage to push myself upright without falling off. He continues to stroke forward, losing speed from exhaustion, and I reach out and ready myself to grab onto the pole.

"Get ready, babe. You got this. Don't let go."

I grip onto the pole as tight as I possibly can, and Kingston heaves me up into the air the second I release Austin. Icy wind whips around me, and I cover my mouth with my hands to stop myself from screaming out.

Strong arms wrap around me, catching me. "Hell yeah, beautiful. That was perfect." Diego combs my wet hair out of my eyes and searches my dripping face for a moment. "You okay?"

I rub my hand across my eyes to dry my eyelashes the best I can. "Yeah, I-I think so. Cold."

Kingston yanks the rod up, sending Austin flying into the air to land on his feet next to him. "Good fucking thing I know—"

A silver arrow penetrates Kingston in the chest, cutting off his words and surprising him so much so that he stumbles backward and into the railing.

He falls over and into the river, getting swept in a current. Another arrow ricochets off the concrete and catches Austin in the leg hard enough to make it buckle out from under him. Diego spins around, taking an arrow in the shoulder.

Footsteps thud on the bridge as at least a dozen rebels start firing their weapons at us. Diego peers to the rebels and then to the open side of the bridge. Austin tugs himself back to his feet, and Diego hands me over to him.

"This way!" Orlando yells. "Hurry. We don't have much time."

My whole body tenses, fear rushing through me in an intense wave the closer we get to Orlando. I don't even have time to point as a figure blurs in his direction. But I don't have to. Orlando spins on his feet, preparing to fight again.

Two vampires charge him, distracting him long enough

for Mitchell to evade him and rush in our direction. Cyprus dashes behind him, firing a gun at us.

Everything happens so fast that my head spins.

I hit the freezing water once again.

WAR

I BREAK THE SURFACE, FLAILING around, my body in shock and doing everything it can to keep me afloat. My mind fares no better, spinning with fear and confusion. Water splashes my face again, and I can't see anything clearly. Something grabs my leg, yanking me a few feet toward the edge of the channel.

"Jewel, swim!" Orlando yells, his voice echoing over the hum of the current. "Fight. Don't let him get you. We're coming."

My attention snaps to my leg, and I screech out, seeing Mitchell dragging me toward him. His long fangs flash with his snarl, his eyes solid silver unlike anything I've ever seen before on him. Bucking my body, I kick my free leg and smash my boot right into his throat. His growl cuts off with his airway, but he still doesn't release me.

"Again, Jewel," Diego says. "Don't make it easy."

I swing my leg and clock Mitchell in the side of the face. Instead of releasing me, he lets go of the wall, and the current takes us. I sink underwater, thrashing and kicking, reaching for anything I can grab onto. My fingers rub against slimy concrete, and I dig my nails across the shallow river bottom along the edge of the channel.

Mitchell drags me back to the surface, and I gasp for air. He latches his fingers to the front of my shirt and heaves me closer to him. I ram my hands into his chest, using all my strength to keep space between us.

"Kingston, up ahead!" Diego shouts from somewhere nearby. "Jewel, dive! Take him under if you have to."

Loud pops echo through the air again, and I jerk my arm at Mitchell and punch him as hard as I can. His fangs sink into the top of my hand, and I thrust myself away, my body reacting to the threat with inhuman strength ignited by the pain.

The movement catches Mitchell off guard, and I arch my whole body in an attempt to dive backward. My boots hit something solid, and I flip and sink under. Mitchell tries to grab for me underwater, but I clutch his wrists and bite him back. His holler breaks through the hum of the water, and he disappears.

I pop up and flick the water from my face, spinning

around to see where he went. More yells sound out from above me, and something blurs past.

"Jewel, swim!" Austin calls. "They're coming up behind you. Get as close to the wall as you can. I'm going to get you out."

I turn myself around, letting the current pull me backward, and spot Diego and Mitchell in a full-on fight, creating massive waves with their punches. I stroke my arms and kick my legs, putting more space between us as Diego slows Mitchell down.

"Arms up, Jewel."

Austin's voice draws my attention to him, and I stretch up as far as I can. Kingston hangs Austin over the concrete ledge, and I swim toward them, pushing through the pain radiating through me, begging me to just float for a minute.

Lacing his fingers around my wrists, Austin tugs me up. We don't make it far. Mitchell launches toward me, kicking off Diego and sending him underwater. Grabbing my legs, Mitchell holds on tight while Kingston heaves the three of us back up. Austin doesn't let go of my arms while Mitchell restrains my legs, and I scream out as my stomach tightens under the pressure. If someone doesn't relent, I could very well be ripped in two.

Growls sound out from around us, but all I can do is flail my body between Austin and Mitchell and hope that someone doesn't come to finish ripping out my middle. Figures blur around us, and Mitchell lets go of one of my legs to grab a blade from beneath his drenched jacket. He swings his arm, surprising Kingston, and slashes across his chest, sending blood splattering over me.

Dropping my other leg, Mitchell sends Austin off balance at the sudden release of me. Mitchell collides into Austin and stabs him so fast I can't even manage a scream. Kingston closes in on Mitchell, but Mitchell kicks him, and he falls back. Two strange vampires drag Kingston a few feet away. Orlando materializes from the fray of things as he fights off the small army of outcast vampires working for Mitchell. He knocks the two guys away and swings his arms so fast that I don't even see him sever their heads from their bodies. It's like one second they're snarling and the next, they collapse, their heads rolling.

My mind spins as I try to keep up with the blurring figures, and I crawl on my hands and knees toward Austin on the ground. Austin extends his hand out to me, and I lock my fingers to his and let him tug me to him. He rolls on top of me and yells out, his voice piercing my ear. Hot pain explodes through my chest, tears burning my eyes. My mouth quivers, my voice dying in my throat with a tightness in my chest that steals my breath.

Mitchell stands over us with a bloody blade aimed and ready to strike down again.

"Jewel, bite me," Austin says, his voice shaking, and he sinks deeper into me like he can no longer hold his weight off me. "Do it now."

I do as he says, latching my mouth the best I can to his

neck and bite hard enough to break the skin. Austin groans as blood fills my mouth, sending tingles through my body with my first swallow. Locking his hands to Austin, Mitchell thrusts him off and pushes him away. Austin lands face first on the ground.

Mitchell stands over Austin and aims his blade at his chest. Austin struggles for a second, trying to get up, but Mitchell stomps his stomach. I push up on my elbows and search around for something, anything. It's then that I realize we're surrounded. Kingston and Orlando work through the group of outcast vampires, sending blood spraying and body parts flying. We're outnumbered. Handling rebels is one thing, but this? I'm not so sure.

"Cyprus, my son. Come do the honors," Mitchell says, his voice bellowing through the air. "Let him through so he can reap the benefits of his loyalty to me. Watch in awe as this magnificent donor rises up as my next Divine Heir."

Ice travels through me at his words. I grind my teeth, fury raging inside me, and I use it to stumble to my feet. The vampires around me growl, but no one tries to grab me. Cyprus pushes through two vampires, not even giving them a second look. We were wrong about him. It wasn't the Vaduvas who got in his head. It was Mitchell. And that's how he got here to intercept and ruin our plan.

I rush forward and collide into Cyprus, knocking him off his feet. "You asshole!" No one stops me as I sucker punch him in the nose, sending blood spraying across the concrete. A few vampires inch closer, and Mitchell rips me off Cyprus and holds me in front of him, flashing his fangs at me. Diego yells my name, and I spot him breaking through the circle closest to the river.

I expect Mitchell to bite me, but he drops me to the ground to cut off Diego. The two of them blur in a fight until Diego roars and hits his knees. Kingston gets through the circle next and rushes toward me, but Mitchell intervenes and shoves him hard. Orlando tackles Mitchell and stabs him in the shoulder, making him fight harder than ever.

"Cyprus, do it now!" Mitchell's deep voice booms with rage. He manages to knock Orlando off, and the two of them go rolling as they try to outmatch each other. It's then that I realize Mitchell's losing confidence. His army no longer fights. My guys are too strong that even a bunch of outcasts vampires can't keep them down.

"Jewel, run," Austin says, heaving himself onto his side. The front of his blood-soaked shirt clings to him, sending my heart racing.

Cyprus rams his foot into Austin's chest, and Austin groans and falls back. His eyes flash silver, and he snaps his teeth in an attempt to bite at Cyprus. Raising his gun, Cyprus shoots Austin a few times, and I scream, the loud noise piercing the night.

I gather all my strength and roll to Austin, making Cyprus hesitate. He glances behind him, and Mitchell shouts his name. I crawl on top of Austin and shield him the best I can.

Cyprus's dark eyes meet mine, his hand shaking like crazy as he aims the weapon at me.

I brace myself for the pain to ensue. I brace myself to die.

"Jewel, get off him," Cyprus says, his voice cracking. "I don't want to hurt you, but this is the only way. I can't live the rest of my life as a donor."

"But you will," I say. "Mitchell's using you. He'll never change you. You know that, right?"

Cyprus aims his gun at me, and I squeeze my eyes shut, feeling Austin's hands slide across my stomach. Loud pops pierce the air, and Austin pushes me off him to lie on top of me. I scream out at his sudden weight squishing me. My ears ring, my head spinning. I can't focus on Austin's breathing or heartbeat. I can't even hear my own.

Stretching my neck, I glimpse at someone approaching at a human's speed on foot. I roll my shoulders, trying to get out from under Austin, my fear running wild.

"Don't move, Cyprus," Liz says, her sharp voice commanding through the air. "Don't you fucking move! Step back. I will shoot!"

Loud pops steal my hearing again, and I press my cheek to the ground. Something shifts in the edge of my vision, making me turn in its direction. I stare in shock at Liz's wide, empty eyes gawking at me from the ground next to us. Blood drips from a wound in her forehead, trailing to pool at her temple. I clench my teeth, suppressing my sob at the shock and pain exploding through me.

A guttural roar rips through the night, striking panic to my heart. I know it's Mitchell without having to see him, my heart working in overdrive as he moves somewhere nearby. More guns go off, and something blurs closer, but Orlando's familiar boots step in the way, protecting us. Austin blocks my view the best he can, shifting to shield both of our heads with his arms, clearly seeing something I can't. Blood splashes the ground in front of me, and I startle at loud screams erupting in the air only to fade into the night.

"Close your eyes," Austin whispers. "Don't look. Please don't look. Just keep your eyes closed until we get out of here."

I groan, reaching my arm up to try to grab Austin's hand. "Austin." It's all I can manage to say. I'm so thankful to hear his voice.

Silence settles through the night, and I tremble beneath Austin until his weight falls off of me. Orlando pulls me onto his lap and bites his arm, dripping blood into my mouth before I can react to what's happening. I suck harder, relaxing in his arms. For the first time in a long time, I don't protest. I don't even think he's that much of an asshole. He protected my guys. He helped me. Damn it if the familiarity of his blood doesn't bring me such relief.

I struggle to sit up in his arms, and he props me against his chest. Kingston and Diego kneel beside Austin, and I reach out for the three of them, and Orlando moves me closer until Diego touches my leg.

"He needs me," I whisper, pulling my lips away from the sweetness of Orlando's skin.

Austin grazes his bloody hand to mine, gazing at me with his glowing silver eyes. "You're too injured," Austin mumbles without getting up.

"Then drink mine." The familiar, masculine voice draws my attention to where Liz's dead body remains, and I watch Hayden approach, his gun drawn, with three other rebels. "But I need something in return. Some of my people are injured and could use your help."

"I'm surprised to still see you around, Mr. Andrei," Orlando says, taking in the sight around us.

And I really friggin' wish I didn't look. I've never seen such a massacre—a mix of human and vampire body parts, blood, weapons, a whole shit ton of things I wish I could unsee.

"I don't abandon my people to die," Hayden says, turning to his men.

Kingston scoots closer and holds his arms out to take me, and Orlando hands me over to get to his feet. I hug Kingston, hiding my face in the crook of his neck, sinking against him while he rubs his hands up and down my back.

"Take care of my brother, and I'll go with your men," Orlando says to Hayden. "Meet us at the bunker. I don't want to stay out in the open for much longer. It seems Mr. Divine has started a war with the Ortega Region."

I groan. "Shit."

A soft hand touches my shoulder, brushing my damp hair away. "Don't worry, Jewel. Tonight turned out better than I expected."

I jerk my head to peer up at Orlando. "People died. A lot of them."

"This unwarranted attack gave us exactly what we need. The other regions are already shifting alliances. Mitchell's reign will fall soon enough."

I don't respond to him. I can't. Instead, I turn my head and rest it to Kingston, listening to the thrumming of his heart. Orlando takes the hint and leaves us to follow the two men that arrived with Hayden. Diego, Kingston, and I sit in silence and wait for Austin to get the blood he needs from Hayden.

"Don't be jealous, babe," Kingston whispers, sliding his fingers through mine. "You can let Austin bite all your favorite spots later. After me. I'm hurt too, you know."

I bump my shoulder into his and puff out my bottom lip. "You can always ask Hayden for some blood next."

He fake growls at me before kissing me sweetly, just grazing his lips to mine without going full-on let's-get-naked-in-front-of-everyone mode. Diego hugs his arms around the two of us since Kingston's pretty dead-set on not letting me go, and I shift and groan at the ache radiating in my chest from the movement. Kingston leans back and fingers the front of my jacket, pulling it down just enough to get a better look.

"I'm going to kill that asshole," Kingston says. Swiveling,

he turns to glance over his shoulder as Austin releases Hayden's arm. "Austin, Jewel got stabbed in the fucking tit."

"Mitchell's blade went through me and into her, but she'll be okay." Austin gets to his feet and closes the space to us, still looking pale, but at least his eyes now remain green. "It's already healing."

Kingston bites his arm and holds it out to me. "Here, drink. Let me help heal you faster."

"Dude," I say. "It's fine. Better my boob than my heart."

He narrows his eyes at me, and Diego whacks him in the shoulder. I tackle them both, pushing them back so I can lie on top of them. I pull Austin closer and let the three of them smother me with their love and affection, not even caring that Hayden shifts awkwardly as eff on his feet while I ignore the grossness of what lies around us just a moment longer to remind my guys how much they mean to me.

I finally pull myself away and let Diego lift me off my feet to hold me in his arms. I hook my legs around him and don't let him set me back down. He encourages me to bite him on the walk toward the bunker where the rest of Hayden's people remain. Keeping behind everyone, Diego hides me in his jacket, letting Austin and Kingston follow ahead with Hayden.

"Don't stop because you think you have to," Diego whispers, sending goosebumps traveling over my skin.

I suck harder for a moment longer, pulling a soft moan from him, and then finally get my body to chill the hell out at the sound of soft voices. "I don't want them to see me do this.

They don't understand me like you do. If my dad—"

"Jewel, your father has left," Orlando says, startling me by interrupting my soft conversation with Diego.

"Left?"

Orlando glances toward the bunker where I follow his gaze to see Kingston and Austin join a few rebels to pull people—mostly dead people—from their hideout. "I didn't want to tell you this earlier, but we weren't Mitchell's target tonight. He wanted the Blood Rebels, and we led him straight here."

"He got to Cyprus," I say. It's not a question. I know it.

"Indeed. It seems that he used Cyprus's desire for a Blood Vow to his advantage. Mitchell got into his mind most likely during our stay at the Blood Match Center. He manipulated him to spy on us. I bet if we had searched his body, we would have found a tracker."

Diego hugs me closer. "Mitchell's been obsessed with rebels for decades. I bet he wasn't expecting all of us to come. We happened to be an opportunity he took advantage of."

"But he'll lose in the end," Orlando says. He reaches out and touches my forehead, pulling strands of hair from my eyes to capture me in his blue gaze. "I promise you, Jewel."

I nod. "I know." Twisting my torso, I glance behind me again. "And you're sure my dad is gone? My cousins too?"

"Ramona is gone as well," he says with a sigh. "As is Brayla."

I press my lips together, puckering my brows. I don't

think he'd lie to me about something like this, but a part of me needs to check to make sure my family isn't among those killed by Mitchell's disgusting, vengeful nature. "Can I look for myself?" I ask, pleading with my eyes for him to let me do it.

"Babe, it's not a good idea." Kingston appears in front of us. "We promise they're not here."

"Brothers," Austin calls from tending to the first woman I've seen tonight apart from Liz. "We can help her through this. It's important to her."

Kingston sighs and rests his hand on top of mine on Diego's shoulder. "I just want to protect her." He looks at me. "I want to protect you, Jewel. I didn't do as good a job as I should, but seeing the aftermath—"

"Kingston, please. I need to see."

Kingston slumps his shoulders and pouts at me. "Okay, but Diego is not putting you down. Got it?"

I pout right back at him. "Hold my hand, too?"

Orlando and Kingston fall into step on each of Diego's sides while Austin meets us at the entrance to the old bunker. A gross stench permeates through the air, a mixture of things I don't want to think of. The dank, concrete and metal underground...house? Well, it most definitely was well lived in. If my dad managed to get people out of here, it looks like they left everything behind. Including the majority of their people.

"These are all males," Austin says quietly, quickly waving against the wall where the ravaged have been lined up.

Against my good senses, I take a peek and immediately regret it, covering my mouth to silence the oncoming whimper. The last thing I expected was to recognize someone among the dead.

"Berto has met his final donation." Orlando's voice remains even, stepping forward to shield me from getting a better look at the boy barely older than my cousins.

"We haven't found his brother, so we can assume he was taken or got out with the others," Hayden says, coming up to drop a sheet over his fallen people.

"Taken?" My voice squeaks as I say the word.

"With so many outcasts, some would take advantage of the situation and grab who they could. Not all shadow vampires kill and run. There are still some out there who..." Kingston's words trail off, and he runs his fingers through his hair. "They all got away. Don't worry, babe."

"We can sweep the area for any stragglers. Hunt down any undocumented covens," Diego says, tightening his arms around me to breathe in the scent of my still damp hair.

"You'd do that?" I ask.

Austin draws circles on my back, staying close to me and his brothers. "Anything for you, Jewel."

"But first." Orlando waves his hand to silently finish his thought, motioning to the rest of the bunker. Metal shelving units section off the open space. Food, clothing, water, blankets, and medical supplies, some looking as old as The Divide, fill the shelves. And who knows? It's possible that some of the stuff might be.

Orlando leads the way while Diego continues to carry me past rooms cramped with more survival supplies. Discarded weapons mix with the destruction, and blood ruins everything. Fresh blood. Human.

"I can't believe this," I murmur, mostly to myself. "My cousins were probably so scared. What I want to know is how they got out." It's clear they're not here. I haven't seen a single female or child, though I fear that females would be most coveted for an outcast to take. The horrifying realization makes me rest my head on Diego's shoulder and squeeze him tighter.

Kingston and Austin stroll away, and Orlando remains by Diego and me, watching the two of them shift bookcases and furniture.

Behind a busted door looks to be another room, a private quarters with a bathroom, shower, closet, and an artillery cage, but it's empty of guns.

"They kept Brayla here," Kingston says, waving us over. "This is flimsy as fuck. She could've easily escaped during the fray of things."

"Perhaps she never planned to," Orlando says.

"I knew we shouldn't have trusted her." Kingston darts his gaze to mine. "And to think you almost applied to a Blood Vow with her."

I can't stop myself from looking at Orlando at the mention of a Blood Vow. I still have so many questions to ask him. "I don't think it was intentional. Brayla's my best friend."

"You mean you're hers."

I shrug. "If she thought my family was in danger, she wouldn't have abandoned them."

"I think Jewel's right," Austin says, swinging the cage door ajar. It wasn't even locked. Someone opened it.

I wiggle in Diego's arms until he relents and sets me on my feet right outside the caged in room. Dried blood stains empty glasses lined up neatly along the cage wall.

I recognize Brayla's jacket folded like a pillow on one side and a blanket sprawled across the concrete ground. Reaching down, I pick it up.

I gawk at the message hidden beneath the blanket. "The Orchards?"

"You were right, beautiful," Diego says. "She knew we'd come here. She helped everyone escape."

I hug myself. "We have to go after her."

An arm drapes over my shoulders, and Orlando pulls me into him. "I'm sorry, Jewel. The Orchards is the last place I'll ever allow you to go. If Brayla and your family make it there, she'll never make it out alive."

Shrugging away, I turn to face my guys. "We have to go."

Without them having to say a single word, I know they agree with Orlando. They don't want to take me there either.

"We need her," I add when no one responds. "You can't officially join the Ortega Coven without her."

"Jewel," Kingston says softly. "We can. We just have to

ou—"

My eyes widen. "Don't say it."

"Think it about it, beautiful," Diego says, "You could change your type of Blood Vow. This gives us the capability without looking like a power play. Brayla chose to go. She abandoned our coven."

I scowl. "For *me*. Brayla's part of our family. We can't do this to her."

Orlando and my guys have a silent conversation, communicating with only their eyes. Turning away, I stare at the mess the vampires left in their wake.

"We can't do this to her," I repeat, bringing my gaze back to them.

"Jewel," Orlando says. "Things are changing. They might get worse. Mitchell will not back off without a fight. The board will—"

"Make an exception," I say, interrupting him. "Make them see how bullshit their ways are. Make them change."

"It's not so simple," Kingston says, inching closer. He slides his fingers through mine and pulls my hand to his mouth to kiss the back. "We don't have any firm allies."

"We have to try," I say. "You guys promised to change the world for me."

"For us," Austin says, taking my other hand.

I straighten my shoulders and look around the room. At the destruction, the devastation caused by Mitchell and his new vampire allies.

What could possibly be the beginning of another terrifying future for humanity if we don't change things. If we don't put a stop to these unfair and unjust ways. "We have to change it for everyone."

BLOOD OF ENEMIES

"ARE YOU TWO GOING TO spend all night in there?" Kingston asks, tapping his finger on the door. "You know we have plans, right?"

Diego drags his fingers up my stomach to rest on my breasts, gently playing with my sensitive skin. "Let our girl relax. She's enjoying herself."

I cup a handful of bubbles and blow the foam into the air. "Very much."

Brushing his lips to my shoulder, Diego kisses a tingling trail to my neck until he sucks my earlobe between his teeth. I release a small moan and shift, feeling the length of his hardness press between my legs as I sit on his lap.

"Me too," he says, his voice lowering.

Reaching down, I trail my fingers along Diego's thighs until I can stroke him in a way that pulls a moan from his lips.

Something thunks on the door. "Damn, I'll stall for you guys."

"Thanks, bro. Our girl deserves it after last night."

I grin and bite my lip, a mixture of desire and amusement sending goosebumps over my exposed damp skin as I shift higher. I never imagined I'd see the day where Kingston wasn't purposely barging in or claiming that the universe was against us.

"Hell yeah, she does," Kingston says without opening the door, though it's unlocked. "I can't wait to give her everything she wants from me."

I close my eyes, my chest rising and falling with my now racing heart. "Mmmhmm. Can't wait either."

Diego chuckles softly without comment, taking his time to kiss my neck, sucking hard enough on my skin to leave a mark. It drags a weird ass noise from me, like a cross between a purr and a laugh, and I gasp and cover my mouth.

"You like that?" Diego whispers.

"Damn it. I'm so fucking jealous," Kingston mumbles through the door. "That was hot."

"You're the one who didn't want to join us," I tease, resting my head back.

Kingston releases a groan. "Have you seen the size of that tub? Plus, I had something to do."

"You still have something to do," Diego says. "If you keep

your word, I'll tell you how to get Jewel to make that sound."

"Shit, yeah. This is getting too weird anyway."

I laugh. "If you continue to stand out there it might. Come in here or leave."

"All right, I'm out. I'll save this weird ass special bonding time for later. Can't leave Austin to fend for himself against the Vaduvas."

"You could grab him."

"Damn it, babe. Don't tease me unless you're ready to be all in."

"I *am* all in, dude." I laugh again and squirm on Diego's lap, enjoying the feeling of his body sliding against mine. "But just give us a few minutes in case."

Diego moans. "Longer."

"Don't forget. You break that tub, it's showers from now on unless you use Orlando's."

"I'm okay with that."

My giggle turns breathless, and Diego gently nips at my shoulder while exploring the skin of my breasts with his fingers. The second we hear Kingston close the door to the room, Diego works his hands lower, building a crazy amount of good pressure between my legs. I arch back into him, sending a wave of water across the tile floor.

"I think I'm ready to get out," I say, slowing my hands.

Diego responds by scooping me up with him and kissing me, not moving farther than the cushioned bench positioned against the wall where our clothes lie in a heap. He knocks them off and sits down with me straddling him. I cup his face and deepen our kiss, moaning into his mouth as his fingers roam down the length of my back to grab my ass. He adjusts my body to his, and I suck in a breath of a moan, opening myself completely. I rock with his guided movements and allow myself to be swept away in the desperation of our desire.

With Diego's lips on mine, his hands combing through my damp hair, our bodies as one, I can forget everything outside the sensations that drag moan after moan from the both of us. I bite him the way he likes, savoring the taste of his blood over my tongue turning my pleasure into pure ecstasy until he finishes and rests his head to my shoulder, breathing as hard as me.

"Whoa," I whisper, smiling before I kiss him.

"I will never get enough of you, Jewel. Every second I see your smile, taste your lips, hear your heart beating—it's my perfect forever."

"It's mine too, Diego."

"I know we can't guarantee that things will get easier, but we'll do our best. We'll always do right by you. I hope you know that."

I hug him, sliding my arms around his broad back. "I know. I do. And I'm going to try my hardest to stop being such a pain. You guys do everything you can for me and us. If tonight doesn't work out like I want it to, then I'll deal with it. I was just so upset—"

"With every right to be," Diego says. "But thank you for

saying that. We're all on edge."

I kiss him and slide my hand down his muscular stomach. "Still?"

He chuckles. "Okay, quite a bit less."

"I guess we should get out of here so I can assure you're completely relaxed—like me."

Diego shifts me off of him, and we quickly clean up and dress to head to the main living area of the house. We heard the Vaduvas arrive an hour ago, but Diego swore that we didn't need to be in a hurry. They're in our household, which means they must wait for us to be ready. The only reason Kingston came to check on us was because he's probably bored as hell.

Voices travel up the stairs, and someone laughs. It was the last sound I expected, but I can't help but be relieved to be greeted by lighter banter compared to grave or angry voices. Diego tugs me closer to him, letting go of my hand to drape his arm over my shoulders.

Orlando materializes in the arched doorway and offers me a smile that lights up his face brighter than I've ever seen it. "Precious Jewel, I'm so happy you decided to join us. Are you feeling better?"

I let his nickname slide and nod. "Much. How is everything?"

Holding out his hand, he waits for me to take it and laces his fingers through mine to tug me into the living room. Diego follows behind us, and I steel myself to face Viorica and her daughters.

Everyone stares at us as we enter, and I try to get my mouth to smile at Viorica, but my lips remain firmly pressed together. I scan the room, finding Austin sitting next to Layla, Samantha, and Evora, and I flick my gaze away. Kingston wiggles his fingers at me from next to Merrick and Heidi, and I can't help thinking about Gabriella and how the Vaduvas are handling it.

Viorica stands from her spot and holds out her hands, surprising the hell out of me. I think it might be the first time she immediately directs her attention to me and not in a way that makes me feel beneath her.

"Ms. Ortega, allow me to offer my regards. Orlando told me what happened." She clasps my hands between hers. "Mitchell has always been so wasteful."

Orlando squeezes my shoulder. "We must offer you our sincerest condolences. His treachery will not be soon forgotten."

I shift on my feet, totally uncomfortable at both their attempts to remain cordial and even-tempered speaking about Mitchell. I can see the blood hunger—hunger for revenge—light Viorica's eyes in silver. It's her deep-seated desire to destroy Mitchell that we're counting on to make all of this work.

"I want to rip his damn head off for what he did to my daughter!" Viorica flashes her fangs, balling her hands into fists. Her sharp voice startles me, and I take an automatic step away, my self-preservation as a human screaming at me to keep some distance.

"And I—we—want nothing more than to help you." Orlando motions his hand toward the couch again. "If we may?"

Viorica nods and retakes her seat on the couch. Her daughters shift their chairs, and Diego pulls one up next to me, allowing Orlando and I to sit with Viorica. Kingston and Austin move to join our cluster, surrounding me as the Vaduvas settle in.

One of the staff members comes into the room with a pitcher of blood and enough glasses for everyone. I nearly offer my blood to my guys, but Orlando smirks at me, shaking his head to stop me from uttering the suggestion.

"Jewel, it's been a while since you've had some blood, allow me to pour you a glass," Orlando says to me, picking up an empty cup.

"I see you're still protective over her mind," Viorica comments. "Do you have something to hide, Mr. Ortega?"

"Most definitely. I can't give away all our secrets now, can I?" he asks.

Orlando flashes his fangs and bites his arm, pouring his blood into my glass without asking my guys to join him. It's now that I realize they're being cautious in front of the Vaduvas. Kingston, Diego, and Austin huddle around me protectively, but none of them touch me like they usually would if it were just the four of us alone.

"We also cannot allow our girl to become susceptible in these uncertain times," Kingston adds. "We suggest Samantha do the same for Evora. It was her heir who betrayed all of us."

"Mr. Divine got into his head," Evora says. "He would've never done this otherwise."

Samantha grabs her hand and stops her from standing up.

"And that's where we must disagree." Orlando hands me the full glass of blood and staunches the bleeding on his arm with his fingers. He leans closer and touches my knee. "Cyprus knew exactly what he was doing. Regardless of whether or not the human heir was manipulated from the start, he still poses quite the threat, and I must insist that for our alliance to work, you must allow his fate to fall into our hands. As a human or vampire depending on Mitchell's next move."

"What?" Evora asks.

Samantha covers her mouth with her hand, and the two of them disappear from the room but not far enough away that we can't hear the start of their argument. And I can't blame Evora. Cyprus is her brother. Out of everyone, I understand the most. Sometimes we can't help the love we have for those who intend to destroy us. That love gives us hope where our good senses know there is none, but like me, Evora is still human. Still full of hope and faith, even if misguided.

Viorica leans back in her chair and gazes in the direction that Samantha and Evora left in. She remains expressionless, just holding her glass of blood between both her hands. I should feel bad about the position we're asking to put herself in, especially after the death of Gabriella, but we need a strong ally that can help influence the board. And she needs a strong ally without Mitchell.

"Evora will never agree to a Blood Vow if we allow this to happen," Merrick says, speaking up. "She doesn't see the future like we do. She still calls herself a donor. This could jeopardize everything. You know how long it took to find her, Mother. Not to mention that Samantha would be devastated if she were rejected."

Orlando removes his hand from my leg and leans forward, linking his fingers together. "Perhaps we can come to another agreement, Viorica. One that could benefit both our covens and make our alliance stronger than any other coven in this territory."

"I'm interested," Viorica says, holding her head high. "What do you propose?"

"It seems Brayla will not be returning to our coven for the foreseeable future as of now, but in good heart, I cannot outcast her. We have a vow to uphold, and as you know, the consequences aren't favorable." Orlando rubs his lips together and looks at me. "You understand the bonds between two sisters, and Jewel very much feels the connection to Brayla."

"Where is she?" Merrick asks.

"I cannot say until we have an agreement that grants us secrecy with each other," Orlando says.

"So what would you like me to do? My hands are tied in regards to the law. That cannot be changed, especially now. I doubt the rest of the board would agree to allow Kingston, Diego, and Austin to join your coven without her here unless she is marked an outcast."

Orlando puffs a breath of air through his lips. "I understand, and unfortunately, as you know, we cannot wait for her. But we'd like to arrange an agreement with you. If Brayla returns, we'd like you to take her into your coven."

Viorica smirks to herself. "I think that sounds reasonable. She would have a happy future with us."

"We'd like the agreement to be temporary. If Brayla decides she wants to return to us after the duration of her time cut off from our coven, you must allow it," Orlando adds.

Kingston stretches, keeping his handsome face surprisingly expressionless. "Or if you prefer to just let us kill Cyprus to uphold our alliance...I'd love nothing more than to rip his throat out."

"Mother." Samantha's voice draws our attention to her as she stands next to Evora. "We'd like you to consider their offer with Brayla."

"Yeah," Merrick says. "Who knows, maybe Brayla won't want to re-join a coven that clearly favors Jewel. I bet she doesn't realize how left out she is."

"Brayla is just as big of a bitch as Mer, so she should fit in," Layla adds, smiling and bumping her shoulder to Merrick's.

Viorica shifts in her seat to look at Heidi, the only one of her daughters who hasn't spoken up. "What do you think?"

"I just want Mitchell dead," she responds, keeping her voice low. "For Gabi's sake."

Viorica nods her head and turns back to us. Lifting her glass, she says, "Here's to our new alliance. May our futures be prosperous, powerful, and brimming with the blood of our enemies."

Orlando clinks his glass to Viorica's. "To the future of Donor Life Corp. May the changes suit our every need."

EPILOGUE

BLOOD LOSS

"DO NOT TEST ME, MR. Andrei!" Orlando's voice bellows loud enough through the wall to drag me from sleep. "We have a mutual agreement but do not mistake where you fall in everything."

I jerk upright only to have Kingston hook his arms around my waist to pull me back to the bed.

"You have to help. It's the third attack this week. You said the board would protect them." The desperation in Hayden's words piques my curiosity, and I wiggle away from Kingston and try to scramble out of bed.

"Nope, not happening, babe," Kingston says, flipping me onto my back. He slides between my legs and presses his hard morning bulge against me. "You're mine right now, and I'm not giving up even a second so that those two assholes can upset you with things we can't control at the moment. It's still light out."

I stick out my bottom lip and clutch his head in my hands. "What are they talking about? It sounds bad."

Kingston groans and rocks against me a few times, testing the barrier our underwear creates between us. "It's...Haven Springs. There have been a lot more incidents lately, but we're working on their security. The board has issued vampire guards to protect the area."

I sigh. "Is this because of Mitchell?"

"Probably. We don't know for sure. He's not making any formal appearances."

"Because you'll rip is head off."

"Damn straight. Now, can you please let me get back to seducing you? I want you so badly. My morning wood is not going to go away until—"

I wrap my hand around him, making him moan and flop next to me as I take initiative to give him what he wants. Hooking his fingers to my shirt, he tugs it off as I shimmy my way lower. I kiss a trail along his stomach until I reach the waistband of his boxer briefs. Talk about a raging boner.

"Come back up here. I want your delicious lips against mine," he says, playing with my billowing hair.

I lace my fingers more firmly around him, feeling the extent of his desire without undressing him. "Are you sure about that?" Carefully tugging down his waistband, I smile up at him and graze my tongue over my lips.

He moans deep in his throat without responding, just sinking back onto our pillows. I take my time teasing him, just tasting the sweetness of his skin as he runs his fingers through my hair, cradling my head but letting me lead the way.

"I love you, babe," he whispers. "You're amazing. I don't know why I was nervous."

"Hmm?"

"Nothing. I love you."

I toss my hair back to peek up at him, catching him smiling. I know how much he loves our moments, but right now, he looks sexy as hell enjoying every bit of my attention with the way he watches me. His messy hair hangs on his forehead, yet he doesn't push it back, never letting his hands get away from me.

Something crashes in the hallway, and Kingston tenses under me. I ease myself away from him and glance at the door. Sliding his hands under my arms, he pulls me up and rolls me back over. He undresses me completely, making me moan with the weight of his body settling on top of me.

"I'm not letting anything ruin your morning," he whispers.

I kiss his neck and wiggle under him until our bodies are perfectly aligned. "Better not."

A thud sounds out from the hall, and Kingston releases a small, sexy ass growl in my ear. He picks up speed like he knows someone might crash through our door at any second, and I release a cross between a moan and a laugh as the head-board thuds against the wall. More voices sound in the hallway, and Kingston starts to slow down. It's Orlando and Hayden arguing about whether or not Hayden's concerns can wait.

"I want to talk to all of them." Hayden's loud voice pulls Kingston's attention away from me again.

"Put your weapon down, Mr. Andrei," Orlando says.

I grab Kingston's ass and tighten my legs around him. "Don't stop."

Kingston kisses me and breaks away to say, "Wasn't planning on it. Just thinking of moving."

With his words, someone bangs on the door, sending Kingston off the bed with me in his arms. A yell sounds out and glass shatters. Kingston ignores whatever is happening in the hall and carries me to the bathroom, kicking the door closed. He flips on shower and music to drown out the noise, and I gasp against his mouth at the feeling of the cool marble of the countertop under me.

I cling onto him, swaying with his motions, savoring every explosive sensation that sends me leaning back against the mirror. Kingston chuckles and slides a hand protectively to the back of my head to make sure the mirror doesn't crack under the strength of his thrusts that tug all sorts of noise from me.

I love him so much in this moment, playful and light-hearted, all smiley like I'm the best thing to wake up to. Slowing down his movements, he tips his head toward the ceiling and finishes with a soft moan. He bends forward to hug me to him, panting as hard as I am.

"I'm going to murder whoever the hell forced us to turn our morning of preferably endless, passionate lovemaking into a quickie," he says, brushing his lips to my shoulder.

"Mmm." My voice vibrates against his neck as I kiss up to meet his lips. "More loving, less fighting. Just keep cuddling me."

"You're right. Hayden is Orlando's problem. He can do the murdering," he says, nipping on my bottom lip. "I'm not giving away my attention to someone else when you're gazing at me like that."

"Like what?" I ask, leaning back to smirk.

"Like you're as hungry as I am. I'd prefer to feed you in bed, but I just heard the door crack so here will have to do."

I squint and stare past him at the bathroom door. Through the loud music and shower, I can't hear anything apart from our breathing. "I'll let you go first but only if I get to bite you too."

Kingston narrows his eyes at me and flashes his fangs. "Mmmm. You're extra hot all bitey, but now someone is clomping across our room."

I snap my teeth at him. "Sure, that's it."

Kingston eases himself away from me and strolls to grab my robe hanging on the back of the door. He tosses it to me, and I cover up in time for him to swing the door open and lean on the frame in all his sexy, naked ass glory.

"You have a serious death wish," Kingston says, lowering his voice to sound intimidating as all get-out. "Austin might be nice enough to control his desire to rip whoever interrupts his time with Jewel into pieces, but I have no such restraint. You better give me a good reason to have interrupted our passion-filled morning."

I chuck my hairbrush at him, and he catches it without even looking.

"With the way you guys have been circling around Jewel and guarding her these last two months, the only way to reach her is to risk my life by barging in here," Hayden says, his annoyed voice practically spitting the words. "So let me talk to her. You guys don't get things like she does."

Kingston growls. "No. Get out. You can make an appointment to see her at another time. We're still busy."

Hayden releases a strangled laugh. "I'll be dead next century."

"Is that when Orlando said you could?" Kingston howls a laugh and glances over his shoulder to me. "You have to admit that was funny."

I raise my eyebrows and shake my head. I guess I should've known that my guys have gone full-on protective mode after everything that happened with Mitchell. After the threats my dad made.

"Please, Jewel. It's important," Hayden says, ignoring Kingston. "I need your help. It's about Mona."

Kingston groans. "Fucking damn it."

I slide off the sink, hugging my robe around me. "You talked to Ramona?"

"Coven meeting," Kingston calls out, exiting the bathroom before me.

I saunter to the doorway, almost afraid to see Hayden again. It's been since the night Mitchell started a war within the board. Since Mitchell slaughtered so many Blood Rebels.

"You couldn't just make him wait in your study?" Kingston asks.

I spot Orlando in the hallway, picking up pieces of glass from the floor runner. None of the staff members are allowed to enter anywhere apart from the kitchen, living room, and the outside grounds with the looming threat over our heads. Orlando would probably release them of their contracts if I hadn't said something, because doing so would assure a terrible fate.

"My apologies, brother. I underestimated his determination. He didn't ask to see Jewel until after..."

I frown as Orlando's gaze meets mine. "You've been giving him your blood?" Because in this type of situation, Orlando could've mind manipulated Hayden to calm the hell down, though I know Orlando doesn't break into people's minds much anymore. Neither do my guys.

Orlando quirks his lips into a half smile, his eyes flashing silver at my remark. "Does that bother you?"

I roll my eyes. "You'd love it if I were jealous, wouldn't you." Orlando resorts to testing and teasing me, sneakily trying to do things to garner a reaction out of me. I try my best not to take his bait as he chisels at my resolve. Things are changing, and I can't help it. I don't even know if I want to help it.

Kingston groans and comes up beside me, carrying his clothing. "You are jealous, babe," he whispers into my ear.

I bat his arm and glare. "Not now, dude."

Kingston purposely balances himself using my shoulder to stay close while he dresses. "You know you'll never go hungry, right?"

My cheeks flush, and I manage to pull my attention away from Orlando to stick my tongue out at Kingston. "Lies. I'm starving now." Turning back to Hayden and Orlando, I wave my hand. "Just sit down. I don't want to hear anything until I get breakfast."

Diego pops his head into the room and smiles. "You're lucky we have perfect timing, beautiful."

I grin and cross the room, opening my arms to give Diego a hug. Austin strolls in behind him, carrying a tray that smells as sweet and as tangy as he is. Kissing my cheek, Austin passes by to set up my breakfast on a tray so that I can eat in bed. I scoot over to the middle of the bed and make room for him. Kingston flops down on my other side, snaking his arms around me to cuddle close, and Diego sits in front of us, pulling my bare feet across his legs.

"You don't get tired of being smothered all the time?" Hayden asks, pulling a chair from the desk. "Your matches might share you, but they're possessive as hell."

I scrunch my brows and glance at Kingston. "You do have a death wish. You're lucky we need you alive."

"I'm sure if we asked around, we could find a replacement rebel to give us the information we need to know," Kingston says, flashing his fangs.

Hayden shifts in his seat and glowers. "I'm sorry. I'm just—I got word from a source about Mona."

It must be serious if Hayden's apologizing. "Is everything okay?"

He leans his elbows on his knees. "I had no idea, Jewel. I swear. Had I known..."

I set my fork down and hand Kingston my tray to sit up straighter. My gaze flicks from Hayden, who rubs his hands across his face, to Orlando, who gives nothing away. I can't tell if he knows or not.

"Spit it out already," Kingston says. "You're scaring our girl."

"I'm sorry," Hayden repeats. "I'm just—your family is okay. They made it to The Orchards. But...fuck. My source told me that Ramona is pregnant. I need your help, Jewel. We have to get her."

I stare in shock, a million emotions fluttering through me, sending my stomach twisting. "Pregnant?"

"That has to be why Brayla left with them," Austin says softly. "That's why she's risking her life."

Orlando straightens his shoulders and catches my gaze.

"It is in our best interest not to help you, Mr. Andrei. Taking the risk to go to The Orchards isn't worth it. Ramona will be fine."

Hayden gets to his feet and risks closing the space to me. "Please, then help me get there. I don't trust Noah. Jewel, your sister is a carrier of your mutation. Our child—"

"Is not our priority," Orlando says.

"Jewel, think of the future of our family." *Our family.* Hayden ignores Orlando and pleads with his eyes, begging me to hear him out, to consider what all this means.

"The chances of Ramona having a female are slim. And even if she does, the chances of her being symptomatic are unlikely." Austin touches my knee. "I agree with Orlando. It's not a priority. The risk is too great."

Diego rubs the tops of my feet. "Yeah, beautiful. We can wait and see."

"I'm with them," Kingston adds.

I nod. "I'm sorry, Hayden. Ramona made her decision and was quite clear about where I stand in her life. If she wants help, she can reach out to us."

"Jewel."

I shake my head. "I have too much else to worry about. The coven vows are coming up and...I'm sorry."

Hayden jumps up, glowering, but he doesn't even get within a foot of me before Orlando grabs him by the back of the shirt. Hayden crashes to the floor, skidding across the room to hit the far wall. The whole place shakes, and I startle.

"You guys hear that?" Austin asks, standing up. "Some-one triggered the security sensors."

Kingston flies across the room and shoves Hayden into the wall. "Is this you?"

Hayden shakes his head, unable to speak.

Diego picks me off the bed before I have a chance to real-ize what's happening. The ground shakes again, and Orlando releases a scary ass growl. Kingston rushes to grab a few weap-ons from a shelf, and everyone closes in to surround me.

"Call Viorica," Orlando says to Austin. He turns to us. "Diego, get Jewel to the basement. Kingston, assist Mr. An-drei."

"What about you, Orlando?" I ask.

Orlando's eyes widen at the sound of an ear-piercing crack. None of us has time to react as the world blurs and the floor drops out from under us. I scream out, clutching onto Diego for dear life until he lands in a crouch on top of a pile of debris.

"You okay, beautiful?" Diego asks, squeezing me tighter.

"Shit balls. What was that?"

Diego doesn't have a chance to respond as a figure blurs toward us. The breath knocks from me as we're thrown back, and a snarling vampire lands on top of me, gnashing his teeth. Pain explodes through my chest, and I stare down in horror at the vampire's hand impaling me.

My guys roar, their growls and snarls ripping through the air.

I try my best to fight, but shadows edge my vision.

"Kingston, stop!" Diego yells. "Don't pull him off. He has her heart!"

The world turns black.

To be continued...

Thank you so much for reading *Blood Loss*! Don't forget to check out the next installment of *The Divine Vampire Heirs, Blood Vows.*

To stay up-to-day on new and future releases, follow Ginna on Amazon or Bookbub. By signing up for the Ginna Moran newsletter or joining her Facebook Group Paranormal Center for Matches and Mates, you will also gain exclusive access to special content on her website, play games, participate in exclusive giveaways, and more!

Other Series by Ginna Moran

REVERSE HAREM
The Divine Vampire Heirs Series
The Royale Vampire Heirs Series
Academy of Vampire Heirs Series
The Pack Mates of Lunar Crest Series

YA PARANORMAL
Call of the Ocean Series
Demon Watcher Series
Demon Within Series
Destined for Dreams Series
Finding Nate Series
Going Ghostly Series
Spark of Life Series
The Merman's Spark Series
When Souls Collide Series

YA CONTEMPORARY
Falling into Fame Series
Life After Lila

ABOUT GINNA MORAN

GINNA MORAN IS a writer from sunny Southern California. She started writing poetry as a teenager in a spiral notebook that she still has tucked away on her desk today. Her love of writing grew after she graduated high school, and she completed her first unpublished manuscript at age eighteen.

When she realized her love of writing was her life's passion, she studied literature at Mira Costa College in Northern San Diego. Besides writing novels, she was senior editor, content manager, and image coordinator for Crescent House Publishing Inc. for four years.

Aside from Ginna's professional life, she enjoys binge watching television shows, playing pretend with her daughter, and cuddling with her dogs. Some of her favorite things include chocolate, anything that glitters, cheesy jokes, and organizing her bookshelf.

Ginna Moran loves to hear from her readers so visit her online at www.GinnaMoran.com. You can also find her on Facebook, Twitter, and Instagram. To stay up-to-date on new releases, sign up to her newsletter. You'll not only get exclusive access to extra stories, but you'll be able to participate in monthly giveaways!